Praise for Nebula Award Winner

JACK McDEVITT

"'Why read Jack McDevitt?' The question should be: 'Who among us is such a slow pony that s/he *isn't* reading McDevitt?'"
—Harlan Ellison

"An intelligent, provocative entertainment by a man who brings energy, style, and a fresh perspective to everything he writes."
—*The Washington Post Book World*

"You should definitely read Jack McDevitt."
—Gregory Benford

"If you love reading good sci-fi and you haven't read a Jack McDevitt book, you're really missing out."
—Wired.com

"McDevitt imagines the far future with precision and believability."
—*Library Journal*

"McDevitt manages to make the odd coupling of the cozy and the cosmic into effective and moving SF."
—*Locus*

Novels by Jack McDevitt

Ancient Shores
Thunderbird

The Hercules Text
Eternity Road
Moonfall
Infinity Beach
Time Travelers Never Die

WITH MIKE RESNICK
The Cassandra Project

The Priscilla Hutchins Novels

The Engines of God   *Odyssey*
Deepsix   *Cauldron*
Chindi   *Starhawk*
Omega

The Alex Benedict Novels

A Talent for War   *Echo*
Polaris   *Firebird*
Seeker   *Coming Home*
The Devil's Eye

Collections

Standard Candles
Ships in the Night
Outbound
Cryptic: The Best Short Fiction of Jack McDevitt

THUNDERBIRD

JACK McDEVITT

ACE BOOKS, NEW YORK

An imprint of Penguin Random House LLC
375 Hudson Street, New York, New York 10014

THUNDERBIRD

An Ace Book / published by arrangement with Cryptic, Inc.

ISBN: 978-0-425-27920-5

PUBLISHING HISTORY
Ace hardcover edition / December 2015
Ace mass-market edition / August 2016

PRINTED IN THE UNITED STATES OF AMERICA

10 9 8 7 6 5 4 3 2 1

Cover art by Tony Mauro.
Cover design by Rita Frangie.

Penguin
Random
House

For Merry McDevitt,
beloved daughter

ACHNOWLEDGMENTS

Thanks to Walt Cuirle, Michael Fossel, Scott Ryfun, Frank Manning, and Les Johnson for advice and technical assistance. To Ginjer Buchanan and Diana Gill, editors past and present. To my agent, Chris Lotts, who asked the right questions. To copy editor Sara Schwager. To my wife, Maureen, and my son Chris, who made major contributions. And to the Spirit Lake Sioux, who, years ago, welcomed me onto the reservation and made it, for a brief period, my home.

How cruelly sweet are the echoes that start
When memory plays an old tune on the heart.

—Eliza Cook, *Lays of a Wild Harp*, 1835

Great Spirit, fill us with the light.
Give us the strength to understand
And eyes to see.

—Mni Wakan Oyate prayer

PROLOGUE

J ERI TULLY WAS eight years old. Mentally, she was about three, and the experts cautioned her parents against hoping for any serious improvement. No one knew what had gone wrong with Jeri. There was no history of mental defects on either side of her family and no apparent cause. She had two younger brothers, both of whom were quite normal.

Her father was a border patrolman, her mother a former legal secretary who had given up all hope of a career when she followed her husband to Fort Moxie.

Jeri went to school in Walhalla, which conducted the only local special-education class. She enjoyed the school, where she made numerous friends and where everyone seemed to make a fuss over her. Mornings in the Tully household were underscored by Jeri's enthusiasm to get moving.

Walhalla was thirty-five miles away. The family had an arrangement with the school district, which was spread out over too vast an area to operate buses for the special-education kids: The Tullys provided their own transportation, and the district absorbed the expenses.

Jeri's mother had actually grown to enjoy the daily round-trip. The child loved to ride, and she was never happier than when in the car. The other half of the drive, when Mom was alone, served as a quiet time, when she could just watch the long fields roll by, or plug an audio book into the system.

Jeri's father worked the midnight shift that night, and his wife was waiting for him when he got home in the morning with French toast, bacon, and coffee. While they were at breakfast, an odd thing happened. For the only time in her life, Jeri wandered away from home. It seemed, later, that she had decided to go to school and, having no concept of distance, had begun walking.

Unseen by anyone except a two-year-old brother, she put on her overshoes and her coat, let herself out through the porch door, walked up to Route 11, and turned right. Her house was on the extreme western edge of town, so she got past the demolished Dairy Queen and across the interstate overpass within minutes. The temperature, which is exceedingly erratic in April, had fallen back into the teens.

Three-quarters of a mile outside Fort Moxie, Route 11 curves sharply south and almost immediately veers west again. Had the road been free of snow, Jeri would probably have stayed with the highway and been picked up within a few minutes. But a light snowfall had dusted the highway. She wasn't used to paying attention to details and, at the first bend, she walked straight off the road. When, a few minutes later, the snow got deeper, she angled right and got still farther away.

Jeri's parents had by then discovered she was missing. A frightened search was just getting started, but it was limited to within a block or so of her home.

Jim Stuyvesant, the editor and publisher of the *Fort Moxie News*, was on his way to the Roundhouse. Rumors that an apparition had come through from the other side were going to be denied that morning in a press conference, and Jim planned to be there. He was just west of town when he saw movement out on Josh McKenzie's land to his right: A small whirlwind was gliding back and forth in a curiously regular fashion. The wind phenomenon was a perfect whirlpool, narrow at the base, wide at the top. Usually, these things were blurred around the edges, and they floated erratically across the plain. But this one looked almost solid, and it moved methodically back and forth along a narrow track.

Stuyvesant pulled off the road and stopped to watch.

It was almost hypnotic. A stiff blast of air rocked the car, enough to blow the small whirlwind to pieces. But it remained intact.

Stuyvesant never traveled without his video camera, which he had used on several occasions to get material he'd subsequently sold to *Ben at Ten* or to one of the other local TV news shows. (He had, for example, got superb footage of the Thanksgiving Day pileup on I-29, and the blockade of imported beef at the border port by angry ranchers last summer.) The floater continued to glide back and forth in its slow, unwavering pattern. He turned on the camera, walked a few steps into the field, and started to record.

He used the zoom lens to get close and got a couple of minutes' worth before the whirlwind seemed to pause.

It started toward him.

He kept filming.

It approached at a constant pace. There was something odd in its manner, something almost deliberate.

A sudden burst of wind out of the north ripped at his jacket but didn't seem to have any effect on the thing. Stuyvesant's instincts began to sound warnings, and he took a step back toward the car.

It stopped. Remained still in the middle of the field.

Amazing. As if it had responded to him.

He stood, uncertain how to proceed. It began to move again, laterally. It retreated a short distance, then came forward again to its previous position.

He watched it through the camera lens. The red indicator lamp glowed at the bottom of the picture.

You're waiting for me.

It approached again, and a sudden burst of wind tugged at his collar and his hair.

He took a step forward. And it retreated.

Like everyone else in the Fort Moxie area, Stuyvesant had been deluged with fantastic tales and theories since the Roundhouse had been uncovered, with its pathways to other worlds. Now, without prompting, he wondered whether a completely unknown type of life-form existed on the prairie and was revealing itself to him. He laughed at the idea. And began to wonder what he really believed.

He started forward.

It withdrew before him, matching his pace.

He kept going. The snow got deeper, filled his shoes, and froze his ankles.

It hovered before him. He hoped he was getting the effect on camera.

It whirled and glittered in the sun, maintaining its distance. He stopped, and it stopped. He started again, and it matched him.

Another car was slowing down, pulling off the highway. He wondered how he would explain this, and immediately visualized next week's headline in the *News*: MAD EDITOR PUT UNDER GUARD.

But it was a hunt without a point. The fields went on, all the way to Winnipeg. Far enough, he decided. "Sorry," he said, aloud. "This is as far as I go."

And the thing withdrew another sixty or so yards. And collapsed.

When it did, it revealed something dark lying in the snow. Jeri Tully.

That was the day Stuyvesant got religion.

ONE

O'er the hills and far away.

—Thomas D'Urfey, *Pills to Purge Melancholy*, 1719

EVEN THOUGH HE'D seen the eerie green glow atop the mountain almost every night on TV, Brad Hollister was still surprised that evening as the hills got out of the way, and he saw it for the first time through his windshield. It was easy to understand why people had panicked a few weeks earlier, had thought it was radioactivity and fled the area. They were mostly back now, of course, assured by official sources that the radiation was not hazardous. The world had been shocked when a structure thousands of years old had been excavated on the Sioux reservation near Devils Lake in North Dakota. And shocked again when, a few days later, it began to emit that soft green light. And completely rattled when investigators discovered it was a star gate. That was the capability, of course, that stayed in the headlines. And kept the phones ringing at *Grand Forks Live*, Brad's call-in show on KLYM.

Scientific teams had been transported to three locations, a garden world that the media immediately branded "Eden," a second location that seemed to be nothing more than a series of passageways in a structure that had no windows, and a deserted space station that appeared to be located outside the Milky Way.

Missions were going out regularly, mostly to Eden and the station. A team of eight journalists, accompanied by two Sioux security escorts, were on Eden now, expected to return that evening. And a group of scientists were scheduled to head for the same destination within the hour. Brad's callers wanted him to make the trip, and he'd been assuring them he would eventually. But before he climbed onto the circular stone, with its gridwork surface, and allowed them to send him off to another world, he wanted to *watch* the operation. Not that he was scared.

The emerald glow brightened as he drew near on Route 32. Eventually, he turned off onto a side road, cleared a police unit, and began the long climb to the summit. A bright moon hung over the sparse land, and a bitter wind rocked the car. Eventually, as he approached the summit, the Roundhouse became visible. A bubble dome, it stood on the edge of a cliff, overlooking the vast sweep of land that had once contained Lake Agassiz. Thousands of years ago, Agassiz had covered most of North Dakota and a large section of Canada.

The building lay below the level of the surrounding granite. Someone had gouged a space in the rock to make room for the Roundhouse. Brad's callers were entranced by the theory that the construction had been orchestrated to place the star gate level with the ancient shoreline. Curved struts anchored it in the rock. The surface resembled a beveled emerald plastic.

It was surrounded by several temporary structures, which had been erected to support the science teams and the security effort. The area was sealed off by a wired fence. A gateway provided access to cars and trucks.

The gates were down. Brad lowered his window as he pulled alongside the security booth. A young man in a dark blue Sioux uniform looked out.

"My name's Hollister," Brad said, handing over his driver's license. "They know I'm coming."

The officer checked the ID, touched a computer screen, nodded, and gave it back. "Okay, Mr. Hollister," he said. "Park wherever you like."

• • •

A SECURITY GUARD opened the front door for him. He proceeded down a short passageway, past several doors, and entered the dome. This would have been the place that filled with water at high tide, allowing the occupants to take a boat out onto Lake Agassiz. That, of course, was very likely the boat found recently buried on Tom Lasker's farm, which had led to the discovery.

There were about twenty people, plus three or four uniformed security guards, standing around talking, a few seated at a table. Most were casually dressed, as if preparing for a camping trip. There was also a TV team. A second entrance opened into the chamber from the far side, where everyone was gathered. During the Agassiz years, it would have provided the access for the incoming tide. It had also been, according to the experts, the preferred entrance for the original occupants, the front door, looking out onto a beach. April Cannon was near the transporter, talking with a reporter. The transporter consisted of a circular grid, large enough to have supported Lasker's boat, and a control device, mounted several feet away on the wall.

April had been the source of his invitation to come in and watch. Brad had known her a long time. She held a doctorate in biochemistry and was a director for Colson Labs, the last time he'd looked. She'd been conscripted by Sioux Chairman James Walker to coordinate the off-world missions, and, as she put it, that had overwhelmed everything else in her life. April had been a guest on *Grand Forks Live* a couple of times. When she saw him come in, she excused herself and started in his direction.

April was an attractive young African-American, with her hair draped around her shoulders, animated features, scintillating eyes, and a persuasive manner. Brad had always suspected that, had she gone into sales instead of chemistry, she would have been wealthy by then. "Perfect timing, Brad," she said. "We've got some people coming in any minute now."

"Hi, April. Where are they now? Eden?"

"Yes. They're all media types. After they get back, we'll be sending out a team of scientists. Biologists and astronomers."

"Have they figured out where the place is yet?"

"No. Maybe we'll get lucky, and they'll do it tonight." She shook her head. "We know it's pretty far."

"I guess it would have to be."

She laughed. And turned away. "It's starting." The front area, near the transport device, brightened though Brad could see no source for the light. "Anyway, glad to see you, Brad," she said. "The show's about to start." She went back to the transporter and joined one of the Sioux, who seemed to be in charge of overseeing the recovery process. A wave of excitement swept through the crowd. A few people started moving closer to the stone grid. The security guards moved in to keep them at a distance.

A TV camera approached, and its lights went on. The illumination was directly over the grid. It expanded into a cloud, and Brad thought he could see something moving inside it. Everybody was leaning forward.

The light kept getting brighter. The cloud enveloped the grid. Then it stalled and simply floated there, so bright it was difficult to look at. And, finally, it began to fade.

It left someone standing on the grid. A young woman in a security uniform. "Welcome home, Andrea," said April, as the cloud disappeared.

It was Andrea Hawk, who, like Brad, ran a call-in show when she wasn't on duty at the Roundhouse. She got some applause, waved to the audience, and stepped quickly out of the way. Moments later, the light was back.

Another woman, this time in fatigues, wearing a knapsack and a hat that would have made Indiana Jones proud, emerged. "Aleen Rynsburger," said a guy standing off to one side. Brad knew the name. She was a *Washington Post* columnist.

One by one they came back, seven reporters and one more security escort. All with wide-brimmed hats. He was relieved to see the process didn't look like a big deal. The light comes on, and somebody steps out and waves to the audience. Nobody looked rattled. When it was over, sandwiches and soft drinks were brought out of a side room, they all shook hands, and there were cries of "my turn next." Then the outgoing science group assembled. They also had a collection of wide-brimmed hats.

"They get a lot of sun over there," April told him. "We're only going to be a short time, unless something develops. It's late afternoon now on Eden, so we'll soon be able to see the night sky. They'll take some pictures, and we'll be back in a few hours. I'd invite you to join us, Brad, except that the chairman doesn't like last-minute changes in the schedule."

"It's okay," said Brad. "No problem."

There would be a total of nine this time, including April and the two escorts. "We always send two," she said.

"They're going to Eden again, right?"

"Yes."

"Is there anything dangerous over there, April?"

"Not that we're aware of. But the Sioux are armed. And so are some of the scientists." She put on her hat and pulled it down over her eyes.

"It looks good," Brad said.

She added sunglasses. "See you later, champ."

He settled back into one of several folding chairs. An escort, a young woman, stepped onto the grid. Somebody yelled, "Have a big time, Paula."

Her family name was Francisco. Brad had seen her picture. She'd been a prominent figure on a couple of the missions. Another of the security people assumed a position at the control unit. He touched something, and lights came on. Brad was thinking how incredible it was that a machine put in place ten thousand years ago still worked. Still generated power.

A group of icons was visible inside the wall behind the grid.

Brad knew the routine, had seen it numerous times on television. You stood on the grid and pressed the wall in front of one of the icons. Or someone did it for you. A luminous cloud formed, and you gradually faded from view. And you arrived somewhere else. It was the story of the age.

He watched. The cloud appeared and enveloped Paula. Then it faded, and she was gone.

Some of those waiting to follow looked at each other with foreboding expressions. They, too, had known what was coming, but maybe being present while it happened was different from watching it on television. Next in line was an elderly guy with white hair. He started forward, but the security officer raised a hand and waved him back. Brad's first thought was that something had gone wrong, but while the security officer watched, the luminous cloud returned. This time, when it dissolved, Paula was back. She delivered a thumbs-up, pointed to the guy at the control, and was sent once again on her way. Okay. So they do a test run first. That seemed like a good idea. He wondered what they would have done if Paula hadn't come back.

The scientists stepped singly onto the grid and disappeared in the swirl of light. The last two to leave were April and the second security guy.

Brad took a deep breath. Spectacular show. But it was over.

He got out of his chair and remembered he'd intended to take pictures but had forgotten. He'd also planned to ask April back onto *Grand Forks Live*, but he'd forgotten that as well. He walked over to the security desk and said hello to Andrea.

She looked up from a report. "Hi, Brad. How you doing?"

He was tempted to ask her to come on the show, too. "I'm good, Andrea. Glad to see you again. It's been a while. How was Eden?"

"Spectacular, Brad. You should go. I'm sure we can set it up for you."

"Yes, I'm looking forward to doing it when I can."

"These are pretty good times for call-in shows, aren't they? Everybody wants to talk about the Roundhouse."

"I know. That and the invisible thing that's been floating around in Fort Moxie scaring everybody."

"I know. You think it's connected to us?"

"Probably." If she came over and did his show, his callers would notice how she was doing missions to Eden while Brad sat in his office. "Gotta go, kid. I'm running a little late."

He left the Roundhouse and was immediately hit by a blast of cold air. The temperature in the parking lot was about ten below, actually fairly warm for North Dakota at this time of year. What kind of technology was able to keep the place warm after thousands of years? Whoever built the Roundhouse obviously knew what they were doing. Except that they'd lost their boat. He wondered if any of them had been casualties when that happened.

TWO

No frigid Northern skies
Chill us from far, mocking our longing eyes
And yearning sympathies,—
Ah, no! the heaven bends kind and clasping here,
And in the ether clear
The stars seem warm and near.

—Elizabeth Akers Allen, "The Dream," 1866

THE MEMBERS OF April's team came equipped with cameras, telescopes, a spectroscope, and laptops. Paula Francisco greeted each on arrival. They were inside a structure shaped like a bell jar, about three stories high. It was much smaller than the Roundhouse, and walls on three sides appeared to be made of darkened glass. The fourth was opaque green, probably a plastic, similar to the Roundhouse. They were looking out at a succulent forest bathed in sunlight. A group of icons were embedded in an earth-colored post. Prominent among them was an arrow. It was the symbol for the Eden transport station.

When everyone had come through, she backed off and made way for April.

"Welcome to the Cupola," April said. "I want to remind you of the guidelines for the operation. You're free to look around. Pick up whatever information you can. But take no chances. We've explored only a few square miles of this place. It seems hospitable enough, and we've encountered no threats. But that doesn't mean there aren't any. We'd like to pin down the location of this place if possible. Anybody going into the forest will be accompanied by either Paula or Adam. Or me." All three carried weapons. "Don't go alone. And everybody stay out of the ocean." She studied the group of scientists. Who'd be crazy enough to go into an alien sea, right? "Our prime concern right now is to take some pictures and get everybody back alive. If we run into anything that could give us trouble, back off and play it safe." The security escorts were distributing gloves. "They're made of polypropylene. Whoever built these places didn't use locks. Once you get outside, you need to be wearing these to get back in. Or something else that's flexible and non-organic. Otherwise, the doors won't open. So don't go anywhere without the gloves. And you'll need your sunglasses."

She signaled Adam Sky to come forward. He was a big, taciturn guy who'd spent his early years in the military. He had riveting eyes and a voice that made it clear everything was under control. The family name was actually *Kick-the-Sky*, but he preferred the shorter version. "Adam's our chief of security," she said. "He has the final say on everything. If he tells us to clear out, we do it immediately with no questions. Clear?"

They nodded and shook hands and stared at the outside world. Jerry Carlucci, an astrophysicist from Jodrell Bank in the UK, said, "Good luck to us all." He appeared anxious to get to work.

Several folding chairs had been brought in from North Dakota, along with two tables and a propane-powered refrigerator. The Sioux had also provided a Porta Potty a few yards from the station.

"We all ready?" said April.

They were.

Garth Chanowitz, a Nobel Prize winner from MIT, walked over to neurologist Michael Fossel and shook his hand. "Hi, Michael," he said. Garth was a big man, almost three hundred pounds, with a gray beard and an expression that suggested he, too, was in a state of near disbelief about where they were. "Bet you never thought you'd get a chance to research alien nervous systems."

"I'm not sure I believe it yet," said Michael. There were doors at opposite ends of the Cupola. One, apparently a rear entrance, was set in the opaque wall. While everybody watched, Adam walked over to the front door and opened it. A lush breeze came in, and the station filled with the scents of pine and jasmine, and the sounds of a million birds. The vegetation was a wild mix of purple, red, and gold.

"You know," said Garth, "I've thought a lot about what aliens might be like. But I never thought I might get a chance to say hello to one."

They went outside and circled the building. The rear exit looked across an ocean.

The beach and the sea had been on all the newscasts. It could have been any oceanfront environment at home, even including seashells. Nobody had any idea what lay over the horizon. Michael stood looking at it, breathing deeply, and listening to the rumble of the surf. The air was considerably warmer, of course, than North Dakota, a blend of South Seas mixed with the scent of a forest after a rainfall. The transport station was at the edge of a ridge, in the style of the Roundhouse, although this one was only a few feet high. Worn stone steps, partially buried, were on the forest side. He looked out across a broad sweep of trees and shrubbery. The vegetation wore a deep violet hue. Enormous silver-and-yellow blossoms hung from thin trees. The sun was just over a group of distant hills. One of the astronomers, Marge Baxter, showed up beside him. "Beautiful place," she said. "Takes your breath away."

"Even the transport station looks good. Better than the one at home."

"Well, the one at home was buried for a long time. This one, according to the experts, isn't nearly as old."

Michael hadn't been certain whether the sun was rising or setting. But he gradually realized it was getting dark. "I understand this place has a moon," he said.

"*Two* of them." Marge took a deep breath. She was excited. "I can't wait to see them. Can't wait to see the night sky, for that matter. I can't believe we're going to be able to sit on a beach and look up at the Horse's head."

• • •

THE OTHER ASTRONOMERS shared her enthusiasm. Jerry Carlucci kept urging the sun to hurry up and set. When finally it dipped below a range of hills, they were all watching from the beach. Even Michael, whose prime interest was in the local life-forms, found himself unable to pay attention to anything other than the gradually darkening sky. "No clouds," said April. "We should get a good view."

"I hope so," said Pat Benson, chairman of the astronomy department at Harvard.

But there's nothing slower than watching the sun go down. A few broke out sandwiches. Garth Chanowitz had coffee, which he shared. Marge kept looking at her watch, causing Michael to wonder if she'd found a way to tune it to Eden's seventeen-hour day.

The tide was coming in. Michael wondered what lived in the ocean. He'd have loved an opportunity to find out. And eventually, maybe he would. First things first, though. He'd already spotted a few birds. They reinforced what he'd expected. Just so many ways to make a squirrel. Or a blue jay.

The sun sank into the hills, and gradually it got dark. Stars appeared, along with a moon. It was not like Earth's moon. This one was fuzzy and bigger. It had an atmosphere.

Garth pointed out over the ocean. "There it is!"

"I think you're right," said Pat. And he looked in a different direction. "That might be Alnitak."

"Come on, Pat," said Marge. "Stay serious."

"Well," he laughed, "who knows? It *might* be."

Michael assumed they were talking about the Horsehead Nebula. Pat caught a questioning glance and nodded. "That's *it*, Michael." Cheers rang out. They stood on the beach and laughed and clapped their hands and congratulated each other.

As the other stars of the nebula appeared, somebody provided music, and they lifted glasses of fruit juice, which was all they had, to the sky. He couldn't remember a party in his entire life so filled with laughter and celebration. "I never would have believed I'd see anything like this," he told Paula.

"Oh, God. How is it *possible*?" squealed Marge. She did not look like somebody who would squeal.

"I'll tell you the truth," said Garth. "I didn't believe this was actually going to happen. I keep expecting to wake up. How different the sky is. To be standing under that thing rather than simply looking at it through a telescope." They were like college kids enjoying spring break. Except a lot more.

They set up their equipment on the beach and began taking measurements while Adam and Paula maintained watch over the forest. Michael spent some time examining the vegetation, but it wasn't his field, and he eventually joined April and the astronomers at the edge of the ocean. He was fascinated by the hazy moon, wondering whether it harbored life. Marge handed him a telescope. He looked at it and saw nothing but open ground. No cities, no indication of structures of any kind. It was disappointing. Ordinarily, he would have simply shrugged the idea off. Now, though, anything seemed possible. The world of Grand Forks, North Dakota, with its brutal winters and routine working days, had been replaced by a cosmos that was suddenly accessible.

Eventually, April and Michael got squeezed out of the conversation. The others were trying to identify individual stars, talking about spectra and angles and checking their computers. They wandered off and talked with the escorts. "Have they figured it out?" Paula asked. "Do they have any idea where we are?" She was slim, young, attractive, but all business.

"I don't think so," April said. "They're still arguing. And holding their hands against their heads."

Michael smiled. "And having the time of their lives."

• • •

A FULL DAY on Eden lasted approximately seventeen hours. Nobody slept that night. As, eventually, the eastern sky brightened, and the stars began to fade, April knew that the moment of decision was near. She'd been told that everything ultimately hung on their ability to identify Eden's sun. So far, at least, that hadn't happened. It was still early in the game, but they had no idea where they were other than being located somewhere in the general vicinity of the Horsehead. That was why they'd really come, to see the nebula. Michael gradually realized that establishing Eden's location was really a made-up claim, something that sounded like a reasonable objective, when in fact the astronomers had been reduced to the status of kids on Christmas Eve. And the nebula was not a disappointment. It was far more spectacular than anything that could be seen with the naked eye at home. Michael readily understood what Marge had meant about standing under the Horse's head.

April had a somewhat different perspective. Not that she didn't enjoy that night sky, but for her, the fact that she was there, on the ground, was all that really mattered. They broke for coffee, and everybody put sunglasses back on. Michael added a Yankees baseball cap. Marge commented that she could really get to appreciate a world that didn't seem to have mosquitoes.

"I'd be surprised if there weren't some bugs here somewhere," Michael said. "Pests of various kinds will probably be pretty common anywhere."

They sat on the ground, propped against the Cupola, usually saying the same thing over and over. "Magnificent."

"My kids would love to see this."

"The real Eden couldn't have had something like this."

April got out of step by commenting that the dawn seemed so ordinary. "It looks like our sun."

"Not really," said Jerry. He was an ordinary-looking guy. Maybe five-eight, his brown hair starting to fade, and a smile that never seemed quite real. "I have a color perception problem, but it looks—?" He turned to Marge.

"You're right, Jerry," she said. "I'd say it's got an orange tinge."

Whatever, Michael thought, the astronomers were behaving as if they'd never seen a sunrise before. "Beautiful," one of them said. They clapped one another on the back and shook hands some more. They were, he thought, trying to show April that she'd taken the dawn for granted.

The sun *was* orange, Michael decided. Unlike Sol.

They trained the spectroscope on it and entered the results into their computers, argued, traded data, and debated some more. The sun moved slowly across the sky and was almost directly overhead before they finally agreed they'd done as much as they could.

"So," asked April, "do you know where we are?"

Marge rolled her eyes.

"Within maybe forty or fifty light-years," said Garth.

Jerry was still consulting his computer. "I think I can make a pretty decent guess."

That got everybody's attention. "So what have you got, Jerry?" asked April.

"It looks like a K5. I don't think anybody's going to argue with that." Nobody did. "I got the angles to several stars in the Horsehead. Now this could be a K5 star we just haven't seen yet. But it looks like—" He checked his laptop again and passed it around. There were a lot of designators, which meant nothing to Michael. "The one at the bottom," Jerry said. 2MASS J05384917-0238222. "Position looks like a match."

"I think you're right," said Marge.

April looked disappointed. "What's wrong?" asked Garth.

"Nothing. I was hoping it would turn out to be a star that people had heard of. You know, one of the stars in Orion's Belt or something."

They all laughed. "You wouldn't want to be living on a world dependent on any of those things," said Jerry. "Two of them are double stars, and Alnilam hasn't been around long enough for life to evolve." He held out his hands, a man who at that moment owned the heavens. "I'd like to stay and spend another night here. Can we do that? It would give me a chance to confirm that this really is 222."

April looked around. "We can, Jerry. If anybody wants to go back, though, feel free."

Nobody did. They broke out some sandwiches and more coffee and sat on the beach talking about whether anybody could figure a way to move one of the big telescopes out here. Maybe one of the Corbins, or the Hobby-Eberly. "There has to be a way to do it," said Jerry.

Garth pressed his palms together and put them behind his head, a man completely at ease. "Just bring out the pieces," he said, "and we can put it together."

"Sure," said Marge. "No sweat."

They talked about people who'd gotten annoyed that they weren't selected to make the trip. Jerry asked April if she knew how the decisions had been made. "The choices," she said in a serious tone, "were based strictly on good looks."

In fact they all knew that most of the decisions, maybe all of them, were being made at the White House level. There was a selection committee in Washington, and the choices had been made on perceived flexibility, by which was meant a willingness to keep an open mind, and on accomplishments and good health. At least those were the theoretical requirements. Garth, hauling around all that weight, did not look to be particularly healthy. Michael had no doubt that April was hoping the guy wouldn't have any kind of attack while they were out here. But his name was as big as his anatomy. Michael also assumed there'd been some political maneuvering to give major scientific figures visibility by ensuring their organizations were represented. That might have been how *he* had gotten on board. He had a lot of connections. However that was playing out, his impression was that they'd gotten a good team.

April told Adam and Paula they could go home if they wanted. "Just send out a couple of replacements."

"That's okay," said Adam. "I don't really want to leave this."

"Neither do I," said Paula.

Marge was watching Paula. "The one thing I'm concerned about—"

"Yes?"

"How can I arrange to bring my kids out here?"

"Check with James," she said. That, of course, was James Walker, the Sioux chairman.

While the sun moved across the sky, Michael wandered into the forest, accompanied by Paula. He saw some small animals, some insects, various flowers, and a wide variety of trees. Birds soared through the sky. Something he couldn't see sat hidden in the branches and yowled at him. And a long, lizard-like creature took time to stare up at him with no indication of fear. He wasn't sure how it would react if he moved so he remained still and cautioned Paula to do the same until it had moved on. It was much too early to begin to draw conclusions about the biology here other than the obvious one: It was similar to the system that had developed at home. But that was to be expected since the environment was similar.

Eventually, he went back to the shoreline and strolled along, just out of reach of the waves, examining shells and whatever else had washed up. April asked if he'd seen any surprises?

"Not yet," he said. "Maybe with a laboratory."

Eventually the sun began to sink again toward the hills. "Beautiful sunset," said Jerry.

Marge's eyes brightened. "I wouldn't have taken you for the romantic type, Jerry."

He smiled. "There's nothing like a beautiful physicist to make me appreciate the sun going down."

Eventually, the night returned. Jerry opened his tablet and began comparing his data with what he could see overhead. Garth sat down beside him.

Marge was staring out toward the horizon as the last faint glimmers of light faded. "Look," she said quietly.

Michael didn't see anything other than a handful of stars.

"What?" asked Garth.

"One of them's *moving*."

For several seconds he was aware only of the barely per-
ceptible rumble of the sea. Then, "Yes." Jerry's voice. "It's a
comet."

"Hell of a show," said Garth.

THREE

For thou art Freedom's now, and Fame's,
One of the few, the immortal names,
That were not born to die.

—Fitz-Greene Halleck, "Marco Bozzaris," 1825

"WE KNOW WHERE Eden is," Jerry told the pool reporters.

"Where?" they shouted.

"Its sun is a K5 orange dwarf." He put the designator on the monitor: *2MASS J05384917-0238222.*

They gave off disappointed sounds. "Does it have a name?" one of them asked.

"That's as close as you'll get."

"We need to give it a name," the *Morning Show* said. "We can't really go live calling it *2Mass Whatever*."

April stepped in: "Since Jerry Carlucci discovered it, I think we should invite him to name it. He suggested *Oyate*."

Jerry tried to conceal his surprise.

The Associated Press pointed a pen at the astronomer. "Brilliant. Exactly the right thing."

April moved close to him. "Named for the tribe," she whispered. "We'll make it up to you later."

"No," he said. "That's good."

"How far is it?" asked a woman from PBS.

"It's pretty far," Jerry said. "A thousand light-years, give or take."

That drew some gasps. "Are you serious?"

"This keeps getting crazier."

"We always knew Eden was pretty far out," Jerry continued. "The Horsehead told us that much."

The *New York Times* asked whether we could assume that whoever built the Roundhouse had come from Eden? "Or can you travel out of the transport station there and go somewhere else?"

Jerry drew back and let April field the question. "The equipment doesn't seem to have been maintained," she said. "At one time, it looks as if Eden had connections with seven other places. Other than Johnson's Ridge. But only two of them still seem to be getting power."

"Can *we* provide power?"

"We don't know. We've been reluctant to tinker with the technology."

• • •

JAMES WALKER WAS uncomfortable taking chances with other people's lives. But since the Roundhouse had been unearthed on Johnson's Ridge, he had no real option. He was fully aware that, at his moderately advanced age, he'd be in the way if he tried to accompany the missions. But to salve his own soul, he would at least have to experience passage through the portal. Or, he thought, maybe he was just making up an excuse to go. To do what he seriously wanted to. There was no reason he should allow others to have all the fun. Especially now since Carlucci had named that world's sun for the tribe.

Nine or ten hours after April's mission had returned with its news about Eden, he visited the Roundhouse. The chairman would not have been easy to pick out of a crowd. He was short, with unremarkable features, and might have seemed more likely to be found repairing rooftops or cars than conducting meetings in a council hall. There was no hint of authority in his mien or his voice, nor was there a suggestion of the steel that could manifest itself when the need arose. His eyes were dark and friendly, his bearing congenial. Those who knew him well understood that his primary strength lay in his ability to get people to tell him what they really believed, a talent as rare among Native Americans as among the rest of the population.

He'd had a television and a computer installed in the transport room. When he walked in the door, CNN was interviewing Carlucci. He was explaining about light-years. Dale Tree was the senior duty officer present. The chairman said hello to everybody and took Dale aside. "I want to see the place," he said. "Eden. I'll only be there a few minutes. Can we manage that without having it become public?"

Dale glanced over at the other two security people, John Colmar and Jack Swiftfoot. "I'll let them know," he said. "When did you want to go, Mr. Chairman?"

"How about now?"

Dale walked over and talked briefly with the others. Then he arranged for Carlucci to take the reporters into the pressroom. When that had been done, he checked his sidearm, strolled over to a table, opened a drawer, and took out two pairs of gloves. He handed one to the chairman. "Ready when you are, sir."

The chairman nodded. "Thanks, Dale. Why don't you stay with Professor Carlucci? In case he needs an assist. John or Jack can go with me. We'll only be a couple of minutes."

Jack got the assignment. He was an average-sized guy who could disappear easily into a crowd. But he was a retired naval aviator who now did tour flights out of Devils Lake Regional Airport. He took the second pair of gloves from Dale, put them on, and walked over to the grid.

Walker had brought a revolver. He checked to make sure it was still in his pocket, donned the gloves, and joined his escort. "Looks as if we're off again," he said with a smile. Jack had been the chairman's pilot on numerous occasions.

"I'll go first," Jack said. He stepped onto the grid and pressed the arrow icon. A sprinkle of lights appeared and expanded into a glowing cloud. It wrapped around him, and he faded from sight.

"Enjoy your trip, Mr. Chairman," said Dale. He shook Walker's hand and left for the pressroom.

Walker knew the program. The luminous cloud reappeared, then faded, depositing Jack's pen on the grid. It was an indication everything was okay on the other end. John came over, apparently to assist, but Walker waved him away. "It's okay, John. I've got it." He picked up the pen and wasn't entirely surprised that as he leaned forward to press the arrow he was pumping adrenaline. The cloud reappeared. It settled over him, the Roundhouse interior faded, John waved good-bye, and he was in a different place.

Jack Swiftfoot was smiling. "Welcome to Eden, Mr. Chairman. Simultaneously our shortest and longest flight."

He opened the front door for the chairman, and Walker looked out at thick forest. He stepped down off the grid, walked across the room, and strode through the doorway into the new world. He'd timed everything to arrive at night. He wanted to see the two moons, but only one of them was in the sky. The night was full of stars, far more than he had ever seen from the Rez. A warm breeze whispered through the trees, and he could hear the dull rumble of incoming tides. He was no longer in North Dakota.

They circled behind the structure, walked through a brief patch of forest, and emerged on a beach. An ocean glittered beneath the Horsehead. This, he thought, would have been an ideal location for the reservation.

• • •

PRESIDENT MATTHEW R. Taylor understood that whatever else he might accomplish during his years in the White House, whatever bridges he might build, whatever boost he might provide the economy, he would always be remembered for what had happened on Johnson's Ridge. It had been an impossible situation. No way to get it right, and in the end he was the guy who had taken the country back to the Indian wars and gotten Walter Asquith killed.

The incident had left him shaken.

The United Nations was voting at that moment on a

motion demanding that the United States declare Johnson's Ridge an international facility. There was no question how that would go. People around the globe were arguing that the Roundhouse belonged to the human race, not to any one nation, and certainly not to those who happened to own the property on which it had been discovered.

Taylor was short and heavyset. He was not as good at hiding his feelings as were most politicians. On that morning, he watched TV images of the scientists talking with the media as they came back in from Eden, going on about the incredible technology and how they now knew where the planet was, and he found himself wishing the whole system would break down. There were too many conflicting issues. If they were able to reproduce the Roundhouse technology, which centered not only on instantaneous, long-range transportation, but also solar-powered energy production, what would it do to the transportation industries, to the car manufacturers, to the oil companies? It would probably wreck the economy. And there were all kinds of other hazards. They might bring a deadly virus back from Eden. Or even an army of invaders.

On the other hand, scientists around the globe were demanding access to whatever worlds were available. And some corporations wanted access to the technology. Handled properly, it could provide an enormous boost to a world with serious energy and population problems.

So what was the proper course of action?

It hadn't been an easy time for Harry Eaton either. The chief of staff was the guy who'd led the charge against all suggestions that they try to buy off the Sioux. It would cost too much politically, he'd told the president. The Indians had shown no inclination whatever to cooperate, and Eaton had argued that the administration had to be tough with them. Show no weakness. Taylor had made a last-minute effort to persuade Walker, the Sioux chairman, to cut a deal. But Walker had backed off, and after that he'd seen no alternative to the use of force.

Eaton had been certain that the Indians would give way at the first sign of armed marshals. And Taylor had bought in. How could he have been so dumb? His buzzer sounded, and Alice informed him that Eaton had arrived. That would probably be with the results of the U.N. vote.

Eaton was African-American, about average size, with an easygoing, if occasionally stubborn, demeanor. He didn't always have the politics right, but he was a genius at handling the media, and he usually got hold of the appropriate course of action. He came in holding an envelope. Even had Taylor not known how the vote would go, his chief of staff's expression made it clear. "It passed," he said.

The president exhaled. "Doesn't matter. We don't have the authority to take the land. And the U.N. can complain all they want, but they're in no position to take any action either."

"Nevertheless, it's a disaster, Mr. President. If we act on the motion, we can expect another armed confrontation. If we don't, if we exercise our veto, the Republicans will be calling it a train wreck."

"And they won't be wrong," said Taylor. "But I'm not going to get anyone else killed."

"That was my fault, Mr. President." He reached into his suit coat and produced a second envelope.

"Put it away," Taylor told him.

"I appreciate your willingness to keep me on board, sir. But somebody's going to have to take the fall."

"Somebody already has."

"Mr. President—"

"Shut up, Harry. If I let you go, I'll look like all those other sons of bitches who make dumb-ass calls, then try to blame it on somebody else. That might have worked in the old days, but not anymore. So just back off."

"Okay, sir. Thank you. But where do we go from here?"

The Roundhouse was a unique global problem. People were terrified of what might happen if its technologies became generally available. Some regional economies were already in a shambles. The auto-parts industry in Morocco was close to collapse. Oil prices had begun to sink, which was not necessarily a bad thing. The stock market was down. Gold was up. Capital investment everywhere had slowed to a crawl.

"I've talked with Walker, Harry. What we need to do is demonstrate stability. Ride it out. He's in agreement. He understands what could happen. He knows we can lend him engineers or whatever the hell else he needs to get through this. We'll do what we can for him. Meantime we hang on, avoid explosions, and eventually everything'll work out."

• • •

WALKER RETURNED HOME and slept for a few hours until his wife, Carla, woke him. "I just couldn't wait any longer, Jim," she said. "It's all over the TV."

He needed a minute to think about it. "Oyate?"

"Yes. I didn't think it was a big deal, but they're going on as if we landed on the Moon again."

"Beautiful," he said. Carla, like himself, was putting on too much mileage. But *unlike* him, she still looked good. Dark hair, gleaming eyes, and the dazzling smile he'd fallen in love with at the Rez school a hundred years ago. "Thanks, babe. I guess we can still do something right."

He watched the cable news while he ate breakfast. Then he headed for his office in Fort Totten. Its walls were decorated with tribal motifs, war bonnets, medicine wheels, and ceremonial pipes. His father's hunting bow was mounted beside the door, and framed photos of Carla and the kids were on the desktop. The boys were ten and eleven, and he wondered what they would see during their lifetimes. The world was changing so fast.

Miranda called. "Mr. Fleury's here," she said.

Jason was his White House contact. "Congratulations, Mr. Chairman. It looks as if you and the Sioux are going to decide what the future looks like."

"That would be nice, Jason," he said. "But I always get a bit uncomfortable when everything seems to be running in the right direction." He pointed at a chair.

Jason sat down and looked at Walker through his horn-rimmed trifocals. He possessed a casual manner that one seldom found in a high-level government official. He had consistently shown an ability to relax under pressure unlike anyone Walker had seen during his working career. Jason had been largely responsible for calming everyone down after the shooting that had occurred when the government had tried to seize the Roundhouse a few weeks before. "Anyhow, finding out where Eden is—that's great. The scientific world is deliriously happy."

"I couldn't help noticing, though, that they gave all the credit to the astronomers. I don't recall anyone mentioning the tribe."

"The astronomers are more visible than the Spirit Lake Sioux. But it'll be there, Mr. Chairman. The president asked me to pass along *his* congratulations, as well. They're having a celebration in the White House tomorrow night. They'd like you to attend."

"I'm kind of busy, Jason."

"Mr. Chairman, I don't want to get out of line here, but this *is* part of your job. You want the tribe to get the credit for their role, you have to show up for the celebration. You're the face of the Sioux."

"But I can't get to D.C. tomorrow night."

"Why not? There's a private flight leaving the Devils Lake Airport at eleven tomorrow morning. Carla's invited, too, of course." He looked happy while Walker tried to digest the news.

He was actually being invited to the White House? He wished his folks could have lived to see this. "Okay," he said. "Tell him I'll be there."

"Why don't you tell him yourself?" Jason produced a cell phone. "It's yours, Mr. Chairman. The president would like to hear from you. And he thought it would be a good idea if you could speak with him directly, without broadcasting to the world."

"There's something special about this phone?"

Fleury nodded. He touched one of the keys and spoke

briefly with someone. When he'd finished he turned it off and handed it over. "It provides a secure connection, sir," he said.

"With the White House?"

"You'll get Alice Worthington. She's the president's secretary."

"Excellent."

"Well, considering everything that's going on, Mr. Chairman, you need to have direct access."

"It might help, Jason. Thank you."

• • •

HE CALLED CARLA, who couldn't believe she was headed for the White House. She said she'd pack what they needed. "Can we get Janet to mind the kids?"

Janet was Carla's sister. "I'll call her. Middle of the week. It shouldn't be a problem."

Then he tried his secure phone. Just push the call button. A woman's voice answered on the second ring. "Hello, Mr. Chairman."

"Alice," he said, "hello. May I speak with the president?"

"He's in a meeting, sir. We'll get back to you when he's clear."

"Okay. And there's a party tomorrow night?"

"Yes, sir. In the East Room. The president would like you to attend."

"Yes. We'll be there."

"Excellent, sir. The president will be delighted. They'll be starting about eight."

The chairman was on his way out the door headed for home when the president reached him. "James," he said, "I'm delighted you can make it." He sounded ecstatic.

First the Horsehead Nebula. Then a party with the president. Life, he thought, was good.

• • •

THEY FLEW INTO Washington in a small government jet and were taken to the Hilton, where they received a call from Alice Worthington. "We'll pick you up at nine," she said.

Walker frowned. "Alice, we were told the party would start at eight."

"It does, Mr. Chairman. But you'll be fashionably late. Okay?"

A limousine arrived at 8:45, and they rode to the White House with a staff escort. They pulled up in front of the East Wing. Music and laughter spilled out of the building. Doors were held for them, and they went inside and were taken to the East Room. The exhilaration that arrived with the invitation was fading, and the chairman had already begun to think he'd be happier when it was over. He didn't know anyone there, and he just didn't feel as if he belonged.

But he and Carla had barely entered the room when President Taylor, who must have been alerted to their presence, was waving at them and summoning them in his direction. He called for everyone's attention and introduced them to a sustained round of applause. He invited the chairman to say a few words, but Walker felt overwhelmed. "I'm proud to be here," he said. "Thank you very much." That brought more applause, but the level of enthusiasm had diminished.

Walker was usually good at social events. One had to be in order to succeed in politics, regardless of what level it played out on. But this was simply too much. He and Carla were introduced to the First Lady, the Chief of Staff, the secretaries of state, the navy, and the treasury. There were half a dozen generals and admirals, the president's science advisor, several physicists and biologists, a mathematician, and two movie stars he'd never heard of. Walker wasn't a fan of films.

Carla was taken away from him and escorted onto the dance floor by the Speaker of the House. Guests drifted in his direction, congratulated him, and wished him well. And, eventually, he relaxed.

He was talking with one of the White House staff, whose name rang no bells, when the president came over. "You've been doing a marvelous job, James," he said. "I was sorry we got off to such a bad start. But you know that. This whole thing is a tough call for us. I can tell you honestly that I'm not sure where we go from here. I wish that thing had never turned up."

Walker managed a laugh. "I know exactly what you mean, sir. I go to sleep every night wondering whether a truckload of Martians will come spilling out from Johnson's Ridge. We're at the beginning of something that will change our lives forever." Somebody brought over a couple of drinks. Walker thought they were rum and Cokes. He wasn't much of a drinker, but whatever it was, it had a soothing effect on him. "I'm trying to stay optimistic," he said.

"Me, too. But we're talking about radical change. And in politics, that's never a good thing." The president drained his glass and set it on a side table. "Right now, whoever's out there has forgotten about us. The smart thing to do would be to leave it that way."

"Mr. President, the technology suggests a highly advanced civilization. I doubt they'd be interested in giving us any trouble. I just wish we could be sure."

"So do I. But I don't think the possibility of invaders is anywhere close to the real danger. If we start transporting people from here to Chicago the way you're doing it at the Roundhouse, it would destroy the automobile industry. The airlines, the oil companies. There are a lot of things that will go seriously wrong, and I suspect a good many that we haven't even thought of. I'll tell you, James, if the Roundhouse suffered a complete breakdown, I'd have no regrets. Sometimes, I'm tempted to think we should arrange it."

Walker stared at the president. "If we do, we'll always regret it, Mr. President. I don't think—" What *did* he think? "In the long run, technology is always beneficial."

"I wonder if Oppenheimer believed that."

In fact, Walker didn't believe it either. But he was trying to keep his head above water. This was an opportunity unlike any ever provided for the Sioux. It was their chance to be at the forefront of the biggest technological breakthrough in the history of the species. To show the world who they really were. "I understand your feeling, Mr. President. But—"

"I know, James. I wish I knew the right way to proceed. I think our best course at the moment is to take our time. Move ahead cautiously. And be ready to close it down if we have a problem."

"This celebration tonight is strictly a political sideshow, isn't it?"

"No. We appreciate what you've done. And we've already made some major strides. I'm just suggesting we be careful not to go over the edge."

FOUR

Vision is the art of seeing things invisible.
—Jonathan Swift, *Thoughts on Various Subjects*, 1706

RANDALL EVERHARDT HAD spent the evening at his daughter's house in Walhalla. He was a grandfather and nothing pleased him as much as playing with the kids. They'd had a casual dinner, and afterward, Pete and Randy had broken out the blocks, and they'd built a fort. But snow began to fall at about eight, and the weather predictions weren't encouraging. Melinda thought it would be a good idea if he stayed with them overnight, but he was supposed to eat lunch the following day with other members of the Winter Group, and that probably wouldn't happen if he waited out the storm. So he said good-bye to everybody and headed home to Fort Moxie, on the Canadian border. It was only about a half-hour drive.

"Be careful, Dad," Melinda said as he picked his way across the icy ground to his car. It was bitter cold. Randall was closing on his eightieth birthday, and everybody had taken to telling him he shouldn't be driving anymore. That was ridiculous. Naturally, he was having some problems with joints and ligaments, but you could expect that. It was no reason for people to assume he couldn't get around.

He opened his car door, waved good-bye to his daughter and her husband, Bill, and slid onto the seat. He had to lift his left knee with his hand to get it in. One of life's little challenges.

He started the engine and the radio came on. It was tuned to KLYM, which was giving round-the-clock coverage to the Roundhouse story. He had actually lived long enough to find out there really were aliens. That was something he had never expected. He blinked his lights and backed out onto Sixth Street.

Everhardt turned north on Route 55, followed it out onto the plains, then east toward Fort Moxie. There was no traffic on the two-lane road. Maybe a car going the other way every few minutes, both cars slowing down until they got past each other. Matt Fanny was talking to somebody who was saying that he wasn't going to deny there was some sort of trans-porter in the Roundhouse. "But there's no way, Matt, it could take them all the way out to that What's-its-name Nebula in a few seconds. You know how far that is? I mean, it's a long walk."

"So what are you saying, Clyde?"

"I'm not sure. It's probably some sort of conspiracy. Maybe the Indians are trying to jack up interest in that place. Make some money selling tickets. I don't know. I know Einstein wouldn't buy it. There's something here that we just need to figure out."

Randall groaned. He was getting tired of the Roundhouse stories. He switched over to NPR, which was doing classical music.

He wondered what he could do to persuade the people in charge to let him make the trip out to Eden? He'd done a lot in his life. Fought in two wars, served as a high-school math teacher, had three kids and seven grandchildren. They were all turning out pretty well. And Melinda was a talented artist.

Fort Moxie was getting close. Its lights were visible in the distance.

He had regrets, of course. Everyone did. At least everybody who'd been paying attention. Most of his missteps were
beyond repair now, neglected friends, failure to realize when
he was needed, women who'd treated him well but that he'd
simply walked away from. He took a deep breath. He'd done
a fair amount of damage over the years. Without meaning to.

The radio voices were still chattering, but he could not
help recalling when Melinda had first settled in Walhalla, and
he and Julie were returning from their first visit. She was their
oldest child, and it had been a new experience. But on the way
back, when the lights ahead had glowed and everything had
been so serene, they'd been congratulating each other, and
laughing, and he'd known at the time it was an unforgettable
night.

Julie had shared his reaction. "Randy," she'd said, "I don't
know when I've ever enjoyed myself more than this."

It would be only a few months later that they'd discover
the cancer.

He crossed Interstate 29 and pulled into town, turned
right onto Second Street, and followed it south through the
ring of trees that circled Fort Moxie, ostensibly shielding it
from the prairie winds, and turned again onto the private
road that led to his garage.

The storm was picking up. He would have enjoyed finding
a good woman he could spend time with. He knew he was
never going to come close to replacing Julie. But it would be
nice to have a woman back in his life. Just someone to have
lunch with occasionally, to talk to, to go to the movies with.
Unfortunately, there were almost no women of an appropriate
age available in Fort Moxie. So he'd been giving thought to
selling the property and moving. To Grand Forks or Fargo.

When spring came, he'd have to paint the garage.

Its door rolled up, and he pulled inside, wondering what
had led him into a morose mood after such a pleasant evening. He turned off the engine, got out, and connected the
extension cord that powered the heater. If you live in North
Dakota, you need something to keep the engine warm during

the night, or you may not be able to start the car in the morning.

They'd been predicting ten below tonight, but it had probably reached that already. He zipped his jacket, left the garage, and started for the house. He'd forgotten to leave the outside lights on. There was no moon, and the sky was cloudy. But that was no big deal. The house loomed ahead, a dark mass wrapped in shadow. He was looking for his key when he put his foot into a hole, stumbled, wrenched his hip, and went down.

The pain was blinding, almost enough to shut off the cold. He screamed. But there would probably be no one close enough to hear him.

Randall closed his eyes. Tried to ignore what he was feeling. To crawl for the house.

It hurt. He lay there, trying to keep his face out of the snow. There were stories every year about people who disappeared during the winter and were found in the spring when the ice melted. Sometimes they were people who hadn't made it in from a garage. Really. There was that guy Eliot Baxter over in Noyes just last year.

He owned a cell phone, but it was in the house somewhere. Even had he taken it, it was probably not charged. He'd been promising himself that he'd start using it. Melinda had given it to him two Christmases ago, but it just seemed more trouble than it was worth. She was going to be angry with him.

He made another effort to get moving, just crawl a foot or so, but it hurt too much.

Somewhere off to the east, as he gave up and slid into darkness, he heard the lonely whistle of a passing train.

• • •

"RANDY, WHAT HAPPENED?" It was a familiar voice. "Come on, pal, talk to me."

It was Brian Collins, who owned the plot of land west of Randall's property. "Hip," Randall said. "Walked into a hole."

"Okay. Just relax. Help's on the way."

"Brian. Thanks." Randall tried to laugh, but his mouth hurt when he talked. "Glad . . . see you."

"Just take it easy." He wrapped a scarf across Randall's face. "The emergency unit should be here in a few minutes."

"Good." Randall closed his eyes. Make the cold go away. And it did.

Then he was awake again, being lifted into a stretcher. Jean Bennett, who lived over by the church, was bent over him. "You'll be fine, Mr. Everhardt. Just take it easy and try to breathe normally."

Brian was still there. "How'd you find me?" There were blinking lights, and the night was closing in again.

". . . Odd business," Brian said. It was all he heard.

• • •

THE THOUSAND-LIGHT-YEAR STORY got the biggest play by the media. Garth Chanowitz mentioned it to ABC's local anchorman, Brock Mellon. "How far is a thousand light-years in miles?" Brock asked.

Despite all his awards, and his obvious mathematical capabilities, Chanowitz was not good in front of a microphone. He needed to think about the question. "There are approximately ten trillion kilometers in one light-year, so for a thousand it would be, ah, ten quadrillion."

"Miles, Professor. What does that equate to in miles?"

"Oh. Six. Six quadrillion. Maybe a better way to think about it is that if somebody on that world had turned on a giant spotlight, bright enough to be seen looking out your window over there, and if they'd done it when Richard the Lionheart was running things in Britain, we wouldn't have seen it yet."

"And you were there yesterday?"

"We were."

"Amazing. What does that tell us about whoever put that thing on Johnson's Ridge?"

Garth frowned as if he were giving the notion serious thought. "Excellent question, Brock," he said, stalling. "I just don't know. All we can be certain of is that they were pretty smart."

Brad Hollister caught the interview in the morning while eating his routine 4:00 A.M. breakfast. The reaction was taking hold around the globe. It gives a whole new meaning to the term spacewalk, Joe Scarborough was saying. Other commentators were asking whether rocket-powered moon flights were now obsolete? "This story just keeps getting bigger," said Loretta MacLeary on CNN. "We're experiencing our first encounter with a nonhuman technological civilization. But who would have ever thought that the aliens would be gone?" On CBS, Joe Pendergast was talking about the impact, and especially the dangers, of meeting another intelligent species. "If we were smart," he said, "we'd close down the Roundhouse. Get rid of it."

Donna, who usually slept until seven, came into the kitchen, poured herself a cup of coffee, and sat down. "You should have invited that guy onto the show," she said, referring to Garth.

"Yeah. I wish I'd thought of it." He shook his head. "You notice, by the way, that we never have a meeting with an alien. It's always an *encounter*."

Brad had been following the Roundhouse story since the beginning, when Lasker dug up the boat on his land out near the Pembina Escarpment, which had once been the western shore of Lake Agassiz. The lake had been there until the glaciers in the north melted. It had then drained, leaving the vast plain that today formed the Dakotas, Minnesota, Manitoba, and Saskatchewan.

Lasker's property, during that era, would have been several hundred feet underwater.

Brad had mocked people who'd speculated about a connection between the ancient lake and the boat, which resembled something that might have been manufactured last week by Dakota, Inc. He'd gone out to the farm to look at it. Whatever idiots had put it together had screwed up the washroom: The toilet and sink were too small and the show-erhead too low to accommodate any adult. He'd used it as a running joke on the air for two weeks. But then the world got a surprise: The sailboat was constructed of an unknown element that was close to plastic but was actually something else. "They're telling us," Lasker had said on Andrea Hawk's talk show, "that it's extremely tough. That they can't tell how old it is."

Adam and MSNBC's Walt Casik were inside the command post that had been set up outside the Roundhouse. Casik was looking at a picture of one of the Eden moons and the ocean. "Tell me, Adam," he said, "do we have a presence on the other side? In the Eden, umm, what do you call it, the Eden transport station?"

"It's called the Cupola. But you mean at this moment?"

"Yes."

"No. We do not. There's nobody there now."

"So the aliens could be there right now, and we wouldn't know it."

Adam might have been looking for a way to evade the question. "Yes," he said finally. "That's correct. But we've been there for a couple of months, and we haven't seen anybody."

"Isn't that dangerous? I mean, what happens if someone goes over there and finds the place full of aliens? And they follow him back?"

"Don't you think that's kind of alarmist? I mean, if they exist at all now, these would be people, creatures, whatever, who have a pretty advanced technology. You're talking as if they'd be barbarians."

"Not really. I'm just wondering why we don't show a little more caution?"

"I'm pretty sure the chairman is aware of the issue, Walt. I wouldn't worry."

Donna's eyes drifted to Brad. She was still gorgeous, with black hair and dark, scintillating eyes and the same come-hither smile that had overwhelmed him when they first met while he was working as a cashier at Hugo's supermarket. But on that morning, the smile had given way to concern. "You okay?" she said.

"I'm fine."

She got up and put some toast on, sipped her coffee, and sat down again. "Life's getting complicated, Brad."

"Yeah." When they'd been doing the excavation a few months earlier, he'd thought about going to Johnson's Ridge and doing a broadcast from the place. He'd decided not to bother. It was at that time just a hole in the ground. It was probably as close as he'd ever come to having a major national news story break on his program. "It'll give us a lift this morning," he said. "Can't ask for more than that, I guess."

"You know what, Brad? This Johnson's Ridge thing is a big deal for you and the station. But I'll be glad when it's over." They sat watching Walter asking Adam how he felt about aliens living next door, and whether he was happy that the Roundhouse was located on the Reservation. Meanwhile the toast popped. Four pieces. Donna arranged them on a plate and brought them to the table.

Brad picked up one, added some butter, and bit down on it. "Why do you want it over, love?"

"Because I'm not sure what's going to happen next. I'm not sure what might come out of the Roundhouse. Doesn't it worry you at all?"

"Not really," he said. "I've thought about it. And I guess there are some weird possibilities. But when they start talking about invading aliens, I begin getting the sense that I'm in a bad science-fiction film. Whoever built that thing, they used it to come here and go sailing on Lake Agassiz. They just don't sound all that dangerous to me."

"You're talking ten thousand years ago. There might be something else coming through there now. What about those stories about a wind creature, whatever it was that was reported in Fort Moxie?"

"Donna, that's a stretch. And I'll believe the stories about the little whirlwind when pictures of it show up on CBS."

He finished breakfast, smiled reassuringly at Donna, and started for the door. "See you tonight, kid. You might want to take a nap before you go over to the school."

• • •

MATT FANNY ARRIVED fifteen minutes after Brad did, which was unheard of. He usually didn't come in before eight. And he was not happy. "I assume you saw what's happening?" His eyes were aimed directly at Brad.

"Yes. I saw it."

"You know this Cannon woman pretty well, don't you?"

"More or less."

"Why don't you explain to her how much it would mean to us if she would give us a call and let us know when she's sitting on a major story? That they'd figured out where that place *is*?"

In fact Brad *had* known. She'd told him how far it was. It just didn't seem like a big deal. A hundred light-years or a thousand. It's way the hell out there. He already knew that. Anybody with a brain knew that. But he didn't want to tell that to Matt, to admit that he'd held back a story of this magnitude and let the major networks run with it. "I'll talk to her," he said. April was due there later that morning, and there was always a possibility his boss would confront her about it. He took a deep breath. "She might have said something about it to me. She mentioned light-years at one point. I don't recall that she put any emphasis on it."

Matt's expression was taking on the aspect of a thunderstorm. "Are you *deranged*, Brad?"

"Matt, she started by telling me the mission had been routine. Nothing unusual had occurred. And she was right. The astronomers took some measurements. Eden was way out there. We already knew that. I mean, you could see the Horsehead Nebula from that beach."

"How the hell long have you been in this business, Brad? Breaking news is what matters. It's all that matters." His teeth were showing. "All right. Make sure it doesn't happen again, okay? Explain to her about stuff like that. What's the goddam point of having a friend on the inside if something like that shows up, and we either don't get the word or we're too dumb to recognize it when we hear it?"

He turned on his heel and headed back to his office.

• • •

DAYLIGHT FILLED THE room when Randall awoke. A nurse was smiling down at him, straightening blankets. Or maybe adjusting the devices he'd been tied into. "Good morning, Mr. Everhardt," she said. "How are you feeling?"

His hip was numb. But otherwise everything seemed normal. "I didn't break anything, did I?"

The smile widened. She looked friendly and optimistic, which was just what he needed. No bad news coming. "No, sir," she said. "Nothing broken. The doctor will be with you in a few minutes."

The doctor was tall and seriously overweight, not exactly setting a good example for his patients. But at the moment none of that mattered. "You're fine, Mr. Everhardt. You'll want to be more careful walking around at night. And I think you might need a hip replacement eventually. We'll keep you here for a day or two, just to be sure you're okay. We don't want you to do any walking for a while. All right?"

"Thanks, Doctor," he said.

"Glad we could help. By the way, you're lucky they got to you when they did."

As soon as he left, Melinda came in. She looked relieved. "What happened?" she said.

He told her, as much as he understood himself.

"So you were out by the garage in the dark? How'd they find you?" She'd grown up on the property and knew how far away everybody was.

"Brian found me. I don't know how."

"Did you have your cell with you? Maybe you called him."

"No. I forgot it."

She rolled her eyes. Some things never change. "He just happened to be back there?"

"I have no idea how it happened," he said.

"You owe him your life, Dad."

• • •

THEY WERE GIVING him painkillers, of course. He slept most of the day. Didn't remember lunch although the nurse told him he'd had one. He was more or less awake that evening, and almost feeling normal again, when Melinda returned. With Bill. "I've been here all day," she said. "Bill just got off work." They'd unhooked him from the machines.

Bill was a firefighter. He looked exactly like the kind of guy who'd rush into a burning building to get someone stranded on the top floor. If somebody was going to show up after he'd fallen down in the snow and do a rescue, he'd have expected it to be Bill. Even if he had no idea how the guy could have known. They were talking about how he should not go anywhere without his cell phone, and how many people just in the Pembina County area had survived near-death experiences because they'd been able to call 911.

Well, of course they were right. And Randall was assuring them for the fourth or fifth time that it wouldn't happen again when Brian walked in. His wife, Mary, was with him. They were both in their fifties, both smiling, both happy to see Randall in good condition. Brian worked at the post office; Mary was a teacher at the elementary school.

Melinda sighed and hugged them both. "Thank God you were there last night, Brian," she said. "I hate to think what could have happened."

Mary sat down, but they were short one chair, so Bill got out of his and offered it to Brian.

"It's okay," Brian said. "I'm good."

Bill insisted. "It's the least we can do for the man of the hour."

It took maybe thirty seconds before Melinda asked the pertinent question: "Brian, how did you happen to be in the right spot at the right time? Did you hear him calling for help?"

Brian glanced at Mary. He was a big guy, broad-shouldered, somebody you'd suspect was a former linebacker. Mary was blond and still had her figure. She had never been a cheerleader, but she could have fooled Randall. They both looked as if the question was somehow embarrassing.

"Tell them," Mary said.

Brian shook his head and exhaled. "I think it was divine intervention."

"Really?" Randall couldn't resist grinning. "Nothing like having the Lord on your side."

"I'm serious. Randy, we've known each other a long time. You know I'm not a wacko, right? At least I hope so."

Yeah. That was true. Brian and Mary were both pretty solid people. "So what happened?" Randall asked.

"We were watching TV. A Western. We don't usually bother with Westerns, but this was a John Wayne movie. Anyhow, I started seeing a picture of you lying in the snow back of your house."

"What?"

"It's true. It was like the living room went away and everything got dark and I was looking down at you. Maybe from the trees. You were lying in the snow between your house and the garage. I knew I was imagining it, and the first thing I thought was that I had a brain tumor. I got really scared." He looked around at the others. "It wouldn't go away. I could still hear the movie. I could feel the chair under me. And Mary was asking me what was wrong. But it was like noise interfering with reality. You were the reality, Randy.

"Then it faded. It didn't completely go away, but I was back in front of the television. I was feeling my forehead, thinking I had a fever. But I thought I better go look outside, just to be sure. So I got out of the chair. I was a little bit dizzy. Mary asked me what I was doing, and I told her about you. Lying out there."

Everybody was staring at him. Except Mary, who was

nodding. Bill glanced over at her. "He told you about Dad? *Before* he went outside?"

"That is correct."

"I grabbed a jacket and told her I'd be back in a minute." He paused and took a deep breath. He had a deer-in-the-headlights look in his eyes. "I don't know what I expected to find. The apparition, whatever it was, went away after I got out of my chair. I felt as if I'd lost my mind."

"That's really weird," said Bill.

"We went over to the rectory this morning," Mary said. "We told Reverend Claude what happened. He was skeptical at first. Thought we'd both lost it, but then he said that it might have something to do with the Johnson's Ridge excavation. That strange things had been reported recently. I don't know. But we sure owe *somebody*."

• • •

IT LEAKED OUT to the media, and Brian found himself talking to television cameras that evening. The story appeared in the *Herald* next morning, bringing a surge of phone calls from neighbors, friends, and relatives. Even his two daughters, one living in Boston and the other in California, got in touch. Most people tiptoed around the divine-intervention theory, not wanting to call him crazy, but they all told him they weren't surprised that he'd shown up where he was needed.

• • •

HIS CONVERSATION WITH the president continued to replay itself in Walker's mind. *"I can tell you honestly that I'm not sure where we go from here. I wish that thing had never turned up."*

Taylor was a good man. But he was on the wrong side of the issue.

". . . If the Roundhouse suffered a complete breakdown, I'd have no regrets. Sometimes I'm tempted to think we should arrange it."

Taylor did not care about the potential benefits for the tribe. Or, more likely, he simply did not grasp the reality. The Spirit Lake Sioux stood at the crux of history. Walker was not going to let the opportunity melt away. But he did not want to force the president's hand. He'd tried to signal the president that he was a player also. That he was willing to reduce the number of missions. But he wasn't going to terminate them. Taylor didn't seem to have gotten the message. Consequently, the chairman would have to make a statement.

FIVE

*The night is more melancholy than the day; the
stars seem to move in a more melancholy
manner than the sun; and our imagination
roams more widely because we suspect
that everyone else sleeps.*

—Bernard de Fontenelle, *Conversations on the
Plurality of Worlds*, 1686

DURING THE FIRST few weeks after the Roundhouse had
been opened, the Sioux had allowed visitors inside during
daylight hours. Walker had never been comfortable with the
policy, but tourists had become a major element in life on the
Rez and, for that matter, around Devils Lake generally. But
the crowds quickly became overwhelming, so Walker had
been forced to exclude them. They could drive past on the
access road, take as many pictures as they liked, but casual
visitors would no longer be allowed inside the building.

Most of the local politicians objected. They wanted him
to permit visitors. Even Devils Lake Mayor Wilma Herschel,
usually a reasonable woman, tried to persuade him to reopen
the place and deal with the risks by hyping security measures. He'd just finished a discussion with Wilma over lunch
and returned to the Blue Building when a call came in for
him. "From a Mr. Osborne," Miranda said.

Walker tried his coffee and picked up the phone. "This
is the chairman," he said. "What can I do for you?"

"Mr. Walker, I represent Caulfield and Barker. The law

firm out of Grand Forks. I assume you know who we are."
Walker had no idea. "Can you make some time to talk with
me this afternoon? It's very important."

"May I ask what it's about?"

"I'd rather not discuss it on the phone. We have an offer to
make. I'd be surprised if you wouldn't find it to your advantage."

• • •

OSBORNE WAS TALL, with a precisely manicured black beard,
gray eyes, and the features of a guy accustomed to having
his way. He was almost bald, probably approaching sixty.
He carried a briefcase, and he wore a coat and tie, a proclivity
not often seen in Fort Totten. "I'm sure you're aware of the
effect the Roundhouse technology would have on the economy if it could be widely applied, Mr. Chairman. I represent
an organization that has been looking into the potential
results. Their conclusion is that the prudent strategy would
be to shut it down. To destroy all trace of the technology. To
make it generally available in the economy would result in
absolute chaos. We already have a problem with the concentration of wealth at the top of the social ladder. Instantaneous
transportation sounds like a great idea, and in the long run,
it might well be. But at the moment, in this economy, in this
society, it would result in the probable collapse of every
industry connected with moving people from one place to
another. Think about that, sir."

Walker wondered if he'd been sent by the president. "So
what are you suggesting?"

"That we take a safe route, one that would eliminate the
negative effects, but still allow the Spirit Lake Tribe to profit
handsomely."

The chairman could see clearly enough what was coming. "And what would that safe route be, Mr. Osborne?"

"We are prepared to offer you three hundred million
dollars if you will allow us to destroy the Roundhouse.
You'll come out of it very nicely. Consider the alternative:
If you proceed on your present course, and the technology
can actually be adapted, I doubt there's an economist in the

country who would not predict a global crash. Not only transportation industries. But the entire defense establishment would be rendered useless. Retailers everywhere would close. Whatever profit you'd glean from the Roundhouse would very likely be worth nothing in a dead economy." He smiled. "I'm sure you recognize that as well as we do."

"And you're prepared to pay us three hundred million to turn everything over to you?"

"I can write the check now." He opened the briefcase and extracted a folder, which he opened and handed to Walker. "This is the agreement. If you wish to settle it, we can bring in someone to act as a witness and sign the deal."

Walker always thought of himself as decisive. But with regard to the Roundhouse, he faltered. He wasn't sure what would be best for the tribe. Three hundred million dollars. Was the global economy really in that much danger?

But if he sold the Roundhouse, and they actually put it to the torch, he had no way of knowing what might be lost. And he'd carry that responsibility the rest of his life. "I'll get back to you," he said.

Three hundred million. He could solve a lot of the tribe's problems with that kind of money. If he played this right, the people on the Rez would prosper. He didn't want to give away the one thing that really mattered: This was an opportunity for the Spirit Lake Sioux to make an historic contribution to the global society. They'd never before been in a position to do that. Ultimately, the money would be there. But a great deal more was involved than simply turning a profit. This was a chance to acquire immortality. To create a world in which he and his people could live with pride. That was the prize being offered, and there was no way he was going to sacrifice that.

They might emerge with the technology to create unlimited instantaneous transportation anywhere on the planet. Or to Mars. Or, for that matter, to the edge of the galaxy. The Roundhouse also possessed an ability to create substantial energy from sunlight, apparently far beyond anything that could be generated by solar collectors. At least, that's what the experts thought was happening. So maybe they were looking at a solution to the world's power issues. The president was concerned about putting airlines and automobile manufacturers out of business. But surely adjustments could be made. Should we have stopped the development of automobiles because of what they would do to the horseshoe industry?

As far as money was concerned, the worst that could happen was that the Sioux would have to settle for transporting tourists to the space station. Or Eden. That process wouldn't produce three hundred million dollars overnight. But he suspected that profits would be enough to provide a pretty decent living for everyone on the Rez.

He sat staring out the window at the snow-covered trees.

• • •

BRAD HAD BEEN under pressure to bring Lasker in as a guest. It was too late now. But he'd had a better idea. He went after Michael Fossel, the neurologist who'd been on the most recent Eden mission. Fossel accepted. He hadn't left the area yet, so he was able to come in the day after the invitation was issued. Brad had seen him on TV, but nevertheless he looked younger in person, with intense blue eyes and the jawline of a TV police detective. He was casually dressed, with an open brown leather jacket revealing a gray rugby shirt.

Brad shook his hand, got him some coffee, introduced him to a couple of the staff, and took him back to the studio. "Professor," he said, "I see you've written a book on life extension."

The visitor delivered a friendly smile. "Call me Michael, Brad. And yes, I have. We're not live already, are we?"

"No, we have a few minutes yet. The title is *Reversing Human Aging*. Do I have that right?"

"Yes. You've done your homework."

"Part of the job, Michael. You're also a member of the Gerontological Society?"

"That's correct."

They sat down at a table with two microphones. Brad looked up at the large clock over the bookcase. It was 7:03 A.M. The news was running. "Tell me," he said, "are we actually going to be able to do that?"

"Reverse aging?"

"Yes."

"In all probability."

"How long before we figure out how to make it happen?"

Michael leaned back in his chair. Brad could see he was tired of skeptics. "It's getting close," he said. "Probably in our lifetime."

"Are you serious?"

"Of course."

"Maybe that's what we should be talking about today. That would be a bigger story than just traveling around in space."

Michael shrugged. "Your call, Brad."

"Do you think you could come back in a few days? Maybe Monday?"

"I think I can arrange that if you want."

Brad asked a few more questions, kept an eye on the time, and finally pulled his headphones down over his ears. They were running commercials. He activated the mikes and leaned over his.

His screener, Cary Elder, took her seat behind the glass in the control room. "One minute, Brad," she said.

• • •

THE SHOW WENT live. "So, Michael," Brad said after doing the introduction, "you've actually walked on another planet?"

The neurologist grinned. He was obviously enjoying himself. "That's what they're telling me."

"But it's hard to believe? Even for a guy who's been there?"

"Sure. Monkey brain at work, right? Teleportation seems like a scam."

"How did it feel?"

"It doesn't hit home right away. When the transporter grabs hold of you, everything tends to freeze. You're just sort of bundled up and carried off. Then I was at the other station, the one on Eden that they call the Cupola. You walk outside, and it feels just like being on the ground here, except that it isn't so cold. By the way, I should add that I lost about fifteen pounds in the process."

"Are you saying the gravity is less?"

"It is. It's hard to be sure just from how you feel. But they've checked it. That place is a little different from Earth."

"I guess none of us would ever have believed something like this could happen. Doesn't it violate basic physics?"

"Apparently not, Brad." He couldn't resist a broad smile. "It's what science is about, I guess. Discovering where we got things wrong."

"Okay. Exactly how does it work, Michael? Do you just go through doors, or what?"

"There's a grid built into the floor. It's *big*. And there are some symbols, icons, visible in the wall behind it. You stand on the grid and press one of the icons. It lights up, and the next thing you know, you're looking at a sky with two moons."

"Incredible." Brad sat back and took a long deep breath. "Did you see other people use the system before you did?"

"One other. Adam Sky went first. He's one of the security guys."

"And what happened with him? Did he just disappear?"

"That's as good a description as any. There was a lot of light, and when it went away, he was gone, too."

"What do the physicists say?"

"I think they're not sure yet what to say."

Brad hesitated. "Michael, when you got onto the grid, were you nervous?"

"Are you serious? I had all I could do not to throw up."

"But you went through with it—"

That large smile reappeared. "No way I could duck."

"All right. Now, they're saying this place is out"—Brad

had to check his notes—"in the general direction of the Orion constellation."

"Yes."

Brad finished his coffee and refilled both cups. "Michael, pictures from Eden are available now. I didn't see anything that appeared particularly alien. The animals looked more or less like squirrels and cats and birds. The foliage isn't quite anything we'd see out back. I mean the colors aren't the same. But it doesn't look all that different. Still, we're being told they *are* different in some basic ways. Could you explain that, please? How are they different?"

Michael considered the question. "Keep in mind that we're in strange territory here, okay?"

"All right. So what do you think?"

"In most cases, when we try to predict what alien life might be like, we are remarkably provincial. For example, our division between plants and animals is not likely to apply perfectly, and maybe not even remotely, to alien biology. There may well be organisms that move and others that don't. There may be some that are equipped with collectors and are able to take their energy directly from the sun. And maybe others that eat the ones with collectors, just as our animals eat plants, but there may also be exceptions that we can't easily predict.

"The individual world will determine what an organism looks like. A planet with an atmosphere whose density is similar to ours, and which approximates our gravity, will very likely have birds. They'll resemble our birds, but that still leaves a lot of room for variation. We have convergent evolution, which occurs when two very different organisms try to fill the same ecological niche. When that happens, ultimately they resemble each other. For example, Australian honey possums, butterflies, and hummingbirds all developed a long tongue to remove nectar from flowers. Humans aren't the only animals that have opposable thumbs. There are hundreds of examples.

"The result is that, even though they may not be closely

related, lots of animals look as if they are. Eden has birds, squirrels, and trees. But, if we take the time to look closely, we'll probably see some major differences. Their sparrows may have fangs. Even though there are creatures that look like squirrels, they may have scales. A maple tree might have bony support material and be hollow. If we look deeper, at microscopic and genetic levels, we'll very likely see that alien organisms are vastly different." He sat back and took a deep breath. "Does that make sense?"

"Sparrows with fangs? That's a bit unsettling, Michael."

"Keep your collar pulled up."

"Did you see anything there that you didn't expect? Anything that surprised you?"

"Brad, I wasn't there long enough to do any serious research. I'd love to get invited back and spend a few weeks in that forest. Or a couple of years. I'd want to establish a laboratory outside the Cupola and bring a staff with me. But we do know a few things. I'm not the first biologist to see the place, and I had a chance to look at some of the material the others brought back." He paused and propped his chin on one fist. "Yes, I got some surprises. On Earth, animals— all free-ranging organisms—have mitochondria. Plants, which don't move around much, all have chloroplasts. Plants make energy from the sun, and store it as sugar molecules. Animals take the sugars from the plants and use the energy. On Eden, things aren't so simple. Some of the birds actually have chloroplasts as well as mitochondria, which is unheard of here. As a result, the birds can glide through calm air and collect energy directly from sunlight. As far as we can tell, they can stay aloft indefinitely.

"We've seen a few of them go above the clouds, so they don't care if it's a cloudy day. They seem to have only two limitations: They can't get enough energy to battle high winds, and they have to come down to mate and raise their young. We've seen them nesting in trees, and we know they eat some of the plants. And we assume they have to sleep. But we don't know for sure."

Brad grinned. "I guess mating on the fly would be pretty tricky." They both laughed. "Michael, do you think any of these animals could operate as pets? Could they blend easily with wildlife on Earth? Except, I guess, that it's colder here. I understand it's winter there now. So it probably doesn't get very cold."

Michael leaned forward and focused on a place somewhere far from Brad. "They might blend in, but most of them couldn't survive on Earth. The birds with the solar collectors would probably do okay though the spectrum's a bit different. But even they need a certain amount of food. Biologies have some fundamental differences. We're probably going to learn that the basic sugars are the same, but most of the proteins and all of the vitamins are different, as are their requirements for minerals. You and I could eat some of the fruits and grains. But except for the sugars, we wouldn't get much nourishment. The same would be true of any Eden animals brought here. Some of the plants would do fine, though. I'd enjoy bringing back some seeds and setting up a garden."

"Michael, we've got some calls waiting. We'll go to them in a couple of minutes when we get back from break." He pressed his fingertips to the earpieces, listened to a commercial for Phil's Jewelry Store begin, checked the time, and removed the headphones. "Brilliant, Michael," he said.

• • •

Janet called every morning. "Hello, Brad. Professor Fossel's a great guest. I'd like to ask whether the animals up there reproduce more or less the way we do? The reason I'm asking is that I heard a rumor they have three sexes? Anything to that?"

Fossel had to smother a burst of laughter. "Janet," he said, "theoretically, the evolutionary costs of having three sexes probably make it impossible to reproduce that way. Imagine that, in order to have sex, you not only have to find one other compatible member of your species, but two—one from each of the other two genders. And you have to find them at the same time. It would make reproduction a bit dicey.

"Which reminds me of another story about two birds and a bee that are out in the jungle when—Well, maybe we better let that one go."

Brad watched him for a moment, trying to decide whether to encourage him to continue, or move on. Finally: "Michael, do they breathe? Can you imagine an advanced life-form that doesn't need lungs or gills?"

"I'm glad to get an easy question. All the land animals we've seen so far on Eden seem to be breathing. We haven't really had much of a look at the sea creatures. Microscopic life-forms can get oxygen directly, but larger forms need a way to absorb it into the body. If the organism is small enough, it can use spiracles, as some insects do. If its metabolism is slow enough, and its active tissue is spread out into the air, like the trees in the park across the street, then it can get by with stoma in the leaves. Once you get a larger organism, particularly a metabolically active one, you always need a way to pull in oxygen, transport it, and get rid of the carbon dioxide. Eventually, we may see an exception to this rule, but I couldn't tell you what it might look like."

Another regular caller was on the line. Mark Collins, a retired guy with whom Brad occasionally ate lunch. "I guess people are interested in lungs and gills and stuff like that, but what we really care about is intelligence, Michael. Have you seen anything that's intelligent?"

"Again, it's early in the game. We haven't seen anything we could talk to."

"So who built the dome? Who was riding in the boat that was buried?"

"We have no idea, Mark. We're going to have to be patient. Whoever built the Cupola is apparently not using it anymore. They may not have used it for thousands of years."

"But it has power, doesn't it?" said Mark.

"So does the Roundhouse. And that was dug out of the ground. Obviously, there are intelligent aliens in the mix somewhere, but we have no details. Except that it's obvious they're much more advanced than we are."

The show continued through two hours. Eventually, the question came that Brad knew was inevitable. "Professor Fossel," the caller said, "we were always led to believe alien life, if it existed, would be radically different from what we see around us. Yet they look very much like the birds and cats and turtles that inhabit our own world. Some people say this demonstrates a purposeful Creator. Without getting into a religious discussion, what do you think?"

"My specialty is neurology, Caller, not theology. In my opinion we've seen nothing that either implies or rules out a purposeful Creator. From our standpoint, you can take your pick. I have to say, however, we are not surprised by seeing life on Eden resemble what we have here on Earth. But an obvious explanation for that is that Eden resembles Earth. Gravity, atmospheric makeup, water, temperatures. They're all similar. There are only so many ways to make an organism fly or swim, so many ways to build an eye or an ear, to build a skeleton or a musculature. Turtles are a good example. If an organism needs protection, then the shape of the shell won't vary much. It's pretty much defined by the fact that an organism has a head and four limbs. Actually, those are good examples of common forms. Most animals will have a head that shares most of the common features found on Earth: a brain, some sensory inputs, and a mouth. They're necessary to survive.

"The universe imposes certain constraints. It may not share a universal seed of life or a universal Creator, but it shares rules of physics. And that seems to be enough to get the job done."

The next caller wanted to know whether we were concerned about bringing back a plague?

"It's highly unlikely," Michael said. "A microbe that emerges from a completely different biological system would almost certainly not be equipped to attack us. We've run some preliminary tests that support that view. The smaller the organism, a virus for example, the more it depends on the host for the equipment it needs to reproduce. Since it's an alien biology, it won't find the right equipment in human cells."

Brad pointed at the clock. They were running out of time. "Michael, is there anything we failed to ask that we should have?"

His guest shrugged. "Your listeners covered a lot of ground."

"Is there a lesson we should take away from this? From what we're seeing on Eden?"

"There's one: The biological rules are always the same, but we should expect the unexpected. Physics—the foundation that underlies biology—will rule life everywhere. You can rely on finding convergent evolution, but there will always be surprises. As in the case of six-legged aliens, it's a poor bet, but odd things happen, and we always make assumptions without even being aware we're doing it. Every new living world will probably make us reevaluate, not the physics of the universe but the way biology uses physics to thrive. If we think we understand an alien biology, we're almost certainly missing something."

Brad leaned over his mike. "Thank you, Michael. That does it for today. This has been *Grand Forks Live*. We'll be back tomorrow at seven. Stay tuned for the *Bill Williams Show*, immediately following the news." He pulled the headphones off and laid them on the table.

Michael sat back in his chair, eyes closed. "How'd we do?"

"That was good. You might consider a career in radio."

He grinned. "No, I talk too much."

"Listen, that was a hell of a show. I envy you."

"Why's that?"

"You're right in the middle of the most exciting story I've ever heard."

"Well, that's true. It's been quite an experience. Have they invited you to go?"

"Ummm, more or less. But I've passed. I don't see much use in my being there."

"But you'd like to do it, right?"

"Sure." Brad got up and started for the door. "I'm not much of a scientist. I wouldn't be able to contribute anything."

"But they're sending media people." Brad looked at his watch, trying to pretend he had to be somewhere else. "I understand you know April." Michael was standing just inside the door. "She could probably set you up."

"The media people they've been taking are the major-network types. I don't really qualify."

"I can't see it would hurt to give it a try." He finally came out into the corridor. "I'll put in a word for you if you like."

That sent a chill up Brad's spine. When he'd been eighteen, a neighbor had gotten him a part-time job with a construction company. They were beginning work on a large building, about twelve stories high, in East Grand Forks, across the Red River. He'd reported for work, and they'd sent him up a series of ladders until he was about eight stories high and out on girders. His job was to run around and recover dropped rivets. But just looking down at the street set his head spinning.

He'd quit the next day. For a moment, while his guest was talking, he was looking down at that distant street again. "It's okay, Michael," he said. "Don't go to any trouble."

SIX

*The causes which most disturbed or accelerated
the normal progress of society in antiquity were the
appearance of great men; in modern times they
have been the appearance of great inventions.*

—W. E. H. Lecky, *History of European Morals, I,* 1869

WALKER WAS ENCOURAGED by what Michael Fossel said.
When the show ended, he called April. "Let's take the
next step," he said.

"What did you have in mind, James?"

"We have two functional links at the Eden station that
we haven't used. Let's pick one and find out where it goes."

"Magnificent!" He knew she was raising a fist as she
tended to do when she got excited. "All right." She was trying
without much success to keep her voice level. "Just one? You
don't want to try both?"

"Let's do one at a time. See where it takes us. Do you
want to lead the mission?"

"I can do that."

"Good. Let's figure on a team of five. Besides you and
security. I'll give you the next five names off the list." The
list, of course, had originated in the White House. "I want
Adam Sky to go on this one. And probably Paula."

"Bad idea," said April.

"What's a bad idea?"

"Sending a *team*. Why don't you let Adam and me make

the crossing? Give us a chance to look around a little. So we don't get any surprises. *Then* send the team."

"April, Adam will go first. If everything's okay, he'll send a message back the way we normally do. If there are dinosaurs or something, we'll just go no farther. Where's the problem?"

"I think it would be safer to know what we're dealing with before we put a crowd together."

"That would be fine if there weren't a political side to all this. Every big scientific name in the country wants to go through the Roundhouse. They've been applying pressure. On me and on the president."

"So put them on a backup team. As soon as we're sure where we're headed, they get to go, too. I doubt anybody will have a problem with that."

"You don't seem to get it, April. Being on the backup team doesn't quite make it with these people. They want to be part of the initial operation. Do you recall who was the *second* person to walk on the Moon?"

"Yeah. Buzz Aldrin."

"All right. You know that, but most of the rest of us have missed it. Everybody wants what *you're* getting. To be first on a new world. Now, let's drop the debate. It's the way the president wants it, and that's the way we'll go. We also have a couple of astronauts coming in to show everybody how the pressure suits work." He paused. "What are the Eden links?"

"What do you mean?"

"What do they look like? The icons?"

"One's an octagon. The other's a set of three parallel lines."

"All right. Which one do we want to use?"

"I hadn't thought about it, James. Flip a coin."

"Okay. Do the parallel lines."

"Good enough. May I ask a favor?"

"You may ask."

"I promised my former boss I'd arrange for him to go along on one of the missions. He's a physicist. Retired now."

"What's his name?"

"Harvey Keck."

Walker put the list on his screen. "There's no Harvey Keck here."

"He doesn't have a political connection anywhere." It was hard to miss the annoyance in her voice.

Walker could add the name to his security force. But no. This was a chance to demonstrate that the tribe had some influence. "All right. Add him as a sixth participant. He won't fall down and hurt himself, or do anything like that, will he?"

• • •

WALKER TOOK THE secure phone out of his desk and made the call. Alice Worthington picked up. "Yes, Mr. Chairman?"

"Hello, Alice. Is the president available?"

"He's in a meeting, sir."

"Can you tell him I called?"

He got back to Walker within the hour. "James," he said. "What's going on?"

"We're sending a mission out. Through one of the Eden links."

"Thanks for the heads-up. But I don't think that's a good idea."

"I thought it was time to take another step forward."

"James, I wish you wouldn't do this."

Walker hesitated. He hadn't expected blunt opposition. "If you insist, Mr. President, I'll shut it down."

"No. God help us, I want to find out what's there as much as you do. But it's unsettling." Walker could imagine him standing there, his eyes staring but not seeing anything. "Do it," he said. "Keep me informed."

• • •

CALLS WERE CONSTANTLY coming in to Sioux Headquarters from people who wanted to travel out to Eden. They kept Miranda and a couple of temporary staffers busy. But one of the calls came from David Woqini, who had been Walker's physics teacher his senior year in high school.

The chairman, and probably most of his classmates, had expected the class to be a long, dreary exercise in calculating rates at which objects fell when you threw them off a building. But Mr. Woqini had started that first day by asking a question: "If you walk off the roof of the school, why do you fall?"

Everybody had yelled "Gravity!" and waved hands. The teacher had stopped them cold with the next question: "That's just a word. What *is* gravity? Why don't you just drift off over the trees?"

Nobody had any idea.

"It's because space is made out of rubber. The Earth is big and massive. So it bends space." They'd started snickering, and a few people laughed. "I'm serious," he said. "We slide down on the curve."

Mr. Woqini had other stories like that, explaining how you aged faster waiting for the school bus than you did while actually riding it. And how you weighed less on that same roof than you did in the cafeteria, which was on the ground floor. He was easily the best teacher Walker had ever known through sixteen years of school. They'd stayed connected.

David was retired now, still living on the Rez. "You have time for lunch?" he asked.

• • •

THEY MET WHERE they usually did, at the Old Main Street Café in Devils Lake. David never seemed to get any older. He was tall and lean, and the amused high-school spirit that had animated his features forty years ago was still there. "Hi, Jim," he said, removing his buckskin jacket and sitting down as a waitress approached. "I see you've become a prominent national figure. How's your friend the president doing?"

Walker grinned. "I *do* seem to have moved up in the world."

"Congratulations." They ordered a round of sandwiches and Diet Cokes. Then, when they were alone, David leaned across the table. "Have you done any of this transporting thing yourself?"

"Not officially. Did you want to try it?"

"Eventually, maybe. You know, a few weeks ago I'd have sworn this teleportation business wasn't possible. I don't think there's a physicist on the planet who has the remotest idea how you can disassemble somebody and move him clear out of the galaxy."

"I'm disappointed."

"Why, Jim?"

"I assumed that, if anybody could figure it out, you could."

He laughed. "It's a nightmare. We thought we had a handle on cosmic reality. Now we know we aren't even close."

"It's not my fault," said Walker.

"Sure it is. It's yours if it's anybody's. Makes me realize I never knew what I was talking about."

Eventually, the sandwiches showed up. The conversation continued along similar lines until, as they sipped the last of their Cokes, Walker felt the mood change. "What's wrong, David?" he asked.

"Jim, you realize you're in dangerous territory?"

"Yes. I know there are risks."

"I'm not just talking about the potential for invaders. Or the possibility of an economic collapse, which I'm sure you've thought of. But, as a result of what you find out there, we may experience a total cultural shift."

"How do you mean?"

"Historically, anytime a technologically advanced culture has connected with a relatively primitive one, a lot of things change. Values, for example. Perception. We could encounter an advanced society that laughs at religion. Or whose individuals have IQs at around two hundred. Or who live for centuries."

"I understand that could happen."

"There are probably hazards we haven't even thought of."

"David, there's a lot to be gained. We can't really walk away from an opportunity like this."

The waitress came and laid the bill on the table. Each

routinely paid his own tab. That was the rule. But David grabbed it. "This one's on me," he said.

"Why?"

"I don't think I've told you this before, but I'm proud to see what you've done with your life, Jim. I like to think I had a hand in it."

"You did, David."

"One more thing? If you can see a way to do it, I recommend you manage things so that we walk away from this. From the Roundhouse."

• • •

THE CHAIRMAN ARRANGED to have April's team of five scientists meet in the tribal conference room, along with the astronauts. Keck was also present, as was Adam Sky. The room was located just down the passageway from his office. A brick, single-story structure known as the Blue Building housed the tribal headquarters, as well as the post office, the Indian Health Service, and the Bureau of Indian Affairs. Outside, the flags of the United States and the Mni Wakan Oyate fluttered in a strong wind.

"Welcome aboard, ladies and gentlemen," he said. "I want to remind you we're going into territory where no human being has ever been before." He frowned. "Sounds like the opening lines for a television series, doesn't it?" That got some laughs. "Our primary goal is just to take a quick look around and get everyone back alive. If anybody's planning on bringing a weapon, it's okay as long as you're certified for it. But we want you to exercise extreme care. Don't use it unless absolutely necessary. Now let's move on. I'd like to introduce April Cannon."

April came forward and opened a folder. "Thanks, James. You already know that we're planning on spending about five hours, assuming everything goes well, at our destination. What we want to accomplish is simply to get a sense of what's on the other side of the link. We'll look around a bit, if we're able to, see if they have life-forms, if it's an Earth-type world, what else is going on. But primarily, we'll be cautious. Nobody is to take any chances. We stay together. The gentleman at the end of the table is Adam Sky." Adam raised a hand. "He will be heading up the security contingent. Anything he tells us to do, we will comply with."

She introduced the astronauts, Melissa Sleeman and Art Coleman. Melissa was a gorgeous redhead who turned the heads of every male in the room. Art, on the other hand, displayed a military demeanor, cool and confident, exactly the guy you'd want in the area if you got in trouble.

"My friends call me *Boots*," he said. "After we've eaten, we'll take a little time to familiarize ourselves with the pressure suits. In case we need them tomorrow." He reached under a table and produced a helmet. "Later today, we'll move the suits to Eden, where they'll be available. Adam will wear one when he makes the initial jump. He'll determine whether the suits are necessary and come back and let us know. If the atmosphere's okay and there is no other problem, we'll ignore the suits and just go."

They served lunch, giving everyone time to become acquainted. Nobody raised any issues about Harvey's presence, for which April was grateful. When they'd finished, Walker reminded everybody that they'd be picked up at their hotel the following day at 11:00 A.M. "We'll take you to the Roundhouse. You'll find Eden a little warmer than Fort Totten. Dress comfortably."

• • •

APRIL SPENT MUCH of the afternoon with them. She was not surprised to hear that their lives, like her own, had been taken over by the project.

"I wonder what we'll see out there?"

"I haven't slept for three nights."

"I don't guess you'd let me go first, April? I know how to use a pressure suit, and I don't think Adam would mind."

"You know, there's been nothing in my entire life to match this."

"Why don't we just go over to the Roundhouse now and get started?"

• • •

WALKER AND CARLA joined them for dinner at the Cedar Inn in Devils Lake. He offered a toast and said he was proud to be associated with them.

Arlene McMenamin, a Canadian astronomer seated next to April, asked about the stipulated five-hour duration of the mission. "I assume that has some flexibility," she said. "If everything's okay, we won't really be rushing to return, will we?"

"Assuming we don't have to wear the pressure suits, yes, we have some flexibility. Though I've promised the chairman that if we go past five hours, one of us will go back to the Roundhouse to let them know what's happening."

"Let's hope that's the way it plays out," said Ray Frontera, a mathematician from Shanghai University.

"I hope so, too, Ray," April said. "James will be waiting to hear what we've found, along with the rest of the planet. Five hours should be enough to tell us what's there. We can play with the details later."

• • •

BRAD CALLED. "YOU'RE headed out tomorrow, April?"

"Around noon."

"I don't guess I could get you for *Grand Forks Live* tomorrow morning before you leave? I can set everything up with our van at the Roundhouse. We can do the show there."

"I don't think so, Brad. Things are going to be a bit hectic."

"Then how about the following day? Friday? Will you be back by then?"

It wasn't the first time he'd asked. She'd been reluctant because she was so close to the project, and it was too easy to say something that would show up on the cable networks and blow up. Everybody had strong opinions about what the country should be doing about the crossover links. And no matter what she said, there was a potential for generating a lot of political heat. "Ask me when we get home, Brad," she said. "Okay?"

"All right. How long do you expect it will be before you get word back to us about what you've found? You think it will be just a few hours? Or—?"

"Brad, what I'm going to try to do is send Harvey back as soon as we know what we have."

"He'll come back to the Roundhouse?"

"Yes. It shouldn't take long. Probably not much more than twenty minutes."

"Okay. Good. Do you think I could get into the Round-house tomorrow? I'd like to be there when you guys head out. And when Harvey comes back."

"I can arrange that. Sure. I've gotta go, Brad. Take care."

• • •

THERE WERE so many troubling issues connected with the Roundhouse that Walker seldom slept soundly. When he closed his eyes at night, he could not get away from wondering who had been responsible for constructing it? Why would anyone with such technology want to visit a primitive Earth to go sailing? How did the place retain power after being abandoned for ten thousand years? Everything not connected with Johnson's Ridge now seemed trivial.

Carla tried to help. "Relax, Jim," she told him. "Everything will be okay. When you're in charge, everything's *always* okay."

"I wish David hadn't been so pessimistic. I could deal with it when the president got worried. But not David."

"Look, nobody moves ahead by backing away from opportunities. You've got good people on these missions. If you shut things down, you'd never forgive yourself."

He had invited the president to send in the engineers he'd earlier said were available. But Taylor had become reluctant. "Not just now," he'd said.

The Sioux had a couple of engineers he could call on. One in particular, Ivy Banner, had a solid reputation. Ivy and her husband lived in Fargo, where she worked for the Renko Construction Company. He didn't remember much detail about her except that she specialized in electrical design.

Next year, he'd be up for reelection, but unless something changed radically, Walker would not run. He'd had enough.

Tomorrow, if the mission went well, he'd call Ivy and ask for her help.

SEVEN

Hitch your wagon to a star.

—Ralph Waldo Emerson, *Society and Solitude*, 1870

ANDREA HAWK WAS on the midwatch at the Roundhouse. She'd spent the earlier part of the evening doing her talk show. She'd have liked to stay and watch April's team set out at noon, but she knew what kind of shape she'd be in after being awake all night.

A couple of media vehicles were parked on the lot, including a van from NBC. Other than that, the area was empty. She wandered outside just to get some fresh air, hoping the media types were asleep. But a door in the van opened. A woman got out and closed the door softly. She had no interest in waking her colleagues.

It was Josephine Costain, who had interviewed Andrea before. She came over and asked the routine questions: What did she think the mission would find when they did the crossover from the Eden link? Had Andrea hoped to go? Was there any possibility that the chairman would go back to allowing reporters to participate, as he had a few—? And she stopped in midsentence, staring up over Andrea's shoulder.

Andrea turned and looked in the same direction. A soft

white glow floated in the treetops at the edge of the parking area. It was rotating slowly. "What *is* that?" said Costain.

"A reflection." What else could it be? But it looked like a small whirlwind that had picked up some loose flakes.

The reporter kept staring. She didn't take her eyes off the thing while she asked whether it might be possible for her to go along on the new mission?

"I don't know," said Andrea. "You'll have to ask the chairman."

"You don't have any input on that?" She seemed surprised. Everybody knew that Walker thought highly of her.

"If I had any serious influence, Jo, I'd be on these missions myself." The little whirlwind was dissipating. Fading. Finally she decided it was probably just moonlight.

• • •

MATT FANNY SAW no point in Brad's visit to the Roundhouse. "They aren't going to let you go along on the trip, are they?"

"No. Not that I know of. But I'll be there today when they leave."

"Well, that's something, I guess." He looked bleary-eyed. It was pretty early for him. "When will we know what they find?"

"They're going to send Harvey Keck back with a report."

"Who's Harvey Keck?"

"He used to be April's boss over at Colson Labs."

"You know, if she can arrange for her old boss to make one of those trips, she ought to be able to manage something for us. Have you asked her to get you on board?"

"We've talked about it."

"It would be a game changer for your career, Brad."

"I don't think it would be a big deal."

"So what's she say?"

"They're sending scientists. I don't qualify."

Matt grumbled something. Then: "So how long's that going to take?"

"Will *what* take?"

"Getting Keck back to the Roundhouse?"

"She thinks about twenty minutes."

"All right. Call us when you have something. And maybe you can get one of those people for the show. This stuff is all anybody talks about anymore."

• • •

BRAD FINISHED *Grand Forks Live* at ten and headed immediately for Johnson's Ridge. He felt a bit out of place since he was not really a journalist. But he liked to think of himself as one, and he'd be crazy not to play this story for all it was worth.

There were dozens of media people in the parking lot when he got there. He bypassed them and headed directly for the front door. April had left his name with security, so he had no problem getting into the transport room. Someone from the tribe was talking to the pool reporters about why *they* weren't being allowed to join the mission. One of the CNN guys was literally yelling. "How can you say that? It's too dangerous for us? We still have people in Syria!" Chairman Walker came in a few minutes after Brad did, accompanied by a man and woman in blue NASA uniforms. April was also there, mingling with the crowd. Walker went over to her and shook her hand.

So did Brad. Over the next twenty minutes, he wandered around, talking with everyone, exchanging business cards, making mental notes of those he thought would contribute to a good show. He knew Harvey Keck, who came over and introduced the NASA people. They were, as he'd guessed, astronauts. And finally it was time for the mission to move out. They were mostly wearing fatigues, and some had brought light jackets. Brad was watching the security people move the reporters back from the transport system when he got a surprise: Max Collingwood came through the door. April spotted him, too, and waved. He waved back.

Max had been the guy who'd short-circuited the shootout between the Feds and the Sioux when the government attempted to seize the Roundhouse. He'd brought a group of celebrities who'd interposed themselves between the two sides, and stayed in place until a compromise had been reached. He was also the second person, after April, to teleport out of the Roundhouse. Eventually, he'd been a guest on Brad's show.

April appeared at his side. "Good to see you, Brad. You're sure you don't want to come?"

Brad saw she was joking, but played it straight: "Thanks. Next time, maybe. Be careful."

She touched his arm. "We will."

Max spotted them, came over, and said hello. "What are you up to these days?" April asked.

He thought about it. "Actually, I'd like to track down our visitor."

"You mean the wind creature?"

"I'm not serious, guys. I'm too busy restoring planes. But I'd like to know if there's something really there."

"If it really exists," said April, "it might be dangerous."

Max laughed. "It might be. But we know it has a sense of humor. And it rescues kids and cares about dogs." He smiled and shook his head. "Who would have thought aliens would be so friendly?"

● ● ●

APRIL WAS ON the ride of her life. Six months earlier, she had been a minor-league chemist who'd been in exactly the right position when the Roundhouse was excavated on Johnson's Ridge. And now, here she was, hanging out with some of the top scientific people on the planet while every major media outlet wanted to interview her. Nobody was drawing more attention at that moment than the Strike Team, which was the name that somebody in the Tribal Council had suggested, apparently because the selected icon consisted of three parallel lines. Three strikes. When she first heard the designation, which had happened when the chairman raised his toast to them last night at the Cedar Inn, she'd winced. Back at the hotel, she'd suggested to Walker that the sobriquet suggested failure. But he'd laughed it off.

Finally, they were moving out. Adam Sky and another of

the Sioux security guys stepped onto the grid. Adam pressed the arrow icon, approximately twenty seconds passed, and the glow appeared, brightened, and wrapped itself around both men. Brad's breathing picked up as he watched them fade into transparency. Then the light went out, and they were gone.

Incredible.

The light reappeared, and another of the security people, a woman, picked up a pen from the grid. Brad knew that was the all-clear signal from Eden.

April and the astronaut Melissa went next. Then Boots, carrying a pressure suit, and one of the scientists. They continued until all were gone.

● ● ●

BRAD WOULD HAVE liked to accompany them to the Eden station. He wasn't so sure about the Strike World. There was a part of him, if he was honest with himself, that was relieved he was staying right where he was. He liked to think of himself as an adventurous type, but the truth was he wasn't big on risks. The notion of getting disassembled, then put back together, made his skin crawl.

Max came over and sat with him. "It's good to see you again, Brad. You trying to arrange to get a booking on one of these missions?"

"Not really," Brad said. "I have to admit that this whole business is a little scary. What's it feel like to go through that process?"

Max was about average size, not quite six feet, with dark hair. He seemed easygoing, but there was something in his manner that suggested his barging into the middle of the Federal attempt to take the Roundhouse would not have been a surprise to people who knew him. "It's a bit unnerving at first," he said. "You just close your eyes and try not to throw up."

"Really? Did you have a stomach problem when you did it?"

He laughed. "No. Not that I can recall. But I *was* jittery." He checked his watch. "They should be moving on to the

Strike World by now. I hate to clear out, but I have to get going. Got clients waiting for me. Brad, you going to stay here?"

"Yes, Max."

"Okay. Do me a favor and let me know when they come back."

• • •

BRAD HAD BROUGHT a photo of the interior of the Eden Station, the Cupola, with him. Eight icons were embedded in a post. The stag's head would take the science team back to North Dakota. The arrow was prominent among them, as the stag's head was on Johnson's Ridge. Neither image would light up and were apparently there simply to serve as reminders of the image that would bring them home.

The other Eden icons were all different from the figures at the Roundhouse. Four of them were geometrical. The remaining two looked like a flower and a pair of wings. Three still generated power. The arrow, an octagon, and a set of three parallel horizontal lines. The Strikes.

If everything went well, Harvey Keck would be dispatched back to the Roundhouse to break the news and describe what they'd found on the new world. That was the moment Brad and the reporters were waiting for.

One of the journalists mistook Brad for a member of the Tribal Council and asked to interview him. Chairman Walker arrived and strolled through the area, talking with everybody. There were a few other people Brad knew, Jim Stuyvesant of the *Fort Moxie News*, Ben Markey from WLMR-TV's *Ben at Ten*, Mike Tower of the *Chicago Tribune*, and Andrea Hawk.

He checked his watch. It had been twenty minutes since the Strike Team had left. That was probably enough time to get Boots into his pressure suit and transport him to the new world, and for him to report back. Then they'd send Keck back to the Roundhouse. He was rushing things, though. They'd probably want to look around somewhat on the new world before dispatching Harvey.

One of the tables was covered with snacks and Cokes. He made a peanut butter and jelly sandwich. The room was beginning to grow noisy again. Everybody was on a cell phone. He bit into the sandwich, and his own phone sounded. Max's voice: "Any word yet, Brad?"

"Nothing. We're still waiting."

"Okay. Thanks. Let me know." .

Eventually, Walker became impatient and decided to go find out what was happening. He approached the wall behind the grid and studied the icons. At that moment the grid lit up. The chairman stepped quickly away, and Harvey Keck's outline appeared. A sense of anticipation spread through the room.

When the light faded, Harvey looked around and waved at the crowd. Walker smiled and extended a hand. But Harvey shook his head no, and whispered something to the chairman. Walker's features hardened. He turned to the reporters. "Everything's okay," the chairman said, raising his voice. "But we need a couple of minutes. We'll get right back to you." Then he was talking to Keck again.

Keck replied, and Walker stared at him in confusion. Brad couldn't hear any of the conversation. Suddenly Keck grasped the chairman's right arm and pulled him onto the grid. Walker waved again to the audience in an obvious effort at reassurance, and pressed the arrow.

The reporters hurled questions at them: "What are you doing?"

"What's going on, Mr. Chairman?"

"Is there a problem?"

"Harvey, is everybody—?"

The luminous cloud appeared. Walker waved and smiled. "Everything's okay." Then they were engulfed by the light.

Everybody in the crowd was back talking into a cell phone. Ben Markey shook his head. "Something's wrong," he was saying.

One of the Sioux security people, a female, jumped onto the grid and pressed the arrow. "Everybody stay put. I'll be back in a minute or two."

"Go, Paula," said another of the security guys. Then, raising his voice: "Everybody just relax, please. We'll have some answers in a minute."

It was more like seven or eight. Finally, Walker and April came back together. The crowd quieted and the chairman came forward. "Ladies and gentlemen, when we transported out on the Strike link, we arrived in a *city*. I say 'we' although the only people who actually made the crossover were Boots Coleman and April. April, do you want to describe what you saw?"

"It's a high-tech place. Big, stretching as far as we could see. We saw some of the inhabitants. They almost looked human except that they were smaller than we are."

The reporters started shouting questions, so she stopped talking and waited for them to calm down.

"We were only there a few minutes," she continued. "Inside a dark building. We saw a river, lights moving through the sky. Skyscrapers. Heard music from somewhere. Actually, we could see a park, and it looked as if there was a party going on. And that was enough. We left. Went back to Eden before one of them saw us."

The grid lit up again, and two of the scientists came back. They looked frustrated.

EIGHT

Oft expectation fails and most oft there
Where most it promises, and oft it hits
Where hope is coldest and despair most fits.

—Shakespeare, *All's Well That Ends Well*, 1602

I T HAD BEEN a long day. President Taylor had attended meetings with a congressional delegation trying to put together legislation to do something about the country's homeless population, with a State Department team trying to calm rising tensions between Gaza and Israel, and with military advisors pressing him to invest more money in a jet fighter the Pentagon did not need. He'd been called to the Situation Room to decide on a response to another terrorist strike in Syria, and had taken time to speak with some third graders who'd been on a White House tour. Whenever the opportunity presented itself, he'd gotten to a television to watch the events playing out in North Dakota. He was glad Walker was on the job out there. Thank God it wasn't some political hack in charge.

Someone knocked on the door. Alice. She looked upset. "Mr. President," she said, "check the TV."

"What's going on?"

"Aliens, sir."

No. Please. He visualized green-skinned creatures wielding hand weapons that fired lightning bolts. He grabbed the remote and turned on the television. April was on-screen, describing what she'd seen, creatures that looked somewhat like us but were smaller and were just out walking around. Their features were a bit different, eyes farther apart, ears a bit larger. The good news was that there was no indication they'd realized we were there. And Walker had shown the good judgment to cancel the mission and pull his people out before whoever was over there found out they'd been visited.

He pressed the intercom. "Alice, get me Chairman Walker."

Moments later, his phone sounded. "Hello, Mr. President."

"Hi, Jim. Looks as if you had an interesting day."

"I'll tell you, sir. It was a scare. But our people handled it exactly as they were supposed to."

"They arrived inside a large building?"

"Yes. Fortunately, it was empty."

"You're sure the aliens don't know we were there?"

"No, sir. There's no way to be certain. A few of them were outside the building. We saw them go by through windows. None of them reacted in any way, or seemed to be in a position to see our people. So it doesn't look as if we were spotted. But there's a possibility there were surveillance cameras. We have no way to know for certain."

"Okay. Can you post a few extra security people in the Roundhouse for the next few days?"

"If the aliens respond, if someone comes back through the link, they'd arrive in the Cupola first. Before they could come here."

"Okay. How about we put some people in the Cupola then? If we were seen, I want to know about it."

"Yes, sir. We've already done that."

"I can send some marshals and beef things up a bit, if you like."

"Not necessary, Mr. President." He hesitated. "Well, maybe it wouldn't be a bad idea. Send about a dozen. Okay?"

"You'll have them before the end of the day."

"Good."

"Something else, Jim. I think it would be a good idea to clear everyone out of the Roundhouse when you don't have a mission running, except the security force."

"I agree."

"Also, please notify me if someone does show up. And instruct your people not to behave in an aggressive manner unless they're attacked, okay?"

"My thoughts exactly, Mr. President."

"Is there anything more? Anything you didn't tell the media?"

"No. They've got everything."

"All right. Thanks, Jim. Your people did a good job. And by the way, I have one more suggestion. It would be a good idea to install a destruct mechanism that would enable you to level the place if you need to. I'll arrange to have my people take care of it."

"Yes, sir. Except that it would be a good idea to give me control of it."

"What happens if there's an emergency, and they can't reach you, Jim? Best would be to assign one of your on-site security people to make the call."

• • •

IVY BANNER HAD been off the Rez for almost nine years, and she'd been shocked to hear from James Walker. She'd been following the stories about the Roundhouse, of course, and had been watching for an indication that *someone* was looking seriously at an electrical system that was still functioning after thousands of years. A few months ago, she would have denied the possibility. And, in fact, she still suspected there was a communication breakdown somewhere in the reports. "Yes," she told him, "I'd be delighted to look at it. Absolutely. When do you want me there?"

• • •

BRAD HAD GOTTEN one of the scientists as a guest for *Grand Forks Live*. That had been the principal reason he'd gone to the Roundhouse. Arthur Lennon, a chemist from Oxford, agreed reluctantly and appeared the following morning.

Brad had seen the switchboard light up before, but on this occasion it exploded.

"Professor Lennon, when are we going back to talk to the aliens?"

"Are they dangerous?"

"Professor, the previous caller wanted to know whether they're a risk to us. Where's his head? How could they not be?"

"I think it's crazy not to destroy the Roundhouse. Are we going to wait until it's too late?"

"Have we made any ground trying to figure out how the technology works? I'd love to be able to step onto a grid down at the bus station and walk out the other end in Fargo."

* * *

"I was able to listen to your show today," said Donna. It had snowed, and the schools were closed. She was a fifth-grade teacher. "Your callers were preoccupied with the alien city, but they're still asking why *you* don't make the trip to Eden."

"It happens every morning."

"Is it really true that April hasn't asked you to do it?"

"Yes, it is. She hasn't said a word."

"Good. Let's hope it stays that way." She was relaxed on the sofa with an open copy of *Time* on her lap. Classical music leaked out softly from the kitchen. Donna was probably the only woman in the country who had to listen to Dvorak before she could make dinner.

"I'm sure it will," said Brad.

"What would you do if you got the invitation?"

He made a face signifying a difficult call. "I know you wouldn't want me to go. But I don't see how I could say no." Mostly because his callers, if they found out about it, would conclude he was afraid.

"Please don't go near it, Brad," she said. "It's crazy. You don't know what might happen. I don't want to lose you. Promise me?"

Brad was aware he looked pretty good, tall, broad-shouldered, strong features, deep baritone. At an early age he'd thought he would have liked to be a firefighter, but then he'd discovered that heights made him nervous. He'd also considered a career as a state policeman. Riding a motorcycle as a member of the Highway Patrol seemed like a much better way to earn a living than sitting in an office somewhere. But he wasn't sure he'd be good during shootouts. Or even pulling people over and giving them tickets.

So eventually he'd become a staff assistant at KLYM, had taken advantage of an opportunity to demonstrate his on-air abilities when two of the station's hosts had come down with the flu at the same time, and became Matt's first choice as a replacement when one of those guys moved on. It was an odd concurrence of events because his old reluctance about confronting people had gone away when somebody handed him a microphone. But he knew that his appearance didn't match his courage. With luck, April would not ask him.

"You're probably right, Donna," he said. "Anyhow, I don't think Matt would want it to happen either."

That was not true, of course. If Brad was given an opportunity to go to the Roundhouse, Matt would have pushed him out the door. And Donna knew that as well as he did. But he went on pretending even though something unsettling had shown up in Donna's eyes.

NINE

Keep your mouth shut and your eyes open.

—Samuel Palmer, *Moral Essays on Proverbs*, 1710

Ivy Banner dismantled the section of wall in which the icons were embedded. Adam Sky, watching her, had not been happy. But the chairman had told him to let her have her way, which, of course, he did. But he thought it was just a matter of time before the lights went out.

Ivy was middle-aged and reminded him of his aunt Shappa, a pleasant lady with chestnut hair and dark brown eyes that could become lasers if someone got in her way. Ivy inspected every inch of the building, climbed onto the roof, where she tried unsuccessfully to scrape samples, took readings of the soft glow that emanated from the structure at night, opened panels he hadn't even noticed in the grid, and removed equipment he'd never seen before.

She took the icons out of the wall. They were affixed to plates. She manipulated the plates and pressed them. Sometimes the luminous cloud appeared on the grid. Sometimes not.

She moved the icons around, placing, for example, the arrow where the one that looked like smoke coming up from a campfire had been. Sometimes the locations that had stayed dark before lit up after the change.

"You having any luck figuring it out?" he asked.

"Getting there," she said. That was about as specific as she got.

• • •

THE ALIEN CITY led the news for the next several days until a pair of lunatics took AK-47s into a movie theater and killed half a dozen people watching a romantic comedy. That sent Brad's callers into one of their periodic debates about gun rights.

He was much more than simply the host of *Grand Forks Live*. He was also the operations manager at KLYM. That meant he handled all of the station's computers and technical issues that did not require calling in an engineer. He was also responsible for listening to the product, that is, to the broadcasts, to ensure the station maintained a reasonable quality level. He oversaw the staff, created their schedules, and provided advice on performances. He supplied tools and equipment, was responsible to ensure that everything was in place and functioning, and to see that it was upgraded as needed.

Relationships with various agencies tended to be his responsibility also, in order to ensure that KLYM maintained a visible presence in the community. If a major charity event was going on—an auction for the battered women's home, a Christmas bailout for the underemployed—he was the face of the organization. On the side, he put together proposals for sponsorship and advised visiting clients on ways to improve their business. In plain English, he assisted with contracts, wrote a lot of the commercials, and even delivered a few of them.

He routinely came in before dawn because he did the early news and weather at five. After that he had to take care of assorted staffing and operational duties. At six, he usually put everything aside to begin prepping for the call-in show, which began at seven.

Two days after the movie shootings, April accepted his invitation and came into the studio the following morning.

Brad reviewed with her the kinds of calls they could expect and asked whether she had any questions.

"No," she said. "I can tell you that I wish there were a way to convey to your listeners what it feels like to stand out there under a different sun. On a world that's never known human visitors. I've watched the coverage on TV, the forest, the ocean, the twin moons, and it just looks like special effects. Pictures don't do it justice. And neither does talking about it. You have to *be* there. The same's true of the Maze. Long passageways, empty chambers. It's overwhelming." The Maze was one of three worlds accessible from the Roundhouse. It was a place that seemed to consist entirely of rooms and tunnels. The other two were, of course, Eden and a space station located outside the galaxy.

"You never saw daylight there anywhere? At the Maze?"

"Well, we never really got outside. We weren't there very long. Just an hour or so. Not much more than that."

"You didn't hear anything either, I suppose?"

"Nothing," she said.

• • •

THE FIRST QUESTIONS were gun-related. Did April own a weapon? How did she feel about efforts to establish tight gun controls? Did she worry about government helicopters coming to get them all? Brad was surprised by that one. His callers were usually rational.

Eventually, he moved the conversation to the Roundhouse by asking about the city on the Strike World. "You were one of the two people who actually saw it, April. That's correct, isn't it?"

"Yes," she said.

"I understand it looked *different*."

"We were there at night, Brad. I'd like to have seen it in the daylight. Assuming they have daylight there."

"Is that possible? Could it be permanently night?"

"Oh, sure. It's *possible*, but I don't think it's very likely. But you have to keep in mind, we're in strange territory here."

"You saw some of the occupants?"

"Yes. We were looking through a door and later a window, trying to keep out of sight. But we saw some of them. We should have taken some pictures, but I guess we got too excited. I know all I did was stand there and stare. It's a beautiful city, what we could see of it. On the edge of a river."

"Are we going back?"

"That's not my call. I believe the chairman's talking it over with President Taylor, and, to be honest, I'd be surprised if we do." She was shaking her head. And while she talked she wrote a note and showed it to him: TRY NOT TO SCARE ANYONE.

"I understand the architecture was different."

"Yes. I don't know how to describe it, exactly. Lots of spires. The upper levels of a couple of the buildings were connected by crosswalks. Lots of soft lighting. And the buildings didn't look as if they were made from stone. Or concrete."

"What *did* they look like?"

"Well, they looked as if they were made from *plastic*. The material was smooth. It even reflected light a little bit."

Brad turned it back to his audience. The first caller wanted to know if the missions were armed?

"Yes," said April. "We have weapons with us."

Then a woman who identified herself as Molly Black: "April, did it scare you, seeing actual aliens?"

April glanced at Brad and smiled. How could Molly possibly think we wouldn't be a bit rattled? But she played the game: "Not really. We don't think anybody capable of developing the kind of technology we've seen is very likely to be hostile."

The calls continued:

"What did the sky look like? Was there a moon?"

"You say you don't think there's any danger because these people make nice-looking architecture? *Really?*"

"Is there any possibility we'll say hello to these creatures? And invite some of them to visit North Dakota?"

And there was the almost daily call from Mark Collins. "How do you feel about this now, Dr. Cannon? Do you wish you'd gone outside and tried to talk to them?"

April had to think it over. "Yes," she said. "I think if I had it to do over, I'd have done just that."

The calls continued along the same line until finally they went to commercial. "Brad," she said, "if I had a replay on that, I would have tried it. The only reason I didn't do it was because it would have been a violation of the protocol. And I know saying hello would have been a pretty dumb idea. But I wish—"

"Sure, April. What could have gone wrong?"

"I know. But it might have resolved everything. These idiots don't understand—"

"Careful, April. Sometimes the mike is live."

"It's not, is it?"

Brad smiled. "No, you got lucky this time. But they aren't idiots. They want to know more about that place. I'm sure you understand that. They're milking it for all it's worth. What they want is for you to go along with them. They're going to go through the rest of their lives without ever getting as close to touching the sky as they are right now. So cut them some slack. They're standing there at that doorway with you, and they know they may never get a chance to find out who those people are. And that's what they want. And they're thinking the chance might have been blown when you and Boots went back to the Eden station. They're thinking they may never know any more about the aliens than they do right now. That the country's going to wrap itself in security issues, and the rest of the story will remain a mystery forever. They want you to give them something they can enjoy. Tell them something they haven't heard already."

There were six callers on the line when they returned.

"Is there any way of getting a car over to Eden? Something you could ride around in? It would be nice if we could cover some serious ground and maybe see what else is there. You say we've only gotten out a few miles from the star gate. That's not very far. Maybe that city's on Eden somewhere."

"Sure," April said. "I don't think that possibility occurred to us, but it could be. Driving around, though, wouldn't work too well."

A caller who sounded suspiciously like Matt Fanny but identified himself as Horace: "Dr. Cannon, all the excitement about this arises from the search for extraterrestrial life. That's what we're looking for, right? Everybody gets excited about it. So why do we back off when we find it? If we scare so easily, why did we ever start pushing the project?"

"You're correct, Horace. That's what really matters. There's a lot of romance involved in the hunt for extraterrestrials. But maybe we tend to forget that there's also a substantial risk involved if we actually find them."

The caller with Matt's voice stayed on the line: "There are two other sites we can reach from the Roundhouse, right?"

"Yes," she said. "One's apparently a space station. And the other just seems to be a group of interconnecting passageways and rooms. That's the Maze. We haven't spent much time at either place. The big news about the space station is that it's outside the Milky Way. Or at least, it's outside a galaxy somewhere. We're beginning to get a sense of the incredible capabilities of the transport system. There seems to be no limit about how far it can take you. And, in case it's your next question, we'll be going back soon. To both places."

"Why so much caution? There must be a lot of people who want to go there."

"There's a long line. But the station's a vacuum. We'll get to it. We just don't want to rush things. We already lost one guy there."

Brad sighed and disconnected his boss. They took a few more questions, until one of the callers wanted to know whether Brad wouldn't enjoy traveling to Eden.

"Oh, I'd love to go." He knew before he'd finished it was a dumb thing to say, but he couldn't pull back. "You're very fortunate, April," he continued. "A scientist in exactly the right spot at the right time."

She turned that glorious smile his way. "Well, Brad," she said, "you had Dr. Fossel on last week?"

"Yes. He talked about life on other worlds, too."

"He mentioned that he thought you'd make a good observer. And that you were interested in going along with us. We're going back to Eden in two weeks. If you like, we'd be happy to include you. We should be taking a journalist with us."

"I know you're not serious, April. And I wouldn't want to be in the way. The truth is, I don't really have any scientific training."

"We'd love to have you, Brad."

Their eyes met. She looked surprised at his hesitation. Maybe disappointed. He saw no easy way out. "Sure," he said. "If it's not a problem. You say you're leaving in two weeks?"

• • •

THE STATION WENT to its top-of-the-hour news, and Brad sat at his desk, staring at April.

"Should I not have done that?" she asked.

"Maybe it would have been a good idea to clear it with me first."

"I'm sorry. It just hit me while I was sitting there that I'd like to have you along. I—I'm sorry if I've created a problem."

"Why would you want *me*? I'm not a biologist or anything."

"I've known you a long time, Brad. I trust you."

"Thanks. I appreciate that. But I don't see how I can be of any help. This stuff is way past my grade level. Anyhow, I'm not on the White House list."

"We can sidestep that. There's always room for a journalist. But I'll back off if you prefer. Let it go. I'm sorry."

"I can't very well do that now. I'd have to explain to my listeners why I'm not going. And no matter what I say, you know what they'll think."

"I guess. I should have thought—"

"Just tell me why you want me out there. You're traveling

with some of the top scientists in the world. And you've got the Sioux security people. What would you expect me to do?"

"Brad, I don't really know any of those people. They live in their own worlds. I've felt alone on these missions. The Sioux think they're there just to make sure we don't get killed. The science guys are caught up in their specialties. I'd like to have somebody along I can talk to. Bounce questions off. And you're already in the public eye. I thought it would give you a professional boost."

Brad got slowly to his feet. "It'll do that," he said.

• • •

MATT CAME INTO his office. "You cut me off."

"What do you mean?"

"You know exactly what I mean."

"You were one of the callers?"

"You know I was."

"I'm sorry. No, I didn't realize you were on the line. Which call was it?"

"Forget it."

"Matt, I'm sorry. April indicated she didn't want to go any farther, so I didn't have a choice."

Matt grumbled something he couldn't make out. Then his eyes locked on Brad. "Well, anyhow I'm glad you agreed to go with her. You handled that right. That should put us right in there with the networks. Do you know how long you'll be gone?"

"No. We didn't discuss that."

"Okay. Give her a call and find out. And don't worry about the show. I can fill in for you if we have to."

Usually, Brad spent the balance of the day researching local news for topics he would focus on during the next *Grand Forks Live*. But after April left, he sat staring at the *Herald* and the other area newspapers stacked on his desk, rehearsing how he was going to explain to Donna that he'd agreed to go through the transport system. And wondering if there was a way he could get out of it.

Maybe call in sick?

• • •

HE HAD NO intention of going off to another world without taking a weapon along. He'd never owned a gun, however. In fact, his only experience with a firearm had come in college, when he'd once accompanied a few friends to a firing range.

He remembered just enough to get by. How to load the weapon. How to handle it. And he'd surprised himself by discovering he was a decent shot.

On his way home, he stopped at Gunmaster Shooting and Hunting Supplies, and picked up a revolver. It felt comfortable in his hands, and he was careful to keep it pointed at the floor.

As soon as he walked in the door, he saw that she knew. Donna was in the kitchen, and she put something down as he closed the door, a plate or a glass, something, and didn't make another sound.

"Hi, love," he said.

She came out into the dining room, staring at him with that glare she saved for special occasions. "Are you crazy?"

"I'm sorry. I didn't know that was coming."

"You promised."

"I got caught in the middle, Donna. She asked me when we were live on the show. There wasn't any way I could get around it."

He listened to her breathing. Then she softened. "I know," she said. "Marcia told me what happened." Marcia was one of the secretaries at the school.

"If I'd backed away, I'd have had to go looking for another job. No decent journalist can decline an opportunity like that."

"Maybe you should look for work as a real-estate salesman." She stood quietly for a moment. Her eyes closed, and her features softened. "To be honest, I'd have been disappointed in you if you had done anything else. But that doesn't mean I'm happy."

• • •

PRESIDENT TAYLOR KNEW why Arnold Bonner wanted to see him. Bonner was even more upset with the Roundhouse technology than the president was. Taylor was weary of trying to mollify him. He was tempted to pass him along to Harry. But there was no advantage to be gained by alienating the Chairman of the Joint Chiefs.

The admiral arrived precisely on time, well pressed, all business, making no attempt to look amicable. He had a slight limp, the result of being shot down over Vietnam. He'd been a carrier pilot and spent two years in captivity, an experience Taylor had never known him to mention.

The president showed him to a chair. "Can I get you anything, Admiral?" he asked.

"No, thank you, Mr. President." Bonner's frustration was written on his face for all to see. "We've had this conversation before, sir. I understand your feelings on this, but I've been hoping I can persuade you to reconsider. This transport device is putting the nation at considerable risk. At the very least.

"You know how we are at keeping secrets. If the transport technology becomes generally available, it will introduce chaos. No nation on the planet will have any defense against it. There are too many lunatics running loose. They'd be able to introduce terrorist forces anywhere. Maybe even directly into the White House." His eyes narrowed. "That might be a bit over the top, but we don't know how big a receiver has to be. All these people would have to do is deliver one anywhere in the country, and they could bring in whoever or whatever they want. A terror group. A nuke. You name it. No place on the *planet* would be safe. Our Navy would become irrelevant."

"Admiral, are you suggesting we move against the Sioux, kill a few of them, take the device, and destroy it?"

"Of course not. Sir, you are the president of the United States. Surely there is a way to take control of the Roundhouse without using force. Eminent domain should work. Or buy them out. Sit down with the chairman and explain the problem. Have you tried to reason with him?"

"I have, Admiral. But he's not the problem."

"Who is, sir?"

"*I* am. Look, the bottom line here is that the Roundhouse technology constitutes the ultimate windfall. As much as I'd like to, I can't simply destroy it. It has enormous potential to carry the nation, and, for that matter, the *world*, into a future brighter than anything we've ever dreamed of. How do I just take that away?"

The admiral's mouth tightened. "So it's a political issue?"

"I resent the implication. I want to get what's best for the country. If that entails a risk, then let's do what we can to minimize it. That doesn't mean a simplistic solution, like just throwing everything out."

"I have to confess, Mr. President, that I'm not all that concerned about a brighter future." Both hands curled into fists. "I'm concerned about surviving the present. We both know there's no such thing as a long-term military secret. When some small group of lunatics gets hold of this technology, as they will, it will negate the carriers, the missiles, everything else we have. I urge strongly that you go in there, explain to the Sioux that they'll be as much at risk as the rest of us, buy the thing if you can, take it if you have to, but get it, and demolish it. *Do it, sir.* We may not get a second chance."

The truth was that Taylor would have been delighted if the Roundhouse would simply go away. If Chairman Walker would destroy it.

But Taylor knew that there'd be outrage across the country against anyone found responsible for such an act. He wasn't prepared to throw his presidency away. Especially when he wasn't even sure that destroying the Roundhouse would be the right thing to do.

Fifteen minutes after Bonner left, the president sat down with several unhappy representatives of the automobile industry.

• • •

Sources close to James Walker, chairman of the Spirit Lake Sioux, are saying that another off-world mission is being prepared. This one will be limited, however, to

Eden, which has already been visited on several occasions by scientific teams. The sources indicate that previous visitors have not gotten more than a few miles from the transport station.

—*NBC Report, April 3*

• • •

WALKER WASN'T HAPPY with the plan to install an explosive device at the Roundhouse. Nevertheless, it seemed like a necessary precaution. They'd only use it if hostile aliens arrived. And if that happened, everyone on Johnson's Ridge would be at risk anyhow.

He hadn't really believed that an attack from another world was anything more than an extremely remote possibility. After all, there'd been no visitors through the transport system since before there was any human civilization on the planet. So everything should be okay, and he should stop worrying. The real risk stemmed from the possibility that one of the security people would hear a noise somewhere, draw the wrong conclusion, and set off the bomb.

He called the security desk. Adam was off, and he got Paula. "We've got marshals coming in today to help. Put three of our guys in the Cupola and keep a presence there round the clock. The marshals stay in the Roundhouse. Okay?"

"Yes, sir."

"Not that this is likely to happen. But just in case. We don't want to be surprised by aliens coming through from the parallel link. That's the sole responsibility of the Eden unit. If any of them show up there, we should try to establish communication if it looks feasible. In any case, at least one of our people is to come back immediately and let us know what's happened."

"I'll take care of it, Mr. Chairman. Are we going to keep them there permanently?"

"I think a few days should be sufficient. Just long enough until we can be reasonably sure we're not going to get a surprise. One more thing. The marshals are going to install a bomb. So we can take down the Roundhouse if there's a serious problem. The trigger will be at the desk."

"Got it."

"Pass the word around, Paula. But we don't want it getting out to the media."

"Okay, sir."

She surprised him. Not only did she not sound a bit rattled by the plan, as he'd expected, but he thought he detected a note of enthusiasm in her voice.

TEN

This world, after all our science and sciences, is still a miracle; wonderful, inscrutable, magical and more, to whosoever will think of it.

—Thomas Carlyle, *Heroes and Hero-Worship*, 1840

THE CHAIRMAN HELD his breath for the next few days. The marshals arrived and joined the Sioux force. Walker watched them cut into the floor and plant the bomb a few feet away from the grid. They tried to keep its presence secret, but it got out into the news within twenty-four hours.

He wasn't comfortable with it. If something unusual showed up, the guy at the security desk, with his fingers on the trigger, might easily panic and blow the place to hell. He'd thought about going over there and installing himself in that role. But he couldn't be there twenty-four hours a day, and anyhow, he wasn't sure he might not panic himself.

He went on *Dakota Brief*, a local TV news show in Fargo, and tried to assure everybody that it was purely precautionary, that no one seriously believed invaders were a likely threat. "But we're covering every possibility," he said.

It was an unnerving time. His social life, such as it was, went away. He didn't sleep well, jumped every time his phone rang, and spent most of his time at home staring at but not watching the television screen. Carla suggested going to the movies, bringing in friends to play bridge, and attending a school play. She did talk him into going to a basketball game one evening, and they sat there only a few rows up with everybody looking in his direction and some people even pointing at him. One night, she brought home a jigsaw puzzle. Ordinarily, he liked jigsaw puzzles. They worked as a distraction and didn't require too much concentration. In the end, though, he put in a few pieces around the frame and left it.

Toward the end of the first week, Adam called him. "A couple of the marshals want to go to the Cupola. On duty. Is that okay with you, sir?"

He found himself trying to think of a reason to say no. But he couldn't come up with one. "Sure," he said. "Do it."

An hour or so later, he was on his way home when the phone rang again. It was David Woqini. "Everything okay, Jim?"

"Yeah. We're doing fine."

"You didn't get to see that city by the river, did you?"

"No," he said. "It didn't seem like a good idea."

"I don't suppose you'd let me go?"

"Do you really want to?"

"Just kidding. I'll admit, though, I'd love to see it."

"Me, too, David."

"Is there any chance at all we'll try to connect with them?"

"I think if I suggested it, the president would have a heart attack."

"You're probably right. I'm surprised. I thought we'd hear from them. It's hard to believe we could ride in on their transit system, whatever you guys call that thing, walk around inside one of their buildings, and they never noticed."

"I'm glad they didn't. I think if we can get through another week without them, we'll be okay."

"It's a pity, though. You know how I feel about all this, but I have to admit I'd love to take a couple of them to lunch at Old Main Street and just sit there with BLTs and find out who they are. Maybe we could talk football."

"It won't happen," said Walker.

"Just as well."

• • •

CALLERS TO GRAND Forks Live were delighted to hear that Brad would be going to Eden on the next mission. They talked about little else that morning. They told him how excited he must be, how they wished they could go, too, and asked whether he could bring back souvenirs. A rock, a flower, anything. A female caller wanted to know whether his wife was still upset about it.

"What makes you think she's upset?" he asked.

"I'm Jennie," she said. One of the secretaries at the school.

Some people wondered what was going to happen to NASA. Or whether cars and planes were about to go extinct. "I'm not so sure that mass teleportation would be a good idea," Brad said. "To tell you the truth. I enjoy getting in my car and driving around. The whole point of traveling is watching the countryside go past. It's not just in arriving at the destination. I wouldn't want to lose that."

People were showing up every afternoon at the station to get their pictures taken with him and to ask for his autograph.

Donna heard about Jennie's call. "I haven't been complaining to anybody," she said.

"It's okay, babe. I understand."

"Sometimes it's just not easy to hide."

• • •

THE SECOND WEEK ended with still no sign of a problem at the Cupola. It was time to go back to normal. Walker called the president. "If it's okay with you, I'm going to bring the Eden security team back and try to return life here to normal."

"Good," he said. "But let's leave the last option in place." The last option was the bomb.

"That was my intention, Mr. President." It was easy to say. Adam was probably the only person he had whom he trusted to keep calm if something that wasn't human came through the link. He had realized belatedly that the only reason he'd had no trouble accepting the bomb was that the occupants of the riverside city seemed to be close enough to human that they would probably not scare anybody.

"Good. So what's the next mission, James?"

"We have another team ready to go out to Eden. We'll do the launch in a couple of days."

"Good. No more surprises, okay?"

• • •

THAT EVENING JOHN Colmar caught a break: His fiancée, Diana Quixon, was a member of the county police, and had been assigned to the unit stationed outside the Roundhouse. John was with the Sioux security unit. It was the first time they'd been on duty simultaneously.

He'd met Diana only a few months earlier at a church dance and had fallen in love with her the moment he saw her. He'd always laughed at people who made claims like that, but it had happened. She was beautiful, and warm, and funny. Not at all what he would have expected from a police officer. And he'd been surprised that the chemistry seemed to be as strong on her side as on his. John never thought of himself as being especially good-looking, but he had seen from the beginning that she'd been swept off her feet. Their first date had been on Halloween, but when he'd gotten to her apartment, she was not there. He'd waited awhile, given up, and in a bleak mood had driven off just as she'd arrived.

Diana, it turned out, had been at a masquerade party, dressed as Wonder Woman, and had lost track of the time. When she realized what had happened, she'd gotten one of the guys to drive her home. She'd seen him leaving, and asked her driver to chase him down. They'd followed for several miles before John realized he was being tailed and pulled over. She got out of the car, and he was startled to see how closely she resembled the comic-book heroine. If I'm ever going to get into trouble with bad guys, he'd thought, now would be the time! It had been a magnificent ride since. Wonder Woman indeed.

Now, on that routinely cold night atop Johnson's Ridge, they managed to spend some time together, on patrol. They had to stay outside the Roundhouse since she wasn't supposed to be in his area of responsibility. That limited the time they had. But it was okay.

The sky was clear and moonless. They were only a few weeks away from their wedding, and the world was a happy place. Mostly, they talked about marriage plans. And the house they were in the process of buying on the west side of the Rez. And Eden. Diana told him she hoped they'd find a way to allow her to visit it at some point. "I'll ask," John said, "after we're certain there's no risk involved. I wouldn't want to lose you."

He didn't like her police career. Too dangerous. They'd had that conversation several times. But she'd made it clear that was what she enjoyed doing, and if he wanted her, he'd have to accept the uniform as well.

They'd been out for about half an hour, and it was time to get back to their posts. They'd both be relieved at the same time, and he was in the middle of suggesting they go to breakfast and asking her to decide on a restaurant when he noticed a movement in the trees. A swirl of snow and reflections from the parking-lot lights.

She saw it, too. She didn't say anything for a long moment. Then: "I think it's that floater that's been in the news."

John put a hand on her shoulder. It was supposed to suggest she not move. But she was already on her way.

And suddenly the world began to rotate. John's head started spinning, and he went down on one knee. A vast globe appeared in the sky. A huge gauzy moon with several vertical shafts that rose high above it and reached down to the horizon. A set of *rings*. He was looking at Saturn, standing on its side.

Diana was down, too.

ELEVEN

*When a man takes the road to destruction, the gods
provide ready transportation.*

—Aeschylus, *The Persians*, 490 B.C.E.

THE CHAIRMAN LOOKED genuinely unhappy while John told
his story. "And Diana saw the same thing?" he asked.

"Yes."

"But nobody else did?"

"No. There were a couple of guys at the gate and two
people in the parking lot. But none of them saw anything."

"Anything like that ever happen to you before?"

"No, sir."

"And you guys weren't drinking?"

• • •

IVY BANNER CAME in less than an hour later. "Have you figured it out?" the chairman asked.

She made herself comfortable and shook her head. "The
technology is beyond anything I've ever seen or heard of.
But I can tell you some of what's happening."

"All right, Ivy. What have you got?"

"The building soaks up power, as far as I can tell, from
wind and sun. Maybe rain, too, for that matter. I'm pretty
sure the circuits would have been down when it was first

excavated. Do you have anything on that? Especially, did it glow those first few nights?"

"I don't think so. I don't remember when the first reports about that started coming in."

"Okay. I guess it doesn't really matter."

"So how does it teleport people?"

"James, I hope I haven't misled you. You're going to have to find someone who's a little more advanced in physics than I am."

"No, I didn't mean that. I was just asking what happens when we push the icons?"

"There's a collector—Here, let me show you." She produced a photo of a gray device with a couple of cables tied into it. "This is the central unit, which acquires all the power that comes into the station and redistributes it according to need. Some of it goes into plates behind the icons. Press the icon, it activates the plate and sends a signal to *this*." Another picture, this time a black device, again with two cables. "This is the feeder. It takes the signal, manipulates it, and relays it to the control box, which activates the grid." She opened a plastic bag and showed him the control box. "More than that I can't tell you. I have no idea how this thing disassembles people and sends them somewhere. I'd be surprised if anybody else will, either."

"*That's* the control box?"

"Yes." She was holding it in one hand.

"You're saying that if this thing is removed, the grid won't function. Is that correct?"

"The grid won't get power. It makes a growling noise, but that's all. So yes, I'm pretty sure it won't function."

"There are no cables attached to it."

"I disconnected it."

"How difficult was that?"

"About the same as disconnecting your computer from the display screen."

"You say it's inside the grid?"

"Yes." She showed him another photo, of the grid with an open panel. "The control box and the feeder are both located in here."

"So right now, it won't work."

"That's correct."

Walker stared. "I was never aware that panel even existed. How did you know to look?"

"There had to be a connector of some kind. Underneath the area where the person being teleported stands seemed like the obvious place."

"Okay. Thank you. Now can we put it back?"

● ● ●

ARI CASTOR COULD not get the Roundhouse out of his mind. It was certainly obvious to him that they should detonate the bomb. Blow the place to hell. It was crazy to leave that door open. No one could predict what sort of aliens were out there, just waiting for an opportunity to come in and take us over. Maybe monsters, maybe something that looked friendly but would still have us for dinner. The government was saying there was little probability that anything like that could happen. But what the hell did they know? And who could trust them to tell the truth anyhow? Even if you could, if there was any chance at all of an invasion, didn't it make sense to stop it now?

Ari had been preparing a bomb for his school. Not that he didn't like his teachers or his classmates. Actually, he did. The other kids were fine, and his teachers were nice. The problem was that they kept talking about treating everybody as if they were the same. It didn't matter to them whether you were white or Indian or Muslim or whatever. And it was time to make a statement.

But the Roundhouse was more significant than racial mixing. He never thought he'd find anything more important to the future than keeping the races separated, but now it seemed trivial. They needed somebody to go up to Johnson's Ridge and take that goddam place out. He sat in the shed behind the garage, which he thought of as his laboratory, and imagined the headlines. ARI CASTOR SAVES THE WORLD. He'd be all over the TV as well, with everybody thanking him for what he'd done. Maybe not right away. But after they had a chance to think about it.

It shouldn't be hard. They'd put a chain-link fence around the place. And there was barbed wire atop the fence. But to get inside all you had to do was pass through an inspection booth with a gate. There was a second, wider entrance for trucks. He saw nothing that would prevent him from pulling up to the inspection booth and then, when it was his turn, hitting the gas. He was pretty sure he could break through the gate. If he set the timer right, all that would be necessary would be to reach the Roundhouse at the right moment, and that would be the end of it.

He wrote a note to his mother:

Mom, by now you probably know what I've done. I know you won't be happy about it, but people will eventually be grateful. Somebody has to do it. If not me, then who? I want to thank you for everything you've done for me. And to tell you how much I love you. In case something bad happens, take care of Robbie for me.

Love, Ari

Robbie was his Boston terrier. He didn't try to explain any further because if she found the note before he had time to complete his mission she'd do everything she could to stop him. He folded the paper and put it inside an envelope, wrote "Mom" on the front, and left it on his worktable. It should be safe. She rarely came into the lab.

The sun was sinking. He studied it for a moment and then took the bomb out of the old filing cabinet that his father had left behind when he ran off with his secretary. He checked it one final time. Then he put it in his backpack, pulled on his jacket, and went into the house to say good-bye to his mother.

You'll be proud of me, Mom. She wouldn't understand at first, of course. Probably wouldn't figure it out until they began talking on the TV about how it was good that somebody had taken action. And the country went into mourning over the loss of a wonderful human being. Thank God Ari had been there. Otherwise, who knows what might have happened?

"Mom, I'm going over to Archie's for a while," he said.

"I thought you said Archie had a game this evening?"

"Yeah. I'm going over to the court and watch the game."

"Okay. Be careful driving."

• • •

HE GOT INTO his car, put the backpack under the front seat, turned on the radio to his favorite rock station, and started west on I-94. There wasn't much traffic. He left the lights of Fargo behind and slipped out into the snow-covered plains. Within minutes he was fifteen miles over the speed limit. Inviting trouble. He took his foot off the pedal and let the car drift back down.

Ari wasn't one of those suicidal nutcases. He was saddened as he drove out of the area in which he'd spent his entire life, knowing he would never see it again. He didn't like the idea of dying. But this was the only way he could think of to make his life count for something.

He didn't know whether there'd be a Heaven, or a judgment. If there was, he was sure he'd be okay. God would certainly understand and be proud of him.

Near Jamestown he turned north on U.S. 281.

The cops were checking people going up to the Roundhouse, but he hadn't seen any indication they were searching people. They'd just be looking for a lunatic, so he wasn't likely to have any problem getting through.

He'd probably come down to the final hours of his life. As he passed Carrington, it occurred to him that he was entitled to a last meal. He'd already had dinner. What he really wanted was a couple of drinks, but they probably wouldn't serve him.

Anyhow, if he got any alcohol on his breath, the cops wouldn't let him through the roadblock.

There was a diner just outside New Rockford. When he reached it, he pulled into the parking area, locked the car, and went inside. There was no point ordering a meal since he didn't have an appetite. But they had lemon pie and milk shakes. And a gorgeous waitress.

That was something else that bothered him: He was eighteen and he'd never taken a girl to bed. He'd tried a few times, but nobody had ever really responded to him. Not to that extent, anyhow. It was the one thing that he would really have liked to do before ending his life.

He settled for the milk shake and lemon pie.

• • •

IT WAS DARK when he arrived at the mountain road that led up to Johnson's Ridge. The police had turned it into a one-way drive, and opened a secondary road for people exiting the area. There were two lines of cars going in. Maybe thirty vehicles altogether. Ari got in line, switched his radio to NPR, and sat back. He wasn't a big NPR fan, but it would help persuade the cops he was harmless. He wasn't at all nervous. He didn't really think there was any chance he'd get caught. This was something he'd been born to do. Protector of the Earth. He suspected that eventually they'd make a movie about this. He began contemplating who would be right to play him.

The police didn't seem to be spending a lot of time asking questions. It took them only a couple of minutes to clear the cars in front of him. Ari pulled up to where they waited and rolled down his window. "Good evening, Officer," he said.

"Hello," said the cop. "Going up to see the Roundhouse?"

"Yes, sir."

"Okay. You understand the parking area is closed now. All you can do is drive by."

"I know, Officer. I was visiting my cousins in Devils

Lake, and I wanted to take advantage of being in the area to see this thing. I just want to get a look at it."

"Okay, son. Go ahead. But be careful. The road's slippery tonight."

Ari eased onto it and started up toward the Roundhouse. It was mostly open country, almost completely devoid of trees or any vegetation other than grass. As he went higher, the plains spread out beneath him. And ahead, along the edge of the ridge, lights appeared.

Gradually, the soft green glow emanating from the Roundhouse rose into the sky. Then the building itself. There was a cluster of lights from cars that had pulled off the road. People were standing around, taking pictures. He saw more lights at the front entrance, which, as Ari had read, would have been a way for the aliens to get in and out when they weren't using the boat.

The gatehouse was also lit up. The gate at the entry lane was down. Four cars and a van were in the parking area. Another car was just leaving. A uniformed guy was walking toward the van. As Ari watched, he climbed inside, started the engine, and began to back out. He was moving slowly, but a cop was already waving him toward the exit. The gate rose.

If he timed it right, Ari might be able to get through the exit before the van got there. That looked like a better idea than trying to crash the entry. He released his belt and reached under the seat for the backpack. After looking around to be sure he hadn't drawn any attention, he set it on the seat beside him and unzipped it.

Traffic was piling up behind him. A horn blew. One of the officers came out of the gatehouse, looked in his direction, pointed to the CLOSED sign, and waved at him to keep going.

A second officer, a woman, came outside. She was a babe.

He reached into the bag for the detonator and set it for thirty seconds. "Good-bye, world," he said.

He pressed the pedal to the floor and surged ahead into

the exit lane. He sideswiped a guard post, hit the woman, and saw that the van had seen what he was trying to do. It was moving to block him. Coming too fast. He collided with it, almost head-on. Ari, who hadn't reconnected his belt, was thrown against the wheel and the front window. Nine seconds later, the bomb went off.

TWELVE

And all who told it added something new,
And all who heard it made enlargements too;
In ev'ry ear it spread, on ev'ry tongue it grew.

—Alexander Pope, "The Temple of Fame," 1714

BRAD'S MOMENT WITH the transporter had finally arrived. The evening before the Eden mission was to go out, he was at home with Donna trying to watch *Rio Bravo* but utterly unable to concentrate on the movie. When the phone rang, Donna picked it up, listened, and handed it to him. "It's Matt."

He sounded excited. "You see the news tonight, Brad?"

"No. What's going on?"

"Somebody tried to blow up the Roundhouse."

"They didn't succeed, did they?"

"No. He barely got onto the parking lot."

Brad had, for just a moment, nursed a wish that the transporter had been wrecked. "That's good," he said. "Anybody get hurt?"

"The bomber got killed. He was a high-school kid. Also one of the Sioux, who used a van to block him. And a police officer."

"Which of the Sioux?"

"Dale Tree was the guy in the van. He was one of their security people. The police officer was Diana Quixon."

Brad knew Dale. "They've announced they're going to increase the security."

"It sounds as if the system they have worked."

"Up to a point."

Ten minutes later, April called. The mission had been postponed.

• • •

KLYM's MONK PATTERSON had the rest of the story in the morning. "Castor's mother found a note saying he was going to do something big. She said she couldn't believe he would ever do anything like try to blow something up. She said he's always been a good boy and stayed out of trouble. His police record is clean.

"She said she had no idea her son had become a bomb maker. She was in tears this morning, but she nevertheless took time to apologize to the families of Dale Tree and Diana Quixon, who died in the attack."

• • •

ED EXETER WAS anxious to get home. He'd been in Grand Forks talking to a specialist about his digestive problems. It was nothing serious, so he was happy. But it was an eighty-mile run back to Fort Moxie. By the time he arrived, he was exhausted. He pulled off the expressway and cruised into town, thinking about nothing other than how good it would feel to get into bed. But directly ahead, just above a cluster of trees, he saw a rotating light. Several cars had stopped, and some of the drivers had gotten out and were staring at it.

Bart Marsh and his wife were on the side of the road. Ed pulled in behind them. It was a small, luminous cloud, at about treetop level, turning slowly. Bart saw him and came over. "You ever see anything like this before, Ed?"

Ed looked at it and scratched his head. "Not that I can remember. You think it's that floater they've been talking about?"

It was probably no bigger than the sign over the front door of the Prairie Schooner, the town's lone bar. People

were coming out of their houses to look. But the illumination
was beginning to fade.

"Crazy," somebody said.

• • •

IN THE MORNING, after his show, Brad drove to Johnson's
Ridge to take a look at the damage. The county police were
more methodical than they had been with their previous
inspections before allowing him onto the road that led up
to the ridge. The two gatehouses and a portion of the fence
were in ruins. Brad saw a couple of the Sioux security people
coming out of the Roundhouse. One was Paula; he didn't
recognize the other. He'd have liked to stop and offer con-
dolences, but a contingent of U.S. marshals had sealed off the
parking area, and he had no way of getting past them. The
building itself had been too far away from the blast and was
undamaged.

He said a silent prayer for Dale and the police officer,
whose name he'd forgotten. Diana Somebody. Then he turned
and drove back to the radio station.

• • •

TWO DAYS LATER, Donna, Brad, and April went to Fort Totten
to attend the memorial service for Dale. His family sub-
scribed to both Christianity and the *Midiwiwin* tradition.
The service was conducted by a tribal holy man who called
on both Jesus and Wakan to grant the dead warrior a better
life in the world beyond the skies.

There was music, singing, grief. Another good man sac-
rificed to the idiocy of the outside world. Brad had been
somewhat uncomfortable since the killer had been a white
man, and he assumed there was still some tribal resentment
aimed at the people who had taken so much Native American
land. There might be an inclination to blame white society
in general for Dale's death. But he and the two women were
welcomed warmly to the memorial.

Walker, of course, was present also.

April, in her role as leader of the exploration effort, was

invited to speak. She expressed her sorrow at the loss, and her admiration for a man who had walked on other worlds and ultimately given his life to stop the attacker. "Had that young man gotten through the gate," she said, "he might have destroyed the Roundhouse, which is a treasure, not only for the Mni Wakan Oyate, but for the entire human race. In their name, I would like to express my appreciation to Dale, and to the courageous people whom he represents."

Most of the same people attended a Catholic ceremony for Diana Quixon the following day in Devils Lake, accompanied by a substantial contingent from the county police force. Mac Doolan, the officer who'd been with Diana at the gate, was also present. Doolan's arm had been broken when the bomb went off, but he had surprisingly sustained no other major injuries.

Everyone knew of the connection between Diana and John Colmar. And while they all came forward to offer regrets, John was beyond consolation.

• • •

WHEN IT WAS over, they returned to Grand Forks, talking about how they wished they could believe that Diana really *was* in a better place. Nothing challenged Brad's faith quite like a funeral. Especially one that was marking the end of a person who'd died too young. He'd visited one of the Canadian Air Force museums once and still remembered walls covered with the names of those who'd given their lives during World War II. And the axiom *They never grew old.*

Eventually, though, as they approached the city, Donna switched the subject to the Eden mission. "How long do you expect to be there?" she asked.

They were scheduled to leave next morning. "We're going to move out a bit this time," said April, "so we'll probably be gone for about two days."

Brad could feel the tension emanating from Donna, and he had no doubt April was aware of it, too. Both women, he suspected, would feel relieved if he backed off. But he saw no way he could do that without losing their respect. And his radio audience would never take him seriously again. "I'm looking forward to going," he said.

"Good." April's smile was perfunctory. "You'll probably want sunglasses and a hat of some sort. Eden gets a lot of sunlight."

THIRTEEN

Point me out the way
To any one particular beauteous star,
And I will flit into it with my lyre,
And make its silvery splendor pant with bliss.

—John Keats, *Hyperion*, 1819

Brad decided to wear the Grand Forks police baseball cap that the chief had given him during one of his visits. He liked being mistaken for a police officer. He wouldn't have admitted that, but it made him feel a bit more like Bruce Willis. He slipped the .38 into the shoulder holster and drew his jacket over it. Donna knew he was taking it, of course. In fact, she *wanted* him to take it, but that didn't mean she quite trusted him with the weapon. "Don't shoot anybody," she said, as they waited for April to arrive.

He succeeded in putting aside his reservations, almost persuading himself he was looking forward to joining the mission. Matt Fanny would be taking over *Grand Forks Live*, but Brad would be the dominant topic of conversation that morning. That was good, and he would have enjoyed listening but could see no way to do that with April in the car. He wondered if there was any chance of another breakdown in the system. Something that would require them to postpone the mission again.

Donna kissed him and smiled and told him to be careful. Then she grabbed her own coat as the mission leader pulled up outside. She was running late for the school. But she paused to squeeze his hand.

Brad said, "I love you," trying not to let them sound like last words. Then he went out onto the sidewalk, said hi to April in the blustery cold, opened the door, and climbed in.

The women waved to each other. Donna was heading for *her* car. There was a final wave as she pulled away.

April handed him a card that identified him as a member of Eden Mission Seven. She was wearing a floppy fedora.

"You going as Indiana?" he asked, as they headed west out of Grand Forks and started across the plains.

"Does it look that good?"

"It's perfect."

"Forgot my whip."

They laughed and talked about movies for a few minutes, but Brad couldn't get his mind off the grid. "It's okay," April said, reading his thoughts. "It's perfectly safe. We've made a number of trips now. Never had a problem. Believe me, Brad, if there were any risk to this, I wouldn't be doing it." She looked especially good that morning. Maybe because she represented a solid terrestrial presence when projected against the mad fantasy located on the ridge.

"Can anyone explain yet how it works?" he asked. "Does anybody have any idea at all?"

"Not that I know of. And to be honest, I don't know if we'll ever figure it out. The technology's on a whole different level from anything we've ever even thought about before."

"When you went through that thing the first time, you were alone, right? You were putting chairs and balloons on the grid and punching buttons and the stuff vanished and you had no idea what was going on. And you just followed it."

"Yeah."

"That's probably the craziest thing I've ever heard. How could you have known everything wasn't being destroyed?"

"We didn't know for sure, Brad. But what would have been the point of putting a device in the Roundhouse that just wiped stuff out? Anyhow, the balloons looked as if they were disappearing. Fading out. Not disintegrating."

She turned into a gas station. "Did you think about using a cat or something first?"

She shut the engine off and opened the door. "Experiment with a cat? If I did something like that, and my mother ever found out—"

• • •

THEY CLEARED THE temporary gate, pulled into the parking area, and checked through the security people. April took him in tow and walked him along the side of the Roundhouse until they were able to look out over the cliff's edge, the section that would have been filled with Lake Agassiz in ancient times. "Thought you'd like to see this," she said. A trench connected the building with the edge of the summit. They descended a ladder into it and followed it back into the building. Doors opened, and a Sioux security guard checked Brad's ID and mission card and stepped aside.

More doors opened electronically, and they walked through the trench that had once been used to launch boats into the lake, entering the transport area. To his right lay the circular grid that was the takeoff point for the teleportation device. A group of pool reporters were present. They would have come in through the front entrance off the parking lot.

She introduced Brad to their two security escorts, John Colmar and Paula Francisco. Brad remembered John from the funeral ceremony for Diana. The five scientists who would be making the crossover with them arrived a short time later. April spent a few minutes with them, explaining the rules, do what the security people say, don't wander off, and so on. She reminded them it was midsummer on the other side.

They talked briefly with the reporters while Brad became aware he wasn't the only person present who was having second thoughts about teleportation. There was a fair amount of whispering going on among the scientists, and people staring at the grid, but April's manner had a calming effect. They were all relatively young. In fact, Brad suspected that, at thirty-two, he was probably the oldest person in the group. And everybody looked in decent shape. Obviously, that was a health consideration when they were choosing participants.

"The plan is simple enough," April said, talking to both scientists and the media. "All we want to do is extend our area of familiarity. We'll proceed south along the shoreline. It'll be shortly after sunrise when we arrive. We'll have about eight hours before it gets dark. When that happens, we'll quit for the night." She paused. "Did anybody bring a firearm?"

The response shouldn't have come as a surprise, but it did. At least for Brad. Among the scientific team, Jeff McDermott, Cornelius Blake, and Chris Gold all had weapons. And Brad, of course. "Is there a problem?" asked Gold.

"No. Just be careful with it. Nothing's threatened us yet. And to tell the truth, we haven't seen anything that looked capable of threatening us. I'll remind you that you should only use it for defense. Don't kill any of the wildlife. And be aware, if you're not already, that the local animals almost certainly would not provide you with any nutrition, so don't even think about having any of them for dinner. Everybody understand?"

Nobody had a problem.

Backpacks, which included sleeping bags, were waiting for them. "Everybody has a food package as well. It's a little bit on the spartan side, but there's enough to meet your needs." Canteens were lined up on a table. "Don't forget one of those." She delivered a reassuring smile.

They looked at one another, and a few took deep breaths, and finally it was time to go.

• • •

JOHN COLMAR STEPPED onto the grid. Paula touched the wall behind it, and the arrow icon blinked on.

Abe Markowitz, a physicist, said, "Wait." He was small, with blond hair, intense eyes, and a neatly trimmed mustache. "Be careful, John," he said. "Your backpack's sticking out over the edge of the grid."

"It's okay," said April. "That doesn't seem to matter. The system has some sort of wraparound effect. You could put a car on there, and the whole car would go. So you don't have to worry about it." She turned back to John. "You ready?"

"Whenever you are, April."

Paula pushed the arrow. It brightened. They stood waiting for about half a minute, but finally an illuminated cloud appeared, enveloped John, and grew brighter. He looked out at them and grinned. And, along with the cloud, began to fade. Then they were both gone.

Brad could not avoid trembling. Everyone in the room had known it was coming, but they all looked uncomfortable. There was a lot of hesitation, until eventually Markowitz stepped forward. But April waved him back. Moments later the glowing cloud reappeared, then faded out again. April bent down over the grid and retrieved John's pen. "Everything's okay," she said. "Abe, you wanted to go next?"

Abe looked as if he were on the verge of changing his mind. But he smiled at his own discomfort, came forward, checked his canteen, and let everyone see he was trying hard to relax as he mounted the grid. Astrophysicist Jennie Parker, from Caltech, joined him, and they went out together. Then Cornelius Blake and McDermott.

Finally, it was Brad's turn. Along with Chris Gold, a biologist. Gold was already on the grid. "Take your time, Brad," said April. "When you're ready."

There were other security people in the Roundhouse, as well as the reporters. He could feel everybody's eyes on him. A TV camera was picking up everything. Donna would see him on CNN later today.

When the grid was in use, it was raised about three inches above floor level. He stepped onto it, trying to laugh at his own fears. Groundless, he told himself. But his stomach was churning. It was one of those occasional moments when he was glad he'd never been part of the military. He just would not have been okay with people pointing guns at him.

"Okay," said April. "See you on Eden, guys."

He wanted to hold on to something, but there was no handrail available. Lights came on, engulfed him, and the Roundhouse interior began to fade. He was having trouble breathing. Then he saw two new figures in the blaze of light. It dimmed, and he was looking at Abe Markowitz and John Colmar. "How you doing?" said Abe.

Brad inhaled. Waited a minute for his voice to steady. "Never been better."

• • •

HE WENT OUTSIDE and found himself absorbed in the quiet and serenity of a lush forest. The only sounds were the melodious singing of a few invisible birds and the rhythmic rumble of the sea. The sun was near the horizon. A few chairs and tables had been brought in by the Sioux. Cornelius Blake had gone around the side of the Cupola and was sitting on the beach, staring out at the ocean. Blake was a climatologist, a lean African-American who could have been a guy fresh out of college. But he had some major awards already though he nevertheless seemed uncertain of himself. That, though, was a quality every member of the team shared. Even April. Maybe this was something you never got used to. Getting teleported across a thousand light-years tends to induce a substantial level of humility.

Jeff McDermott, another biologist, stood at the front door taking pictures. Jeff was close to seven feet tall. Probably, Brad thought, a basketball player at one time. John was beside him, watching to make sure nothing unexpected came out of the forest. Paula stayed close to the grid and the icons. The security people had informed everyone to keep away from the transport equipment when it wasn't actually being used. The Sioux escorts were the only ones permitted to manipulate the system. "They want to make sure," said Paula, "that if somebody drops out of sight, they can limit the search perimeter."

Like the Roundhouse, the outside of the Cupola did not maintain its transparency.

A few small birds, all apparently of the same type, came

in from somewhere, landed, and began walking across the grass. When Brad moved in their direction, they scattered. "There's no hurry here," April said. "If anyone wants to stop and look more closely at the vegetation or something, just give a yell. Whatever you guys want to do is okay."

• • •

THE AIR WAS fresh, and a steady breeze blew in off the ocean. Red, gold, and purple flowers bloomed everywhere. Something that looked like a turtle looked up, saw them, and hurried into the waves. They picked up their backpacks. April took the lead, and they started walking along the beach. Paula dropped behind and wished them luck. "Isn't she going with us?" Brad asked.

"No," said April. "She's our contact with the Roundhouse. If something happens, and we need help, John will let her know, and she'll take the message back."

"So she's going to sit back there for a couple of days?" asked Markowitz.

John shook his head. "She'll be here about six hours. Then she'll be relieved by one of the guys from the Roundhouse. Okay?" His voice suggested Abe sounded as if he thought the Sioux weren't smart enough to take care of their own.

Abe nodded. "Makes sense," he said. "How many radios do we have?"

"Three," said April. "The escorts each have one, and I have one."

Jeff, wearing a sidearm inside his belt, moved up front with April, while John assumed a position in the rear.

Save for the color of the vegetation, they could have been in Southern California. The sand was warm and crunched underfoot. Shells were scattered near the water. Long-beaked birds fluttered over an incoming tide, looking for dinner. The only thing missing was sunbathers.

A cluster of about a dozen small lizards came out of the forest, traveling together and headed toward the water. They made no effort to avoid the humans. Instead, April paused to let them pass.

There wasn't a lot of conversation because they were so overwhelmed by what they were seeing. Cornelius kept saying it was gorgeous. And incredible. And unbelievable. He kept dropping behind to get pictures.

Jennie, walking beside Brad, remarked that she was trying to visualize where they were, how it could be that they were out here by an ocean located in the Belt of Orion. "Do I have that right?" she asked. The others just smiled at her. "When I was a kid," she continued, "my folks took me to see a magician, and I watched him make things appear and disappear, and it left me with a sense that magic really happens and anything's possible. That's a little bit the way I feel today." She bit her lower lip, and her dark eyes sparkled. "This is the wildest day of my life."

The temperature was rising. They'd gone about two miles when April called a halt. "Okay, everybody," she said. "It looks as if it's going to get warmer than it was last time we were here. Let's get out of the sun." They left the beach and went into the forest. That forced them to climb through shrubbery, but the cooler air was welcome.

• • •

THE CUPOLA WAS the only structure in the area. Other than that, Brad could see nothing but forest and ocean. The shoreline was a long collection of gently rolling hills. At home, given the summer weather, the area would have been filled with villas and châteaus, and the ocean would have been covered with boats.

The ground was uneven, and the grass was thick, so they were moving more slowly than they had been on the sand. Eden had insects, including some that resembled spiders. But none seemed interested in biting. Fruit in a wide variety of colors hung from the trees. The red ones especially looked juicy.

They came to a stream and decided to take a break. "I wonder," said Chris, "if they had dinosaurs here? It would be interesting to get a history of this place."

"Or maybe have them *now*?" said Brad. "There's an uncomfortable thought."

"I'm not suggesting we do anything that would cause any

damage. But having a second living world to study? It opens up all kinds of opportunities."

Brad watched another turtle stroll past. "Just like home," Chris said.

Jennie nodded. "It wouldn't surprise me to find a lot of animals with similarities to Earth life. This place has the same kind of environment."

"The big question for me," said Abe, "is the Cupola. Who put it there? And the Roundhouse?"

Cornelius didn't like the occasional sunlight, so he covered his eyes. The sunglasses weren't quite enough. "Little green men did it," he said. Then, changing tone: "Hang on. We should get an answer soon." He looked out through the trees at the ocean. "I keep expecting to see a ship or maybe a plane coming in from somewhere."

It got warmer as the sun moved across the sky.

They passed a large, fallen tree. A broken branch had been laid across it. "This is as far as we got last time," said April. "From here on, we're in unknown territory."

• • •

THE SUN WAS sinking into the hills as they arrived at the edge of another stream. "Why don't we stop for the night?" said John. "This would be a good spot."

April looked around. "That okay with everybody?"

"I'll be glad to get off my feet for a while," said Jeff, leaning back against a tree.

"How much farther will we go tomorrow?" asked Chris.

"Probably another four hours. Then, if we don't see anything, we'll go back. But by a different route."

They unrolled their sleeping bags and made themselves comfortable. Except John. "I'm going to take a quick look around," he said, "before we settle in. Anybody want to come along?"

Abe was sitting with his arms wrapped around his knees. He looked tired, but he surprised Brad. "Yeah. I'm with you."

"Good. Let's go."

It was time for Brad to play his role and show some energy. "I'll go along, too, if it's okay." John would make a perfect guest for *Grand Forks Live*. So far he'd only been thinking in terms of the scientists. But a security guy, if he was asked the right questions, could be a pretty interesting interview.

John told April they'd be back in about twenty minutes. Then they set off along the stream, following it inland and gradually uphill until their way forward appeared blocked by some heavy shrubbery. But John pushed through the bushes, finding a narrow strip of rock to walk on. Brad followed and was just getting back into the clear when Abe stopped. "Look!" he said.

A fish. It could easily have been a trout. They watched it swim past, headed downstream. It was quickly followed by several more. Abe, trying simultaneously to get hold of his camera and balance himself, dropped it into the water. "Damn!" he said.

Abe would have fallen in himself while trying to retrieve the camera had Brad not gotten hold of him. But he wavered on the edge of the rock. "I want to get the camera back. It's got some great pictures."

"Is it waterproof?" Brad asked.

"I don't know. I doubt it."

"Maybe you can save the memory card," said John.

Abe indicated Brad should let him go. He jumped in, got the camera, waded upstream a few steps, and climbed out. "Not very good planning, I guess," he said.

●　●　●

THEY FOLLOWED THE stream around a bend and arrived at a waterfall. If you could call it that. It was only about six feet high. "I don't think we're going to see much here," said John. The trees were getting thicker and moving through the shrubbery was becoming a serious challenge.

There was no trail or path of any kind. The stream narrowed down to a few feet. And they came out onto a trail. Directly ahead, they saw a wooden bridge.

FOURTEEN

Curiosity is one of the permanent and certain characteristics of a vigorous intellect.

—Samuel Johnson, *The Rambler*, March 12, 1751

PAULA FRANCISCO HAD been blown away when the tribe originally accepted her application to join the Johnson's Ridge security force. She had a passion for science, especially for astronomy, and she'd wasted no time taking advantage of the opportunity to get involved in the force that would be protecting the Roundhouse. She was a natural for the assignment. She'd spent two years with the county police after having been forced to leave college as a sophomore because of the overwhelming cost of tuition.

She would have preferred to go exploring with John and the others, but somebody had to stay at the Cupola. It took a lot of the joy out of the assignment. At least, she thought, she could get out and walk around a little. She checked to make sure she was wearing her specialized gloves. Didn't want to get locked out. Then she went out to look around. She strolled through the forest, wandered onto the beach, took a call from John informing her everything was okay. Finally she returned to the Cupola, took one of the Sioux chairs outside, and made herself comfortable.

The forest was different from anything she'd seen before.

Enormous blossoms hung from trees that looked half-human, like people who had defied the gods and taken root. Occasional wind gusts moved the branches.

She'd expected more. If she closed her eyes, she could easily have been back on Earth. The rumbling tide, the squawking birds, the dead shells scattered near the surf line. The only thing that was missing was a Pizza Hut. And that probably wouldn't be long delayed, once the tribe began selling tickets to tourists.

She wasn't used to so much sunlight. Eventually, she went back inside, where a cooling system controlled the temperature. Somebody had left a couple of books on one of the tables, but they were spy thrillers. When they got home, she'd recommend a TV be installed in the place.

John checked in with her again. Still nothing going on. They'd abandoned the beach and sought protection from the sun in the trees.

She'd become bored. And she was having a problem. Paula could not get out of her mind the look on the faces of Boots Coleman and April when they'd returned from the Strike mission. Now it was pretty obvious that the tribe would not be going back. At least not anytime soon. Though that decision hadn't been formally announced, she had no doubt it had been made. Chairman Walker had been unable to hide his shock at the time. She would have given anything to have been with April and Boots when they opened that door and looked out on the alien city. Now, she would never get the chance. The order had come down from the chairman's office: Nobody was to use the parallel-lines link under any circumstances. Or the other link, the octagon, whose destination remained a mystery. Or any other link not formally approved. Her responsibility as a security escort was to enforce the directive.

She had less than an hour left before her relief would arrive. That would be George.

She went inside the Cupola and stared at the icons. She went over to the post that contained them and waved her hand in front of the parallel lines, the way one does with a movement detector in a washroom. It lit up, and she shivered. But the luminous cloud that actually seemed to do the transporting didn't appear. That was probably because she hadn't *pressed* the icon.

She wanted to see the city.

The icon blinked off.

Her radio sounded. "Hi, Paula. How's it going?"

"Okay, John. Just trying to stay awake."

"I have some news."

"Everything okay?"

"Yes. But be alert. We found a *bridge*."

"A bridge? Really? What kind of bridge?"

"It's pretty primitive. It's built across a stream. So there's *somebody* here. Don't go to sleep."

"I won't."

"And don't forget to pass it on to George when he gets there." That would be George Freewater.

"Okay."

"Tell him I'll keep him informed. We're all going over now to take a look. Before it gets too dark."

• • •

PAULA HAD ALWAYS played by the rules. She'd never been in trouble during her school years. Had received only one traffic ticket in her entire life. Had performed her policing duties by the book. But she really wanted to see the city by the river. She could go take a look, probably without any real chance of anyone's ever finding out about it.

The downside was that if she found something especially exciting, she might not be able to keep quiet about it. But if she had to compromise herself, so be it. And if she didn't make the effort, it would be something she'd regret the rest of her life.

She stared at the three parallel lines.

Okay. She'd take her rifle. Just in case.

She stood for a minute, giving herself a chance to back away. But she wasn't going to do that. So: Take a deep breath.

She climbed onto the grid, checked that her flashlight was still on her belt, and touched the three lines. They lit up.

She fought down a sudden inclination to jump off.

Stay. Don't move. The first glimmers of light appeared around her. They grew more luminous. Her heart was pounding. And the Cupola interior began to fade.

The light dimmed to a gentle luminescence, faded out, and the world went dark. She was on another grid, but she was inside a large chamber filled with shadowy objects. She turned on her lamp. Her immediate surroundings had a luxurious ambience. A wall stopped well below the ceiling. And enclosed her on only three sides. The fourth side opened onto a vast space whose darkness was interrupted by occasional dim lights. Framed landscapes hung on the wall. Three armchairs and a couch that could have been leather were placed around the grid. And two tables held lamps with purple shades. They were turned off.

She took a moment to find the icon that would take her back to Eden. The arrow. Then she examined the eleven other images done in a style similar to those in the Cupola.

Good so far.

The chairs and tables were too small to accommodate her. She walked over to the couch, reached down, and touched the seat. It was firm and inviting.

The landscapes included a view of a dark ocean from an escarpment. And a surprise: a depiction apparently of Saturn with its rings rising out of an ocean. And another surprise: a desert with a pyramid in the background.

They were beautiful. She thought about taking one back with her. But how would she explain it? If the chairman found out what she'd done, she'd be fired. Disgraced.

The lights outside her immediate area were distributed among glass cases and tables. She could see a small aircraft, a boat, a circular structure that might have been a satellite of some sort except that it had a comfortable-looking interior that resembled someone's living room. There was also something that might have been the interior of a car. The place looked like a museum.

The building was silent. She wandered through it. The artifacts, if that's what they were, were mostly unlike anything she'd seen before. The plane had jets, but the wings didn't look big enough to support it in flight. The boat had a cabin, but there was neither a mast nor a propeller. An array of what appeared to be electronic devices occupied display cases.

A window looked out across a river. And she also had a view of the city, which occupied both banks. The sky was full of stars and a multitude of lights. Some were moving. Some were connected to buildings. For a few moments, she had trouble catching her breath. The museum was located near the edge of the river, immediately off a walkway. Two benches stood near the water for anyone who just wanted to relax and enjoy the view.

A large moon floated on the horizon, but of course it wasn't Earth's moon.

Where was she?

Something passed overhead. It was drifting slowly and, as she watched, it dipped down close to the water. It was getting smaller, crossed the river, and disappeared among the myriad of lights on the other side.

Domes, towers, complex structures all rose high into the sky. Bridges connected many of them. And aircraft, like the one that had just passed, moved between and above them. But the aircraft were moving too slowly to stay aloft.

She found a door to the outside, but it wouldn't open. The museum had several enclosures as large as the one in which she'd arrived, and a lot of windows. Clustered among the skyscrapers were a few small structures that might have been private dwellings. One was especially close, an A-frame variation, two stories high. Its windows were lit, but curtains were drawn.

Overhead, a quarter moon floated among the stars. The museum looked out across a park, where a fountain sparkled in the light. It was surrounded by more benches. Most of them were occupied. But not by *people*. They were bipeds, with moderately dark skin, but too small to be human. And there was something different about their features, about the way they moved. She wished she'd brought binoculars.

She looked at her watch. Better get back to Eden. She was supposed to be on duty, and hanging out here was putting people at risk. She wondered if the museum housed a security system. Was anyone watching her at that moment?

She hurried back, hoping she hadn't forgotten where the grid was located. But she heard voices outside the building and stopped by a window. They sounded like children, approaching on the walkway. After a minute they came into view, and she saw they *were* children. Except, of course, not human. Their eyes were too large. And they seemed too muscular for kids. Despite the alien appearance, they looked extraordinarily good. Two handsome boys, two beautiful girls.

They were watching the traffic on the river. One was pointing at a boat. It didn't have sails, and Paula couldn't hear an engine, but something was driving it. They all started laughing though she had no idea why. She stayed back in the dark, not moving, watching them pass.

Music was coming from the boat. A stringed instrument. It could have been a violin. And someone was singing. The voice sounded almost normal. She watched as it went past. Silver hull, blue cabin. Somebody, some*thing*, at the wheel. Except for the music, it proceeded silently, leaving a widening wake. Three occupants were seated in the after section. None of them seemed to be providing the voice or the music.

The children on the walkway passed, as did the boat, going in opposite directions. Then she heard more voices. Adults this time. It sounded as if they were all talking and laughing. From a distance, they almost looked like ordinary people, dressed in pants and pullovers. She counted nine of them, of both sexes. It was unlikely any were as tall as she was. Her first thought was that there was a medical issue of some sort, but they moved smoothly and gracefully.

Their heads seemed oddly shaped, narrower and longer than human heads. Their throats were longer, noses sharper. She watched them pass, impressed again by their almost classic features despite the alien quality. They were *almost* human. Somehow, the design had just missed. When they were gone, she hurried back to the transport station. She got on the grid and was about to activate the arrow when the other icons caught her attention. Not that she considered trying another one, but she wondered how large this transport network was? How many destinations were available?

Okay. Time to go home. She put her fingertips atop the arrow and pressed. After a half minute, it lit up. Within a few seconds, the luminous cloud appeared and wrapped her in its embrace.

Moments later, she was back on Eden.

• • •

SHE WAS FEELING lucky. The only other working icon at the Cupola was supposed to be the octagon. It looked inviting, and she was on a roll. It had been a few scary moments in the world with the river, wherever it was. *Riverwalk,* she thought. Scary, yes. But she had never felt more ecstatic. There was no way she could resist this other one. This time, though, she'd be more careful. No walking around and inviting trouble. Just take a quick look, see where she was, and come back. Paula got up on the grid, adjusted her rifle strap, put her fingertips on the post, and pressed the octagon image. It lit up. She waited, counting the seconds until the glowing cloud began to form. Then she said a prayer and took a deep breath.

The interior of the Cupola lost definition, and suddenly she was underwater. The reflexive action of holding her breath probably saved her life. At least for the moment. Where was the arrow?

Don't panic. It was dark, but she was still standing on the grid. Or actually she was holding on to something and trying to keep her feet planted on it. She reached directly ahead with her free hand and touched the wall. But she couldn't see any icons. Not enough light. She pushed off and made for the surface. And collided with a ceiling.

My God. She let go of her rifle and slammed her hands against the overhead, and then moved across it, feeling desperately for an opening.

There had to be one somewhere.

She fumbled at her belt, got her flashlight, and pressed the button. *It worked.* But she saw no break above her, brought the light down, and aimed it at the murky walls. Her heart was pounding. The light moved across a door on the other side of the room. She swam to it, found a pad and pushed it. The door opened, revealing a corridor, but it, too, was submerged.

She was running out of air.

Her instincts screamed at her: *Get the hell out of there. Swim for it. Down the passageway. It's your only chance.* But do that and if she got out, she might not be able to get back to the grid. And it wouldn't take long for the water to get into the flashlight. Without that, she wouldn't even be able to find the arrow icon.

She turned the light back on the transport device. It looked slightly different from the ones at the Roundhouse and on Eden, but not much. She swam over to it. The light picked up the icons. They were in the wall. She found the arrow, which was all she cared about. No time to think. She pushed it, pressed hard, waited, fought the urge to inhale, and got her feet down on the grid. Would the damned thing work underwater? Yes. It *had* to. It had brought her in.

The arrow lit up. Twenty-three more seconds.

She didn't think she could hold on that long without sucking water into her lungs. Her instincts wanted her off the grid, go somewhere, find *air.* But she held on and waited for the light.

Please.

She'd heard about what people think of during their last moments. Regrets. Friends they'd never see again. Things left undone. She experienced none of that. There was only cold terror, a gathering need to breathe, a sense that nothing else mattered.

Then the luminous aura appeared and formed around her. *It was working.*

She reached the end of her endurance as the lights came on, and she collapsed, coughing and choking onto the floor of the Cupola.

• • •

SHE WAS STILL lying in a puddle of water when George Freewater found her. "You okay, Paula?" he asked, down on one knee. "What happened? You're drenched."

She coughed. Brought up more water.

"Take your time," he said.

"Never realized," she said finally, "how I took breathing for granted."

"What did you do?" He looked up at the post and the icons. "You went somewhere?" There was an accusation in his tone.

"Don't let anybody use the one with the octagon."

"It's underwater?"

"Yes."

"Okay." He hesitated. "What were you doing, Paula? You know they don't want anybody screwing around with that stuff."

"I know."

"Did you use the other one, too? The lines?"

She looked at him for a long moment. She had never been a good liar. "Yes, George. I did."

He took a deep breath. "So you saw the city?"

"Yes."

"Did any of them see *you*?"

"No. I don't think so. I never really knew—" She gagged. Brought up more water. When she got herself together, she tried again: "I never had any idea what it looked like. It's incredible over there, George."

He leaned over her. "You *are* okay, Paula?"

"Yeah. I'm fine."

He got her off the floor and settled her in a chair. "So what do we do? We're going to have to warn everybody about the water."

"First person over will be wearing a pressure suit. So there shouldn't be a problem."

"Paula, I'm going to have to make a report. I won't mention that you told me about going to the other place. The city. But we wouldn't want somebody else repeating what you did. I don't see a way to handle it without giving you away."

"I know, George." Her eyes closed. "Do you what you have to."

"Can I make a suggestion? Go to the chairman and tell him what happened. Get out in front of it. Maybe he'll let you stay on."

"There's something else."

"What's that?"

"They found a bridge."

FIFTEEN

Don't monkey with the buzz-saw.

—American proverb cited by H. L. Mencken, 1921

EVERYBODY WANTED TO see the bridge. John cautioned them to make as little noise as possible and led them upstream past the waterfall and around a couple of bends, broke through some heavy shrubbery out onto a trail, and there it was. It wasn't very big, probably only fifteen feet long. John examined the ground. "Footprints," he said. "They look a bit large for any of us. Somebody wearing shoes."

They took pictures. Of the bridge, the stream, and the footprints. "Do we follow the trail?" asked Chris, his face suggesting he didn't think it would be a good idea.

Jeff and Abe were concentrating on the bridge. "It's pretty primitive," said Abe. Wooden planks and struts were held together with rope. But it felt solid when they walked on it. It was about ten feet wide, and it had handrails. The handrails were shoulder high.

"So what do we do now?" asked Brad.

April was looking at the sky. "I don't think we want to be stumbling around in the dark," she said. "Let's go back to the campsite. We'll deal with it in the morning."

John used his radio to call the Cupola. But no one answered. "That's not good," he said.

"She's probably asleep," said Jeff. "Give it a little while and try again."

· · ·

CHRIS AND ABE had collected some firewood, but it seemed like a good idea not to attract attention to themselves. Jennie asked whether any of the previous teams had spent any overnights away from the Cupola?

"Yes," said April. "We've done it several times."

"And nothing ever noticed you were here?"

"Not as far as I know."

Brad opened one of his food packs. Dried beef entrée and assorted vegetables. With some cheddar cheese for dessert. He began eating, and they sat almost in silence, listening to the forest.

Abe started on some chicken. "You know, there's an interesting possibility that no one's suggested." He kept his voice almost to a whisper.

"What's that?" asked Brad.

"Maybe the tech came from our end. Maybe there was an advanced civilization in the Dakotas back in ancient times."

"You're not serious?"

"No," he said. "Of course not. Although it would probably make an interesting theory to expound on your radio show. But it's pretty likely it didn't originate here either."

John tried calling Paula again. George answered. "She's gone back home," he said.

"Everything okay?"

"Yeah."

"Good. All right. She told you about the bridge?"

"Yes. You figure out yet who put it there?"

"Negative. We'll take a closer look in the morning."

"Okay. Guess this is the season for surprises." George signed off before John could ask him about the plural.

Cornelius seemed annoyed. Or maybe scared. "What do

we do in the morning? Do we actually try to make contact with whoever's here?"

"This is why we came," said Abe.

"I understand it's maybe why *you* came." John obviously didn't think saying hello would be a good idea. "The protocol says we don't do it."

"Look," said Abe, "I'm not suggesting that we go barging in anywhere. But eventually somebody's going to have to face up to it. We don't really want to go home and tell everybody that we found a bridge but were too scared to find out who built it."

"I agree," said April. "Let's try to track it down. Get it settled. But I don't think all of us should be involved. We'll play this carefully."

Jennie did not look happy. "So who gets to sit here while somebody else does the mission?"

April's features tightened. "Since we don't know what we're facing, Jennie, I think we should save the bravado and show a little common sense."

"I don't think anybody would disagree with that," said Abe. "What's the plan?"

April looked around at her team. "First, we get a good night's sleep. John, I don't want you up all night doing lookout duty. Who wants to volunteer?"

Everybody was willing.

"Okay," April said. "Let's go back to the camp. We'll run two-hour watches. I've got the first one. Brad, you're on next. Then Jennie. Then Abe has it until dawn. Okay? Everybody got that? In the morning, six of us will go up and follow the trail. The other two will make for the Cupola. Who wants to go back?"

Nobody.

Brad thought it would be a smart move. But, of course, he wasn't going to say that.

"All right," said April. "We'll draw straws in the morning."

"Do it now," said Abe. "We don't want to try to sleep with that hanging over our heads. I don't think anybody here wants to go back while the other guys go up and make history."

"All right." She rolled her eyes and sighed.

They found eight sticks, and passed them to her. She discarded two of them. "We only need six. John and I will not be drawing."

"That's about what I figured," said Abe.

She ignored him and cut the tops off two. "You pick one of the small ones, you go back, all right?"

"I can understand John," Abe continued. "But how come *you* don't get to draw?"

"Because it's my decision. No way I can send somebody else up there while I stay back. And, John, I'm assuming you don't have a problem with this?"

"No," he said. "It's why they pay me so well."

That broke the tension. April arranged the sticks in her hand and offered Jeff first pick.

He studied his choices with an air of uncertainty, and drew a short one. "Damn it," he said. "Let's wait until morning."

Chris got the other abbreviated stick.

Brad never got to draw.

• • •

IT WAS A pleasant, cool place to sleep. Brad lay for a while looking up at the handful of stars visible through the trees. Both moons were in the sky. He was telling himself that the bridge certainly hadn't been built by savages, that they'd be okay in the morning, when Jeff showed up beside him. He shook him gently and put a finger to his lips. "Brad," he whispered, "I need a favor." It wasn't hard to guess what it would be. "Would you be willing to trade places with me in the morning? Please?"

Oh, yes, Brad would have been delighted to trade places with him. To go back to the Cupola and let someone else track down the aliens. If there was a way he could do it without looking like a coward. "Jeff," he said, "I'd like to. But I'm going to be doing broadcasts about this. There's no way I can back off."

"Is there anything I can do to change your mind?"

"No," said Brad. "I have to do this. Sorry."

Jeff closed his eyes. "Okay. Thanks anyway. I understand."

No, you don't, thought Brad. *You don't have a clue.*

● ● ●

JOHN AND APRIL took the lead. They went back to the bridge but found no fresh prints. They turned right on the trail, away from the bridge. It moved gradually uphill in a more or less straight direction. As they approached the summit, the trees thinned out, and they got more sunlight. More flowers appeared, and small furry creatures peered at them from behind bushes. Then the trail divided, left and right, but still rising. They went right. John informed Jeff, who'd been given April's radio.

He'd just disconnected with the biologist when April raised an arm and stopped. "Heads up!" she said. Between the trees directly ahead, Brad saw a *cabin.*

They all ducked, trying to lose themselves in the foliage.

The cabin resembled one that would not have been out of place in a national park. It was one story, made of logs, and it had windows and a chimney. No smoke came from the chimney, and no light was visible in the windows. Brad couldn't see any movement inside.

The trail split again, an offshoot leading directly to the front door, which was about thirty yards away.

"Another crazy first contact," said Jennie. "Who'd've thought it would be like this?"

John was motioning for quiet with his right hand.

Brad looked back over his shoulder to see whether anything was coming up behind them.

"What do we do now?" It sounded like Abe, but the voice was high.

Brad heard something scurry through the overhead branches.

John took his rifle down from his shoulder. He was kneeling behind a tree, the weapon pointed at the ground while his right hand curled around the trigger guard.

"April?" Abe again. "What now?"

"Are you kidding?" said Cornelius. "Back off. Let's get out of here."

"I know this sounds crazy," said Jennie, "but why don't we go up and knock on the door?"

"Not a good idea," said John. "Whatever's in there won't be expecting visitors. Especially not anything that looks like us. We'll scare the hell out of it. Or maybe worse."

"We're getting too loud," said April.

"I vote," said Cornelius, "we don't touch this. Let's go back to the Roundhouse and let the experts figure out what to do."

"We're supposed to *be* the experts," said Jennie. Brad hadn't taken much notice of her during the hike from the Cupola. She looked reserved, not at all the sort of person who'd show up on a project like this. She'd presented a generally reclusive manner until they'd found the bridge. And suddenly she seemed to become the leader of the pack. "April," she continued, "don't we have guidelines on how to respond to this kind of situation?"

"My instructions," April said without taking her eyes off the cabin, "are that we should avoid chance encounters if we can. If we can't, be nice to them. And defend ourselves if necessary. To be honest, I don't see how we can walk away from this."

"It sounds to me," Abe said, "that James would prefer we avoid them."

"This is not a call for us to make," said Cornelius. "I think we've gone far enough. If that's what the chairman would want, that's the way we should go."

"The chairman's a politician," said Jennie. "You know what will happen if we clear out? They'll send somebody else to go knock on the door. Then they'll classify everything, and we'll go to our graves without knowing who or what is in the cabin."

Brad finally stepped forward. "The story will get out as soon as we get home. Either we go say hello, or it'll be all over the news cycle that we ducked." Brad couldn't believe he'd just said that. But he didn't want to go back with such a huge question hanging over his head. In any case, he'd known April a long time, and he couldn't imagine *her* walking away from this.

Jennie nodded. "I'll go up and knock on the door. Everybody else stay here." She started to get to her feet, but John stopped her.

"I think we're overreacting," said April. "There's not much chance that whatever's up there would seriously try to harm us. It lives in a cabin, and it builds bridges. So it's probably not a savage. This is an opportunity that most of our colleagues would kill for. And we're talking about walking away from it? That's crazy."

Cornelius shook his head. "Things could go seriously wrong. We're eight hours from the Cupola. April, I don't think there's a serious option other than to go back. Preferably leave now. And let higher authority make the call."

"You know," said Jennie, "we have a chance to make history here. Get our names up there with Darwin, Galileo, and the rest of those guys. I don't know about you people, but it's the only shot I expect to have. Ever."

"All right," said April. "If anybody wants to clear out, go. We'll wait a half hour. That should provide a decent head start. Then we'll go say hello. John, have you informed Jeff yet?"

"I was going to do that now. Just waiting for you to make the call."

"Okay. Who wants to start back?" She looked around. No response. "Cornelius?" she said.

"No. I'll stay if the rest of you are."

Nobody else spoke.

"Okay," said April, "Then there's no reason to wait. Let's do it. "

"How do we manage this?" asked Abe.

April stood. "I've got it. The rest of you wait here." John moved up beside her and gestured for the others to stay down out of sight. "You, too," she continued, indicating the Sioux escort. "Stay. I've got this."

"April, no."

"Do it, John. If we have a problem, I want you back here where you can cover me."

"No. You're not going up there alone."

They stared at each other. "It might be a good idea," Brad said, "if you guys got back down out of sight until you decide how you're going to handle this."

April stepped out onto the path that led to the door and began walking. John followed her. There was no further debate. Brad was trying to recall if he'd ever seen a movie first contact event that had gone well.

The cabin had a porch. She was tempted to look in one of the windows first. But if she got caught, it would not be a good way to start the proceedings.

April was considerably more nervous than she'd let anyone see. She would have been happy to stay back and watch while John or Brad or any of them did this. But she was in charge, so she really couldn't allow that. She resisted the impulse to look back. Straight ahead, baby.

"You all right?" John's voice. She raised her right hand, wishing he'd stay quiet.

"I'm good. Stay back. Give me some space. And don't point the rifle at anybody."

"Okay. When you get to the door, keep off to one side. In case I need a clear shot."

Three wooden steps led up onto the porch. She climbed them and faced the door. It had a lever. She paused and listened. Something was moving around inside.

Tree branches moved in the wind. She knocked. Softly.

SIXTEEN

Ships that pass in the night, and speak each other in passing,
Only a signal shown and a distant voice in the darkness,
So on the ocean of life, we pass and speak one another,
Only a look and a voice, then darkness again and a silence.

—Henry W. Longfellow, *Tales of a Wayside Inn*, 1863

SOMEONE WAS COMING. April heard a click, a latch probably. Then the door swung open.

She looked up at a gorilla.

Well, not really a gorilla. It stood straight, its arms were no longer than hers, and its face, despite the fur, bore no resemblance to a simian. Its eyes went wide, and its brow creased. It stared down at her. She would have bolted had she been able, but she was frozen in place. It looked as shocked as she was. They stared at each other. April tried to back away, but she lost her footing and went down. The thing hurried out after her, grabbed her arm, and prevented a hard fall.

It growled. That was when April saw the fangs. But then it released her.

She tried to scramble away. Its eyes were looking past her now, over her shoulder, and she heard John coming. He had the clear shot he'd wanted.

April's eyes were locked on the creature, which was still holding out a hand to her, as if to invite her to stay.

Suddenly, April realized it was *wearing a robe*!

"Don't, John," she screamed. She caught her breath, grabbed the hand, and steadied herself. She tried to get between the creature and her security escort. "Don't shoot." And she performed what probably was the gutsiest act of her life. She threw herself into the creature's arms.

"April," he shouted, "what are you doing? Get out of the way."

She stayed where she was, waving at John to stop. "Put it down," she said. "For God's sake, put it down."

The creature stared at the weapon, breathing hard. "Get away from it," said John.

It growled again. Or, rather, it *spoke. "Kiballah di santo."*

"Hello," said April, hanging on to the creature. It was also wearing *slippers.*

It backed away from her, withdrawing a step into the cabin. *"Kumenta dirk."* And it closed the door between them.

The others had fallen in behind John and were all moving cautiously toward the porch, urging her to run, to get out of there. Other than a few red marks on her right arm, she was fine.

"Come on," said Brad. "Let's clear out while we can."

April retreated back onto the grass. The creature appeared at a window. It looked afraid. "What the hell was that?" asked Abe.

"I have no idea. It's a simian of some sort. But look, how about if everybody goes back to the trees, and we try again?"

"I don't think that's a good idea," said Cornelius.

April held out both hands. "It's trying to talk to us."

"Maybe." Cornelius fixed April with a warning glare. "Even if you're right, you don't exactly speak the language."

"Let's give it a try, okay? Everybody get back out of the way."

"A lot of good that'll do now," said Brad.

April watched them retreat into the trees. John stayed where he was, a few steps behind her. The creature was still watching through the window. April raised her right hand. "Hi. How are you doing?"

It didn't move.

She went back to the door and knocked softly.

It drew away from the window and, after a few seconds, the inside latch clicked again. The door opened. April removed her fedora. "Hello," she said.

It stared down at her, then glanced back at John, who was still holding the rifle but pointing it off to one side. And it said something that sounded like *Shall eye.*

"Shall eye," April said, hoping she'd gotten the pronunciation right.

The creature replied: *"Shalay."*

April understood. *"Shalay* to you." She pressed a hand against her breast. "April."

It hesitated, looked past her again, toward John. It showed a set of fangs, but she wasn't sure it hadn't been a smile. *"Ay-pril,"* it said. It hesitated, and backed away, leaving room for her to enter. She saw two large armchairs, a framed painting hanging on a wall, and a shelf with *books*. The creature stood watching her. Waiting for her to enter. It tightened its robe and she saw it had breasts. She placed a claw over them. *"Solya,"* she said.

The radio buzzed. "You okay?" John's voice.

Solya looked startled and shifted her focus to the radio, which was clipped to April's belt.

"Yes. I'm fine."

"Be careful."

"I'm okay." She left it on so John could overhear everything and smiled at the creature. "Solya?"

"Gont." It added a question, which of course April couldn't translate. But she could guess. *Where are you from? Who are you?* What *are you?*

She showed her a picture of the Cupola. But it simply

looked puzzled. Or maybe shocked. "Glad to meet you," April said.

"Gont." Yes. And, holding both hands to her head: *"Loka."*

That might have meant *Welcome*, or *Glad to meet you.* Or that she didn't have a clue what April was talking about.

She went inside and pulled the door closed. There was a sofa that April had missed. Other than being oversized, the furnishings looked comfortable. Solya indicated she should take a seat. April had some reservations about sitting, but she said thanks and eased into one of the chairs. She could see into two other rooms. The gorilla went into one and came back a minute later with a basket of red-and orange-colored fruit, which she held out for her visitor. The instructions were not to eat the local food. But April didn't want to offend her host. She selected something that looked like a lemon. "Thank you."

"Bana ki." She was trying to commit to memory the words she was reasonably sure of. This was probably *You're welcome.*

Solya asked her something, but it was completely unintelligible. April looked up at the bookshelf. There were nine volumes, and another one lay open on one of the chairs. She wanted to ask whether there was a city nearby. Where had the books come from? How many neighbors did she have? April took a photo of Solya and showed it to her.

Solya's mouth dropped, and her eyes went wide.

Obviously, these weren't the people who'd created the Cupola. "I would like to take some more, if I may?" She spoke slowly, hoping that Solya would grasp the meaning. The creature waved her hands—*claws* was the wrong word; she had fingers—in a manner that suggested April could do as she wished. Meantime, she slipped out of the room again. April busied herself taking photos of everything, especially the paintings. (She'd discovered a second one.) Both were landscapes. When Solya came back, the robe was gone. She was wearing orange slacks and a blue knit blouse.

"Your home looks very nice," April said, smiling and extending her hands toward the furnishings.

Solya shook her head and looked puzzled. She had no idea what April was saying.

There was no sign of electrical power. Two lamps were visible, but both appeared to be oil-based. She couldn't keep her eyes off the books. She got up from the chair and walked over to get a better look. They were bound, with titles on the spines in exotic characters. They were *printed*. She reached for one, touched it, but the shelf was high, and the books were large. She was afraid she'd drop it if she tried to take it down, so she picked up the volume on the chair. Solya said something but all April could do was smile and nod. What had she said? Probably *Are you familiar with it?* Maybe *You can have it if you like.*

What kind of book was it? A novel? A history? A philosophical work? Whatever it might be, it was priceless. She looked through the pages. The print was a bit larger than would have been found in a book at home. She held it against her breast to indicate that she was entranced by it.

Eventually, she put it back on the chair, watching Solya for any signal that it would be all right if she kept it. But none came.

Solya pointed at the door, held her hands out, and shook her head. April translated it as *Maybe you should leave now.* Or *Where did you come from?* She decided to go with the second reading and tried to indicate very far away. But maybe it was time to back off. She asked whether it would be okay if she returned later so they could talk some more. She pointed to her lips. "I would like to get to know you better. Learn your language. "

Solya smiled. It was a bit unsettling, that smile. Too many fangs in it. But yes, she seemed to understand. The smile widened. She pointed at the door and moved her arms back and forth. Come and go. As you like.

Eventually, April got to her feet and glanced at the book, still without a reaction. "I should be leaving."

Solya also got up. *"Gormana,"* she said, as April started for the door.

"Gormana, Solya." And for one wild moment she thought about grabbing the book and making a run for it.

SEVENTEEN

It is prudent for a man to abstain from threats or contemptuous expressions, for neither weaken the enemy: threats make him more cautious, and contemptuous remarks excite his hatred and a desire to avenge himself.

—Niccolò Machiavelli, *Discorsi*, II, 1531

WHEN GEORGE FREEWATER heard the news about Solya, he was delirious with joy. He jumped on the grid and went back to North Dakota. The security detail and a handful of pool reporters watched him arrive. He was off schedule, so they knew something had happened. "We found *aliens*," he told them. "Well, *one* alien, really. It doesn't look much like us, but it's friendly." He waved and laughed. "They look like oversized monkeys." The audience was torn between cheering and laughing. "They have books," he added. And the laughter went away. Then he went back to the Cupola to serve the final hours of his watch.

Jack Swiftfoot heard the story on his car radio while on his way to the Roundhouse. He was scheduled to relieve George in an hour for the next watch. Johnson's Ridge was usually pretty quiet at that hour, but when he arrived, it was jammed with reporters. None of April's team had gotten back yet, but the chairman was there, shaking hands, smiling, giving statements to interviewers, commenting on the courage of those "who put themselves at risk to explore new worlds." Jack was delighted. They were talking to aliens, and the Spirit Lake Sioux had been the ones who'd pulled it off.

The media took pictures of him as he arrived, asked for comments, and stayed with him until he got into the Round-house, where he was greeted by the pool reporters. He said hello, commented that he was proud to be part of the oper-ation, picked up his rifle, and made his way to the grid. The questions continued, including one asking why he was car-rying a rifle. He responded "Safety first," and pressed the arrow icon. Questions were still coming at him when the system activated. Moments later, he arrived on Eden to find George stretched out in a chair listening to an audiobook. It was midmorning there.

George smiled, looked at his watch, removed the head-phones, and put them on a side table. "Glad to see you, partner."

"Are they really monkeys?" Jack asked.

"John says they're a pretty good imitation."

"And they wear *clothes*?"

"Well, there's only been one. *She* does. April says she's a female."

"Any hostility?"

"No. None whatever. It even gave April some food." He reached down on the side of the chair that Jack couldn't see and raised his rifle. "So everything's okay. Jeff and Chris should be here in about fifteen minutes. The rest of the crew started back a half hour ago. They'll be a while."

"Okay." Jack noticed a large puddle on the floor. "Where'd that come from?"

"Glad you reminded me. In case you get bored—"

"Yeah?"

"Don't go near the octagon, okay? It goes underwater."

"You're kidding. How do you know?"

"Let it go. Just stay away from the icons. Like the boss says." He started for the grid, stopped to pick up his audio equipment, and pointed at the radio, which was also on the table. "There are a couple of extra batteries here in case you need them."

• • •

JACK'S FIRST ACT was to call John. "Is everything okay?"

"We're fine, Jack. On our way back now. So far, at least, the aliens are friendly. Or I should say *the* alien. We've only seen one."

"That's what George was telling me. A monkey."

John laughed. "She was wearing a bathrobe when we first saw her. April says they tried to talk. And she has a library in her cabin."

"A *library*?"

"Yeah. Books. They *read*, too."

"This is not exactly what we expected, is it? Is there just one cabin?"

"We only saw the one."

"Well, I hope they're all friendly."

"So do I."

"All right. I'll see you when you get here. *Cupola* out." Jack enjoyed playing the role. He smiled and sat down, facing the door. The sweet sounds of singing birds and the wind in the trees provided a sense of exhilaration. Life was good!

He was enjoying the cool air when Chris Gold and Jeff McDermott showed up. He saw immediately that they weren't happy. Both had their hands jammed into their pockets. Their faces reflected gloom, like people who'd just experienced a seriously bad night at the casino.

"Everything okay, guys?" he asked.

"Yeah, we're good, Jack," said Jeff. "Damned sons of bitches."

"What's the matter?"

Chris turned angry eyes on him. "You know what happened back there, right?"

"I know they talked to a monkey."

"First contact."

"So what's wrong?"

"You know where we were when that was happening?"

"On the road, I guess."

"We were a mile or so away, headed back here."

"Why didn't you stay for the—umm, conversation?"

"Because," said Chris, "April didn't think it was a good idea for everybody to be there. So we got sent back."

"As a safety precaution," added Jeff. He delivered a series of expletives.

"I'm sorry, guys. But I can understand why she did it."

They walked directly past him. He followed them into the Cupola, where Chris pointed at the icons. "They don't want us touching these damned things either. So, if you don't mind—" He climbed onto the grid. "Please just send us home."

Jeff got on beside him. Jack pressed the stag's head.

"Sorry, Jack," said Chris. "It wasn't *your* fault."

• • •

HE WASN'T GOING to let their attitude bother him. There was some open ground off to one side of the Cupola. That would be the place where field, beach, and woods all came together, where Jack would have enjoyed building a cabin. He'd been thinking about it all along, but of course it wouldn't work. He'd have no way of getting groceries, no electrical power, no way to get around. No place to go, really. He'd always dreamed of living on an island somewhere, or a mountaintop. But when the opportunity actually arrived, it no longer looked very inviting.

He clipped the radio to his belt, swung the rifle over his shoulder, and went outside into the wind. He headed for the beach.

Jack was in love with a nurse he'd met when he was taken to the hospital with a broken arm. The fracture had resulted from a collision in a baseball game. Her name was JoAnn Sanders. Unfortunately, the chemistry wasn't working on her side. Although they still dated periodically, he knew the end was coming. It was just a matter of time before she would explain why they couldn't continue. So he was enjoying her company while he could, resisting the temptation to be the one who broke things off. He couldn't help thinking, on that bright sunlit day, what life would be like if he and JoAnn had a cabin on *this* beach. With its occasional twin moons. What a great place it would be to visit on weekends.

The surf was rolling in. He went down to the water's edge and stared at the horizon. They needed to bring a boat and find out what else was here.

• • •

APRIL CALLED. THEY were four hours away.

"What did it feel like talking to a monkey?" he asked.

"She's not a monkey, Jack. I'm not sure what she is, except that I think she's as smart as we are. And I don't think we should be talking about monkeys when we get back."

"Okay," he said. It was a little late to head that off. "What did she have to say?"

"It's a little hard to communicate. But she let me know I was welcome. Told me her name, waved at everybody, and invited us back."

"She doesn't speak English, does she? How'd you manage all that?"

"A lot of communication is nonverbal, Jack. You can read people pretty well from expressions, their eyes, their tone, you name it."

"But monkeys aren't people."

"This one is."

He didn't like the accusatory tone she was taking. And he guessed she'd had no problem picking up the nonverbals from Jeff and Chris. "I wouldn't think you'd be able to do much interpretation with a gorilla, though. I mean—" He tried to imagine himself walking up to one of the animals and saying hello.

"I know what you mean, Jack. And in case I didn't make it clear, Solya's not a gorilla."

• • •

HE WAS BACK staring at the ocean, thinking how magnificent it would be if he spotted a ship out there somewhere. Another historic moment. Jeff and Chris would probably get annoyed about that, too. The thought seemed cruel, but he couldn't resist smiling.

Something that resembled a crab with six spindly legs came out of the water. It moved steadily along just out of reach of the incoming waves, inspecting shells.

Jack sat down near the beach on the edge of the forest and watched the sun climb higher. It was getting warm, so he moved farther back to get some shade. He'd just gotten resettled when he saw movement in some trees near the Cupola. Something wearing olive-colored short pants and a gray shirt came out into the clearing. Another monkey. Or whatever we're calling them. But this one clearly wasn't a female. He briefly considered showing himself, waving, and saying hello. But that idea vanished quickly as he got a better look. The animal was a good bit bigger than he was. And it did not look friendly. Fortunately, Jack was carrying his rifle.

The thing walked easily, straight up, relaxed, chewing on something. It appeared to be wearing a necklace. And sandals. Jack squeezed down lower into the bushes, hoping he hadn't been seen. It strolled across the field toward the Cupola and paused before the front door. And Jack saw with horror that the door was *ajar*. He hadn't closed it. It put a claw, or a hand, against it and pushed. It opened, and the creature went inside.

He had to make sure it did no damage. But he didn't know how it would respond to him. And he didn't want to have to shoot something wearing clothes. Killing it was against the protocol anyhow. *What the hell do I do?* If it broke something, they might all be stranded on Eden.

The open door was probably what had drawn the animal in the first place. Stupid. He thought about firing a shot into the air, but that seemed more likely to cause it to hole up in there than to come out. Damn it.

He kept the rifle pointed toward the ground. Oh, Lord, he did not want to get into a fight with this thing. We make first contact and on the same day kill one of the aliens. How could he ever explain that to the chairman? Finally, he took a deep breath, came out of the trees, and approached the door at an angle that eventually allowed him to see inside. The gorilla was looking at the transporter.

Jack raised his right arm. "Hello!"

The creature flinched and turned in his direction. For a long moment, it remained still. Then it took a few steps as if to come out. But it stopped just inside the entrance, its eyes fixed on him. It took hold of the door.

Please. Don't close it.

It pulled the door shut.

Jack called John. "What do I do?"

"Maybe it would be a good idea to just get out of sight for a while."

"Suppose it breaks something in there? I was hoping I could scare it off with the rifle."

"It probably doesn't know what a rifle is."

"Can it open the door from the inside? Or does it need the gloves?"

Then he heard April's voice: "It can open the door if you ask him nice," she said. "Listen, Jack, I hate to ask you to do this, but you're going to have to go do it for him, open the door, then just back out of the way. Don't make any aggressive moves. If you don't scare him, or threaten him, I think you'll be okay."

"You *think*?"

"No guarantees, kid. How'd he get in there in the first place?"

"I guess somebody must have left the door open."

"Good move."

All right. Stalling wasn't going to get the job done.

April again: "Leave the transmitter on so we can hear what's happening."

"Okay." He walked to the door and knocked gently. "Hello," he said, raising his voice slightly. Trying to sound friendly. "You mind if I open up?"

He heard something he couldn't understand, not a growl, maybe just a grumble.

Then April was back: "Jack, I wasn't thinking. Its word for 'hello' is *shalay*."

"You don't happen to have the word for 'friend,' do you?"

"Unfortunately not."

"Okay." Jack faced the door. "*Shalay*, old buddy." It occurred to him that *old buddy* might translate into a threat. He raised his voice: "I'm going to open up, pal." He heard movement inside as he reached out and touched the pad. Pressed it. Then he backed off as the door opened. The creature was just a few feet away.

He lifted his left hand. "*Shalay*."

It stood a few feet back from the door, watching him.

"What's happening?" asked April.

"It's standing in there looking at me."

"Wave."

"What?"

"Wave at him. You know, friendly gesture."

Jack raised his right hand, palm open. "Hi. *Shalay*."

The creature said something back.

"Jack," said April, "where's your rifle?"

"On my shoulder."

"Maybe it can sense it's a weapon. Why don't you back off? Give it some distance? Maybe it'll come out."

"That sounds like a good idea." He turned and walked back toward the trees, stopping at the edge of the forest. "April?"

"Yes, Jack?"

"You have a word for good-bye?"

The creature's eyes were focused on him. Fangs were visible. April gave him the word, and he repeated it. "*Gormana*."

He took a few more steps into the woods.

The creature came out into the sunlight. "*Gormana*," it said.

EIGHTEEN

The ice of life is slippery.

—George B. Shaw, *Fanny's First Play*, 1911

PAULA WAS HAUNTED by the vision of the city on the river. She'd said nothing to her mom. Or to the guy she'd been dating. He was also a member of the security detail. And she certainly didn't want to tell the chairman. But she had no choice.

She liked Walker. And she loved being part of the security unit. It was painful to know she'd put all that at risk, but if she had it to do again, she wouldn't change a thing. The prospect of being dismissed hung over her like a dark cloud. She'd wanted to get it over with, to tell the chairman what she'd done, but he wasn't present when she got back to the Roundhouse, and she took advantage of that to go home and put off facing him.

She lay awake most of the night framing what she would say. Nothing sounded very convincing. In the morning she called Sioux Headquarters and asked for an appointment with him.

"May I ask why you want to speak with him, Paula?" said his secretary.

"Security issue, Miranda."

"Can you be here at two?"

• • •

THE TRIBAL HEADQUARTERS was only ten minutes from her home, but it was one of the longest drives of her life. She finally got there, pulled into the parking lot, and, after a long moment, got out of the car and walked into the Blue Building. Miranda notified the chairman that she had arrived and invited her to have a seat. Several minutes later, a man she didn't know came out of Walker's office, glanced her way, and left.

Then the chairman appeared. His expression suggested he was not looking forward to the interview. *He already knows,* she thought. Normally he would have said, "Come in, Paula." But on this occasion he simply stood aside and looked back into his office.

She entered and sat down. He turned to the secretary. "Hold any calls, Miranda."

"Yes, sir."

Walker closed the door, circled the desk, and settled into his chair. "Are you okay, Paula? I heard about the underwater episode."

"Yes, sir," she said. "I'm fine."

"Good. What can I do for you?"

"You may not have the whole story, Mr. Chairman."

"What am I missing?"

She cleared her throat. "I used the Strike link, too. Don't know why I was so dumb. But I wanted so much to see what was there. And I thought nobody would ever know."

His expression darkened. "And what did you see?"

"Probably the same city you did. Riverwalk."

Walker had not crossed over. But he let that pass. "Have you told anyone about this?"

"No, sir."

"You're sure? What about—?" He stopped, picked up a folder, and looked through it. Then his eyes targeted her again. "George? You told George, didn't you?"

"Yes, sir. He made me promise to come here and tell you what I'd done."

"I see."

"I'd have done it anyway. Come here, I mean. I'm sorry, Mr. Chairman. I don't know what got into me. It's very exciting to be over there. And I felt that if I didn't do it, I might not get another chance. And I'd always regret it. But I won't do anything like that again. Not ever. And I won't say anything to anyone. I'd like very much to keep my position with the security unit. If you'd be willing to trust me again. I'll understand if you don't. "

"When you were there, at this place, were you seen by any of them?"

"No, sir. Not that I'm aware of."

"Tell me about the city."

"It's beautiful. The transport station is in the middle of a park. There are lights. Music. People walking around. They're like us, but not really people. They're different. I'd love to drive around in the place. To really get a chance to look at it."

"You mentioned people? Did you get a good look at them?"

"No, sir. It was nighttime. And I couldn't get close without their seeing me. Their faces are different. The features are sharper. Eyes are farther apart, I thought, though I couldn't be sure. And they're smaller. I didn't see anybody who appeared to be over five feet. The males would probably come up to about my shoulders."

"You called it Riverwalk."

"A made-up name, sir. Of course."

"It's a good fit, judging from what I've heard. You're sure it wasn't a city on Earth?"

"No. It wasn't one of ours. For one thing, they had a different moon. And the inhabitants are certainly not human."

"Anything else you can tell me, Paula?"

"It looked like a nice place to live."

"Would you say they're more advanced than we are?"

"Oh, yes. It's maybe the way our cities will look in the far future."

"That was April's reaction, too." Walker chewed on his lower lip for a moment. "Thanks for coming in, Paula. It's probably too late to stop this from getting around. But I don't want you discussing it with anyone. I've sent out an update warning the security unit about the octagon icon. And also stipulating that anyone else who violates the protocol will be terminated. You may keep your job, Paula. But I won't tolerate a second offense."

When she was gone, Walker sat staring at the framed photos of Carla and the kids. It seemed inevitable that eventually something would go wrong. And the Sioux knew too well what happens when a high-tech civilization shows up and moves in. You lose everything. Even with the best of intentions.

* * *

APRIL LOOKED ACROSS a bevy of television cameras. Chairman Walker reached out to shake their hands as she and John got down off the grid. John joined the other members of the team who were standing off to one side. "It's good to have you all back," he said. "Welcome home. And congratulations." He stepped out from behind the lectern, making room for April.

She nodded. "Thanks, Mr. Chairman. It's been an incredible experience."

The reporters wasted no time shouting questions at her. "How does it feel to be the first person to shake hands with an alien?"

"Did it scare you?"

"Are they really apes?"

She raised both hands and waited for them to quiet down. "First off, they are *not* apes. Or anything like that. I'm sorry that got back to you, but it's not accurate." She handed her cell to Andrea Hawk.

"What did it have to say? Were you actually able to talk to it?"

"Is there a civilization up there?"

"Did you see any planes or cars?"

April started to explain that they had a printing press but she was interrupted when the screen lit up and a picture of Solya literally took over the room. She was in shirt and slacks, with bright eyes and a wide smile. The photo minimized her fangs.

A long minute passed before the questions resumed. "Is that *her*?"

"When will you be going back?"

"Weren't you afraid of her?"

For the next ten minutes, everything was about Solya. "Will you guys be bringing her back here at some point?"

"She just invited you inside? And you trusted her?"

It became absolute chaos. Questions from all directions.

April let it run for a while before eventually taking control. "Nobody asked her name," she said. "It's Solya. And she asked me to say hello to everybody."

That brought some skeptical laughter.

"It's true," said April.

Jim Stuyvesant waved a hand. "How about sending one of *us* to Eden? It's been a while since you let any of us go. You must have figured out by now that it's safe."

"We've sent Brad. But I hear you, Jim. Eventually, I think we'll get back to providing better exposure for the media. At the moment, though, we're still concerned about the risks."

Photos of Solya and her cabin continued to appear on the screen. The TV cameras recorded everything. When the series had finished, the room filled with applause again.

When it ended, Walker took the floor. "I have some additional news for you," he said. "We've had a team working here, trying to pin down a more precise date when the Roundhouse was built. We have a tentative result. They're saying it was constructed approximately twelve thousand years ago. So it's a little older than we thought. But not by a whole lot."

April by then knew a substantial number of the reporters. One, Mike Tower of the *Chicago Tribune*, asked how they'd come up with that number. "I thought the materials used to make this place," he added, "were completely foreign to us."

"They didn't actually date the building," said Walker. "They did an analysis of the soil. Don't ask me to explain it. It had something to do with melting glaciers and Lake Agassiz retreating. When the lake drained, it left sediment layers. The sediment layers tell us when a given area was a coastline. Anyhow, they say the date is correct within a few centuries."

"Close enough," said one of the reporters.

The grid lit up, and Jack appeared. "Just the guy I've been waiting for," Walker told the reporters, motioning him to his side. "April wasn't the only one who had a conversation with an alien today. Jack Swiftfoot welcomed one to the Eden station a few hours ago. Unfortunately, he wasn't able to get the kind of photos April did." They put up a picture of the second creature. It was walking away, toward a cluster of trees. "This one was inspecting the Cupola. But before you ask, they don't seem to know anything about it other than that it exists. So we still have no idea who developed the technology."

• • •

WHEN IT WAS OVER, April asked James if they could go out to his car for a few minutes. "Of course," he said, realizing more was coming. When they got settled in, he started the engine to get some heat. "So what else do you have?"

"You saw the pictures of Solya's library."

"Of course."

"We should do some rethinking. Eden has a civilization. It may or may not be high-tech. We don't know. Solya didn't seem familiar with electricity, and she almost fell out of her chair when I showed her the photos. But they have the printing press. We shouldn't get so locked down on the city by the river that we don't try to find out something about Solya's culture as well."

"Of course. What's your suggestion?"

"We start by learning the language. We need somebody who's good with this kind of stuff to go back and spend some time with Solya. And maybe eventually we could even bring her *here*."

"How about *you*? That would give her somebody she's familiar with. I think she'd be more comfortable with you than with anybody else we could send."

"I'd love to do it. But I barely got through my French courses in college. No. We need somebody who has some serious linguistic talent."

"Okay. I think I know who to ask."

"Who's that?"

"The Snowhawk."

"Who?"

"Andrea. She's—"

"Oh, yes. Another talk-show host. Yes, I know about her. She's good with languages?"

"As far as I can tell. I'll ask her. You got anything else?"

"Solya's library. We should try to make a deal to get hold of one of the books. Do a trade of some sort. Whatever it takes."

"I'll do what I can, April. Listen, one other thing?"

"Yes?"

"I think, considering what we've accomplished, we should do a celebration. Get some public relations out of it."

"Sounds good to me."

"We'll set it up for next Friday night in Fort Totten. If you want to suggest some people we should invite, let me know, okay? But let's get right on it."

• • •

APRIL RODE BACK to Grand Forks with Brad. She was usually a quiet sort, inclined to let others carry the conversation. But that afternoon, as they crossed the prairie, she couldn't stop talking. "Absolutely historic," she said.

"You don't think there's any possibility that Solya's ancestors could have built the Roundhouse, do you? Could you develop that kind of technology and then lose it?"

"I suppose anything's possible. The technology probably came from Riverwalk, though."

"You'd really like to go there, wouldn't you?"

"Sure I would. Who wouldn't? Imagine having an opportunity to sit down with a couple of them and talk about their history. I wonder what they've seen? With that kind of technology they'd have no need for starships or anything like that."

"But they *do* have vehicles, right? *You* saw them. Boats and aircraft."

"That's true. And what it tells me is that they enjoy traveling. And not just arriving in different places. By the way, the tribe's doing a celebration next weekend. Friday evening. You'll be getting an invitation from James."

"Great," he said. "Donna, too, right?"

"Of course."

"Okay. We'll be there."

"He hasn't said yet, but I suspect it'll be formal."

"I'm for it. Haven't worn a tux since my prom."

"There's something else. We'll be sending another couple of missions out during the next month."

"Back to Eden?"

"There'll probably be another one to Eden as a follow-up. But the ones the chairman has in mind will be going to the Maze and to the space station."

"What's the purpose?"

"We just want to look around a bit."

"Okay. That's as good a reason as any, I guess. Good luck."

"I think you'd especially enjoy the view from the station. Are you interested in going?"

A tractor-trailer roared past, headed in the opposite direction. "Sure. I'd love to." Brad's fears had disappeared.

"Good."

He was surprised by the invitation. He'd assumed she was disappointed in him. He'd stood aside and let her go up alone to the cottage. What a missed opportunity that had been. What if *he* had gone? Brad Hollister makes first contact. But it was just as well. April had fallen down when Solya had opened the door. Had he been with her, he'd still be running.

• • •

DONNA SIGNALED HER reaction by gazing at the ceiling. "The space station?" she asked, in a flat voice.

"They just want to take a look. See whether it really *is* a space station. That's still up in the air." He chuckled at his own joke, but she wasn't buying in.

"The place without any air?"

"We'll be wearing space suits, so there won't be a problem."

"Brad, when was the last time you wore a space suit?"

"It's been a while. They've got a couple of astronauts who've been helping them. They'll provide some training."

"What's the point of this again?"

"They want to find out what the place is. Where it is."

"Brad, I wish you wouldn't get involved in any more of this stuff."

"I understand, Donna. But it's safe. And, you know, I love doing it."

• • •

THEY SAT THAT evening plugged into cable news, watching Brad materialize again and again out of the transport system at the Roundhouse. She'd caught her breath the first time she'd seen it. It still unnerved her. She'd reached over and taken his forearm, holding on as if he might slip away. It was unsettling for Brad as well.

"Okay," she said. "I'll admit it. I'm proud of you, love. But if something happens, I'll never forgive you."

Media vans were showing up. For most people, it would probably have been a nuisance. But this was Brad's business. And he enjoyed attention. It's what he was about. He was always at his best when he had an audience. So he did what he could to accommodate them.

They watched the interviews play out on the various

networks. Every time the phone rang, he hoped it was someone calling from *The Tonight Show.* Or Stephen Colbert. But usually it was just a local media outlet. Toward the end of the evening, Donna picked up a call, listened, and handed it to him. Her lips formed Matt's name.

"Hi, Matt," he said.

"Hello, Brad." There was a stiffness in his boss's tone. Not the all-out congratulations he was expecting. "You did a good job. Well done."

"Thank you. I was just lucky enough to be there when stuff was happening."

"Yeah. Look, you'll probably be doing more interviews. When that happens—"

"Yes?"

"Do you think you could mention the station's call letters once in a while?"

"Oh. Sure. I guess I got so caught up in all this, I forgot."

"Naturally. Now, you're going to be here in the morning, right?"

"Yes, I'll be there."

"Good. See you then."

He disconnected. Brad stared at the phone. "He's never satisfied."

"Brad, he probably thinks he's going to lose you."

It was true that Brad was hoping he could turn all this into a job as an anchor at a local TV station. If that happened, who knew where he might go from there? "He's a crank, Donna." He flashed that big happy grin that told her not to worry, everything was fine.

• • •

WALKER DIDN'T REALIZE he'd left his secure phone in the desk drawer until he was several blocks away from the Blue Building, so he was not entirely surprised when, on the way home, Carla called and told him the White House wanted to talk to him. "Call them right back, okay?" She sounded nervous.

It was early evening. He turned around and went back to the office, which was deserted when he arrived. But Alice was still at her White House post. "He'll be right with you, Mr. Chairman," she said.

He expected a show of annoyance, but the president congratulated him on the first contact and on getting through it without any dire consequences. "You have a good operation out there, James," he said.

"Thank you, Mr. President. April and the people on the ground deserve the credit."

"I know. But so do you." There was a long pause. Then: "I'm sure you're aware that we got lucky."

"How do you mean, sir?"

"That everything went well. As you know, I've been concerned since the beginning of this about who we might run into out there. James, is there anything at all I can do to persuade you to slow this thing down? I don't see any way these continuing operations can end well."

Walker looked toward the windows. It had begun to snow. "Mr. President, I wish I could oblige you. I've cut back as much as I can—"

"I appreciate that. I'm taking a lot of heat from the scientific community. They want acceleration. Missions going out every day."

"I'm aware of that, sir. I'm getting a lot of complaints, too. And there are people who are desperate to get a look at the technology."

"Just tell them I'm the one responsible. No need for you to absorb any of the fallout. But the reality is that we have to get away from this. James, I really think we need to bring this to a halt. Take the equipment down. Do whatever you have to."

"Mr. President, for the first time in my life, I love coming to work. The reservation is *alive*, as I've never seen it. We're making incredible discoveries, and the Spirit Lake Sioux are leading the way. I can't take that away from them." He watched the snow coming down. "I can't see that any harm is being done."

"I understand, James. But if something goes wrong, and it could happen easily enough, you wouldn't want your people associated with it."

NINETEEN

Sight is the keenest of the senses.

—Cicero, *De Oratore*, c. 80 B.C.E.

LLOYD AND MABEL Everett loved bingo, which they played regularly on Friday nights at the Spirit Lake Casino in St. Michael, North Dakota. St. Michael was part of the Sioux reservation. It had been a good night for them. Largely thanks to Mabel, they still had $120 of their winnings after buying pizza and Cokes for themselves and their neighbors, Chuck and Amy Benson, at the Snack Bar.

They hung around the casino for another hour, enjoying the music, the conversation, and the views of Devils Lake. Lloyd was a psychiatrist and Mabel had been a full-time mom. But the kids were gone now, off to school, and the household seemed unduly quiet. Chuck and Amy were both retired Customs officers, whose children had also left home.

Ordinarily, they'd have talked about movies or who was coming back for Lloyd's birthday or whatever oddball news event had shown up on TV. But on that night, nobody was talking about anything other than the star gate, or whatever it was, that had been found buried atop Johnson's Ridge, which they'd passed on their way to the casino that evening.

Chuck and Amy had driven onto the ridge a week earlier, hoping to get a look at the interior of the thing, but the police had been keeping everyone at a distance. "What really blew my mind," said Amy, "was watching the Feds back off after they tried to seize the thing."

"You guys believe the Roundhouse story?" asked Chuck. "You think they've really been able to do that *Star Trek* thing? That they're actually opening doors to other worlds?"

"They've got pictures," Mabel said.

That wasn't exactly news, of course. "But it looks pretty ordinary. Just woods. Everything looks like Colorado. You notice they've got blue jays?"

"You might be right, Lloyd," said Chuck, "but I'll tell you, I'd love to have a portal to San Francisco. But sure, it's going to turn out to be an illusion, or a fraud of some kind. When it does, I'll be disappointed." His oldest son, Jess, lived in San Francisco with his wife and two kids.

Amy smiled. She was in her sixties but still pretty. "Chuck," she said, "you watch too many science-fiction movies."

They had another round of drinks and lifted their glasses to the happy gorilla who'd been all over cable for several days.

• • •

WHEN THE EVENING was over, Lloyd went out onto the parking lot under a full moon while everyone else waited inside. The temperature was down close to zero, which was a bit brisk for this time of year even by Dakota standards. He tracked down the car, climbed in, and drove back to the front entrance. Mabel, Amy, and Chuck came out.

Chuck was having minor problems with his left leg, but his wife helped him into the backseat. Then she got in beside him. Mabel climbed in, and Lloyd pulled away. He made his way out to Route 57, turned left, and almost slid into someone's mailbox.

"Heads up!" cried Mabel. "It's icy."

Lloyd came off the gas, straightened the wheel, and

discovered he'd been holding his breath. "Wait'll you see me on the mountain roads," he said.

That produced laughter in back. "So," said Amy, "if they open the Roundhouse to the public, are you guys going to go up and go through the star gate?"

"I'm not so sure I'm ready to try that," said Lloyd.

Mabel laughed. "I'm not big on it either. What do they call it? Teleprompting?"

"Tele*port*ing," said Amy. "You'd rather take the bus?"

"I'd rather make sure that I actually get where I'm going. How do you know that the person who gets reassembled at the other end is actually *you* and not somebody else with your memories?"

"I don't think that makes any sense," said Chuck.

"Neither does a building that's been buried for ten thousand years but still lights up at night."

• • •

ROUTE 57 TOOK them north across the lake and into the city. "I can see it," said Chuck.

Mabel swung around in her seat so she could look through the rear window. "The Roundhouse?"

"Yes. See the glow?" Nobody knew why the place put out that eerie green light. There'd been a panic at first, and people had fled the area. But the Geiger counters had registered nothing dangerous, and after a while everybody had become accustomed to the radiance. Had even come to admire it.

Lloyd turned right on Twelfth Street, passed the Northern Plains Railroad offices, and turned left on Fifth Avenue. He was about three minutes away from Chuck's house when something changed. He was simultaneously holding on to the steering wheel while he drifted through the night, looking down on his car from a height of about thirty feet. The car began to swerve. He could still feel the wheel in his hands and the gas pedal under his foot. But he was *out* of the car. Somebody screamed. He came off the gas and tramped down on the brake. He watched the car angle off to one side and jump the curb. It barely missed a telephone pole and plowed into the piles of snow.

"Oh my God," said Mabel. "What was that?"

He was beside her again. Back in his seat. "You guys okay?" asked Amy from the rear of the car while Chuck demanded to know what the hell Lloyd was doing.

"Don't know," said Lloyd. "What happened?"

"You mean *you* don't know?" asked Amy.

"I have no idea." He was having trouble breathing. "Did you see that, Mabel?"

"Yes!" she said. "Yes. I was outside. Up with the trees."

"What are we talking about?" Chuck asked.

"I don't know," said Lloyd. "I don't get it. I didn't have that much to drink."

"What happened?" Chuck sounded shaken.

"I was up there." Mabel pointed at the roof. "Above the rooftops. Looking down. Damn son of a bitch!" She rarely used language like that.

"Me, too," said Lloyd. "I don't— There must have been something in the drinks."

"What?" Chuck was seriously upset. "You were up in the air? *Both* of you."

Both shouted, "Yes!"

"I know it sounds crazy," said Lloyd.

"*Sounds* crazy?" Chuck was breathing heavily. "It *is* crazy. You didn't drink that much."

A blinking light showed up in the rearview mirror. "Uh-oh," said Lloyd.

A police car pulled in behind them. Amy advised him to just relax. "Don't say anything about being up in the sky," she said.

One of the patrol car doors opened. An officer got out and approached. Lloyd lowered his window. "Everybody okay in there?" he asked.

"Yes, sir," said Lloyd. "We're good, Officer."

"May I see your license and car registration, please?"

He produced the documents. The officer studied them. "What happened?"

"I guess we slid a bit."

"On what, Mr. Everett? It's not that slippery here. Would you step out of the car, please?"

"Why, Officer? We didn't do any damage."

He sniffed a couple of times. "You've been drinking."

"Not very much. I'm sure I'm not over the limit."

"Would you step out of the car, please?"

Lloyd exhaled and climbed out into the street. He felt okay. "You want me to walk a straight line?"

"No. Let's not waste time." The other patrolman was getting out of the police car now. He was carrying a small black device. "I'm sure you wouldn't have any objection to a Breathalyzer test?"

Lloyd had never been much of a drinker. On this night he'd had two rum and Cokes. But, depending on the type of rum, it might be enough to set off the alarm. "Officer," he said, "I'm a psychiatrist. Can't we just move on?"

"I'm sorry, sir. But I think we need to be certain you're okay. We can do it here, or we can do it at the station."

Mabel turned in her seat and looked at their passengers. "You guys really didn't see what happened?"

Amy and Chuck both looked puzzled. "I have no idea what happened," said Amy.

Chuck nodded. "Me either."

Mabel frowned. "That was no dream, Lloyd," she said in a rising voice. "Maybe you should tell them what we saw."

"Yes," said the policeman. "Why don't you do that? What did you see?"

"Mabel," Lloyd said, "please be quiet. Let me handle this."

"Mr. Everett, this is going to go a lot better if you cooperate. Now, what happened?"

"Something took us out of the car," said Mabel. "Both of us. We were up there somewhere, looking down, and I know how crazy this sounds. But we're not drunk, and I don't mind going down to the station if that's what it takes to prove it."

The policeman with the Breathalyzer approached.

Lloyd submitted to it. They took the reading, studied the results, and looked surprised. "You're okay," the cop said. "But when you get home, you might want to get the lady some help."

TWENTY

Our doubts are traitors,
And make us lose the good we might oft win,
By fearing to attempt.

—Shakespeare, *Measure for Measure*, 1604

"HAVE YOU SEEN the latest Quinnipiac poll, Harry?" The president looked tired. "The voters want us to go into the river city and say hello. By a thirty-eight-percent margin."

Eaton nodded. "The voters will support anything if someone gets them excited. The cable news people are pushing it." They didn't dare send anyone out to take on the cheerleaders. They couldn't do that without scaring everybody. "When that thing first showed up, I thought we might get a serious technological boost out of it. But the more I think of the ways it can do us in—We need to find a way to get rid of it."

"Harry, if I weren't sitting here, I'd be with them. I'd want us to go in and find out who they are. Send April What's-Her-Name in to say hello. It worked with the gorillas; it should work with the river city. Maybe we could sit down and have a few beers with them." He sat quietly for several minutes. Finally, he shook his head. "Why the hell did this have to happen on *my* watch?"

• • •

ANDREA HAWK LOOKED surprised when she came into Walker's office. "You wanted to see me, Mr. Chairman?" she said.

"Have a seat, Andrea."

She was a beautiful young woman, long dark hair, intelligent eyes, perfect features designed more for TV than for radio. She sat down on the couch. "Would you by any chance like to come on the show, James? My callers don't want to talk about anything other than you and the Roundhouse."

"I know. I'm a regular listener. But I think I'd better pass for now. They'll be asking questions I'm not ready to answer." He leaned forward, put his elbows on the desk, joined his hands, and balanced his chin on them. "Speaking of the radio show, I've noticed how good you've been with foreign visitors. How many languages do you speak?"

"Spanish and French. A little German."

"Very good. And you handled a Chinese visitor pretty well last year."

"Thank you. I have some work to do on that, though." She flashed that all-knowing smile.

"You know about Solya."

"The gorilla? Sure."

"I have a favor to ask."

"You want me to learn the language?"

"Yes. Do you think you could take the time to do that?"

"James, I'd love to help. But something like that is way beyond what I could do."

"I think you're underestimating yourself, Andrea. But if you don't want to attempt it, I understand."

"It's not that I don't want to try. I just don't want to waste our time. Something like this needs a professional."

"Do you have anyone in mind?"

"No. But I have some contacts. Let me call around. I suspect with this kind of project, we can get pretty much anybody we want."

"All right. There's something else. You know that Solya reads books."

"Yes. Are we going to be able to get our hands on some of them?"

"We'll do what we can."

"How do we manage that? We're not going to try to steal them, are we?"

"No, of course not. We've picked up some coffee-table books with lots of pictures. Landscapes. Astronomical views. Cabins at sunset. That sort of thing. If we can find the right person, we'd like to have him, or her, go to Eden, get to know Solya, and execute a trade."

"Good. Give me a little time, James. I'll get back to you as quickly as I can."

• • •

WALKER HAD GOTTEN word that an Eden movement was under way in the tribe, so he wasn't surprised when a delegation showed up at his office. It consisted of three people, only one of whom he knew personally: Walter Billings, who owned Walt's Electronics in Fort Totten. His companions were Chaska Good News, who was probably in his nineties, and Wichahpi White Eagle, whose angry eyes suggested she expected no nonsense from the chairman. They introduced themselves as representing a group that wanted access to Eden. "There's no reason to keep our people out of there," Walter said. "It's a chance to get away from the cold, a great place for a vacation. Why aren't we letting our own people take advantage of this?"

Walker's secretary brought coffee in for the visitors.

"I would like nothing more," said Chaska, "than to make the area available as a legacy to my grandchildren. We have a clear obligation here, Mr. Chairman, and I'm sure you will not try to sidestep it."

"There are a couple of good reasons for my hesitation," said Walker. "The major one is that it's dangerous. We don't really know enough about this place to sanction casual visitors. There may be predators that we haven't seen yet."

"That's hard to believe," said Wichahpi.

"He's talking about the gorillas," said Chaska.

"I'm talking about *tigers*. We don't know yet what we're dealing with. And just so we're clear, Chaska, the real reason is that there *are* inhabitants. We don't know how they'll react—"

"They're *gorillas*, for God's sake," said Walter. "Why would we give a damn about a bunch of gorillas?"

Damned idiots. "They're *not* gorillas. They're intelligent creatures. I understand what they look like, which by the way is not very much like gorillas except for the fur."

Chaska jabbed a finger at him. "Chairman Walker, we're serious about this."

Walker told himself to stay calm. "I hate to say this, but you're suggesting we just go in and take the place over, right?"

"No, I'm not saying that although I can't see that there'd be a problem if we did."

Somewhere nearby a woodpecker was at work. "You know," Walker said, "I suspect that was pretty much the way the whites talked about us when they first showed up. Look, people, you're going to have to trust me on this. Let me handle it. For the time being, we're not going to allow anybody to go in there for anything other than scientific purposes. When we get the information we need, *then* we'll think about what our next step will be."

"Have your way," said Walter. "Hell with the tribe."

"Try to open your mind, Walt."

Wichahpi was wearing a smug smile. "Mr. Chairman, did you know they are now selling gorilla action figures?"

"No. I hadn't heard that."

"They were advertising them on TV today."

"Well, I guess that's no surprise."

She was watching him as if he were a deer. "Mr. Chairman, I hate to criticize, but are we getting a share of that, by any chance?"

• • •

ARTHUR WOODS WAS approaching eighty, but he'd filled his life with workouts and had never been ill. Unfortunately, good things don't go on forever. His daily walks, which used to consist of strolling three miles while he listened to audio thrillers, had grown stressful as he'd become more vulnerable to the weather, and he'd ended them. Now he restricted himself to about fifteen minutes in an aerobic chair, and a half hour on a stationary bike. He especially liked that because he could read while he pedaled. Despite growing problems, he refused to admit, even to himself, that he was getting old. Eighty, he'd decided, was the new forty.

Arthur's breakfasts usually consisted of two pieces of toast and a lot of fruit. He especially liked grapes. But on that morning, there was no fruit in the refrigerator. "Sorry, dear," said Rosalie, his wife. "I forgot to get some yesterday."

"I'm going down and take care of it," he said.

"Why don't you have some cereal?"

"I'm not in a cereal mood, love."

"All right. Just give me a minute to change, and I'll take care of it."

"It's okay. I got it."

She watched him take his overcoat and trapper hat out of the closet. "You going to take the car, Arthur?"

"We're two blocks from the store, babe, and I'm just getting some grapes and, probably, strawberries."

"Be careful," she said.

The sky was clear. He walked south on Phillips Street, hands pushed deep into his pockets. Like many of the people in Fort Moxie, he'd once been a Customs officer. But that was a long time ago.

Across the street, Marie Stone was just pulling out of her driveway. She saw him and waved. Then she turned right on Main and was gone. He turned left. The sidewalks had been cleared of snow. He passed Lock 'n' Bolt Hardware and noticed his neighbor Frank Brantlow coming out of Jerry's Gun Shop. Frank's appearance distracted him, and he stubbed his right foot against a piece of uneven pavement. It sent him hurtling through the air. He threw out his hands in an effort to protect his head and suddenly it seemed as if a cushion had formed under him. He came down on his nose and mouth, but the landing, impossibly, was almost soft. He was lying flat on the ground, on cold concrete when Frank Brantlow knelt beside him. "Arthur," he said. "You okay?"

One knee was bent under him, but it didn't feel as if anything was broken. Dottie Cassidy appeared on his other side. "Arthur," she said, "what happened?"

"I tripped."

She stared at him, then at Brantlow. "Did you see that, Frank?"

"I'm not sure," he said. "What did *you* see?"

"It looked like he *floated* down onto the pavement."

Frank nodded. "Yeah. I saw something like that, too."

Arthur laughed. Then realized he couldn't get up on his own. "Frank," he said, "could you give me a hand?"

"Sure. You okay? Want me to call the EMTs?"

"No, no. I'm fine."

"You went down face-first, Arthur," said Dottie. "How did you not get hurt?"

"I think I blocked the fall with my hands."

Frank reached under Arthur's right arm and lifted him to his feet. "You better be careful out here. It's slippery." They stood back and watched him to be sure he was okay. "How about I take you home?" said Dottie. "I'm in the parking lot."

"No, thanks. I'm good." He made sure everything was still working, then limped down to the end of the block and went into the supermarket.

• • •

DOTTIE HAD LUNCH that day with Diane Freewater at Clint's Restaurant. She mentioned the incident with Arthur, whom Diane did not know. "It just amazed me that he could absorb a spill like that and not get hurt."

Diane took a bite out of her tuna sandwich. "Well, if he got up and walked away, he was obviously all right."

"I guess. But I was there. He didn't really fall. It was like he stopped short of the sidewalk. And something happened to the light where he was. It changed color or something. I don't know. It just looked different. And somehow he got a soft landing."

"Really?" Diane recalled George's mentioning something like that when one of the science teams had come back from the place they called Eden. And, of course, there'd been other stories lately about a spirit, or a ghost, or something drifting around town. She'd assumed it was just the media playing stuff up. George, she'd thought, had imagined seeing something. Now she wasn't so sure.

TWENTY-ONE

*Language! The blood of the soul, sir, into which our
thoughts run, and out of which they grow.*

—Oliver Wendell Holmes, *The Professor at the
Breakfast Table*, II, 1859

THE SKY WAS still dark when Brad rolled into the deserted
KLYM parking lot and let himself into the building. A
few minutes later, he was putting together the five o'clock
news and weather report, which he would read live. On this
unique morning, he smiled as he worked. It was the first
time in his career that he was part of the story. He would be
using an extract from the IPA:

> *The scientific team that left Johnson's Ridge for Eden
> returned after an encounter with the first alien to appear
> in human history. The alien gave no indication of hos-
> tility although it resembled a gorilla. Incredibly, it lives
> in a cabin and owns several books, written, according
> to team leader April Cannon, in a language she did not
> recognize.*

There was no mention of the creature that had entered the
Cupola. Brad thought about adding that part of the story but
decided to let it go. One alien works better than two. And
the books were an explosive element. Even better than the

bathrobe. Brad reread the extract and wondered whether someone had expected Solya's library to be in Spanish. His name showed up at the conclusion of the account, in the general listing of the team members: *"—and Brad Hollister, a local talk-show host."* He resisted the temptation to insert "popular" into the report, but did replace "local" with "Grand Forks."

When he went live at five o'clock, he read it straight, or at least tried to. But it was impossible not to add a little false modesty.

The staff members all congratulated him. And there was something new in their voices. He was no longer just the guy who ran *Grand Forks Live* and wrote commercials. Most asked how it felt to travel to another planet. Two of the secretaries and their sports guy still claimed it had to be some sort of illusion.

At seven, after the hourly news, he went on with the talk show. No guest today. But there was nothing unusual about that. And from the moment he sat down at the mike, the line was backed up.

From Roger: "What did you think, Brad, when the gorilla opened that door?"

"I'll tell you the truth, Roger. My heart stopped. I expected a little green man, maybe. But a gorilla? No way. Although, in all honesty, I could see immediately it wasn't really a gorilla. There was a resemblance. But it stood there straight and it moved—I don't know how else to say this—it moved gracefully. And it was dressed."

And Marie: "Is there any way I can get a ticket to go to Eden? I'd love to visit the place."

"Marie, you'll have to ask the Spirit Lake Sioux. But I doubt they'll let anybody go for a while. Other than the science teams."

And an unfamiliar voice: "How did *you* get an invitation, Brad? You're not a scientist, are you?"

He thought about turning it into a joke, about how he had friends in the right places, but realized that would get him in trouble. So he played it straight: "They wanted a journalist."

Then another unfamiliar voice, belonging to a male: "How come you guys all hid in the woods and let a woman go up and knock on that door?"

He'd known somebody would bring that up. His reply was ready: "Because she was in charge, and she said that was the way we were going to do it."

Larry O'Brien was next: "Brad, what do you think about this apparition people have been seeing? The one that lights up? Any connection with the Roundhouse? Is it maybe something that came through from Eden?"

"I doubt it. But who really knows what's going on? There have been some strange stories about it." The conversation continued along that line for several minutes. People were seriously interested in the apparition. Some sounded worried.

Then Marie: "You deserve a lot of credit for going out there, Brad. To Eden. You're my hero."

"Marie, the hero of that operation was April Cannon. She took her life in her hands when she walked up to that door. We had no way of knowing what was behind it."

Mack: "You know, Brad, sometimes I think women are tougher than we are. I'll tell you, I wouldn't have gone up there without at least a gun in my hands."

That stung a bit. "I know, Mack. I know exactly what you mean."

Unknown caller: "Do you think they'll invite you to go out there again? And if they do, will you go?"

"I don't know, Caller. I don't know whether they'll ask me to go back to Eden. Would I go if they did? Yes. There's nothing I would rather do."

They hadn't officially announced the trip to the space station, so it was best he keep quiet about it. But he liked being in the spotlight. So yes, he would certainly want to go on the next mission. Wherever it went. He'd never known anything like this. And he wasn't sure he would be able to survive when it all went away.

He'd never enjoyed *Grand Forks Live* as much as he did that morning. When, at ten, he signed off and the theme music, Carl Orff's "O Fortuna," took over, he felt its power in a way he never had before.

• • •

AT THE END of the day, the chairman was getting ready to leave when George Freewater arrived. He looked uncomfortable. That was unusual for George. Walker had known him since George's high-school days, when the chairman had been one of his English teachers. George was a combat veteran. He'd been through a lot, but he'd never let it get to him. There'd been a line in one of his essays that had stayed with the chairman: "No matter what you do, things always end the same way." A dark comment to see in a high-school assignment.

Walker waved him into a chair. "So, George," he said, "what can I do for you?"

"Mr. Chairman, you're going to think I'm crazy."

Walker smiled. "Then you've nothing to lose, George."

"I'm serious." He opened his jacket, leaned back in the chair, and crossed his arms. "I was in the Roundhouse when one of the teams got back from the Maze a few weeks ago."

"And—?"

"I think something came back with them."

"What? George, we already went through this story once. I thought we'd put it behind us."

"I guess not, sir. My wife had lunch yesterday with a woman who saw an old guy fall down in Fort Moxie. But he didn't get hurt. Dottie said—that was the woman—that the light around him changed, and it was like something grabbed him and let him down slowly."

"And you think this is the same kind of thing you saw?"

"I don't know. But it's an explanation. What else could it be?"

"Tell me about it again. What you saw."

"Okay. A mission had just come back from the Maze. We also had people on Eden at the time. At one point, after the last people from the Maze had come in, the grid lit up, but nobody arrived. The lighting changed, though. It got brighter or something. Then I got dizzy. And one of the people who'd just arrived fainted. That's all that happened. Cass Deekin—the guy who passed out—came around. He said he was all right. I thought it was over. Maybe it wasn't."

"George," the chairman said, "who else was there with you?"

"You mean on the mission?"

"The security guys."

"Jack and Adam."

"Did they see this thing?"

"No, sir. They just saw me and Cass start to act funny."

"And you say it came across from Eden?"

"No, sir. We also had people on Eden at the time, and we were expecting them. But the wrong icon lit up. I thought somebody was coming in from the *Maze.*"

"But there was no one?"

"That's correct. Everybody who'd been on the Maze mission had come back. But it was the Maze icon that lit up."

"It's hard to make sense out of that, George."

"I know. It's why I've hesitated about this. But Diane's been saying all along that something probably came through. Anyhow, for what it's worth—"

• • •

APRIL WAS IN her office when the chairman called. "It's getting spooky," he said.

"What is, James? You talking about the alien stories?"

"Yes. George Freewater was back with that account of something coming through from the Maze. You were on the Maze mission. You sure nothing happened?"

"At the time, we thought we were being tracked by something we couldn't see. Some breezes started blowing. And—Well, I remember feeling spooked. But we never really saw anything." He could hear her breathing. "Now I'm not so sure."

"George says the Maze icon lit up, and the lights got funny. Two of the people who were in the Roundhouse at the time—George was one of them—got dizzy. Passed out. It sounds like the symptoms we've been hearing about."

"The wind creature?"

"Yes. I don't know what's going on, but I don't want us looking at liability claims if this turns out to be something we caused."

"If we really do have an alien drifting around, it doesn't seem to have been a threat to anyone. In fact, it's been helping."

"I'm not comfortable with this, April."

"I know. Tomorrow morning, on his radio show, Brad will have the Grand Forks chief of police as his guest. That's going to be the subject."

"The floater?"

"Yes."

"That's all we need. More publicity about this. I don't guess you can talk him into discussing something else? Don't they have a crime wave or something over there?"

"I don't think he has much control over the topics. I'd guess Matt Fanny's got the lead on that these days."

"Matt *who*?"

"Matt Fanny. He's Brad's boss."

"April, I've been planning a new Maze mission. Don't know whether I mentioned it to you. Now I'm not so sure it's a good idea."

"I wouldn't back off, James. If the place really has some sort of windblown life-form, it's worth looking into, isn't it?"

"You think it's safe?"

"At some point, we're going to *have* to do it. I say go ahead with the project."

"Some of the people who've seen the thing in Fort Moxie think they've been in touch with a spirit." Walker sounded tired. "I think I'd be happier if that were actually the case. Why the hell does Brad keep stirring things up?"

"James, he's a talk-show host. It's what he does."

"I wish we could get him to wait until we know what's really going on."

"That would take all the fun out of it."

"The requests from people demanding we destroy the Roundhouse are heating up. Some people are worried primarily about economic consequences. But the alien is getting some attention, too. April, life would get easier if that thing went away."

"I know."

"Any idea how we could send it back where it came from?"

• • •

TOWARD THE END of the afternoon, Brad called her. "Tell me," he said, "about that other place. The Maze."

It wasn't hard to guess where this conversation would be going. She stared at the phone before answering. "Why do you ask?"

"Just curious. I know you guys said there was nothing other than passageways. And chambers. Nothing else. All the rooms were empty, you said, right?"

"Yes. It's bare and empty."

"As far as you could tell."

"Brad, we didn't really stay that long. Why do you want to know?"

"There's a story going around that it might have been where the little whirlwind originated."

"I've heard something about that. But I have no idea."

"I'm hearing that they're going to take another mission out to the Maze. Is there any connection?"

"You're looking for a story."

"Is there one?"

"Not that I know of. You want to come and take a look?"

• • •

DONNA'S BROWN EYES wouldn't leave him. "So now it's the Maze? What happened to the space station?"

"I think we'll be going there later."

"Tell me again why you want to do this, Brad?" She'd come in the door with an armload of essays. He'd taken them from her and put them on top of the bookcase beside another stack. Then they'd sat down on the sofa and she'd asked him how his day had gone and he'd told her. It had gone downhill from there.

"Donna, there are people all over the country who would give anything to have the opportunity to do this stuff. They have whole crowds trying to persuade the Sioux to let them make visits."

"And why don't they let them do it? Why don't they sell some tickets?"

"I don't know. I think it's an abundance of caution either by Walker or the president."

She did not look happy. "Why exactly are *you* getting all these benefits?"

"They see me as their P.R. guy. Donna, the Maze is perfectly safe. April's been there. All that happened is that they walked through a lot of empty passageways, then came home. That's it. That's all there is."

"Then why are they sending another mission?"

"They want to figure out what the place is."

"So they really don't know much?"

"Not really."

"And that makes it safe?"

"They haven't seen any kind of problem."

"It doesn't sound as if they've looked very hard."

"Listen, love, I'd give anything to be able to make a contribution of some sort to one of these projects. Maybe I'd see something the rest of them missed."

"When are you going?"

"The end of the week."

"Wonderful." She closed her eyes. "Do what you want, Brad. It's your call."

• • •

LLOYD EVERETT ROUTINELY allowed himself to sleep late on Thursday mornings, the day on which his office opened at eleven. He was enjoying a leisurely breakfast with Mabel when the phone rang. They were watching the news, and the caller's number showed up on the screen. It was local, but unfamiliar. Probably a sales pitch.

"Let it ring," said Mabel, knowing he wouldn't. They only ignored unknown numbers with unfamiliar area codes.

He was still chewing a piece of toast when he picked up.

"Dr. Everett?" said the caller.

"Speaking."

"My name is Victor Sedgwick." The voice was unfamiliar. "I'm associated with the Sedgwick and Kane realty office. I don't know whether you'd be interested in selling your house, but I'm in a position to make a very generous offer. I wonder if it would be okay if I dropped by to discuss it with you?"

Lloyd looked over at Mabel, who was finishing her scrambled eggs. "Our property's not up for sale, Mr. Sedgwick. But thanks." He touched the disconnect but didn't press it.

"Doctor, please, hear me out. We have a company that is planning to do some reorganization in your area. They're offering sixty percent more than the current retail value of your property. I strongly recommend you at least consider it."

"Who is it?" Mabel asked.

"A real-estate salesman."

She shook her head. "What's he want with us?"

"Hold a second, please, Mr. Sedgwick." He watched a FedEx truck stop across the street and covered the mouthpiece. "Mabel, he says he has an offer for the house. Sixty percent over current value. Are we interested?"

She put her tongue in her cheek. "That's a serious amount of money, Lloyd. How much would it cost us to move?"

Lloyd didn't really care about the money. He liked the house and the neighbors, and he had no inclination to go somewhere else. He and Mabel had more than enough income to support their lifestyle. His wife had grown up down the street, and she loved this house. Since that wild night when they'd been extracted from their car, when he'd become someone else, *something else*, looking down from the sky on the vehicle that he was driving, the world had changed. Thank God she had been through the same event.

That they'd been able to talk about it, and reassure each other that it had actually happened. Had she responded the way Chuck and Amy had, talking to him from the back of the car with scared voices and asking him what the hell he was doing, he'd have drawn the only possible conclusion: that he'd suffered a mental meltdown. The house, with its familiarity, had become their anchor in the new reality. Whatever had happened that night, they felt safe near their fireplace. "You know what this is about?" he said. "There's a lot of talk that real-estate prices here are going to go through the roof."

Mabel took a sip of her coffee. "Because of the Roundhouse."

"Yes. And I'd be surprised if that doesn't happen."

"Okay. So that's one more reason to stay put."

Lloyd took his hand from the mouthpiece. "We're really not interested, Mr. Sedgwick."

"Dr. Everett, opportunities like this don't come every day."

"Thank you, but we'll pass." He'd just gotten back into his seat when it rang again. Mabel was getting up. "I've got it," she said.

"Tell him to go away," said Lloyd.

He took another bite of his toast and heard Mabel say, "You're kidding." A silence followed, then he heard the channels being changed. And Mabel was saying, "Lloyd, you want to see this."

He grumbled something, got back up, and returned to the living room. Mabel was pointing at the TV. They were interviewing Chuck.

Then the phone was ringing again.

• • •

WALKER WAS IN his office attending to final details for the Fort Totten ceremony when Andrea contacted him. "I think I have the person you want."

"Good," he said. "Who?"

"Dolliehi Proffitt. She's a Ph.D. at Princeton. She's considered one of the top linguistics experts in the world. Has written several books on the subject. One of them, *A Brief History of Symbology*, was a finalist for the Pulitzer a few years ago."

"Is she willing to go spend some time with Solya?"

"She says she'd love to. You want her number?"

"Please. Do you think we could persuade her to come in for the celebration?"

TWENTY-TWO

*I go into my library, and all history unrolls before
me. I breathe the morning air of the world while
the scent of Eden's roses yet lingered in it, while it
vibrated only to the world's first brood of
nightingales, and to the laugh of Eve. I see the
pyramids building; I hear the shoutings of the
armies of Alexander.*

—Alexander Smith, *Dreamthorp*, xi, 1863

THE SPIRIT LAKE Tribal Council wasn't scheduled for its
regular meeting until the end of the month, but Chairman
Walker wanted to get things moving. So he called a special
conference at their Fort Totten headquarters. The council
consisted of the chairman; Jane Martin, the treasurer; and
representatives from the tribe's four districts. "You've all
been invited to the celebration tomorrow," he said. "We're
looking forward to seeing you there.

"We've been aware from the beginning of the possibility
of finding another civilization out there. And it's happened.
In fact, we've found *two*. One appears to be in an early stage
of development. The other, Riverwalk, is highly advanced.
At least technologically. Unfortunately, we didn't get any
photos of Riverwalk. And we won't be going back anytime
soon. Nonetheless, we know it's there now, and *we*, the Spirit
Lake Sioux, made the discovery."

"James," said Dorothy Kalen, who represented the Woodlake district, "some people in my area are interested in

moving to Eden." She laughed. "Not that we don't love the weather in North Dakota, but life over there looks pretty inviting. When can we expect a green light?"

"It'll take some time, Dorothy. For one thing, we need to be certain it's safe. Tell your people that all options are open, but I don't want to rush into anything."

Bobby Reynolds, who hailed from Crow Hill, raised his hand. "Who could ever have believed this would happen?"

"I don't think we can talk about *two* civilizations," said Rack Colby, from Mission. "Eden has a cabin with a gorilla. That's all we know." Colby glanced at the chairman. "Or at least all we've been told."

Bobby rolled his eyes. "Let's not get into that again, Rack."

Jane usually maintained a discreet silence when they weren't discussing monetary matters. But not this time: "They have somebody out there producing books," she said. "That would seem sufficient to establish that there's something more than just a gorilla in a cabin."

Walker tried not to let his annoyance show. "I don't think Solya qualifies as a *gorilla*. Just for the record, I'd agree that the weather on Eden is pretty nice. But even if no one were there, it would not be a good place for us. I'm not sure how well we'd do without highways, TV, and an electric company. Let's not try to go back to the eighteenth century, okay?"

Dorothy had a weight problem. Somehow, when she was digging in, as she was now, it made her look a bit more intimidating. "I don't think that was anybody's intent, James. But let's try not to be so negative. We'd have a land of our own again. Imagine what we could do with it."

"We're probably out of practice," said Walker. "That stuff sounds good at a rally, but I think there are some difficulties once we get beyond the hand-waving."

"Okay," said Les Krider, the Fort Totten representative, "where do we go from here?"

Walker took it: "We've been thinking too much about the Roundhouse as a source of cash."

"Right," said Rack. "We don't have any use for a gold mine."

"All right," said Walker. "Let's keep it serious. What's the single biggest problem the Spirit Lake Sioux have? I'm talking about the people now, not the organization."

They looked at one another, and everybody had the answer: "Jobs."

"The same as the rest of the country," added Rack.

"Except that *our* unemployment is around fifty percent."

"But the Roundhouse," said Bobby, "can fix that. Permanently. Sell the damned thing."

Walker frowned. "I'm not so sure."

Dorothy looked as if she were ready to throw something. "Come on, James. How can we *stop* the Roundhouse from fixing it? We'll get more than enough cash to provide for everybody on the Rez."

"You really think," said Walker, "that handing out a ton of money will help us long range? What happens when the money runs out? And it would, eventually. We give everybody a large handout, and the only thing it buys for us is time. Look, why do we have a bigger unemployment problem than the country at large?"

"Maybe," said Les, "we need a better education system." Les would one day, because of his passion and eloquence, be a serious political asset. But he was still too young, and would have to grow into it. But, as usual, he had a point.

"Okay." Walker sat back in his chair. "Isn't the real problem here that we live in a part of the country that has a very low population density? The towns are small. And they're thirty and forty miles apart. And between them it's virtually empty space. If we were living in, say, central Pennsylvania, or outside Seattle, how much easier would it be to find work? Or better yet, to establish the Lester Krider & Associates Real Estate Agency? Or to open Rack Colby's Hardware Emporium? Or the Kalen Café? You try starting a new restaurant here, what are your chances? We need a system that provides a way for people to support themselves. Not just handouts. We need something that gives purpose to our lives."

"I don't have a better idea," said Jane, "than taking the best price we can get for the Roundhouse."

"All right." Walker allowed himself a complacent smile. "What do you think this area will look like in ten years?"

Rack was nodding as if he could see exactly what it would look like. "I know where you're headed with this, James. But it probably won't be much different from what it is now. It never changes. And that crazy door isn't going to have that big a long-term effect. I mean, it might become a theme park. But there'll probably never be more than one narrow entrance. And now that we know someone's there—" He turned and grinned at the others. "Even if we're talking about gorillas with books—all that's going to happen is more of what's *been* happening. Government control. Sure, they'll talk about coop-eration with us, like they do now, but we all know they're leaning on you constantly, James. They are not going to allow us to open it to the general public. Not now. Especially not after that city. And the whatever. The gorilla."

"That's correct," said Walker. "And I have no problem with that."

"You don't?" Bobby looked surprised. "You were the guy who kept talking about asserting our rights."

"I was thinking small. I was thinking about establishing our own country on the other side. But that was crazy. There's no way we can make it work. We're in the Communications Age. There's a global economy out there."

Dorothy cleared her throat. "What exactly are you saying, James?"

"Johnson's Ridge has become the most visible, and remarkable, place on the planet. In ten years, this area will be overrun."

"By tourists?"

"Sure. And by industry."

"You know," said Rack, "they're still going to have to squeeze through that damned grid."

"It doesn't matter," said Walker. "They don't have to go *anywhere*. *All* that matters is that they show up here and look at the Roundhouse. They'll be everyplace. As will developers. Ladies and gentlemen, the world is coming to Fort Totten. We'll need a new airport. More restaurants. Hotels. Real-estate values will go through the roof. We need to advise our people about what's coming. Anybody who can pick up property should do it this afternoon. No casino will be big enough to hold the crowds. Jane, maybe you should establish a sight-seeing tour that finishes up at the Roundhouse. If we play this right, the tribe is headed for glorious times. But the smart thing to do is for us to keep control to the extent we're able. Sell it to the corporates, and they'll take care of themselves, and we'll only survive until the cash runs out."

"So what's first, James?" asked Les.

"We're going to try to acquire the language of the Eden inhabitants. It would help if we could get a name for these creatures. Something a little sexier than 'gorilla.' But don't worry about it. We'll come up with something.

"Also, we have a few other working links at the Maze and the space station. We have no idea where they'd take us. I'll admit to being a bit uncertain about sending teams to unknown places. That's something we need to think about."

"Mr. Chairman," said Jane. "What are you hearing from the president?"

"He's offered whatever assistance we need. He has also, as you would expect, made it clear that, if we wish, he will take over the operation and assume all risks."

That drew some laughter.

"I think you're right," said Bobby. "We should maintain control. Why'd you let the marshals in?"

Walker sighed. "I thought that was clear to everybody."

• • •

AFTER THE MEETING, the chairman returned to his office and was just sitting down to take a look at the reservation's latest employment statistics when Miranda informed him of a visitor. Her name was Cynthia Harmon, and her business card identified her as executive vice president of the Black-well National Bank in Minnesota.

She was middle-aged, with amber hair and features that implied she was accustomed to being in charge. "Mr. Chairman?" she said. "I need a favor."

He invited her to sit down and had his secretary bring in some tea. "How may I assist you, Ms. Harmon?"

"This may be hard to explain, sir. I grew up in Minneapolis. When I was a child, I was a huge *Star Trek* fan. I remember asking my father one night if we'd ever go to the Moon." She smiled. "He told me we'd already gone. That it was just a big rock.

"So I asked whether we'd ever go to Mars. He said no. It's too far, and it doesn't matter because there's nothing there either. He showed me some pictures of the place. And he was right. It doesn't look anything like what showed up in the stories. Have you ever read Ray Bradbury, Mr. Chairman?"

"Yes," he said.

"It's a heartbreaker when you learn the truth. But most people never really look past the rooftops." She paused, and her eyes grew intense. "You have a door that opens onto other worlds. All I've really wanted during my life, other than my family, of course, my kids, was to find out whether there was life somewhere else. It's something I've always cared about. Don't ask me why."

"And now you know," said Walker.

"And now I know. My dream has been realized. But there's something else. I mean, I have the opportunity to actually *walk* on another world. On a place that's—what?—a thousand light-years from here. What I'm asking is that you let me pass through the star gate. Just make the transit. Or whatever you call it. Let me go through for a few minutes and see one of these places."

"Ms. Harmon, I wish I could help you, but we simply don't allow anyone to pass through the link unless they're part of one of our scientific teams."

"I'm willing to pay, Mr. Walker. Please."

"I'm sorry—"

She took out a checkbook. "How much would it take to persuade you?"

"I would if I could. It's complicated, but we just can't do it. For one thing, it would set a precedent."

"I wouldn't tell anyone. You have my word."

Of course not. This rabid enthusiast would make it out to the Belt of Orion, but she'd never mention it to anybody. "I'm sorry, Ms. Harmon."

"Two hundred thousand, Chief."

"I'm not a chief, Ms. Harmon."

She inhaled. "I'm sorry, Mr. Chairman." She took another breath. "One million."

Walker thought about what could be done with a million. Business incentives. A few more teachers and a load of supplies at the schools. "I wish I could help, Ms. Harmon. But I think, if you're willing to show some patience, the opportunity may arrive in the near future. We are still feeling our way."

"I don't have a near future, Mr. Chairman. I have breast cancer."

Walker froze. "I'm sorry," he said finally.

"They're giving me three months."

A terminally ill woman passes through into Eden? There was no way that could be kept from the media. And it would be followed by an endless horde of special cases. It would be the first step. And, eventually, April's friends in the cabin would find their land taken over.

Still, there was no way he could refuse her. "Okay," he said.

She broke out into a relieved smile, thanked him, and began writing the check. It was one of those moments in which he realized how much he loved his job while simultaneously wishing he could retire.

• • •

THE GRAND FORKS chief of police was Juan Cavalos. He'd been an occasional guest before on the show, where they usually talked about ongoing traffic issues or current efforts to curb juvenile delinquency. But now nobody had any interest in traffic problems around Grand Forks, or measures the police were currently taking to reduce the recent rise in the number of burglaries across the city. All they cared about was the wind creature.

"Brad," he said, answering the host's usual leadoff question, "we're doing fine. Crime in the city continues to be low, and the biggest single automobile problem we have is tailgating. If we could break that habit, we'd get rid of probably fifty percent of the accidents. But that, I suspect, is not what either of us wants to talk about today."

"You're referring to the illusions?"

"Yes. We've been handing out more tickets than usual lately. And we're beginning to see a pattern."

"What's the pattern, Chief?"

"Drivers who are behaving as if they've been drinking too much or are on drugs."

"And—?"

"They test negative. We had a collision last night at the intersection of Columbia Road and University Avenue. Fortunately, nobody was hurt. But a pickup ran the red light and hit a car. The driver of the pickup claimed that he'd lost his vision. Well, that's not quite correct. He said that he got pulled out of the truck. That he was suddenly above it. Above the intersection. And that he watched the collision from overhead."

"And he tested negative?"

"That's correct. But that's not the strangest part of it. The other driver told us the same story."

"He was above the street, too?"

"Yes. But the accident seemed to put them both back inside their vehicles."

"That's incredible, Chief. It's hard to believe they weren't both on something."

"And even that is not the end of it."

"Go ahead," said Brad, who knew what was coming. As did probably most of his listeners. "Tell us the rest."

"We've had a series of similar incidents over the past week or so. The sky illusion isn't always there, but it usually is."

"I've seen some of the accounts," said Brad.

"Yeah. I've never seen anything like it. And it keeps getting weirder. I've been in touch with area law enforcement, of course. The same kind of thing's happening in Devils Lake, Cavalier, Fort Moxie, Fargo. There've been other kinds of incidents as well. People having illusions that sometimes turn out to be real."

"For example?"

"One guy, at home, imagined he saw a neighbor lying out in back of his house. In serious trouble. The illusion was so strong he went out to look."

"And the guy was there—"

"Yes."

"I know. I saw the story. So what do you think's going on, Chief?"

"I have no idea, Brad. The only theory I can offer: People started seeing these stories in the papers, and it kind of takes hold. You do something dumb and get ticketed for it, and you're looking for an explanation, so you make something up. Then other people start to join the parade."

"So you think all these people are lying?"

"I'm not saying that. But I think you'd have a better chance with a psychoanalyst here to explain this."

"Okay, Chief," said Brad. "Let's go to the callers."

Mark Collins was first up: "What we're hearing, Chief, is that there's an alien running around causing all this. Presumably he can't be in two places at once. I wonder if we've checked to see whether any two of these incidents have occurred at the same time?"

"Actually," said Cavalos, "we have, and we can't match any of them. No two have occurred within an hour of each other. But that's not a surprise in any case because there haven't been that many incidents."

They were about ten minutes into the calls when they got

the first claim of a personal experience. "It happened to me," a woman said. "I was coming out of the supermarket with my son. And suddenly I was in a gray, drab corridor. My impression was that it was like an abandoned hotel. No windows anywhere, though. I fell down, I heard my son screaming, but I couldn't see him. He's eight years old. Then the daylight was back. The groceries were all over the pavement. And my son had lost his as well. He said he saw the same thing I did."

"Did you actually fall?"

"Yes."

"Were you injured, Caller?"

"No. A bruise on one leg. That was all."

Before the show had ended, there were seven similar calls. People who suddenly found themselves floating through the night sky, two who repeated the abandoned-hotel account, two who found themselves in open country. The landscape they described sometimes sounded dreary, a swollen sun, wide gray plains, no sign of habitation; at other times, there was an ocean, and a ringed world dominating a sky full of stars. One caller described a conversation with a dead husband.

Brad's show routinely drew its share of deranged calls. But he prided himself on knowing them when he heard them. These sounded legitimate despite the content. "Whatever else might be the case," he told Chief Cavalos when they were off the air, "they're not making it up."

Cavalos agreed.

That afternoon, when Brad was preparing to leave the station, the chief called. "You remember the question about simultaneous incidents?" he asked. "I checked it out. There have been three, but they happened in the same area."

"So you're suggesting that, whatever's going on, whatever's causing it, there's only one."

"Brad, I'm not sure I have any idea what I'm suggesting."

TWENTY-THREE

*This solemn moment of triumph, one of the
greatest moments in the history of the world . . .
this great hour which rings in a new era . . . and
which is going to lift up humanity to a higher plane
of existence for all the ages of the future.*

—David Lloyd George, speech in London,
November 11, 1918

APRIL RODE OUT with Donna and Brad to the Fort Totten celebration. The party was well under way when they arrived. A reservation band was playing "Between Me and the Mountain" while people danced and sang. The chairman came over to welcome them.

Everybody knew April. They crowded around her, and she was obviously enjoying herself. Brad got a lot of attention, too.

The music was a mixture of blues and pop. It worked fine, setting exactly the upbeat tempo for the evening. Tables were loaded with chocolate croquettes and zucchini parmesan crisps and roasted tomato salsa and strawberry brownies and lemon meringue tartlets and a host of other treats. "I'm going to be two pounds heavier going home," said Brad.

Donna laughed. "Now there's some technology I could buy into."

"What's that?"

"Eat as much chocolate cake as you like, step onto the grid, and it just ships the extra weight to Eden."

He and Donna were introduced to the mayor of Devils Lake and the governor of North Dakota. Several former *Grand Forks Live* guests were present, including Michael Fossel. Some of the celebrities who'd flown in and blocked the looming shootout between the Feds and the Sioux at the Roundhouse also circulated through the crowd. Among them were Charles Curran, Gregory Benford, Ursula LeGuin, and Stephen Hawking. He'd have loved to invite some of them onto the show. He thought of himself as a guy who wasn't easily intimidated, but that night was a bit too much.

"You okay?" Donna asked him after they'd spoken a few minutes with LeGuin. She'd told him how fortunate he was to have been able to do the crossover to Eden and to have been there when they found Solya. "I envy you," she added.

• • •

WALKER CAME OVER to their table and introduced Dolly Proffitt. "You're taking on a major assignment," April said. "I can't imagine how you'd even start."

"*You're* the one who got us started," said Dolly, as she and Walker sat down. "What is she like?"

"Actually, she's very nice."

"For a gorilla," added Brad, who couldn't resist himself.

"When you see her," said April, "say hello for me."

"Do we know how to do that?"

"The word is *shalay*. Give the second syllable from deep in your throat." April demonstrated as best she could.

Dolly tried it a couple of times. And laughed.

"No, that's not bad," said April. "When you hear *her* do it, it'll be easier for you." She braced her jaw on her fist and smiled. "You know, learning to talk with Solya is probably the most important thing we'll do. I'd love to do it myself, but I've never been that good with languages, and I'd just make a mess of it."

"I'm looking forward to meeting her," Dolly said.

Walker studied her for a moment. "One thing to keep in mind: When you *do* get the communications down, be careful not to let Solya know what the Cupola really is. What its capabilities are. We've been fortunate that they apparently haven't tried to break into the thing. Or tear it down."

"Do you think they could do that, James?"

Walker passed the question to April. "Don't know," she said. "We left a door open on one occasion and they took advantage of it to go inside. Other than that, we're not aware of any effort to get in."

"Does Solya eat our kind of food?" Dolly asked.

"I don't know that either. I had a couple of meals with her. Everything tasted okay. So sure, try taking her something." April smiled. "Maybe some chocolate."

"That's all we'd need," Brad said. "Give her something that makes her sick."

Walker stood quietly for a moment. Then, without making it clear to whom he was speaking: "Something you can do for me."

April and Dolly traded glances. Both said, "Okay."

"Get us a name for them. For the aliens. Please. No more gorillas."

• • •

ONE OF THE guests took Dolly out onto the dance floor, where they were joined by Brad and Donna. Walker was standing off to one side with April, looking as if he was trying to make up his mind about something. "I hope she can make some progress," he said. "Though it's going to take a while. I can't imagine how she's going to learn both the spoken and written language in any reasonably short time."

"Dolly's pretty good, Mr. Chairman. She'll do fine."

"I hope so." He looked at his watch. "Getting late." And finally he came out with it: "I thought I'd go along, too."

"To the Cupola?"

"To the *cabin*. I'd like very much to meet Solya."

"That's not a good idea, James. It's just too far. The ground is uneven."

"The gravity's less over there, April. I don't think there'd be a problem."

"It's not that much less. And the cabin is four hours away.

I doubt the EMTs would be happy walking all that distance to bring you home."

"Yeah." He nodded. "I didn't think you'd care for the idea. But I'd like to be part of this."

April leaned forward and squeezed his arm. "You *are* part of it, James. As much as any of us."

• • •

BRAD ENJOYED SOCIALIZING. During the course of the evening, he spent time with the Tribal Council members, introduced Donna to the other members of the team that had been on the Solya mission, with the exception of Jeff McDermott, who hadn't come. He spent time with Boots Coleman and Melissa Sleeman, inviting both onto the show. Melissa asked if he knew that Boots was from the Rez?

Brad had not heard that before. Boots had a military demeanor, but he mixed it with an amiable personality and a sense of humor. Both would make good guests.

• • •

MAX COLLINGWOOD WAS an ordinary-looking guy. Average size, nothing remarkable about his features. Had he not known Max's history, Brad would never have guessed the heroic part he'd played in bringing the handful of celebrities into the middle of the Roundhouse standoff. "You were a central part of the operation during the first few months," Brad said. "You've sort of gone missing. What happened?"

"This is just not my area of interest. I restore warbirds." Brad understood he was referring to military aircraft. "I told April she could call on me if she needed me. But the reality is I don't have any expertise that would be of help to her."

"I suspect she'd like to have you back."

"Well, maybe. Brad, the reality is that I watched Arky die saving us at the space station. He was first across. And it was a vacuum. Well, you know all that. Anyhow, I've never really been the same since."

"I understand, Max. If you get a chance, I'd enjoy having you come in and participate as a guest on the show again."

"Sure," he said. "I don't know that I'd have anything new

to say. But let me know when." There was something in his tone that suggested Brad should just let it go.

• • •

EVENTUALLY, WALKER STEPPED up to the lectern to welcome everyone. He invited all those who had gone off-world to stand. About twenty got to their feet. The chairman read their names while the audience applauded. Then those who'd flown in with Max Collingwood and faced down the guns were recognized, and the response took the roof off. "And I have to mention Walter Asquith, who gave everything he had." Which produced another standing ovation. "I should also mention," he said, "that eighteen members of the Sioux security team have accompanied the missions.

"We don't know where the world will be going from here. We can only be sure that history will never forget what has happened on Johnson's Ridge. On the territory of the Spirit Lake Tribe." He paused and looked out across his audience. "And now, we have one more guest I'd like to introduce." A door opened on his right. "Ladies and gentlemen, please welcome the president of the United States, Matthew Taylor."

The president came through the door as the audience rose to its feet and applauded. The band broke out with "Hail to the Chief." Taylor shook hands with the chairman, waved to his audience, and waited for them to sit back down. "Thank you," he said. "Makes me wonder why I don't come to Spirit Lake more often."

He expressed his appreciation to the tribal members, to the people who had traveled off-world from the Roundhouse, and to those who'd stepped in to stop the armed faceoff. "That was my fault." He paused and took a deep breath. "Someone else I would especially like to recognize: Max Collingwood, the pilot who delivered these folks to Johnson's Ridge in the nick of time." More applause. "Max, you here?"

Collingwood was seated on the far side of the room. He rose and waved.

"This should be an interesting week. We'll be doing three missions over the next few days. We'll be going back to Eden, to start an effort to learn the inhabitants' language. Dolliehi Proffitt will be spearheading that effort. Professor Proffitt, are you out there somewhere?" She stood to a round of cheers. "We'll be taking another look at the Maze, and then we'll be heading for the space station. We have no idea where it is, but hopefully we'll have figured it out by the time our team returns. And who would have believed we'd be saying such things. Sending people to a space station or to an underground place, and we have no clue where either is located. Whenever I think about the money we poured into all those rockets down on the Cape, I wonder why we didn't just build a star gate?"

Brad wasn't sure whether he'd expected to get laughs. In any event, the room stayed quiet.

TWENTY-FOUR

Or like stout Cortez when with eagle eyes
He stared at the Pacific—and all his men
Look'd at each other with a wild surmise—
Silent upon a peak in Darien.

—John Keats, "On First Looking into Chapman's
Homer," 1816

THEY WERE BOUND for the Maze. John Colmar picked up
his rifle, walked over to the grid, activated the g-clef icon,
smiled at April, and disappeared into the light. Moments
later, the emblematic pen came back. Paula picked it up, put
it into a pocket, and signaled she was ready. April and one
of the scientists went next, then the other two team members.
All were women.

It was Brad's turn. He got into position, was joined by
Paula, and moments later he was looking at a large gray
chamber.

It was devoid of furniture or anything else. The walls were
covered with a light green fabric, decorated with represen-
tations of flowers and vines. A dull light with no visible
source provided the only illumination.

The others were already leaving the room. John looked
at him and shook his head, indicating there probably wouldn't
be much to see. The place was deathly quiet. He stepped
down onto a red carpet whose color had faded somewhat and
was surprised when it sank softly beneath him.

"What the hell kind of floor is this?" he said.

"The whole room's like that," said John.

It provided sufficient support, but walking on it was annoying.

The room was L-shaped. There were exits on opposite sides, both opening into shadowy passageways. On the wall behind the grid, Brad saw the by-now-familiar set of triggers, located in an angled panel. There were nine this time. One of them was the stag's head. The way back.

The ceiling was high. Sections of it were lost in shadow, behind a network of beams. A rectangular hole opened almost directly above him, but when he aimed his light through it, he couldn't make out anything other than another ceiling.

The others had dispersed into the two passageways, which were illuminated by the same dull light. John took a quick look at each. "Everybody stay together, please. April, don't get too far in front of me."

The air was cool. A few degrees below Brad's comfort level. "I feel as if I've lost some weight," he said to Paula.

"You're right," she said. "I feel lighter, too."

April picked an exit, and they all followed her out into a corridor. Its walls were constructed of burnished gray rock. Brad watched while April decided which direction to go. The passageway was long and straight to the right. In the opposite direction, it continued past a few more open chambers, then curved out of sight. One of the scientists commented that it felt like the bottom of a skyscraper. Paula commented that it looked like the inside of a pyramid. Brad wondered if she'd ever been in one, but he let it go. The place *did* feel like an ancient building despite the soft floors.

"Let's go this way," said April, turning left. She was starting a map in her notebook.

They passed several rooms, all empty, all of different designs and dimensions. There seemed to be no pattern to them. Finally, they found a chamber with another set of icons in the wall. But no grid.

There were three of them, a cube set at an angle, a vertical bar with four horizontal lines, and a leaf. But no stag's head.

"I don't think I've seen any that looked much like these before," Brad said. The style was different also, no curves anywhere. Everything was designed from straight lines and right angles. Even the leaf.

"I didn't notice this one when we were here before," said April. "Not paying attention, I guess."

Brad moved closer until April reached out and restrained him. "Why don't we try one of them?" he said. "See what happens?"

"I wonder how I knew you were going to say that?"

"Well, there's no grid. How much trouble could we get into?"

"Right. What could possibly go wrong?"

Brad was feeling good about himself, as if he were benefiting from an unusual flow of adrenaline. "Which one do we try?"

John moved up next to him and raised empty palms. He wasn't having anything to do with it. "I don't think it's a good idea," he said.

April surprised him. She pulled Brad out of the way. "One way to settle it." She pushed one of the icons. Her arm got in the way so Brad couldn't see which it was. He was hoping it wouldn't light up.

But it did.

John glowered at *him*, not at April.

"That might not have been a good idea," said Paula.

Eleanor Johnson was probably the best known of the three scientists. She was an astrophysicist from the University of Pennsylvania who was known primarily for her work in string theory. She was a small woman, barely five feet tall, probably in her sixties. But her inordinate success over a thirty-year span had given her a take-no-nonsense approach. "I can't think of a better way," she said, "to find out—" The lights dimmed. "To find out what the hell this place is about."

Something moved. It was out in the passageway. Wheels turning. Around the bend.

John ignored his rifle in favor of his .38. "Everybody

back in the room. April, I told you this wasn't a good idea."
Paula had drawn her pistol also.

The noise was getting louder. "Keep cool," said Brad. He
loved talking to the security people like that. Not that he
didn't feel jittery himself. But this was another chance to
play the action hero. He pulled his own weapon from his belt.
He had done some training since the last mission and now
almost felt comfortable with it.

The noise didn't sound threatening. It was, he thought,
only a vehicle. And not a heavy one.

They were still watching, holding their collective breath,
as it came around the bend. It was *empty*.

Brad's first thought was that it looked like a golf cart.
Four wheels, open top, front and rear seats. Room for four.
It slowed as it approached. The passageway was almost
twice as wide as the vehicle. It stopped outside the chamber.
Bars along the side swung up, inviting them to climb in.

"What do you think?" asked Brad.

The question was directed at April, but John responded:
"Absolutely not. Everybody stay back. Keep away from it."

"Ridiculous," said April. "Eventually, somebody will
have to get in and see where it goes." She started to climb
on board, but John grabbed her arm. He hesitated when she
resisted but finally pulled her back. Then *he* started to get
in. "I'll let you know what happens."

April looked over her shoulder at Paula. "Wait here for us.
If you don't hear from us in twenty minutes, go back home.
Okay?"

"Yes, ma'am," she said.

John was in the front. April eased herself into one of the
rear seats. "What do you have to do to start it?" she asked.

There was no visible set of controls. "Damned if I know,"
said John.

Brad saw himself watching again as April knocked on
the cabin door. He pulled himself together and joined her
in the rear.

"No, Brad," said April. "Stay clear."

Eleanor took advantage of the confusion to signal John to move over. He shrugged and complied, and she took his seat. One of the other women wanted to get on board, too, but there was no room. The bars came down and became handrails. And the vehicle began to move. "Damn it." John's frustration had risen to fury. "You guys are going to get me fired."

"Shut up, John," said April, as they started to accelerate. "They wouldn't install something like this to harm anyone."

"I hope you're right."

Belts clicked into place, locking them into their seats, and somebody behind them was yelling "Good luck!"

• • •

THERE WAS NO indication of tracks, but the cart remained in the center of the passageway. "Everybody okay?" John asked. Other than being a bit nervous, they were fine. The area ahead of them brightened somewhat, then dimmed again as they continued to roll. The overhead was low. Brad could almost have reached up and touched it. They were still seeing occasional chambers on both sides. And suddenly the slick gray walls and overhead had been replaced by rock. They were in a tunnel. The vehicle continued to accelerate. "You see any brakes anywhere?" John asked, in an I-told-you-so tone.

"Negative," said Eleanor.

The air was getting cooler. "Great," said Brad. "No brakes and no steering wheel. How could this possibly become a problem?"

"Relax," said April. "We're committed."

Despite the harness that secured him, Brad by then was hanging tightly on to his seat. As were they all. "We'll be okay," he said though he was close to screaming.

The doorways had become a series of blurs. The effect was enhanced by the light that raced along with them. But, finally, the acceleration eased off.

"Uh-oh," said John.

They all saw it at the same time. Ahead, the corridor curved sharply left. *Not gonna make it around the turn.* But the cart braked. Threw them all hard right against their seat belts. Something under the vehicle squealed.

Then the passageway turned right, and everybody was hurled in the opposite direction.

"My God," said Eleanor. And, incredibly, she started giggling.

John was damning everything in sight.

They had a couple more sharp turns and then straightened out. "April," Brad said. "I just figured out what this is."

"Really? So what the hell *is* it?"

"A roller coaster."

The cart accelerated, then slowed down and ripped around another curve. They screamed and howled. Then it was tearing along a straightaway. "How the hell is it making those turns?" gasped John.

He got no response.

The light that had been tracking them went out, and they were plunged into total darkness. But the cart began to slow. "April," said John, "first chance we get, we've got to get out of this thing,"

"And go where?"

"Anything's better than this."

Ahead they saw a sprinkling of stars. "Tunnel's ending," John said.

"Thank God."

A three-quarter moon appeared off to one side. Brad held his breath as they raced out under a dark sky and rolled along a narrow shelf on the face of a cliff. A bright light was coming from somewhere behind them. On Brad's left, a rock wall rose seventy or eighty feet over their heads. On the other side, April's side, they were looking down at an ocean.

He was scared silly. The ledge seemed narrower than the cart. But the pace had at least slowed to a reasonable level. Although *any* movement on that roadway seemed like too much. He closed his eyes as they went around another curve. "We are *never* going to get back to the grid," he said.

"My God!" John's voice. It had gone up a couple of octaves.

"Ohhhh." Eleanor gasped. "Look at that!" She had twisted around so she could look behind them, over her shoulder, and she sounded as if she were ready to jump out of the cart.

Brad turned in his seat, too, and saw another moon. But *this* moon was enormous, dominating the sky. It had *rings* that reached down and vanished beyond the horizon. Its surface was gauzy, hidden inside clouds.

John Colmar gasped. "*That's* the thing I saw that night with Diana," he said. "Outside the Roundhouse."

April was still hanging on. "What are you talking about, John?" Her voice was up a couple of octaves.

"We saw a light in the trees that night, the day before she got killed. Diana and me. We were both on duty at the Roundhouse. Out in the parking lot, and *this* is what the sky looked like."

"Not possible," said April.

"I don't give a goddam. It's what happened. Ask the chairman. I described it to him. He can tell you."

"You told him this story?" said April.

"Yes. He didn't mention it to you?"

"No."

"He probably thought I was being delusional. I pretty much thought so, too, until just now. But, damn it, that's the same sky."

"And Diana saw it, too?"

"Yes." He took a deep breath. "Oh, God. Is that really *Saturn*?"

"It's not Saturn," said Eleanor. "But it's the same kind of world."

Brad began to struggle with his harness.

"What are you doing?" said John.

"Trying to get my camera."

"Forget it. Sit still."

"John, that's the most spectacular thing I've ever seen."

• • •

HE WAS STILL trying to get his camera out when that glorious sky vanished, and they were back inside a tunnel. The cart accelerated again, but Brad had concluded that the objective was not to kill the passengers, but to provide a thrill ride. At least that was what he was telling himself. They descended to a lower level, turned back in the direction from which they'd come, and emerged again along the ocean. This time Brad was on the outside, and his grip on the handrails tightened.

The alien Saturn was back. In front of them this time and consequently easier to see. They cruised along the face of the cliff, and Brad, overwhelmed, would have stopped the vehicle had he been able. A cool breeze was blowing in off the sea, and he wanted to just sit for a few minutes and enjoy the view. He finally got his camera out and started taking pictures.

"I'm not sure they'll ever let me come back here," Eleanor said. "But I'm glad I was here."

"I wish Donna could see this."

"Your wife?" she asked.

He nodded. "She'd love it."

They were approaching another tunnel entrance.

"Who wouldn't?"

• • •

THE VEHICLE STOPPED outside a chamber much like the one in which they'd arrived. The L-shape configuration was now simply a cube. But it had a grid and icons, one of which was the stag's head. Their ticket home.

John used his radio to contact Paula. "We're okay," he said. "We should be able to go back from here. See you at the Roundhouse."

April signaled for the radio. "Paula," she said, "if you guys get a chance to take the ride, do it. It's a little unnerving at first, but you wouldn't want to miss it."

TWENTY-FIVE

The spirit of the age is the very thing that a great man changes.

—Benjamin Disraeli, *The Infernal Marriage*, 1834

DONNA WENT INTO a state of near shock as Brad described the experience and showed her the pictures. "It *is* beautiful," she said. "But I'm glad you're back alive."

"I know. And I'm sorry it's such a problem for you. But it's just a ride. There's no danger there anywhere."

Suddenly, she was smiling at him. "That's not why I'm upset. Do you think you could arrange for *me* to go? I'd love to see that thing in the sky."

"You've always said you don't like roller-coaster rides."

"I could maybe allow an exception for this one."

"You're serious now?"

"Yes!"

"Okay. I'll see what I can do, Donna. But I don't think they'll be open to the idea. They're already buried with requests from people who want to go out to these places." He didn't want to finish: "To be honest, there's no way to be sure how safe it is."

"But you just said—"

"I know. Because that's how it seems. But—" He didn't want her going. "I'll try to arrange it."

He gave her a day to think about it. She was even more adamant when he raised the subject again, so he called April. "Funny you should ask," she said. "The chairman wants to go on the ride, too. And every physicist on the planet. I'm sure he'd be okay with Donna if there were a way to keep it quiet. But—"

"I understand."

"I'm just wondering what all this is about, Brad. Boat rides on Lake Agassiz. A galactic space station. Eden. Now we have a roller coaster through the Maze. We're missing something here."

• • •

GEORGE AND ADAM took a couple of bicycles to Eden in an effort to eliminate the long walk to Solya's cabin. But they proved useless. There was no forest trail available, and the sand always seemed damp. In addition it possessed a general softness that reduced pedaling to a constant battle. It was easier to stay on foot.

April reported the results to Dolly, who laughed it off. "I enjoy walking," she said.

"That's good. You'll need it." The purpose for the meeting, which took place in April's office, was to discuss what they knew of Solya's speech patterns and vocabulary. There wasn't much. "I left the radio on while I was there," April said. "I should have recorded everything, too. I just wasn't thinking."

"That's okay," said Dolly.

"How do you plan to do this?"

"I want to just have a chance to sit and talk with her for a couple of hours. You think she'll be amenable to that?"

"Yes."

"All right. Good. I'll record everything. Then I'll come back and see what I can make of it. After that, I should get at least a little capability. Once that happens, we can try to extend things. I'd like eventually to spend a few evenings with her. Sit around the fireplace and just talk without putting a lot of strain on her."

"That sounds as if it might work."

"You're coming with us, right?"

"Yes."

"Excellent. I'll need you at the beginning to introduce me and break the ice."

"It'll be a pleasure. She seems to be friendly, but I think we still need to be careful."

"I know."

"What I'm saying is that there may be a risk. We just don't know. When you go back the second time, I understand you're planning to stay overnight. So you'll have a sleeping bag with you. Solya may offer to have you stay in the cabin, but don't do it. It's a chance we just don't want to take."

"Adam's already warned me." She smiled. "As if I needed it."

"You have a story for her in case you get the invitation?"

"Sure. I have to report every night to my boss."

"Good enough. Now, what can I do to help?"

• • •

GRAND FORKS LIVE had been lit up for weeks. A fresh eruption began Monday when the Rev. Arnold Restov, a Fargo preacher appearing on *Dakota Brief*, stated that "we need not fear the implications of the Johnson's Ridge story. It in no way calls into doubt the Genesis account of creation. For one thing, this whole business could be a hoax. It certainly sounds like one. Or it may be that the so-called portal to the stars is actually a gateway to hell."

The story went viral. Brad and Donna were Presbyterians, and he wasted no time inviting their pastor, the Rev. Martin Axler, to the studio. He came in, and the lines were overloaded before they got past the opening notes of "O Fortuna."

Martin had been at the church as far back as Brad could remember. He was generous, amiable, easygoing. A little guy with a magnificent baritone. But he was clearly in his declining years. "I don't pretend to be a theologian," he said after Brad had introduced him. "I can't speak for the church, but I'll tell you what I think."

"That's all we can ask," said Brad, opening the line to the first caller.

It was Larry O'Brien: "If there really are aliens, Reverend, does that mean the Bible got things wrong? How do they fit, for example, in the Jesus story? Did he die for them, too?"

"I think, Caller," said Martin, "as we learn more about the universe, what we're discovering is that the biblical God is much greater than we'd imagined. I can't begin to connect the Crucifixion to beings living on other planets. The important thing is that Jesus delivered a timeless message here. Imagine what the world would be like if we actually lived as He suggested. Beyond that, I'm inclined to leave the details to God."

Janet was next: "So is the Genesis account wrong? Are we more than six thousand years old?"

"The scientific evidence indicates we've been here a long time. Keep in mind that the Bible is a collection of attempts by a people living long ago to make sense of their notion of a loving God and a life that included a lot of pain."

"Then it wasn't written by God?"

"It's obvious there isn't a single author. I prefer to think of it as inspired by Him. If we are certain of anything about His character, it is that He has tried to show us the way, how we might live together in peace, but He allows us to make our own choices."

When it was over, Matt was ecstatic. Brad couldn't help noticing that his own upcoming departure for the mysterious space station barely got mentioned.

• • •

WALKER'S FIRST EXTENDED off-world trip came a day after the Reverend Axler's radio appearance. George Freewater took him and three members of the Tribal Council on what had now gone viral as the roller-coaster ride. When it was over, and he was still trying to catch his breath, the chairman knew that his perceptions had changed again. He'd acquired an appreciation for the power and beauty of the universe that could never be acquired through a mere telephoto lens or a slice of poetry. He was in his office the following morning, still unable to get the spectacle out of his mind. A couple of reporters were waiting. He provided them with some generalities, about how we don't know where the human race is going from here, but the future looks very bright.

He showed them a video clip of the ringed world. Somehow, displayed on a television screen, it lost a lot of its majesty. It felt like special effects.

The reporters weren't exactly overwhelmed either. Their questions went right back to the roller coaster. "Is that supposed to be a theme park of some sort?" asked a Fox reporter.

"You know as much as we do," he said.

"Well," the reporter continued, "let's get to the heart of this thing. Who built it? And are they still around somewhere?"

TWENTY-SIX

*Language—human language—after all, is but
little better than the croak and cackle of fowls, and
other utterances of brute nature—sometimes
not so adequate.*

—Nathaniel Hawthorne, *American Notebook*,
July 14, 1850

APRIL AND DOLLY made the transit accompanied by three security people. John Colmar would establish a base at the Cupola, while Adam Sky and Sandra Whitewing accompanied the women to Solya's cabin. That was the day they discovered there was rain in Eden. It was torrential when they opened the Cupola door and looked out.

"You say this place is about four hours away?" asked Dolly.

April nodded.

Sandra's features scrunched together. "We should have brought a car."

"There has to be a way to do that," said April. "The people who built these places transported a boat." They laid their knapsacks on the table. April and Dolly had chosen eleven coffee-table books for Solya. Adam would carry four. The other six were divided among the three women.

The rain pounded on the domed roof.

"We could bring a boat," said Adam. "The cabin's not that far inland, but dealing with the surf might be more of a battle than it would be worth."

Dolly shook her head. "I'm in a place I never expected to be," she said. "I'm not sure how I'd tell my grandkids our biggest problem was rain."

"We've got about another hour to get started," said April. "After that, we wouldn't arrive until it's almost dark. We don't want to do that."

• • •

EVENTUALLY, THE STORM subsided. It was still drizzling lightly, though, when they packed up and set out, leaving John behind to act as their contact point. But after an hour, the sun broke through, and the skies cleared. They were drenched by then, of course, and April was thinking how Walker would never have been able to make it. At about the same time, Sandra pointed toward the woods. Three gorillas were watching them.

"We have to get a name for them," April said.

They stood just inside the line of trees, about fifty yards back, staring at her.

"Maybe we should just keep moving," said Adam.

Dolly caught her breath. "They're carrying towels. Are they going swimming?"

"Maybe," said Adam. "Don't stop walking."

"You sure?" said Dolly. "Maybe we should go back."

April tried waving, but none of the gorillas responded. "What do you think, Adam?"

"Keep going. I'd be surprised if they haven't heard of us by now. They probably know we're headed for Solya's. They're a little bit shocked, though, since this will be the first time they've seen us." One of them waved.

Dolly's breathing picked up. "This place is going to take some getting used to."

They walked calmly on, leaving their visitors in the rear. April heard some grunts. She knew her companions were all listening for footsteps coming behind them, as she was. "Don't look back," she said.

The beach curved around a bend ahead, and eventually it seemed safe. They were out of sight. Adam notified John.

"I doubt you'll see them, or even that they'd be a threat if you do. But be aware."

"Roger that," he said.

Dolly laughed. "I'd have liked to stay and watch them in the surf."

"You think they had a beach umbrella?" said Adam.

• • •

THEY WERE ALL weary by the time they got within range of Solya's cabin. Adam took Sandra's books. "Stay here," he told her. "Out of sight. We'll keep the radio on so you can follow everything. Anything happens, call John."

"Okay," she said.

Dolly had known what was coming, but she still seemed surprised at the equanimity of the cabin and its grounds. She stood for a moment surveying trees, bushes, and some colorful flowers. The cabin itself possessed a quiet, dignified ambience. Here they were in this impossibly distant place, and somehow it seemed like home. At least it would have if it were a bit cooler. April led the way up onto the porch and knocked on the door. Footsteps sounded inside, the door opened, and Solya appeared. No, *not* Solya. It was someone else. A male.

April flinched but held her ground. "Hi," she said. Then, gathering her wits: "*Shalay.* Is Solya here?"

Apparently disarmed by their appearance, he stood staring at their bodies, or maybe their clothes. Maybe he'd thought Solya was kidding about the visitors. Then he returned the greeting, said something else she didn't recognize, stood aside, and made room for them to enter.

"We're here," Adam said, speaking to Sandra via the radio. "We're going in."

Dolly had brought a recorder with her. She switched it on. *"Shalay,"* she said, extending a hand to the male. April was impressed. She hadn't seen her even blink.

The creature took it and pressed it against his breast. *"Shalay a tiko,"* he said. Then he released her and backed away.

Solya came through from the kitchen and showed two rows of teeth in her equivalent of a smile. *"Ay-pril,"* she said. *"Kala Morkim, tel aska."*

"Shalay, Kala," said April. But Solya indicated something was wrong, and she repeated herself.

April decided that *"kala"* probably meant "this is" instead of being the male's name. She looked up at him, smiled, and tried again. *"Shalay, Morkim."*

That induced smiles all around. Then April introduced her companions.

There was a brief exchange between the aliens. Solya looked at April, pointed outside in the direction where Sandra had stationed herself, and said something in a soft voice. "She's inviting Sandra in," said April. So much for staying out of sight.

Adam shook his head no.

April nodded. Do it.

No way.

"Do what I'm telling you," said April.

Dolly smiled at Solya. "We're a bit nervous."

Solya seemed to understand. *"Korvik,"* she said, closing the door.

Morkim had his eyes on Adam's radio. Solya put a hand on Morkim's shoulder and said something to him. Both laughed. Then she looked at the chairs. *"Bowa Mach."*

April interpreted it as *Please sit*. She did, pulling Adam down beside her. Morkim and Dolly also sat down. Solya said something else, probably "excuse me," and went into the kitchen.

Morkim looked lost. He said something and made a gesture that might have been a shrug. "Probably," said Dolly, "he said how hard it is to talk under these circumstances."

Solya returned quickly with several mugs. She filled them from a jug and passed one to each of her guests and to Morkim. Dolly raised hers, in an effort to determine whether the gorillas did toasts. Apparently they didn't, and both of them looked momentarily confused. Then Solya demonstrated how to drink from the mug.

That got a laugh from the humans. "They think we're pretty dumb," said Adam.

The liquid was not alcoholic, but it filled April with a contented warmth.

• • •

THE CONVERSATION WENT easier than it had during April's first visit, and not only because she had acquired a bit of the language. Solya showed a talent for making everyone feel relaxed, a skill one wouldn't have expected from a gorilla. The fact that they had trouble understanding one another was parlayed into a running joke.

Dolly and April brought the books out. They were filled with photos of open countryside, cruise ships, cities, cows, mountains, planes, and animals both wild and domesticated. The one that particularly caught Solya's attention was *Natural Wonders of the World*. The Grand Canyon was on the cover. There were a couple of people looking down into it, so she was able to get a sense of its size.

Solya flipped pages and shared pictures with Morkim, periodically clapping her hands with delight. April found the meanings easy to pick up. *"Amazing." "A beautiful river." "A place I would love to visit."* And, looking at Yosemite Falls: *"Dolly, have you and April actually been to this place?"* She lifted her hand to indicate her reaction to its height.

Both creatures were dressed, the male in a brown pullover, boots, and pants that looked like fatigues. Solya wore a red blouse with, incredibly, a yellow flower stitched across the front. She had on a pair of shorts that came to her knees. And slippers.

Dolly and Solya continued to carry the bulk of the conversation. And the struggle to clarify what they meant consistently drew laughs and, in the case of Morkim, occasional snorts. April indicated that she would like to look at Solya's books.

"Tario." Of course.

Nine volumes were lined up, one leaning over into a space

left empty. That had probably been occupied by the book she'd seen last time lying open on a chair. She wondered what their level of quality was. Yes, they were alien literature. Everybody at home had been behaving as if April had discovered the lost plays of Euripides. But there was a distinct possibility that Dolly would go to considerable length to learn the language, then discover that the books were juvenile, at best.

Morkim took down three volumes and gave one to each of his guests. The layout was much the same as one might expect. They were bound with paste boards covered by a silky fabric. There was artwork on the covers. The one given to April had a flower with three leaves. There was also a title and either a byline or the name of an editor. The letters, fortunately, did not look complex. Dolly, after turning some pages, commented that the aliens used an alphabet, rather than a system in which each character had a meaning. "That'll make it easier to deal with," she added.

Solya said something to Morkim. He went into the kitchen and returned with a large basket of fruit, which he set down for his guests.

Adam took something that looked like a watermelon slice. Dolly leaned toward him and lowered her voice. "*Sala*, Morkim."

"Pardon?" Adam said.

"*Sala*. It means 'thanks.'"

Adam, who now seemed more relaxed, relayed the comment. Morkim smiled. "*Tunkol*."

Adam understood. "Yes," he said. "It's delicious."

April looked at several of the books. She couldn't even figure out whether they were novels or histories or books of philosophy. Solya could not get away from the book of natural wonders. She loved the pictures and sat for a long time staring at the cover. "*Jarvik?*" she said.

Dolly indicated she did not understand.

Solya pretended to write something in the air.

It didn't help.

She opened the book to the photo of Yosemite. Showed it to Dolly. And did the same with a picture of a snowcapped mountain. Everest. She made the hand gesture again.

Dolly looked at her colleagues. *Does anyone know what she's trying to say?*

April studied the mountain, the towering peak, the glittering snow. "I think," she said, "she's asking whether someone *drew* those pictures. Whether they're pieces of art."

"That can't be," said Adam. "They're obviously photos."

"As far as we know, they don't have photography."

That brought a long silence. Morkim said something that got past April, probably asking whether anything was wrong. Dolly glanced at Solya, reached into her pocket for her phone, and took Solya's picture.

Solya smiled complacently. She'd seen this routine before.

Dolly showed her the photo and pointed at the book. "They are the same."

Solya nodded. *"Ork kabalo."* She understood.

Their two hosts paged through a travel book that contained pictures of railroad engines and churches and cabin cruisers and people riding hay wagons. They grunted and laughed and threw up their arms in astonishment. At one point, Morkim looked up from a photo of a volcano, grabbed Solya, and hugged her.

Eventually, they closed the book. *"Sala, Dolly,"* said Solya. She added something else that was probably along the lines of *Spectacular*. Then she handed *Natural Wonders of the World* to April.

"Bana ki," said April. She gave the book back, signaling that it was Solya's, if she wanted it. As were the other volumes.

Solya understood at once. Her eyes closed and she bit her lower lip. *"Sala,"* she said. And something more. It felt like *How can I repay you?*

Dolly drew the same conclusion. She got up and walked over to the bookshelf, studied the volumes for a minute or two, and selected one from the middle. She looked briefly through the pages, wrapped an arm around it, held it to her breast, and let everyone see that she wanted it.

Solya got out of her chair, moving with far more grace than April would have believed possible from such a creature. She said something that could only have been *Yes, it's yours.*

Dolly thanked her. Solya went back to examining the other volumes they'd brought.

Their hosts were impressed by the technology of the books, as well as baffled as to who April and her colleagues were, and where they'd come from. Nevertheless they maintained a relaxed attitude throughout the balance of the afternoon. They continued to provide fruit and drinks. And something that came close to tasting like lemon pie.

April had been thinking about her flashlight throughout the day, wondering how Solya and Morkim would react to it. Did they know about electricity at all? It could be a shortcut to getting a handle on the level of Eden technology. Eventually, she took it off her belt and showed it to them. Both toyed with it, exchanged remarks that made it clear they had no idea what it was. When they handed it back, she aimed it at the only wall with no windows and turned it on. It would have been more effective had it been dark rather than early evening. But nevertheless Solya grunted, and Morkim almost fell out of his chair. Both got up and hurried over to the wall to examine the circle of light.

She gave the flashlight to them without turning it off. And they obviously enjoyed shining it in one another's eyes while delivering cackling sounds. When they tried to return it, April told them to keep it, and was able to convey the notion that it would lose power. "I should have brought extra batteries," she said.

Adam contributed two that he had, and demonstrated why they were necessary and how to insert them.

• • •

EVENTUALLY, SOLYA SHOWED them through the cabin. There were two bedrooms, and they had indoor plumbing. April thought they were going to receive an invitation to stay over, but it didn't happen. And the truth was that she would not have been comfortable sleeping in that cabin, no matter how friendly Solya and her mate were.

Each of the bedrooms sported a painting. An exchange between Dolly and her hosts indicated that Morkim had been the artist. They were both surprisingly good. One was simply a landscape, a mountaintop at sunset. The other depicted one of their species looking lost and alone on a moonlit ridge. There was a dining room, containing a small, framed portrait of a smiling Solya. She was wrapped in a soft blue knit sweater. It was hard not to laugh, but there was something intensely congenial in those eyes.

The two landscapes in the living room fit into the general pattern. Dolly turned back to Morkim. "All your work?"

"Gont," he said. Yes.

"Beautiful." She turned to April. "I can't see any problem with staying here if they invite me."

April didn't approve, but it didn't matter. The invitation didn't come.

TWENTY-SEVEN

*I do not pin my dreams for the future to my
country or even to my race. I think it probable
that civilization somehow will last as long as
I care to look ahead.*

—Oliver Wendell Holmes, speech in New York, 1913

WALKER CALLED CYNTHIA. "I know you wanted to visit Eden, but you've probably seen the pictures from the Maze. If you'd prefer, we can take you for a ride on the roller coaster."

She literally squealed. "Yes, yes! I was going to ask. Absolutely. When do we leave?"

"Will tomorrow work? Say two o'clock?"

• • •

LATER, ANDREA HAWK called from the Roundhouse. "James, April and Dolly Proffitt should be back within about an hour," she said.

"Great. Did they get a book?"

"Say again, Mr. Chairman?"

"They were going to try to get one of the books from Solya's library. Do you know if they managed to do that?"

"I don't know. I can ask them if you want."

"No, that's okay. Thanks, Andrea. I'll be over shortly."

When he arrived, he had to navigate across the parking lot through the usual crowd of media people. Questions were shouted at him. "Are they okay?"

"How are they making out with the language?"

"Are they bringing Solya back with them?"

More reporters, the pool, were inside. They also wasted no time surrounding him. But Andrea called everybody's attention to the luminous cloud that had just appeared on the teleporter. "Somebody's coming in," she said.

Colmar was already standing on the grid, smiling. That took everyone's attention. He waved to the crowd. "They're only a few minutes out." Then he spotted the chairman and gave him a thumbs-up.

"John," said Walker, "welcome home. Can you tell me—?"

John smiled. "Yes, sir. They did it. Professor Proffitt had a conversation with them."

"Beautiful. Are they bringing back a book?"

"Yes. They got one."

"Did they say whether it has any pictures?"

John made a clicking sound with his tongue, as people do when they're trying to stall. "I don't know, Mr. Chairman."

• • •

THEY CAME IN fifteen minutes later. Dolly and April arrived first, followed by the security people. They all looked tired, even Adam. Walker was watching for the book but it must have been in somebody's backpack. "Congratulations," he said, as Dolly slipped her bag off her shoulder. He was expecting to see her produce the book, but it was Adam who held it up for everyone to see.

It was a large volume. A TV camera zeroed in on it. There was a title and a byline, and a drawing of something that might have been a duck. "Did we find out anything about them, April?" he asked.

April passed the question to Dolly. "Solya has a mate," she said. "And I don't think they've ever seen electricity before."

"What else have you got?" asked one of the reporters. "What do we know about the book? Is it a history? A novel? What?"

"I can't be sure, but it looks as if it might be a collection of plays. If so, they're by different playwrights, assuming these are actually bylines and titles." She showed him an example. "No way to be sure yet."

"All right. That's fine. Do you have anything on the language?"

"We've picked up bits and pieces of the *spoken* language, but I can't relate any of that to this." She looked over at the volume. "I'm going to have to match letters to sounds first." She played recordings of Solya and Morkim speaking. To Walker, they could have been humans speaking a foreign language. *Very* foreign.

"Okay." Jim Stuyvesant jumped in. "That's not bad for one day's work, I guess. Thanks much, Professor. Anything else you picked up that we didn't know? Do we have a name for them yet?"

"Not yet. I need time." Her face softened. "I can tell you that we showed them a copy of the *Fort Moxie News*. They're interested in a subscription."

The *Florida Times-Union* was next: "What can you tell us about the mate?"

"His name's Morkim. He's an artist."

That produced an avalanche of responses. Dolly handed a memory card over to the desk officer, and moments later, pictures first of Morkim and then of the artwork appeared on the monitor.

For Walker, this did not feel at all the way first contact was supposed to go. Questions about Morkim and his work tied up the next six or seven minutes. Then MSNBC asked Dolly whether they'd be going back. "You have to, right, if we're ever going to figure out the language?"

"Sure, we are. I suspect the chairman will want me to move in over there."

• • •

AFTERWARD, WALKER MET with them in the conference room, where he showed his displeasure. "April," he said, "I thought I made it clear that nobody stays over in that cabin."

"Nobody will, James. I didn't even know there'd been an invitation."

"James," said Dolly, "April told me about your feelings on this. And the fact is that I didn't get a direct invitation. But it'll happen next time I'm there. And if you want me to get the job done, you'll go along with it."

Adam broke in: "That's not a good idea, Mr. Chairman."

"I agree," said Walker.

Dolly pushed her hair back from her eyes. "They're friendly," she said in a tone that suggested she was talking to a child.

"It's hard to get past the way they look."

Dolly rolled her eyes. "James," she said, "they're civilized. I don't much care what they look like. They read books, Mork-im's a pretty decent artist, and they treat strangers well. I need time with them. Right now, there's too much walking back and forth."

"I understand. But we could set up a tent. I'll leave a couple of the guys with you to make sure you're safe."

"Damn it, James, there's no way I can do that without insulting them. If this is going to work, we need them to trust us. And that means we have to trust them."

"It's too dangerous."

"Then call it off. I'm not going to waste my time if you're going to get in the way of letting it happen."

• • •

WALKER MADE COPIES of some of the pages and turned the book over to Dolly. He took the pages back to his office and spent time looking through them. There was an alphabet, and the words were separated by spaces. By midday he'd counted twenty-seven letters. He determined which characters were used frequently, and which were not. He doubted that detail would make much difference, but it gave him a sense of accomplishment.

TWENTY-EIGHT

*There are many intellectual beings in the world
beside ourselves, and several species of spirits, who
are subject to different laws and economics from
those of mankind.*

—Joseph Addison, *The Spectator*, 1712

CHAIRMAN WALKER PICKED Cynthia up at her hotel. She signed a document recognizing that there were risks involved in traveling to the Maze and releasing James Walker and the Spirit Lake Tribe from all culpability in the event of an unforeseen occurrence. "The Roundhouse will be surrounded by the media," he said. "Don't stop to talk to any of the reporters if you can help it. If you get cornered, and you probably will, tell them you're an electrician. You're there to fix some of the lighting gear we brought in. There's a tool kit in back. Take it with you. Okay?"

"Sure."

The media presence was considerably less than the previous day because nothing was officially scheduled. The Roundhouse wasn't open to reporters at such times, but there were always a few in the area. As Walker pulled into the parking lot, several of them came over to meet him. "Hello, Mr. Chairman," said one accompanied by a CNN cameraman. "Anything happening today?"

Cynthia reached into the back for the tool kit. "I have a statement," Walker said. "Just hold one second, please." He turned to Cynthia. "Terry, see if you can get it fixed. I'll be with you in a minute." They made room for her to get through. "Okay," he said, "you already know that we have a mission going out to the space station this weekend."

"Of course," said a reporter from Fox. "What will they be doing?"

"Just looking around. We haven't really done a thorough exploration of the station. It's time."

"It's more than time," grumbled a woman from the *Wall Street Journal*.

"Look, the problem is that the hatch leading out of the transport chamber was closed, and we haven't been able to figure out how to get it open. We've been reluctant to cut our way through because we didn't want to cause any unnecessary damage."

"So what *are* you going to do?"

"We're out of other options. We'll be taking a laser along this time."

"So you *are* going to cut through?"

"Yes."

A guy from the *Boston Globe*: "Isn't it time you gave us access to the space station?"

"One at a time, guys," he said. "Some of you were at the space station several months ago. Nothing's changed." The Roundhouse door opened, and Cynthia slipped inside.

"Who's she?" asked the *Fargo Forum*.

"Teresa is one of our electrical experts. We had a circuit breakdown in our lighting equipment. It's minor-league stuff."

ABC asked whether they'd been able to interpret the gorilla book?

"We just got the thing. You'll have to give us some time."

And from the *St. Louis Post-Dispatch*: "There's another set of links in the Maze."

"Yes, there is."

"When are you going to try some of them to see where they go?"

"In due time." He laughed. "I know what you guys are thinking, but caution is my middle name."

"You can say that again, Mr. Chairman," said the *San Francisco Chronicle*.

Walker raised his left hand. "Gotta go, people." He broke away and headed for the door. It opened as he reached it, and he hurried inside.

There were four security people, one of whom, Jack Swiftfoot, had gotten Cynthia a cup of coffee. Walker watched him stand talking to her. Jack and his partners were being paid minimal salaries for risking their lives. But that was about to change. The tribe was on the verge of cashing in. He'd finally gotten past all the talk and had a million-dollar check in his pocket. The Roundhouse was paying off.

No. *Starlight Station*. That had a much better ring to it. From now on, that would be the official reference.

He said hello to everybody. Then: "The lady is a close friend of the tribe. Officially, she's an electrical worker. Repairing some lights in back." He grinned. "She and John and I are going over to take a look at the Maze. We'll only be gone a short time. An hour or so."

No problem. A couple of them told him to be careful.

• • •

WALKER HAD NEVER seen anyone waiting to be teleported the first time who hadn't looked at least mildly nervous. He liked to think of himself as a guy who didn't scare easily, but he recalled his own feelings that first time, when Harvey Keck had grabbed him and whispered something about a problem and all but dragged him onto the grid. Cynthia Harmon was the exception. If she was even slightly rattled, she hid it extraordinarily well.

John went first. He sent his pen back, and Walker and Cynthia followed. They arrived in an empty chamber and she immediately stepped off the grid and began examining the place, pressing her hands against the walls, studying the carpeting that sank underfoot, and proceeding to each of the two exits and looking up and down the passageways. Cynthia was going to make it count. "What *is* this place?" she asked. "You guys have any idea at all what it is?"

"As far as we can tell, it's a theme park." Walker shrugged. "It's a place where you can get the ride of your life."

John took them to the room with the roller-coaster icon, and a few minutes later they were riding wildly through the tunnels, with Cynthia and Walker both holding on for their lives, while shrieking with laughter. Then they came out onto the face of the cliff, and she reacted to the sky exactly as he'd expected.

• • •

WHEN DOLLY ARRIVED at the Blue Building, she informed Walker she'd made some progress, but most of it consisted of linguistic technicalities like separating vowels and consonants. And she'd started a vocabulary. So far it consisted of ninety-seven words, some of which she'd been able to spell in Solya's language. "Something else of interest," she said. "They live on an island. They're about thirty miles—if I have the terminology right—from the shore of a continent just over the horizon. They also have some big cities. Though I have no specific idea about size. Or their technology."

Eventually, they circled back to the book. "Did she tell you what the title is?"

"Yes, but it was in her own language, and I didn't get it clearly. So, no, we don't have the title. It's obviously an anthology. I counted twenty-one plays. If that's what they are."

"She said it was plays?"

"I'm still working on it."

"Okay. Thanks, Dolly, for what you've done. As far as your staying at the cabin: I'm going to leave that to your best judgment. Whatever you choose to do, I'll support to the fullest extent possible. I'll get a volunteer from the security force, and he'll accompany you when you go back. I hope you won't take any unnecessary chances. And I'd prefer you don't do this. But it's your call. As long as your relatives don't sue us."

"I assume," she said, "you have a document for me to sign?"

He passed it over to her, and while she was looking at it, he asked whether she'd gotten their name? A species name?

"No. I tried, but I just couldn't find the vocabulary. We couldn't get past 'Solya.' I got the impression she doesn't think I'm very bright."

Damn. "How do we know the cities are *big*?"

"The word for big is *kowala*."

"That covers a lot of ground. Does that mean a large population? Or a lot of land?"

"Not sure. I heard it applied to her husband, so it indicates physical size, but there's no way to be sure it's limited to that. I'm sorry, James. It's just going to take time."

He had an idea. "You mentioned a continent. Do they have a name for it? Or do they just call it 'the continent'?"

"The term they use is 'Arkonik.' It's not used with an article, their equivalent of 'the,' so I suspect it's a name."

"Arkonik?" He raised both fists. "Dolly, I think we've discovered that our aliens are *Arkons*."

"I like that," she said. "It has a ring to it."

• • •

THE CHAIRMAN WAS getting ready to close up for the day when Cynthia called. "Thank you," she said. "It was the most riveting experience of my life."

Walker had grown to like her. "I'm glad I was able to help. And I appreciate your donation."

"It's a small enough price to pay for that kind of ride. Mr. Chairman, I should mention that I'm not comfortable doing this by phone. I'd have preferred to go back to your office today, but I suspected someone might identify me and cause a problem for you."

"I appreciate your thoughtfulness."

"In any case, I'm grateful. I'll confess to you that it's been difficult not telling anybody what I did, but I've kept my word. And I'll continue to. If eventually you change your mind and open the place up a bit more to the public, would it be okay if I talk about it then?"

"Cynthia, if we reach a point where it's okay to say something, I'll let you know."

"Good. Thank you, Mr. Chairman."

"My name's James," he said.

• • •

RACHEL BRADFORD WAS the host for *Dakota Brief.* "It's good to have you with us, Brad," she said. It was his first appearance on the very popular Fargo TV news show.

"Pleasure to be here, Rachel."

They were seated in separate armchairs in front of several rows of filled bookshelves. Rachel was attractive, as female TV hosts inevitably are. Her black hair was cut short. She had expressive green eyes and a congenial smile. "It's nice to have a real space traveler on the program."

Brad wasn't accustomed to TV productions. He reminded himself of the advice Matt had given him: Don't stare at the cameras but talk to them as well as to Rachel. "Who would have believed it?" he said.

She smiled. "Before we get off on that, Brad, we have a clip we'd like to run."

He looked across at one of the monitors. A blank screen gave way to a white panel truck with the call letters KLMR on its side moving slowly along a narrow street with a lot of trees. It passed mostly dark houses, each set well back on a wide lawn. The truck's location appeared at the base of the screen: Fort Moxie.

"As you're aware, Brad, we've been getting reports of apparitions in Devils Lake, Grand Forks, some of the smaller towns, and especially Fort Moxie. We sent a team up there last week to see if they could get a look at what the fuss is about. They stayed several days and saw nothing out of the ordinary until last night."

The time of the film clip blinked on: 11:46 P.M.

"For anyone who hasn't been to Fort Moxie, it's a *small* town. Population is under a thousand. It's only a mile or so from the Canadian border."

The time moved to 11:47.

The truck turned right. "It's now on Harper Street," said Rachel. "They are two blocks north of the center of the main street." Suddenly, a light became visible in the trees.

They pulled in closer and got a clear view of the source. It was a small whirlwind, though it seemed to be rotating slowly. "At first glimpse," said Rachel, "you get the impression it's a reflection of the streetlights."

"You could read it that way," said Brad.

Rachel nodded. "That's our floater, but my question to you is: Where is the wind coming from? There was no serious wind last night. And in any case, why would it be spinning?"

"Well," Brad said, "you know as well as I do, Rachel, there's never a night without wind. Not in this part of the world."

"Is that your explanation?"

"I don't have one. What happened next?"

"Hang on."

A couple of people came out of their houses to watch. Then the film moved ahead, and the floater faded away. "It was there for about five minutes before it disappeared," Rachel said.

Brad was looking directly into the camera. "I have no idea what it is."

"Well, let me ask you straight out, Brad: Do you think we have an alien running around Pembina County? Or maybe I should say *floating* around?"

"I just don't know, Rachel."

"What do you think?"

"If I run into it, I'll ask it what's going on."

• • •

RACHEL BRADFORD HAD become entranced with the floater aspect of the Roundhouse story weeks earlier, and since then *Dakota Brief* had pursued it relentlessly. Consequently, Walker had become a regular viewer. He'd seen the stories about people experiencing illusions and light distortions. But this was the first time he'd seen them come up with pictures. He could not get George Freewater's account out of his mind.

He called April. "No, James," she said. "I did see the show, but it was probably just an ordinary small whirlwind. What's probably happening is that stories are getting around, and people's imaginations are heating up. The notion of a meta-physical alien loose in the area is Hollywood stuff. I don't think we should allow ourselves to get caught up in this. Look, tomorrow we'll be headed for the space station. Hopefully, that'll change the conversation."

TWENTY-NINE

Thou, nature, art my goddess; to thy law
My services are bound.

—Shakespeare, *King Lear*, 1606

BRAD AND APRIL were in the Roundhouse, as were the media, when Walker arrived to see the space-station mission off. He wished them luck, spoke briefly with Jack Swiftfoot, the mission's security escort, then got back out of the way when Jennie Parker came in, followed by astronauts Melissa Sleeman and Boots Coleman.

The pressure suits were already laid out on one of the tables, along with a laser that Jack would use to get through the door that had blocked egress to the rest of the structure. Melissa did a brief introduction, explaining that they weighed about 110 pounds, so they would be bulky until the wearer got into a zero-gee environment.

"We've checked the radiation levels," she said. "Since we don't know where this place is located, we didn't want to take any chances. But they're lower than they'd be if it was in Earth orbit. In fact, the level's only about half what we have. So there shouldn't be a problem."

"They must have had life support," said Jennie. "I wish we could get it up and running again."

"Me, too," said Melissa. "Eventually, it'll probably get

done. But you'll be fine. The only thing you want to do is watch where you go and don't crash into anything. Don't play with anything that has a sharp edge." Brad wasn't sure whether she was kidding.

They pulled the suits on, and Walker watched as Melissa and Boots made the connections for them, lower to upper torso, then added the gloves. Everything seemed to be a matter of just twist and lock. "It's simple enough," Melissa said, "if you line it up. But you have to get it right, or you'll lose air."

Jennie grinned. "Okay, I'm for that."

They handed out communication rigs that looked like hats with wiring. "This is your 'Snoopy cap.' It has a mike and earbuds and plugs into the comm unit *here*." She connected it to the upper torso segment. "Put it on and say hello."

Brad pulled his down around his head. "Hello."

She nodded. "Good. Be careful about movement. The place *has* gravity, but it's only about a third of what you're used to. So be careful. Low gravity is a whole different environment from what you're used to. If you push something that doesn't give, it'll push back, and you'll go flying. So no sudden moves. Just keep everything low key, all right?"

"All right," they said.

Andrea Hawk was standing just behind Brad. "You're really lucky, big guy. I wish I'd been able to persuade the chairman to send *me* on this mission. I could use a bigger audience, and I can't think of a better way to get one. Though I don't guess I'm telling *you* anything new, am I?"

"No," Brad said. "I don't expect it'll hurt the ratings."

"Okay." Melissa took a stance in front of them. "Everybody hold out your helmet." They complied, and she walked past them carrying a yellow canister, spraying the interior of each unit.

"What's that?" Brad asked.

"Reduces fogging." She took his helmet and placed it over his shoulders, twisted, and locked it down. "Take a deep breath." Her voice was coming in through the earbuds. "Everything okay?"

"It's good."

She repeated the process with Jennie, April, and Jack. "It's pure oxygen," she said when she'd finished. "The tanks are in the backpack. Your helmet has lamps if you need them." She demonstrated.

The visor was tinted. But the suit was extremely awkward. Brad's hands were muffled in thick gloves, and everything else was layered in protective materials. "Hope I don't have to go anywhere in a hurry," he said.

Melissa was all business. "So do I. The suit will remain stiff, Brad. Just sitting down can be a hassle, so whatever you decide to do, take your time." She looked down at her notes, then at the four of them, checking to make sure she hadn't forgotten anything. "Okay," she said, "you're all set. Am I missing anything, Boots?"

"I think we're good."

"Anybody have a question?"

"I think I've got it," said Jennie. She and Brad were dressed and ready to go.

April and Jack were just getting their helmets on. Melissa and Boots watched until they were in place, then started getting into their own suits.

Brad looked around at the security crew. There were three of them, all signaling thumbs-up, good luck. Chairman Walker sat down at the desk and leaned over a mike. "Don't take any chances out there, people. Keep in mind, you've only got a six-hour air supply. Be back here in *five* hours. At the latest." He stood. *"Tókhi wániphika ní."*

Jack's voice broke in: "He's saying *good luck*."

• • •

JACK WAS SCHEDULED to make the initial crossing. He picked up the laser and stepped onto the grid. Andrea activated the rings icon. Brad watched the light turn on and gradually fold around the Sioux escort. Then he was gone. A minute later, a notepad came back.

Boots and Jennie were next. Then Brad and Melissa. Brad was doing what he did when he went to the dentist, or had a blood sample removed: He tried to think about the topics he'd try to emphasize during the next *Grand Forks Live* and the questions about the space station that he could expect from callers. *Was there any indication anyone other than you guys had been there recently? Could you see anything that suggested what the people who built the place looked like?* And somebody would ask whether there was any possibility the Arkons could have been responsible? (*Arkon* was now, at direct order, the official terminology.) As he tried to think of a clever response, the light enveloped him.

He was slow stepping down off the grid. The weight of the pressure suit went away, and he was back to normal. *Better* than normal. Had he been home, he could have jumped onto his rooftop.

"Careful," said Melissa.

They were in a long, gently curving chamber filled with machines, illuminated by a magnetic lamp that Boots had attached to the wall. Additional light was provided by their helmets and wrist lights. There was a single room-length window on one side of the chamber and a cluster of windows on the other side. At first he thought they were only black panels. Then he realized the panels *were* windows but that everything out there was so dark it was easy to miss. Was absolutely without light. A sky with no stars.

April arrived next, completing the team.

Jack was already kneeling in front of the sealed hatch.

Jennie stood near the window. "Can't see a thing," she said.

Melissa was staring. "That *is* a window, isn't it?"

"It *is*," said April. "But it's an empty sky."

"Where's the galaxy?" asked Boots.

"When the first missions came here, they all saw it. But as the station rotated it gradually slipped down out of the window."

"Pity," said Melissa. "I'd love to see it."

Jennie pressed as close to the window as she could. "It certainly isn't out there anywhere."

Jack activated the laser and began cutting.

Brad took a minute to examine the wall behind the grid. It had the stag's head, the rings, and five other icons, none of which duplicated those at the Roundhouse. Two were geometrical figures, both based on curving lines. There was also a backward E. Another resembled a flower, and the last one was a circle with an X in the center. April came over, told Brad to stay clear of the grid, and tested the icons. The geometrical figures were nonresponsive, but the backward E, the flower, and the X all lit up.

"It's called an existential quantification," said Jennie.

"What is?" said Brad.

"The turned E."

April's face suggested they had better things to talk about. "Let's just go with the backward E and pass on the explanation."

Okay. Jennie turned on her wrist lamp and aimed it out the window. Brad did the same. Both shafts of light simply faded out. There was nothing whatever to see out there, like an overcast sky at midnight. And that didn't even describe it. With an overcast sky, you were at least aware of the clouds. This was simply a dark vacuum.

"All right," said Jack, "it's working. It'll take a while, but we're getting through."

• • •

THEY REMOVED THE hatch and passed into a large room furnished with chairs and tables, and, against one wall, a set of control devices, though what they controlled Brad had no idea. "Nobody touch anything," said Jack.

The furniture was small. Seats and tabletops were low. "These were designed for kids," said Boots. The chairs were padded and looked comfortable. Boots put a hand on one of the seats and pushed. It was rock hard.

"Frozen," said April.

Brad touched it, too. "Well, it obviously wasn't the Arkons who were using this place."

The windows continued, the long one extending the length of the room on one wall and the clusters on the other. Jennie was looking outside, trying to find something. "Darkest thing I've ever seen."

Brad didn't like the suit. "This thing is seriously awkward."

Jennie would have been delighted to get rid of hers, too. "It's like walking around in an outfit made of brick."

"I know," said Melissa. "Sorry about that. It takes a little getting used to. But you wouldn't want to be traveling through here without it."

There was another hatch. They were happy to see that this one was open. The windows continued but stayed dark. Jennie was getting frustrated. "What happened to the damned galaxy?"

A pair of ramps led to upper and lower levels.

"Jack is right," said April. "Stay away from anything that looks like a switch or a button or whatever. There'll be a follow-up team later with a better idea than we have of what's going on. Let them do the experiments." She was taking pictures while Jennie walked across to the far exit.

"Looks like a chow hall," she said. "And the window keeps going."

"Which way do we go from here?" Brad asked.

"Let's do the ramp. Try down," said April. "Maybe we can find a ground floor somewhere."

• • •

THEY DESCENDED THREE levels through identical chambers. Each had a version of the long window. "That's enough," said April. "I wonder how far down it goes?"

"It might go twenty floors," said Jack. They got off the ramp and moved through another doorway. Chambers that had apparently been living quarters appeared. They were equipped with chairs and storage cabinets and probably pull-down beds though the team couldn't get any of them to work. The cabinets contained a few odd pieces of clothing, shirts and slacks. They found one pair of shoes. It was all on a scale that would have fit young teens.

Eventually, the passageway passed what appeared to be a theater. They aimed lights directly forward, across a floor filled with chairs. There was a stage at the far end. A dark curtain was drawn back on either side.

"What kind of shows," Brad said, "do you think were performed here?"

"Maybe musicals?" said Melissa.

The stage was higher than Brad would have expected. "I wonder," he said, "if one of the basic characteristics of an intelligent species will turn out to be an appreciation for music?"

April was beside him. "I have no—" She delivered an "*oops*" and grabbed his arm. He should have been okay, but his head started to spin, and they both went down.

Jack hurried over to help. "You guys okay?"

"Yes," April said. "I'm—"

"Something's wrong," said Jennie. "I feel dizzy."

And Boots: "I keep trying to fall on my head."

Melissa was playing her lamp across the dance floor. "It's tilted," she said. "The floor slopes down."

Light beams flashed in several directions.

Melissa took a few more steps across the room, walking parallel to the stage. "We're on top of a hill." She swung her lamp around and pointed it at the rear doors, where they'd entered. "Look at it." It was downhill all the way.

Jennie reached out to Boots and held on to him. "How could we not have noticed that when we came in here? I mean I was sure the floor was level when we came in the door."

Boots started back, taking careful steps to avoid falling. "This isn't possible," he said.

Jack was looking at the stage. "Why the hell," he asked, "would they tilt the place? If you were sitting here watching a show, you'd be looking uphill all night."

"Dancing would be fun, too," said Melissa.

Jennie retreated into the passageway. Then she turned around. "What the hell? The place looks flat from here."

They stared at her. "What do you mean?" said Jack.

"The floor's *flat*. Normal. No tilt at all."

Brad could see that she was well below where he was standing. It wasn't a steep decline, maybe only ten or fifteen degrees. But you couldn't possibly miss it.

"Come on," she said. "Look for yourselves."

They trooped back. Brad felt the floor leveling out as they went. As if it was moving. By the time they crowded into the corridor, his stomach was giving him trouble. The angled floor was almost gone. He thought for a bad moment that he was going to throw up.

"Maybe," said Jack, "we should get out of here."

Jennie took a deep breath and walked carefully back into the theater. "I think I know what it is. The gravity's screwed up."

"How do you mean?" asked Brad.

"Okay. We've been talking about whether we've got artificial gravity, or whether this place is actually on the ground somewhere. I think this settles it."

"The system's breaking down," said April.

"I think that's exactly right. The gravity we're getting everyplace we've been is generated from beneath the floor. Somewhere. This place out here"—Jennie waved her light around the ballroom—"isn't getting the feed. So when we walk across it, the only gravity we feel comes from behind us, and is angled. The farther we get from the source, the steeper the angle seems. I suspect if we were to try to get up on the stage, we'd have a good chance of breaking our necks."

Brad was trying to imagine himself during *Grand Forks Live* trying to explain this to his audience.

• • •

THEY CONTINUED ALONG the corridor, passing more empty chambers, and were relieved that the gravity issue did not reappear. Eventually, they saw light begin to show in the window.

They all crowded over. "It's up ahead," said Boots. It was little more than a glimmer in the distance. But it was *something.*

They kept moving, following the gently curving wall. "You know," said Boots, "I'm beginning to think this place is a lot bigger than we thought."

They went through a series of rooms. The area began to feel more like a concourse, periodically divided by hatches. But they were all open, and, gradually, the source of the light came into view. It was a magnificent oval cloud of stars and gas. And obviously at a considerable distance.

"The Milky Way?" asked Brad.

"No way to be sure," said Jennie, "but it's as good a guess as any. You saw this when you were here before, didn't you, April?"

"Yes," she said. "We saw it."

There was a second starry cloud, not too far from the outer edge of the big one. And a third one, smaller, a bit closer in. "Those might be the two Magellanics," Jennie said.

"So how far are we," asked Brad, "from North Dakota?"

Jennie laughed. She said something about not being in Kansas anymore. Then: "But how is this possible? This is *crazy.* I thought it was absolutely nuts when we decided that Eden was out in the Orion Belt somewhere."

"How far?" asked Brad again.

Jennie couldn't take her eyes off it. "If that's really the Milky Way, I'd guess a hundred thousand light-years, at a minimum. You know what this *is*? We're at some sort of tourist spot. Or at least that's what it used to be."

"Like the Maze," said Brad.

• • •

THEY WALKED INTO another chamber, with a central desk where a clerk might have been stationed, half a dozen cushioned seats, and several side tables. A purple banner hung on the wall behind the desk. It was in folds, frozen like everything else. "What's that in the center?" Boots asked.

"Don't know," said Brad. He couldn't separate the folds to get a decent look. "It's a monogram of some sort." He took some pictures. "It looks like a bird."

"With its wings spread," said Melissa.

They proceeded into another control area. "We should be able to get something valuable out of this," said Boots. "April, this is another place where we need to send in some engineers to look at the technology. Maybe we can figure out how to read their hard drives and find out what this place was all about."

"Maybe," said April. "Don't get your hopes up."

Brad had thought it might be a breakthrough as well. "Why not?" he asked.

"Everything here's almost certainly ancient, Brad. I know the Roundhouse still works, but it may be yesterday's equipment compared to this."

"It can't be too old," said Jennie. "The place still has power."

• • •

THEY ENTERED A chamber that was bent and broken. The wall with the long window was torn away. April went over to it and looked outside. "Careful," said Melissa.

"Something crashed into it," she said.

Jennie joined her and leaned out. "An asteroid or something. That accounts for the Schleffer question." Harry Schleffer was a physicist who'd asked why, if this was a tourist spot, visitors couldn't see the galaxy whenever they wanted to. Why did they have to wait for the equivalent of a moonrise? "Apparently," she continued, "the station was knocked into a rotation." Finally, it was time to start back. "First thing we should do here," Brad said, "is install some lights."

"And repair the window," said April.

"I'd suggest," said Melissa, "they get the life support up and running."

They returned the same way they'd come. And they paused again at the theater entrance.

They aimed their lights through the darkness, fascinated by the gravity disparity. Yes, step inside and the floor *did* seem to tilt slightly uphill toward the stage.

Brad played his light across the curtains, which were drawn back on either side. And he saw something he'd missed earlier. Something they'd all missed. They were the same color as the purple banner in the lobby. More to the point, when Brad put his light on it, he saw the same monogram. At least, it would have been the same had the curtains been drawn together, closed as they would be prior to a show.

"Hold on." He entered the theater and moved forward. The floor began to angle uphill. The slope became steeper as he approached the stage. April told him to come back, but he kept going until he'd reached the curtains. By then he was using the chairs for support. The rear entrance, where they all waited, looked a long way down. But he was okay. He'd gone all the way to the stage, so he'd expected it. Knowing the cause made it easier to navigate.

"What are you doing?" April said.

"It *is* the same image." He grabbed the lip of the stage and used it to balance himself while he reached for one of the curtains, but he couldn't get hold of it without falling.

Eventually, he rejoined the others and looked at the photo from the lobby. He held it up and compared it with what he could see on the curtains. It showed different sections of the monogram. And yes! It was clearly a bird.

"It reminds me of something," said Jack.

"What?"

He frowned. "Well, nothing really. Ridiculous idea."

• • •

"THE REPORTERS WILL be waiting for us when we get back," said Boots. "What do we tell them? They're going to think we're crazy."

Melissa laughed. "Just show them the pictures." But the photos gave them nothing. They revealed a flat interior no matter where the pictures were taken.

"No point keeping it quiet, though," said Brad, "even if we can't show it to them." He was thinking how this story just keeps getting bigger.

THIRTY

Break, break, break,
At the foot of thy crags, O sea!
But the tender grace of a day that is dead
Will never come back to me.

—Alfred Tennyson, "Break, Break, Break," 1842

SCIENCE TEAM VISITS INTERGALACTIC SPACE STATION
by Jim Stuyvesant

Devils Lake, May 3—*A group of scientists led by April
Cannon used the Johnson's Ridge technology yesterday
to visit a structure that appears to have once been a
space station located outside the Milky Way. Professor
Alex Ridgeway, of North Dakota State University, said
that "if the cited location is actually the case, the potential we may be able to derive from this technology is
even greater than anyone has dared imagine. We can't
know whether the photographs and data brought back
are an accurate depiction, or whether it's all a fabrica-
tion of some sort by whoever created the station. In any
case, we seem to be on the edge of a new era. Life on
Earth may never be the same."*

*Pew Research has released data showing a rising
tide of disenchantment with the president for failing to
pursue technological development at the Roundhouse.
Many of his critics charge that the nation is proceeding*

*at the convenience of James Walker, the chairman of
the Spirit Lake Sioux. Representatives from the National
Science Foundation are scheduled to meet with the president tomorrow in an effort to persuade him to put pressure on Walker. They have already released statements
indicating that allowing a private group of persons to
make critical decisions regarding technology that they
happened to find on their property has been a pathetic
strategy.*

—The Fort Moxie News

• • •

"Does it remind you of anything?" Walker asked, handing
the photo to Carla.

She frowned at it, at the dark curtain and the figure
trapped in its frozen folds. She held the picture sidewise.

"Maybe this will help." Walker showed her the one they'd
seen in the lobby.

She shrugged. "It's a bird."

"Jack thought it looked like the thunderbird." The pow-
erful sky spirit of Sioux legend.

She began to laugh. "It's a *bird*. Whoever designed that
place out there lived on a world that had birds. In fact, it
would be hard to imagine a living world that *doesn't* have
birds."

"I'm not saying that *is* a thunderbird. But look at the way
the wings are arched. The design. And it's carrying lightning
bolts in its claws."

"It's an interesting coincidence, love. I hope you're not
suggesting that one of our tribes put the station out there."

"Oh," he said, "I'd give a lot to be able to believe that's
what happened. But no, I haven't completely lost my mind.
Still, I can't help wondering about the coincidence."

• • •

The evening news was running clips of the floater. Oliver
White had never paid much attention to the news, but he'd
become intrigued with the alien stories. Especially since he

had actually *seen* the thing. It had shown up several times in one of the trees at the end of the block. It was never quite visible from his house, but he knew it was there when the crowds assembled. At night in Fort Moxie, a crowd tends to be any gathering over six people.

Oliver had three children, two boys and a girl, ranging in age from five to ten. The kids in Fort Moxie didn't go out much at night to play. It was too cold. Even in May. But they traveled to one another's houses. And that meant that if there really *was* an alien creature, they were exposed to it, at least for a short time.

The situation scared him. Since it had developed, he or his wife accompanied their kids whenever they went outside. And for all he knew, their presence might not be sufficient protection if the thing turned lethal.

It was also not exactly convenient. His wife worked at the post office, and he was the manager of the town's super-market.

Fort Moxie was normally an ideally safe place for fami-lies. No living person could remember the last time a crime had been committed in the town. They didn't even have a police presence. The only law-enforcement people available were the Feds, who worked the border. If a police officer was actually needed, he would have had to be brought in from Cavalier, a distance of about thirty miles.

He'd tried reporting the issue to Cavalier law enforce-ment. When he'd explained that the floater was in one of the trees, the dispatcher hadn't laughed, as expected, but simply told him they'd look into it. "We get these calls all the time, sir. There's no indication that what you're seeing is in any way dangerous. Until we get it figured out, we suggest you keep inside and stay away from it."

He had friends in Grand Forks who were telling him the cops there paid no attention either. But who really knew what this thing was capable of? He'd walked down on several occasions to look at it. He even tried to talk to it, to tell it that people would feel safer if it went somewhere else, to warn it that eventually he might have to do something he'd prefer not to. The creature never responded in any way. The gently whirling snow and the lights never accelerated or slowed down. They simply continued to turn through the branches.

Oliver never went out to confront it without taking his .44 double-action Magnum with him. Finally, one night, he ran out of patience standing under the tree and produced the weapon. Cass Engle and Joe Wendell were already there. "Probably not a good idea," said Joe, while Cass urged him to put the gun away. Which he did.

A week later, on the evening he saw the report about the mission to the space station, the thing was back. He decided he'd had enough. He got the weapon and waited until the crowd had dispersed. Then he walked to the tree, looked around to be sure he was alone, and got directly under it so the bullet wouldn't go through someone's second story. He aimed for the center of the thing. "Go away," he said.

It ignored him.

"Get the hell out of here." He showed it the gun.

It continued to rotate.

He waited about seven seconds, said "Okay," and raised the weapon. "Last chance." He felt like an idiot standing there talking to the wind.

A door opened. Tony Tully's house, which was across the street. Tony's two sons came out onto the porch. They were watching him. And his wife, June, joined them.

Better not pull the trigger, he thought. Don't want to scare anybody.

• • •

Plans are in the works for a television series based on the Johnson's Ridge events. The cast hasn't been decided on yet. But it's expected the series will arrive in the fall. Its projected title: Worlds Apart.

—The New York Times, *May 6*

• • •

CNN LED EVERY half hour with the bird-symbol story, described it as breaking news, and brought in "experts" to offer theories on what the image signified. "It has a hawkish demeanor," Roster Arbuckle said. "Especially when you look at the lightning bolts. Whoever they are, we don't want to get connected with them."

• • •

PEOPLE WERE STILL coming into KLYM to get Brad's autograph. Matt had put a security guard in the reception area to make sure they didn't get deeper into the station. He was happy about the skyrocketing ratings *Grand Forks Live* was collecting, but he obviously wished the fans would go away. Or maybe he was annoyed that they didn't know who *he* was.

Brad was seated in his office after signing a few autographs, getting ready to quit for the day, when Elizabeth Hardy put her head in the door. Elizabeth was a staff assistant. "You have a phone call, Brad," she said.

"Who from, Liz?"

"Somebody named Hendin." She smiled at him. "He says he's one of the producers for *Face the Nation*."

THIRTY-ONE

Life is a game of chance.

—Voltaire, letter to M. Tronchin, 1755

O N SATURDAY EVENINGS, Kohana Brenner and Hank Stackhouse routinely stopped at Ramsey's Bar on the reservation for a couple of beers. Both were retired. Kohana had worked most of his life for a real-estate developer in Fort Totten. Hank had been a Customs officer at the Fort Moxie border station. In another era, both had played baseball for Spirit Lake High School.

Those had been good days. Life had gone a bit off the tracks since. Kohana had never married, and most of his family had left the Rez, so he was effectively alone now. Hank had lost his wife to cancer three years ago, and he was still trying to deal with it. He had two sons and a daughter. One of the sons and his daughter were in the Navy; the other son had married and now lived in Seattle. Consequently, they both looked forward to their evenings at Ramsey's, where they talked about politics and the Minnesota Twins and the craziness going on atop Johnson's Ridge and what they were currently watching on TV. Other old friends hung out there, too. Hank usually had some news about one of the kids. Kohana was still actively chasing women around the reservation.

Normally, they spent most of the evening at the bar with a couple of the other guys. Kohana always enjoyed himself but usually couldn't have repeated much about the conversation. This particular evening, though, was an exception. They'd talked mostly about the space station and tried to figure out what was meant by a broken gravity field.

A framed picture of a Spirit Lake High School baseball team, the Indians, from forty years ago, hung on one wall. It wasn't the one he and Hank had played for. Theirs had been active a couple of years earlier. The guys in the picture had won a championship. Kohana had known a few of those kids, though. They'd just been starting during his senior year.

His team had never won a title, and in fact had barely finished over .500 during the two seasons he and Hank had been playing. Nevertheless, those had been gloriously good times. He hadn't realized it then, that it wasn't all about winning. It was about being there, being on the field with friends, with plenty of girls in the stands, living in a world full of enthusiasm.

Most of those people were gone now. Some had moved off the reservation. Others had died. Some had simply become strangers. And the reality was that he would have given almost anything to be able to go back and play one of those games again. Damned idiot, he thought, I never realized at the time what I had.

About midnight, they wrapped up the conversation, paid the tab, and headed for the door. He and Hank lived almost across the street from each other, not quite three blocks from Ramsey's. They collected their coats, buttoned up, and left. By then, they'd left the broken gravity field behind, and Hank was going on about the cop shows, that they weren't as good as they used to be.

The sky was clear. A steady wind was blowing out of the north.

"I mean," said Hank, "the action's okay, but I never really get involved with the characters anymore. I don't know; maybe it's me."

Hank had been an outfielder; Kohana had played second base. In those days, he'd dreamed of going to the majors, playing eventually for the Twins. There'd been a pitcher with Devils Lake, Derek Grayson, a left hander, with a curve ball like a whip. It had been almost impossible to *see* what he threw, let alone hit it. After graduation, Derek had been signed by the Cubs and gone off to the minors. Two months later he was back. According to the story, everybody in Class D had hammered him. That was when Kohana realized there was no major-league career in his future. Eventually, he'd discovered a talent for moving property.

There was still some loose snow left over from the winter. A gust picked it up and formed a small whirlwind. "I don't enjoy the cop shows that much anymore either," Kohana said. "I think it's because there are just so many ways you can do them, and we've seen them all." They were walking past Bantam's Hardware. The store was dark, but music was coming from inside. Something that sounded like hip-hop. "Don't know why anybody listens to that stuff."

Hank nodded and kept his hands jammed in his pockets.

"What've you got on for tomorrow, Hank?"

Hank was a volunteer for the Humane Society. "I'll be at the shelter most of the day," he said.

Kohana couldn't get the baseball team out of his mind. The squad's captain, Ben Windrider, had been one of his closest friends. Ben had served in the army, had come home and gotten married. They were all playing ball together again in one of the independent leagues. But one evening, Ben, who'd been pitching, collapsed on the mound. He made Kohana and Hank promise not to tell his wife. "It's nothing," he said, "and I don't want to worry her."

They'd kept their word. Ben had died two weeks later from a brain aneurysm. They'd both wrestled with a sense of guilt for a long time after that, but they never talked about it. Kohana had eventually put it behind him. He wasn't sure why it was surfacing again while he walked those cold, empty streets.

"Do you think," said Hank, "the Twins are going to turn it around this year?"

"They're off to a slow start," Kohana said. He couldn't see it happening. But suddenly he was back in the daylight, charging a slow ground ball hit to his left. He didn't think he could get to it, and neither did Tawachi Lynch, their first baseman, who was calling him off. Ben, who was pitching, had broken for first to cover.

He pulled off to avoid a collision and watched the play unfold. Tawachi gobbled up the ball and flipped it toward the bag, where it arrived just as Ben did. The batter crossed a half step late, the umpire signaled out, and somewhere a crowd began cheering.

Kohana looked past first base at the stands. They were all on their feet. They'd retired the side. Ben circled around and started back across the infield toward the home bench, which was located on the third-base side. He glanced over at Kohana, and their eyes connected. Ben said something. He was too far away, and the noise too loud to hear it, but he recognized it anyhow. "Good move, Kohana."

• • •

THE NIGHT WAS back. And the frigid air. They'd both stopped walking. "What was that?" asked Kohana. "What just happened?"

"You saw it, too?" said Hank. He sounded shaken.

"Ben?"

"Yes! Ben and Tawachi! They were there." Tawachi had long since moved to Minneapolis and dropped out of sight.

"Yeah. I saw it. The play at first."

"Must have had too much beer."

"No. Close play at first, right?"

"Yes."

"How could we both have seen the same thing?"

• • •

BRAD FLEW INTO Washington Saturday night and arrived at CBS News Headquarters forty minutes before *Face the Nation* was scheduled to air. They sent him to one of the makeup people, a young woman who asked him if it was really true that they were doing that *Star Trek* thing. "It's hard to believe," she said. "Who figured out the technology?"

"That's a good question," he said.

She patted his cheeks with powder. "Yes, it's really amazing. Anyhow, Mr. Hollister, you look great. Just use that smile when you're out there."

She turned him over to one of the staff, who took him to the green room. Brad was shocked to discover that Bill Clinton, along with a couple of guys who were obviously Secret Service, were already there. "Mr. President. I didn't—" Brad stumbled over the words. "Uh, am I in the right place?"

Clinton smiled. "Sit down, please. I'm happy to meet you, Brad."

"You're happy to meet *me*?" He looked around at the agents. Neither showed any reaction. He extended his hand. The former president *knew* who he was.

"I can't believe what's been happening these last few months. And I should tell you that I admire your courage, Brad. Is it okay if I call you *Brad*?"

"Sure. Yes, sir." Brad caught his breath. "You can call me anything you like, Mr. President." *Dumb,* he thought.

Clinton grinned. Then one of the agents pointed to the door. Another staff member had arrived. "Mr. President," he said, "it's time."

Clinton got up and shook his hand. "Good luck, Brad. Be careful out there."

A young woman came in, bringing coffee and chocolate chip cookies. When she'd set them down she produced a remote and aimed it at a TV that Brad hadn't noticed. She turned it on to the CBS channel, which was running commercials. "I'll be back for you when it's time, Mr. Hollister," she said. "It'll be about fifteen minutes."

• • •

BRAD HAD ALWAYS thought of himself as cool under pressure. *Grand Forks Live* was ecstatically successful. He'd gone through his appearance on *Dakota Brief* smoothly, and had come in for *Face the Nation* without missing a beat. But he sat frozen in his chair, watching as former President Clinton settled in with John Dickerson to discuss the Clinton Foundation's efforts to protect defenders of human rights in countries where those rights were routinely abused. "Sounds like dangerous territory," said Dickerson.

Clinton nodded. "It is. And, unfortunately, there's an enormous amount of work still to do. I just met the young man who will be your next guest today, Brad Hollister, and I couldn't help thinking that we might actually be on the verge of moving out to other worlds, but we haven't yet made our own a safe place to live. And I'm not only talking about Africa and Asia. The United States has a long way to go, John. We still face a substantial level of racial prejudice. Women are still treated as second-class citizens—"

Brad was startled to hear his name mentioned. Okay, he told himself. Calm down. You can talk to John Dickerson. Just relax. He'll do the work, and all you have to do is respond. Nevertheless, for the first time since he'd started his career, he was scared of going on a public venue. Normally he *loved* having an audience. What was different this time?

The former president was still on-screen when the door opened. "Mr. Hollister? They're ready for you."

• • •

JOHN DICKERSON POSSESSED an abundance of that most critical capability for an interviewer: He knew how to provide his guest with a sense that everything was okay. When the camera lights came on, and he welcomed Brad onto the set, the radio host found himself breathing again.

"Well," said Dickerson, "we've had a lot of guests on *Face the Nation* over the years, but you're the first who can tell us what it's like to look back on the Milky Way. What was running through your mind when you were standing out there on that space station, Brad?"

A monitor was mounted on the wall so those on the set could see the broadcast picture. Brad and his host were currently on display, but they suddenly blinked off and were replaced by a picture of the long space station window and the galaxy.

"There's no way I can put it into words, John. You have to actually *be* there."

"I can believe it. Is that really the Milky Way?"

"The experts are still trying to decide. But what I'm hearing, unofficially, is that they'd be shocked if it isn't."

"So tell me what you were thinking, Brad."

"I got a sense, for the first time in my life, how small the place is where we live. I grew up with the notion that we were the center of the universe. Grand Forks. The USA. Whatever. And, of course, eventually I read some books on astronomy and came to realize we're only a speck on a beach. But I never before really understood what that meant. You talk to some of the astrophysicists, and they'll tell you that people who walk around saying how we will eventually make ships that are going to take us to other stars have no clue what they're talking about. I had somebody on my show back home who told us that, moving at the speeds we have now, it would take fifty thousand years just to get to Alpha Centauri. That's the nearest star.

"And there are *billions* of them in the Milky Way. So we were standing in that station, wondering who built it, how it got there, and we could see the Milky Way, and there are *billions* of other galaxies, but they're so far you can't see them at all. Without a telescope, that is."

"Yes," said Dickerson. "I wonder if it ever ends. Or does it go on forever?"

"I don't think anybody knows."

"Brad, who *did* put it there? The space station? Are there any theories? I assume there's no connection with the gorillas on Eden?"

"I don't think so, John. We've only been in touch with two of them. And by the way, we found out who they are."

"And who are they?"

"Arkons. I hope sometime you get an opportunity to have one of them on the show. I think your audience would be pleasantly surprised."

Dickerson smiled. "I'd love to have one of them, Brad. Any chance you can arrange it?"

"We might be able to do it later. You'd probably want to wait until one of them can speak English."

"I understand they have books."

"That's correct."

"Amazing. So what's next on the agenda? What about that Riverwalk place? Are we ever going back there?"

"I don't think so. Not for a while anyhow. But there *are* other links."

"Yes. We know one takes you to the space station. And the other to the place you call the Maze. Where they have that incredible view of Saturn. Or whatever." The images Brad had secured while riding the roller coaster appeared on the monitor, which meant the audience was seeing them. "That's an absolutely incredible sky."

"I know. It gets hard to breathe when you're out there."

"What's the temperature like? It looks cold."

"No. Actually, it was very nice. We were getting a cool wind off the sea."

"Lovely." He sat quietly for a moment letting the clip play out. Then: "Where *is* this place? Any idea?"

Brad smiled. "Not a clue. Some astronomers have tried to do an analysis of the sky to see if they could match a cluster of stars with something they can identify, but I don't think they're having much luck."

"Is that where the alien, the floater, came from?"

"If there *is* one, yes, the Maze is a good guess. But that's something that's still up in the air."

THIRTY-TWO

*The investigation of nature is an infinite pleasure-
ground, where all may graze, and where the more
bite, the longer the grass grows, the sweeter is its
flavor, and the more it nourishes.*

—T. H. Huxley, "Administrative Nihilism," 1871

THE AVALANCHE OF requests from those who wanted to visit
one of the off-world sites forced the chairman to hire additional people to respond. People with children tended to
favor Eden, a consideration that drove Walker crazy. Who
would take a kid to a place with intelligent gorillas? And
even if we now called them Arkons, they still should have
induced some concern in parents. Others were more interested
in the roller coaster. Relatively few seemed to care about
the Milky Way.

At first Walker thought that Cynthia Harmon had broken
her word and let everyone know she'd gotten to the Maze. But
her name never came up. "I'm surprised it didn't start earlier,"
said Miranda, her eyes twinkling. "I think people at first were
a little scared about the way the transport system worked. But
that's obviously changed. I'll tell you, James, *I'd* like to go.
Put me on the roller coaster and send me to the Moon."

"That's not what happens."

"I know that. But the point is we've got a gold mine here.
We should start selling tickets. And I'm not sure there's any
limit to how much we can charge."

Complaints continued to come in from people upset that the Roundhouse activity was endangering the world or violating divine law. Walker's e-mail was clogged, the telephone line was constantly tied up, and the post office delivered a fresh pile every day. In the early days of the Roundhouse, he'd allowed a few tourists to visit Eden. But it had been a foolish decision because he couldn't guarantee their safety, and it had been a dangerous precedent. After a couple of weeks, and a suggestion from the president, he'd stopped it.

Despite his reluctance, there was no way the chairman could continue indefinitely to decline these opportunities. But he wasn't comfortable about allowing people on board the roller coaster. And he didn't want to turn a pack of tourists loose on Eden. The space station seemed like his best bet. He began looking into the possibility of getting heating units installed, along with an oxygen supply.

• • •

APRIL, OVER THE course of a few months, had become one of the most famous persons on the planet. She'd signed a multimillion-dollar deal to write an account of her off-world experiences, bought a new house, and left her job at Colson Laboratories. Walker had heard her joking that she could now *buy* Colson Laboratories. She took her secretary Barbara along with her. Requests from scientists who wanted to join one of the missions continued to arrive by the busload. One of the calls came from Lloyd Everett, whom Barbara described as "another physicist."

"No," he said. "I'm a *psychiatrist*, Dr. Cannon. I'd like very much to talk with you about the reports of apparitions in the area. May I come see you?"

"I'm extremely busy, Doctor."

"I may be able to tell you something about what's actually happening."

An hour later, he walked into her office wearing a large woolen sweater. He sported a carefully trimmed black beard and had intense blue eyes. "I wanted to talk to you about the alien that's been all over the television lately."

She invited him to sit. "Doctor, there's really not much we can do about that. We don't even know for certain that it exists."

"*Something* exists," he said. "And I suspect you're aware of that, or you wouldn't have agreed to see me."

"All right. What did you want to tell me?"

"I was involved in an incident with it. Dr. Cannon, it took over my mind."

"In what way?"

"Since then," he said, "I've spoken to a number of the people who showed up in the news after their own encounters. I don't pretend to know what we're dealing with. But these people all had the same kind of experience. If they were making it up, or imagining it, we wouldn't get descriptions that share certain details."

"Like what, Doctor?"

"The overhead perspective, for one thing. People involved in these incidents are consistently looking down from a position that seems to be twenty or thirty feet in the air."

"How do you know?"

"I've talked to a dozen of them. All but three had the same airborne experience."

"But there's no way to be sure they aren't playing off one another. Picking up the standard story."

Everett exhaled. "As I said, Dr. Cannon, I've spoken with these people. I'm pretty good at knowing when someone is lying to me. Or to himself. And there's another reason."

"What's that?"

"I've been *through* the experience. It never made the newspapers, but what they're describing is exactly what happened to me."

"Floating in the sky?"

"To a degree. The reality is that I, somehow, acquired the perspective of someone else. Some*thing* else."

"All right. So where do we go with this?"

"That's where it gets tricky, doesn't it? It's hard to believe we actually have an alien loose in the area, but it's hard to account otherwise for these events. You probably know more about this than I do, so this may come as no surprise to you. Several of these people experienced another effect. A couple of guys who used to play baseball when they were teens spent an evening reminiscing in a bar. On their way home, they found themselves on a field, playing ball again."

"Both of them?"

"*Both* of them. One of them came to see me about it. It was the first time he'd experienced anything like that. I've since spoken with the other man. Same thing. Look, Dr. Cannon, something really strange is going on." He took a deep breath. "My name's Lloyd, by the way."

"You might as well call me April. Have you any theories? Other than that it's an alien?"

"I've seen shared delusions before. You'll find a few cases on record, but the people involved inevitably have a common history of instabilities. The two former ballplayers—" He took a deep breath. "I can't see it happening. April, if it really *is* an alien, nothing's off the table. You asked about theories— Yes, I *do* have one. A number of the people who have had these encounters have also experienced a delusion that includes a return to a place they once loved, the home where they grew up, a farm their family once owned. The baseball field."

"And that tells you what, Lloyd?"

"It tells me the alien does not communicate verbally. I know this sounds off the charts, but obviously it connects more directly with us."

"You're suggesting it can read minds? Or, rather, project thoughts?"

"Maybe not thoughts so much as emotions. I think the creature is empathic on a scale that leaves us pretty far behind. That would explain why, on several occasions, it seems to have intervened when someone was in trouble. It may be that it transmits emotions directly to the brain. I have to confess I don't know whether that's even possible."

"Any particular emotion?"

"Good question. In the baseball case, apparently, sadness. A lot of it seems to be about something of value that's been lost. I think your alien would like to go home. That it misses where it came from, and it doesn't know how to get back."

The idea had occurred to April, but it just seemed too far out to take seriously. "You really think that might be true?"

"I wouldn't want to be quoted. But yes, try to imagine any intelligent creature, cut off and alone in an alien world."

"That could be fairly depressing."

"Especially if it came from a place like Eden."

"We don't think it came from Eden."

"Really? Where then? The space station?"

"No," she said. "We suspect it came from the Maze."

"The place with the moon that looks like Saturn?"

"Yes." Barbara brought in some coffee.

"April, have you any idea how we might be able to get this thing back to the Maze?"

"There's no easy solution that I can imagine."

"Were *you* there when it got loose?"

"Probably. We're not sure about any of this."

"It's been showing up a lot in Fort Moxie. In fact, there are all kinds of media vehicles up there, hoping to get lucky. And I imagine the townspeople have been looking out their windows a lot. In any case, it is obviously intelligent. If you were able to show up and talk to it, maybe say hello—" He smiled. "Do that, and there's a good chance it would connect with you. Maybe recognize you."

"It sounds like a colossal waste of time, Lloyd. It's not as if it's out there on a regular schedule."

He pressed his fingertips together. "There might be a way to make it happen."

"And what's that?"

"Mount a large TV screen in back of a truck. Drive the truck around Fort Moxie at night, running some of the images of the floater that have been on TV. Or maybe images from the Maze. The ringed world would look pretty enticing to it, I suspect. I'd be surprised if it didn't realize that we are trying to contact it."

• • •

"James, the evidence suggests it might have telepathic capabilities."

Walker broke out laughing. "Mind reading? Come on, April, let's leave the witchcraft out of it."

"I'm not talking about witchcraft. The creature seems able to establish a mental or emotional connection with us. Are we sure we can do it? Of course not. But it's worth a try. If nothing else, maybe we can show that we want to help it."

"Then what would you do?"

"Dr. Everett thinks it's lost and wants to get home. We're responsible for its being here. I think we should try to help it."

"Okay. So what do you want from me?"

THIRTY-THREE

O the snow, the beautiful snow,
Filling the sky and earth below!
Over the housetops, over the street,
Over the heads of the people you meet,
Dancing, flirting, skimming along.

—Joseph W. Watson, "Beautiful Snow," 1858

OLIVER STILL FEARED for his children. Even Becky, who was usually inclined to ride through life without worrying, recognized the potential for trouble. "It just amazes me," she told him, "that so many people don't take this more seriously. Who knows what that thing really is?"

Oliver had always thought of himself as a hardheaded guy. Not the type to take seriously reports of aliens and flying saucers. And the truth was he still hadn't really seen anything other than a glimmer of light that might have been a reflection and wind blowing in a tree. Still, somehow, he had *felt* a presence. "I don't even like going out," he said, "and leaving the kids alone in the house."

"It looks as if the damned thing has settled in here," Becky said.

"We need to get rid of it."

"That would be great if you could think of a way to do it. But no more with the gun, okay?" She didn't like guns in the house to start with, and she'd damned near gone into convulsions when he told her what had happened.

"You have a better suggestion?"

"Try hosing it down. Maybe it'll get the point."

"I don't know. You think water might have an effect?"

• • •

THE APPARITION CAME back that evening. It had settled in a tree on Jay Spangler's property, two blocks away. Jay was a butcher at Mike's Supermarket. "Let me get that again," Spangler said on the phone. "You want to chase the thing by squirting a hose at it?"

"Right. I can't say that it will work, but it's worth a try."

"Okay by me. When were you planning on doing it?"

"Might as well do it now."

He could hear Spangler breathing. The guy was obviously not comfortable. "All right," he said finally.

"Can we use your gear? You have a hose?"

"Sure. Just be careful."

"I'll be there in a couple of minutes."

It was about seven thirty, but they'd just gone on Daylight Saving Time, so there was still plenty of light. Becky was upstairs. "I'll be back in a bit, love," he said.

"Ollie?" Her voice drifted down the staircase. "Are you going chasing after that thing again?"

"Just an experiment."

"I wish you'd leave it alone. You have no idea what it is, and there's no way to know what might happen if it gets mad."

"I'll be careful. Be right back." He tugged on a jacket and gloves and went outside. The walkway was covered with a light dusting of snow. The winter just wouldn't go away.

Jay's wife, Mary, didn't think it was a big deal. She'd tried to convince her husband not to worry about it. After Oliver had waved the gun around, though, she'd told her husband that Ollie was probably a bigger threat than the floater. She was a good woman, but if it had been left to her, they'd all wait around until something happened, somebody got hurt. Then her attitude would change.

He turned the corner at Twelfth and waved to the McColloughs, who were standing at the edge of their property pointing at the tree down the block. The Donoughs were there as well, and a couple of kids. The floater was spinning slowly, lodged in the same tree it had occupied before, where the branches were thickest. He saw little more than rotating mist.

Jay came out of the house, bundled in a woolen coat, with a hunting cap pulled down over his ears. The hose was on a reel. The outside spigots were frozen, so he'd attached it to a faucet in the kitchen. As Oliver approached, he dragged the hose forward. "Okay," he said. "We could make a lot of people happy if this works." He fired a test blast into some bushes.

A door opened across the street, and Tony Tully's two sons came out again, both pulling jackets over their shoulders. June was right behind them.

Oliver looked up at the floater and took a deep breath. "Whatever you are," he said, "go away. We don't want you here."

"Yes, we do," said June. "Leave it alone."

"June, I know you think that thing got Jeri out of a bad situation. But we don't know *what* it might do. We're not going to hurt it."

"Just stop it, Ollie. Please."

A gust blew in from the west. Oliver's eyes met Jay's. He grabbed the hose, raised the nozzle, and squeezed the trigger. The water soared through the mist and blew it away. But some of the stream got caught up in the floater's rotation. Water was flung in every direction. And suddenly the thing wasn't there anymore.

"How about that?" said Jay. "I think it worked. I think we got rid of it." He let the hose go a minute or two longer, then shut it off. The two boys came down and stood beside their mom. The older one, Ted, was shaking his head in disapproval.

Dumb kid.

"I'm sorry, June, but it's best this way."

"I think it's gone," said one of the McColloughs.

Oliver was still looking up at the dripping branches. "Ask me in a week whether I think it really worked."

"You're a born pessimist, champ."

June just stared at him.

The gusts that had been coming in from the west picked up a bit. While Oliver rewound the reel, Jay walked back to the house, went inside, and disconnected the hose from the kitchen spigot. When they'd finished, they shook hands. "Thanks, Ollie. I'm sorry about June, but she'll come around. Anyhow, I owe you one."

The wind intensified while they congratulated each other. June said nothing more, but simply walked back to her house. The kids followed, and the wind began to churn and suddenly a load of cold snow blew out of the branches and landed on Ollie's head. He fell forward.

Then Jay was helping him to his feet. A couple of kids down the street started laughing.

• • •

THERE WERE NO reports of further sightings that night in Fort Moxie. April expected it to come back to the small border town. But it had been seen frequently in Devils Lake also. And occasionally in Grand Forks. She wanted to get the thing away from North Dakota and return it to its home in the Maze. She couldn't imagine why anything like the creature Dr. Everett had described would want to go back to those dreary tunnels, despite the incredible night sky, but she was determined to assist the creature if she could.

She decided to cover both Devils Lake and Fort Moxie.

A majority of Brad's callers were saying they liked the floater and wanted it left alone. But a lot of people wanted it gone. And the police chief thought it was just a matter of time before somebody was killed on the highway.

Brad did not take sides, nor did he voice his own opinion, which was the same as April's: It probably wants to go home, so we should assist it. When she asked him why he was holding his tongue, he said that he needed to maintain his image as a skeptic who wasn't prone to buying into the latest crazy theory.

April already owned a pickup truck. The morning after

the hosing incident, she bought two wide-screen TVs, leased a second truck, and picked up a cover for each. The Spirit Lake Tribe produced a team of electricians to install the televisions on cradles in the truck beds.

She asked the chairman to make George Freewater available to her. George could be the key because he'd been present in the Roundhouse when the floater had come through the port. Which meant that it might recognize him and would hopefully associate him with its arrival. She was assuming that the creature had blundered into the teleporter and had no idea what had happened after that.

She and her colleagues had sensed a presence in the tunnels during their first visit. They'd never talked much about it because there'd been no evidence it had been anything other than their imagination. But if it had been the floater, it might recognize her as well.

The electricians connected the cradles to the hydraulic system, which could raise them to whatever angle was needed to ensure that a viewer at the top of a tree would be able to see the screen. Both the cradles and the televisions could be operated by the driver.

April inserted disks containing the footage that had been appearing on the news shows: the little whirlwind slowly rotating, its barely visible glow that seemed always to nestle in or near trees. And videos from the Maze, of the tunnels, and the giant moon. "It's set to go," she told George, two days after the hosing incident. "All we have to do is find the thing. If you see it, park as close as you can, aim the TV in its direction, and start the clips. Hopefully, it will get the point."

"Which is what?" asked George.

"That we can take it home. It would also be a good idea to get out of the truck and let it see who you are. It might remember you. You might even try thinking about the Roundhouse, and about the Maze. There's a chance it could pick that up."

"You're kidding."

"I never kid, George. I know how this sounds. But right now, it's all we have."

"Whatever you say, April."

"If you find it, or hear about a sighting, let me know. I'll do the same. Try to get under it with the TV, give it a few minutes, and then drive slowly away. Head for the Roundhouse. With luck, it'll follow you."

"What do I do if it doesn't?"

She had no idea. "I suppose you could get out of the truck again and try to talk to it." She shrugged. "I don't know. If it wanders off, it wanders off."

"Sounds like a long shot."

"For now, it's all we have. We've set up quarters for you." George would be in Devils Lake. She gave him the name and address of a local motel. "They've got a room for you. Or go home. Whichever works. Don't forget you have a wide-screen TV in the back of the pickup. When you're not in it, keep the cover down."

"How do I get my car back?" They were in her Grand Forks home, where she'd treated for a take-out meal of Philly cheese steaks and baked potatoes.

"I'll see that you get it tomorrow."

"All right. You want me to do these patrols at night?"

"Yes. It's easier to spot at night. Unless you hear that it's shown up somewhere. In that case, we don't care what time it is. Keep me apprised of whatever happens."

The pickups were in the driveway. "If there's no sign of it, you might try turning the TV on and just drive around. We've cleared it with the police, so they won't give you a problem." She handed him a set of keys. "Keep the radio on to one of the local news shows or whatever you can find. With a little luck, it'll show up again tonight somewhere."

"Let's hope it turns up in Devils Lake. That's closer to the Roundhouse."

"By the way, if it *does* show up, you may experience some emotion. Maybe a sense of sadness, or who the hell knows? And I know how that sounds. But it's been happening." She paused. "If you start seeing illusions, like the roadway from sixty feet overhead, it's nearby. But stop the truck, right?"

"Of course."

"Try to concentrate on the purpose of the mission: that we want to establish contact and help it. To help it get back home."

"April, do you have a problem if I take someone with me?"

"No. Although I'd prefer we not broadcast what we're doing. Who did you have in mind?"

"I think Andrea would love to be part of this."

"Okay."

They finished the meal, shook hands, and wished each other luck.

• • •

A FEW HOURS later, April rode I-29 north to Fort Moxie, which was still quiet.

At the top of the hour, she turned on KLYM in Grand Forks. A woman had confronted police with a rifle in Cavalier on the outskirts of town. The gun, it turned out, wasn't loaded, but nevertheless the standoff had lasted three hours. So far, no motive was given. A former member of the city commission was charging that real-estate taxes were higher than necessary, that the money was being wasted, and that the commission chairman should step down. Two boys were injured when a car crashed into a moose. And a student who'd gone missing from UND had been found partying in Hawaii. No explanation had as yet been offered. An investment advisor had been scamming clients. And a politician had delivered some racist remarks during a TV interview in Devils Lake. The politician was now saying that he apologized to anyone who might have been offended. He was claiming he had misspoken. There was no mention of the floater.

When the news report ended, she started an audiobook, Stephen Hawking discussing the nature of time.

But she wasn't able to pay attention to it. She was too distracted, too anxious to see the floater taken home, too reluctant to see Fort Moxie lose the creature. Did that make any sense?

Dusk was settling in as she exited the interstate at Fort

Moxie and pulled into a gas station. The pickup had three-quarters of a tank, but she wanted to talk to one of the locals. And if you didn't have a police force to supply information, who better than the guy behind the counter at the town's only fuel stop? She went inside, scanned the shelves for treats, picked up a couple of lemon pies, and wandered over to the register. There was no other customer in the store. "Hi," she said, "is this Fort Moxie?"

The cashier smiled. He was middle-aged, overweight, with a bald head and glasses. His badge identified him as Ernie. "It is," he said. "You looking for somebody?"

His tone suggested he knew everyone in town.

"Just passing through." She dug out a ten. "Seems like a nice quiet place."

"That would tell me you don't know much about us. But aren't you the woman who keeps showing up on television?"

"Uhhh, yeah. I guess so, Ernie."

"You looking for the floater?"

"Actually, yes. Any sign of it today?"

"No. Not that I know of." He took the money, rang up the sale, and handed her the change. "You need a bag?"

"No, thanks."

"What will you do if you find it?"

"We're going to try to take it back where it came from."

"And that's one of those places up on Johnson's Ridge, right?"

"Well, yes. In a way."

"Why do you want to do that? It hasn't done any harm. Don't misunderstand me, but why don't you just go away and let it be?" A car pulled up to one of the gas pumps.

"Have you seen it?"

"Down by city hall a few days ago." He sucked his cheeks in. "One of our people wouldn't be alive if it hadn't been here."

"This isn't its home," she said. "Look, I've got to go."

"I wish you would."

• • •

SHE PULLED ONTO Bannister Street, which ran through the center of town, and parked in front of the post office. If anything generated some excitement in Fort Moxie, she would surely see traffic moving from that vantage point. As the sky grew darker, lights came on, and the few pedestrians dwindled and disappeared.

Nothing was open save Clint's Restaurant and the Prairie Schooner. April left the engine on. She sat for a while and eventually threw a U-turn and parked in front of Clint's. She climbed out, went into the restaurant, got a table near the window, and ordered coffee and a grilled cheese.

She took her time eating, nursed her coffee, and finally went back outside, got into the pickup, and began patrolling the town. At 8:00 P.M. she caught the KLYM news again. There was nothing of substance. She continued cruising through the empty streets and, after about three hours, returned to the gas station, said hello to Ernie again, and refilled the tank.

The stars were disappearing as heavy clouds moved in from the west. She listened to some more of Hawking, heard nothing on the midnight news, and wandered into the Prairie Schooner. A TV was playing, carrying a game from Los Angeles between the Twins and the Dodgers. April wasn't a fan, but she wondered whether there was a chance they'd break in if somebody spotted the floater. But that was crazy. She began to think maybe she should call it a night. The place was quiet as bars go, a few people watching the TV, two or three drinking alone, and occasional laughter at a couple of tables.

She had a beer. April didn't usually drink much and consequently didn't have any capacity to speak of. She quit with one and returned to the pickup.

Every street in Fort Moxie was empty and quiet. She pulled up again outside the Prairie Schooner as two guys were coming out. One stumbled, but his buddy caught him before he went down. They climbed into a black Buick and left. April waited a few minutes before swinging back out into the street. She was moving slowly, watching the trees pass overhead. "Come on, pal," she said. "Where are you?"

Once you got away from the center of town, there were few streetlights, and the houses at this hour were mostly dark. Someone working in a garage looked up and waved as she passed. Within a couple of minutes, she reached the tree belt on Fort Moxie's northern limit.

When the first gray light of dawn appeared, she was back on Bannister Street, near the post office. Her head was bent over the steering wheel and her eyes were closed. The radio was on, somebody talking. Time to go home.

THIRTY-FOUR

*The main of life is, indeed, composed of small
incidents and petty occurrences; of wishes for
objects not remote, and grief for disappointments
of no fatal consequence; of insect vexations which
sting us and fly away; impertinences which buzz a
while about us, and are heard no more; of
meteorous pleasures, which dance before us and
are dissipated; of compliments, which glide off the
soul like other music, and are forgotten by him that
gave, and him that received them.*

—Samuel Johnson, *The Rambler*, November 10, 1750

APRIL WAS ASLEEP in her office when Barbara walked in.
"Sorry," she said, "but you might want to take this call."
"Who is it?"

"June Tully. She's the mother of the special-needs child.
From Fort Moxie. The one who's been in the news."

The child, Jeri Tully, had been all over the media a few
weeks ago when she'd wandered out of her house and somehow gotten onto Route 11, apparently headed for her special-
education class in Walhalla, which was thirty-five miles
from her home in Fort Moxie. It had been a Saturday.

According to the parents, it had been the only time in
Jeri's life she'd done anything like that. She'd gone almost a
mile in near-zero temperatures before getting off the highway. A frightened search had developed in Fort Moxie, where

nobody thought to look on the road. Fortunately, Jim Stuyvesant, the editor of the *Fort Moxie News*, was on his way to the Roundhouse when he spotted what appeared to be a churning wind in the middle of a snow-covered field.

"Yes, Ms. Tully, what can I do for you? How is Jeri?"

"She's fine, thank you. Are you the Dr. Cannon who's connected with the Roundhouse?"

"Yes, I am."

"I'm going to be in Grand Forks this afternoon. Do you mind if I stop by?"

• • •

JUNE TULLY, A few years earlier, could easily have qualified as queen of the prom at most schools. She had soft chestnut hair, bright blue eyes, and classic features. "I appreciate your taking time to talk to me, Doctor."

"My pleasure, Ms. Tully." April gave her a hand with her coat, led her into her office, and invited her to sit on the couch. "What can I do for you?"

"You know about my daughter? And the floater that called attention to her?"

"Yes. It was a remarkable incident."

"It was." She laid her purse on a side table. "I promised myself I wasn't going to bring up the rest of the story, but I probably have no choice."

"What else is there?"

"Jeri's life has always been very limited. Mentally, she's still three years old. And that's probably an optimistic appraisal. The doctors tell us she's never going to improve. She doesn't talk and doesn't understand anything that's said to her. And she has no clue what's going on around her."

"I'm sorry."

"Aren't we all? We've never had an explanation for the problem. The doctors have never been able to tell us what's wrong with her, or what caused it." Her eyes closed for a moment, then opened again. "Something happened the day she got lost. I'm not sure what it was, but when she came back she was different. For one thing, she was talking. And

when I asked her if she was okay, she said, 'Yes, Mommy.'
Dr. Cannon, you have no idea what that meant to me after
all those years. She's eight years old and she had never before
put together even a two-word sentence. Her eyes had come
alive, and for the first time I could see that there was somebody looking out at me. I know this makes no sense, but she
told me about being afraid when she was out in the snow.
She thought she might die, and she didn't know where she
was. I wouldn't have believed she'd had any idea what death
was. She looked at me and said, 'What's wrong with me?'"

"Did you report this to the doctors?"

"Yes. But they never *saw* it. The condition went away
after a day or two, and she went back to being what she had
always been. The doctors offered no explanation, other than
that the shock of going through the experience had forced
her to recognize reality. They said we still don't really know
enough about how the brain works. But I could see that they
thought I was making it up. Or imagining it."

"I'm truly sorry, Ms. Tully. I wish there was something
I could do."

"There might *be* something."

"Really?"

"Yes. This is maybe a bit off-the-wall. But I had a long
conversation with Jim Stuyvesant."

"The guy who found her."

"Yes. He pulled Jeri out of a snowbank. He's convinced
that the alien, if that's what it really was, deliberately led
him to Jeri."

"So what is it that I can do?"

"The floater not only saved Jeri's life but opened her eyes
for a couple of days. Made her who she was supposed to be.
And it's happening again. When it's nearby, she comes
alive." Her voice was breaking. "When it goes away, Jeri goes
with it."

"Can I get you anything, June?"

"No. Just, please, don't let them take it away. Some people
are scared of it. It's something they don't understand. And

I'm hearing that there's a lot of pressure on the Sioux to find a way to send it back to wherever it came from. I don't know whether anybody knows how to do that, but it would be a terrible mistake. That creature, whatever it is, has helped a lot of people in the area. Especially Jeri." Tears ran down her cheeks. "If you have any influence on the reservation, please don't let them drive it away."

"But it's a hazard, June. It's just a matter of time before it gets somebody killed in a car wreck."

"I know what you're saying, Dr. Cannon, people suddenly finding themselves outside their cars, floating in the air. But if you talk to them, they'll tell you they were always aware that their hands were still on the steering wheel, and they still had access to the brake pedal. When something like that happens, all we have to do is stop the car and wait for the problem to go away. I understand it's dangerous, but we stand to gain so much. This thing, whatever it is, opens our minds. People are getting a new perspective on what really matters to them. It's like having an angel in town. Please, Dr. Cannon, do what you can."

April sat for a long moment before she could bring herself to reply. "June," she said, "what would you do if the evidence indicated that the angel was lost and alone, and wanted to go home?"

"No," she said. "Please, no."

THIRTY-FIVE

Fare thee well! and if forever,
Still forever, fare thee well.

—Lord Byron, "Fare Thee Well," 1816

"So what are you suggesting we do?" said Walker. "I understand your feelings, but if someone goes off the road and gets killed, they're going to come after *us*. The police are telling me it's inevitable."

April wanted to take the phone and throw it through a window. "I don't have a choice that I like."

"Then why don't you back off this thing? I can send Sandra Whitewing over to your place to pick up the truck, and she'll take it from here. You just find something else to do and let us handle it."

"I can't do that. I told Mrs. Tully I'd be taking the floater home if I could. And I tried to explain why."

"What did she say?"

"She told me to do what I have to and walked out."

• • •

APRIL WATCHED THREE more sunrises from the vicinity of the post office. George saw nothing in Devils Lake, and there were no more reports anywhere of the floater. One of Brad Hollister's callers thought that the creature had probably moved north into Canada to stay with the snow.

She arrived in Fort Moxie for her fifth night there. It was getting dark, and she was pulling out of Ernie's gas station when two cars hurried past on Bannister Street, headed into town. They all turned left on Twelfth. She followed, drove one block, and saw a few people gathered under a tree.

She slowed to a crawl. Cars were parked on both sides of the street, leaving no space for her. Everybody was looking up, pointing at the tree. It was the same tree where the hosing incident had occurred. She needed a minute to find it, but there *was* an incandescence floating in the branches. It might have been a reflection from a streetlight. Whatever it was, the thing rotated at a leisurely pace. Precisely like the one everybody had been watching on cable news. She drove slowly past, looking for a place that would allow her to stop and angle the TV so it would be visible to the creature. The only thing available was a driveway.

She pulled into it and sat for a minute, waiting to see if anyone inside the house would react. Its outside lights were on, but the door stayed closed. Good enough. She got out of the truck and looked up at the creature. Damn. They needed a name for it. *Floater* didn't exactly hit the right note. And she wished the crowd would go away. It would be easier to talk to it if she were alone.

"Hey," somebody said, "that's the woman who's been on TV."

April tried to think happy thoughts, *it's good to see you again, do you remember me?* She tried visualizing the ocean with the giant planet and its rings reaching down below the horizon.

"You need help?" someone asked. A woman was crossing the street to get to her.

I need a name. She had a particular affection for her uncle Louie. He entertained her with his guitar and always took time to play games with her. *Can I call you Louie?* She tried to project her thoughts. *Hello, Louie. Are you reading me? Can I do anything for you?*

The woman arrived. "Aren't you Dr. Cannon?"

"Yes," she said.

"I'm glad to meet you."

A door opened behind her. June Tully came out onto the porch and stood watching with her arms folded.

April looked away, looked *up* at the rotating light in the tree, and decided she might as well say it: "Louie, if you're reading me, if you understand me at all, could you give me a sign? Please? Anything?"

It continued to turn quietly among the branches.

April went back to trying to project thoughts: *Follow me, and I'll take you back to Johnson's Ridge. You can go home if you stay with me.*

A crowd was gathering. They hadn't been making much noise to begin with, but now they'd gone absolutely silent. April pressed the remote, and the cover over the pickup bed began to rise, exposing the television. "What are you going to do?" asked a guy with a fur hat pulled down over his ears.

"Just hang on." She used the remote to adjust the angle of the TV toward the creature. Toward Louie. "I'm going to try to get it away from here."

"With a television?" The guy snorted. "How in hell are you going to do that?"

April touched the remote again. The screen blinked on, and the floater appeared. It could have been a live image of what was actually happening.

"You think it watches television?" someone across the street yelled.

"Louie," she said, "can you hear me? Do you remember who I am? I can get you home if you'll just follow me. Okay? If you can hear this, if you understand what I'm trying to tell you, show me."

A man said, "We don't want it to go away."

A few people clapped their hands.

Someone wanted to know whether his name was really Louie.

Another guy, wearing a Border Patrol uniform, touched her arm. "Pardon me, Dr. Cannon," he said, "but that thing could be dangerous. You might want to stay clear of it."

Louie kept spinning at the same quiet rate.

Several members of the crowd were talking into cell phones.

A man standing in the middle of the street yelled, "Great. This is just what we need, for you people to show up and try to help."

"We might be able to get it back where it belongs," April said.

"Please don't," said June. She was walking across the grass, coming in April's direction. Jeri stood silently on the porch just outside the doorway.

Okay. Lloyd said it was empathic. It might be able to feel her emotions. The problem was that the only emotions she was feeling at the moment were frustration and a growing sense of guilt. She was trying to imagine what Louie was feeling, might be feeling, an awareness of being lost, of everything that comes with being cut off in a strange world.

The Border Patrolman moved closer. "Why do you think it comes here?" he said. "Jeri loves it."

She remembered having heard that June's husband was a Border Patrol officer. "I'm sorry, sir," she said. "We don't have a choice." She thought of June Tully fighting back her emotions, and of the damaged child lost in the snowbanks. Of the man lying in the snow outside his garage, helpless in the freezing night. *Louie,* she thought, *I love you.*

For the moment at least, it was true.

A pained sadness came over April, and it was as if the world had stopped. Memories flooded in of guys she'd liked but left, of friends who were no longer in her life, of her mom, who'd died too soon. Of one guy who'd simply stopped calling. Where was that all coming from?

The hazy glow continued its methodical rotation.

April had had enough. She screamed "Stop!" and glared

at the tree. And suddenly she was aware again of June and the little girl standing on the front porch.

"Are you all right?" June asked.

"Yes. I'm okay. I'm sorry. Don't know what happened."

"We're used to it." June did not take her eyes from April. "Please don't take him away."

April looked at her, at Louie, at the television, now running images of the ringed moon. And at Jeri.

I'm leaving, Louie. Make up your mind. Follow me if you want to go home. Maybe she should have said it aloud, but she was too much of a coward to do that. She got back into the pickup, turned off the television, lowered the cover, and started the engine. She eased out into the street, turned right at Bannister, and headed out of town.

• • •

AFTER A FEW blocks, she stopped, got out, and looked behind her. No sign of Louie. All right, she thought, I'm done with it. She reached into a pocket for her phone.

George picked up on the first ring.

"I'm giving it up," she said. "You might want to do the same. I'll explain to the chairman in the morning."

"Explain what? Why are you quitting?"

"I'm not really sure, George. I just know I've had it. I got within thirty feet of that thing and had no luck at all communicating with it. It's useless."

"You're okay, right?"

"Yeah, I'm fine. It's still in the tree, by the way. At least it was last I looked."

"The TV didn't work?"

"Not that I can tell."

"Why are you giving up, April?"

"Look, let it go for now, George, okay? I'll explain when I see you. In any case, you might as well quit for the night."

• • •

IT WAS CLEAR to June that using a television to lure away the floater was a crazy idea. But April was one of the lead scientists in the Johnson's Ridge project, so it was possible she'd known what she was doing. Consequently, June was relieved when the television got turned off. She knew April couldn't hear her, but she nevertheless whispered a *thank-you* as the engine started, and the pickup backed into the street and pulled slowly away.

She stood at the edge of the driveway, looking at her husband, and friends and neighbors, not knowing how to explain any of what they'd witnessed. Probably it didn't matter. She glanced back at Jeri, still on the porch, watching the crowd. The pickup's lights disappeared around a corner. The *thank-you* stayed in her mind, directed now toward the floater, which had not moved.

Jeri came down from the porch, walked across the grass, smiled, and hugged her. Smiles and frowns were the only language Jeri knew. Years before, she'd had a small vocabulary, maybe a dozen words, like "hot" and "ice cream" and "stop." But they'd long since gone away.

"You okay, Jeri?" she asked.

The child squeezed her tightly while Tony came up the driveway. She smiled up at him. "Daddy."

June had read enough about her daughter's condition to know that she was trapped inside a narrow world in which stars were no more than lights in the night sky. That she didn't recognize neighbors and lived in a place where almost everyone was a stranger. That she couldn't communicate, couldn't ask to be taken for a walk, couldn't say, at least not directly, how much she liked their two cats. The cats, in fact, were sometimes afraid of her.

She would have given anything to protect the child from the environment in which she lived. And gradually, as she stood with Tony at the edge of the driveway, holding Jeri while her neighbors asked if she was okay, she realized she was looking at the world through Jeri's eyes. In that moment, June wanted to tell everyone she was okay, that she was happy because her family cared for her. But June couldn't remember the words. She wasn't sure who she was. Couldn't remember why the crowd had gathered.

She wondered why everyone kept talking to her mother.

But they were talking about *her*, about *Jeri*, and it was nice to have all that attention. She was having a good life. She couldn't have described the emotion, or even named it, but she started laughing. She loved to laugh, loved her life, and wished for nothing. Wanted for nothing.

Then the dichotomy was gone. June was staring at her neighbors, trying to grasp what had just happened. One of the men was holding her, keeping her on her feet. And Tony was wearing a confused expression.

Jeri was still holding her tight. She wasn't laughing, but she wore a large smile.

Above them, the branches were empty.

• • •

APRIL WENT HOME to Grand Forks, put on the TV, and watched CNN reporting on the latest eruption in the Middle East. She killed it after a few minutes and sat down with Henry James's *Roderick Hudson*, which she'd been trying to get to since her college days. She'd barely opened it when the phone rang.

It was George. "It's at the Roundhouse!" he said.

"What? Louie?"

"Who the hell's Louie?"

"The floater."

"Yes. It's there."

"How's that possible?"

"Don't know. Maybe it read you better than you thought. Anyhow, I just got a call from Paula. It's out on the edge of the parking lot, in the trees."

"Where are you now, George?"

"Devils Lake. Where I've been most of the week."

"Okay. Call them back. Tell Paula to open the door." She stared across the room at an award she'd received from Colson Labs several years before. "If they get a chance, try to bring it inside."

"Will do."

"Yeah. If it comes in, close the door. They want to get it

to the grid. If it goes anywhere close, they need to hit the rings icon. Send it back to the Maze, if they can. Tell them I'm on my way."

• • •

THE NEXT CALL came after she got on the road and was headed west. It was Paula this time. "It's just sitting out there," she said. "We've had the door open, but it's not showing any sign of coming in."

"Okay. Leave it open, Paula. I know that makes things a bit cold, but—"

"I understand, April."

Ten minutes later, as she moved across the wide, sprawling plains, George called again. "It's still outside. I'm looking up at it now."

"You getting any reaction?"

"I don't know if you'd call it a reaction, but I spent a couple minutes out there with it, and I kept feeling as if I was inside the Roundhouse."

"Good. You've connected with him, George. He recognizes you."

"How do you figure that?"

"That was where he saw you when he came through from the Maze."

"Wonderful. I almost threw up."

"Try visualizing the roller-coaster ride. You need to get it inside."

"Okay. I'm trying."

"You're standing close to it now?"

"I could almost reach up and touch it. And I'm doing the roller coaster. Whoooo, look out, baby."

April had gotten only one speeding ticket in her life. Several years earlier, while traveling on I-29, an NPR broadcast of "The Ride of the Valkyries" had gotten her up close to ninety before she noticed. It was happening to her again. *Get your foot off the gas pedal.*

"It's not responding, April. It's just sitting up there."

"Is the door still open? To the Roundhouse?"

"Yes. And I think it's getting a bit drafty in there."

"Okay. Stay with him. I'll be there as soon as I can."

"What can *you* do that's any different?"

"I have no idea, George."

• • •

JOHNSON'S RIDGE HAD never seemed so far. George reported in every few minutes to tell her nothing had changed. Eventually, he'd gone back inside the Roundhouse. The door was still open, just barely ajar. Nobody was happy. He told her that Adam Sky had arrived. "He's out there now, but I don't think he's trying to talk to it. He's more inclined to yell at it. Thinks it's just an animal of some kind."

The countryside was flat and empty except for an occasional farmhouse or barn. Finally, the land ahead began to rise, and Johnson's Ridge came into view.

George called again. "We had to close the door," he said. "Everybody was freezing in here. And nothing was happening. There's just no point leaving it open."

"Okay."

"Where are you?"

"Ten minutes out." A tractor-trailer rumbled past her, headed east. "He *is* still there, right?"

"Yes. He hasn't moved."

She was approaching eighty. Way too fast for this road, especially at a time when it had icy stretches. She cut back down and tried to keep it below fifty.

And, finally, the access road came into view. Walker had been trying to persuade the local authorities to give it a name. This seemed to be the season for names, but he wanted something to make it easier for the flood of tourists to find it. It hadn't happened yet because there was an argument of some sort going on. Someone had suggested they were having trouble deciding which politician to honor.

She cleared the police, pulled onto the access road, and climbed toward the top of the ridge. Even at this late hour, a few cars were there, all slowing down as they approached the Roundhouse. One got off onto an embankment. Its occupants started climbing out to get a better look. April passed the car, rode up to the gate, and saw a group of reporters and a couple of guys with TV cameras all looking up at Louie. He was not in a tree but simply adrift over the parking lot. Just barely visible. She showed her ID, rode into the parking area, and got out of the truck. Reporters immediately surrounded her.

"I can't talk right now," she said. "Everybody please stay clear."

They delivered a surprise by accommodating her. Except for a couple of questions about Louie, accompanied by laughter, they backed off. The name, obviously, was getting some attention. The Roundhouse door opened. Adam appeared and came out. And the chairman.

Walker came over to her and looked up at the slowly rotating mist. "I guess you've got a friend," he said. "You think you can coax him inside?"

Her mind suddenly filled with images of long tunnels and the ringed planet.

She put a hand on Walker's arm. "Glad you could make it, James."

"I wouldn't miss it. Are you seeing that?"

"The rings?"

"Yes. Lord, that's incredible."

She raised her left hand. "Louie. It's good to see you again." George came out and just stared. "Leave the door open," she said. Then she returned her attention to Louie. "Come on, pal. Let's go inside." She strolled toward the entrance as if she knew he would follow.

"He's coming," said Walker.

"He's my buddy." She was picking up images of Louie in the Maze tunnels. Or maybe it was another floater. And yes, it *was* another *floater*. She had no idea how she knew, but she *did*.

Paula was waiting inside, breaking into a broad attagirl smile as Louie followed her in.

"Careful," said April. "Don't make any sudden moves. We don't want to scare him." She stopped in the middle of the room. Louie was just inside the doorway. She picked up a sense of uncertainty. *You can trust me. This is the way back.*

"How," asked Walker, "did this thing become a *him*?"

"Don't know, James. Maybe it's a female."

"That's not what I meant." The chairman turned his attention back to the creature. "Go in, Louie. Go in and say hello."

An owl hooted.

"*He* must realize," said Walker, smiling as he delivered the pronoun, "that we can't do him any harm."

"Not sure what he realizes." April turned to Paula and Adam. "How about if you guys go into the conference room for a minute? And close the door behind you?"

Adam did an eye roll. But they both filed out of the transport area. The mist was still revolving, but it was barely noticeable.

The owl hooted again.

Walker stood by the front door. "You want me to close this?"

"No," she said. "Let it be." But Louie wasn't moving. Maybe there was too much light. She turned off three of the four lamps. The one she left on was near the grid, set on a table beside a copy of *Newsweek*. An astronaut was on the cover.

A sense of confusion and remorse settled over her. As if she'd done something irrevocably wrong. Or dumb. Like letting the only guy she'd loved, whom she'd married, walk out of her life because she couldn't balance her marriage with her career.

Mike. Where the hell are you now?

She was fighting back tears mixed with a sense of victory. Then Louie began to float toward her. But he stayed near the overhead, out of reach. Walker and George followed. Neither made any move to close the door.

April tried again to frame the roller coaster and the giant moon in her mind while she climbed onto the grid and looked back at Louie.

Come on, pal.

It was coming toward her. Descending, until she could have reached out and touched it.

Follow me. She pressed the g-clef and waited for the light to come. *Stay where you are. Please.*

She was still seeing Mike. The Mike from the good times.

She waited, looking at the place where the transport beam would form. And finally it ignited. April took a step toward it, waiting for Louie to come closer. He did, and she backed into the illumination, still facing him. He became hard to see, blended with the light. She couldn't be certain whether Louie had come far enough, but as the interior of the Roundhouse faded, she felt a sense of triumph. Then she was in the Maze, in the same bleak chamber. *And Louie was with her.*

She stepped down off the grid, and he came, too. Beautiful. She would have hugged him had she been able.

"I'm going back, pal," she said. "Thanks for what you've done. You've made a lot of friends on the other side. If you ever want to come back, we'd be happy to see you. There'll be visitors here. All you'd have to do is just follow somebody out." He hovered, barely moving, a few feet from her. "So long, Louie."

She raised a hand to say good-bye, got back on the grid, and pressed the stag's head. He was still floating there when the chamber faded, and she returned to the Roundhouse.

THIRTY-SIX

*Solitude, the safeguard of mediocrity, is to genius
the stern friend, the cold, obscure shelter where
molt the wings which will bear it farther than
suns and stars.*

—Ralph Waldo Emerson, *The Conduct of Life*, 1860

CNN REPORTED THAT the floater had been sent back to its place of origin. Everyone was grateful, the network said, because a serious danger had been removed. It was good news as far as the chairman was concerned. One less thing to worry about. The experts on the various cable talk shows agreed with his assessment. But, as Walker got ready to leave for the office, there were some dissenting voices. Calvin Woodward, on *First Strike*, commented that the alien had given every indication of being friendly, had in fact attracted assistance for several people who'd gotten into trouble. While Walker drove over to Fort Totten, he turned on *Grand Forks Live*, and the first caller he heard asked Brad who could ever forget Jeri Tully?

By the time he'd arrived at the Blue Building, it had turned into a catfight. Well, however it played out, it was over. And he was grateful for that.

He had a relatively quiet morning. There were some congratulatory calls, others from scientific groups asking when he would allow them to send someone to the space station, and a request that he do another appearance on *Dakota*

Brief. He didn't like doing TV interviews, where it was so easy to say the wrong thing. But this was a critical time, so he accepted. He was about to go out for lunch with a couple of the council members when his secure phone sounded.

President Taylor never called with good news. Usually, he was being pressed for tickets through the Roundhouse by the head of the biology department at Princeton or somebody who had put together the Primal Simulation Theory. Or fielding calls from the Republicans, fearing what the alien technologies would do to the economy, wanting him to shut down all operations.

Walker was confronted regularly by the same people, who could not understand why they couldn't buy him. They thought he was holding out for the maximum amount of money to be wrung from the discoveries.

He couldn't remember the last time he'd had a decent night's sleep. In the beginning, when the Roundhouse was first uncovered, he had been juggling tribal concerns. How best could he manage things for the general welfare of the Mni Wakan Oyate? That alone had been enough to cost him any sense of tranquility. Now, however, the stakes had risen astronomically. It wasn't just the tribe at stake. It was the planet. Advanced technologies were almost certainly available. But what would the side effects be? They'd already experienced the fallout from the presence of *one* alien, who had never really shown any sign of hostility. What if something from outside came to take over? Or if they simply appeared and were more generous, more reliable, more truthful than we were? Would that be a good thing?

"Yes, Mr. President," he said. "What can I do for you?"

"Hello, James. How is it going?"

"About the same, sir. Do we have a problem?"

Taylor laughed. "How could we have a problem? James, I wanted to be first to congratulate you on arranging to have our visitor sent back."

"Thank you, sir. Actually, I was pretty much a bystander for that operation. It was carried out by April."

"The result is all that matters. Also, I promised I'd get back to you on the medical question."

"You mean about the possibility of a plague coming through?"

"Yes. The experts tell me there's no certain answer. But they don't think any disease arriving from an alien biological system would be likely to do us any harm."

"Well, that's good to know."

"Keep in mind it's only an opinion."

"I understand."

"One other thing: You know I'm taking a major beating from the Republicans. They're all over me for not taking control of this issue."

"I know that, Mr. President. But they should understand that the U.S. government doesn't *own* Johnson's Ridge."

"Oh, there are steps I could take. There's a public-safety issue for one thing. We need to let people see that we're working together on this. The scientific community is still pushing very hard for us to find out where else we can go. You mentioned a new mission or two. What's coming up? Are we going somewhere new?"

The chairman hadn't made up his mind yet. But he gave the president what he wanted. "I can arrange one, sir, if you like."

"Good. Put something together. When you do, I have a couple of names for you. People I'd like to see go along. If you can accommodate them, it'll take some of the pressure off."

• • •

THE DAY AFTER Louie had reached home, Walker took April to dinner. "I didn't think you'd be able to pull it off," he said. "You know, I experienced some of that telepathic stuff myself when I got near it." They were sitting in Culver's, in Grand Forks, drinking coffee, waiting for a couple of steaks to arrive. "I wouldn't have believed we'd actually be able to get rid of that thing." He couldn't bring himself to refer routinely to the alien as Louie, even though the name had gone viral overnight.

"James," she said, "how's Dolly doing with Solya?"

"It's still pretty early in the process. You know they have an alphabet, right? The Arkons?"

"Yes, James. I was aware."

"Well, she's concentrating right now on getting the spoken language down. Once she has that, she's going to try to learn to read. But it'll take a while." He shook his head. "I don't know how she does it. I've looked at that book. How anybody could ever make sense out of it—? Anyway, it's time to move on."

"What did you have in mind?"

"I want to get another mission out. The president has a couple of people he wants included, which I will do, naturally. Are you interested in leading it?"

"Another mission where?"

"I thought we'd use the transport system at the space station."

"That sounds interesting. Who are the president's people?"

He pulled out a notebook. "Patrick McGruder. He's an astrophysicist from MIT. And Lynda Russell, a biologist from Wesleyan. Do you know either of them?"

"I've heard of McGruder."

"Okay. They'll probably be in touch with you. I'll forward their e-mail addresses."

• • •

APRIL WASN'T SURPRISED to receive a call from Brad. "I hear you're heading out again," he said.

"Yes. We're going to use one of the space-station links."

"Well, I'm glad to hear it. Be careful."

"We will."

"Will the astronauts be going with you?"

"Yes."

"That's good. Melissa and Boots know what they're doing." He hesitated. "I have a favor to ask."

"You want to come, too?"

"How'd you know?" She couldn't miss the energy in his voice. "Can you arrange it?"

"For the big star of the Sunday talk shows? I think we can do that."

"Beautiful. When do we leave?"

• • •

PAULA WOULD HAVE enjoyed being included in the space-station mission, but so would most of the other Sioux security people. In any case, she had a conflicting assignment as one of the two Eden escorts. One stayed with Professor Proffitt at Solya's cabin, and the other remained in the Cupola to provide a connection with the Roundhouse. That would be Paula.

She'd been there about two hours when John Colmar called from the cabin. "Everything's going okay," he said.

"Are they making any progress, John?"

"I guess so. When Solya and Dolly sit down to talk I can't understand a word they say. Anyway, just wanted to check in. Nothing's changed."

She'd thought about bringing a book with her, but that would have raised some eyebrows. The instructions were to remember that she was on a strange world and maintain constant vigilance. It was just past midnight on Eden. Both moons were in the sky. She took a chair outside and sat down.

She couldn't resist taking a minute to scout through the radio frequencies on the off chance she might pick up something. Someone had undoubtedly tried that by now. And she knew that the Arkons were not supposed to have electrical power, but you never really knew. She would have loved to take that kind of surprise back to the Roundhouse. An artificial radio signal. Maybe a domestic comedy, performed by gorillas. Umm. By Arkons. Unfortunately, she picked up nothing.

It was painful. They were making such a big deal about a couple of these creatures in a cabin and paying no attention to the high-tech civilization at Riverwalk. *That* was what she really cared about, and so did everybody else. It drove her crazy that the chairman wasn't doing anything. It made her wonder why Walker had taken a chance, trusted her, and even

put her back at the Cupola. She'd love to travel back and go
outside on the walkway and say hello to a few of the inhabitants. They didn't look at all threatening. But there was no
way she'd betray that trust.

The sky was clear, and the stars glittered. One of the
moons floated directly overhead, and the other was hanging
out near the western horizon. The only sounds were the wind
in the trees and the gentle rumble of the retreating surf. She
wondered what had happened at the place where she'd almost
drowned? Rising oceans, maybe? Or simply the worst plumbing in the universe?

THIRTY-SEVEN

*If you are an artist at all, you will be not the
mouthpiece of a century, but the master of eternity.*

—Oscar Wilde, lecture, Royal Academy,
London, 1833

DOLLY LOVED BEING with Solya and Morkim. They surprised
her on the third day when roughly a dozen Arkon neighbors showed up for a welcoming party. She'd learned that
they were out there but hadn't expected to see them. They
brought drums and string instruments, and laughed, sang,
and danced into the night. They took turns swinging and
pirouetting with her, and in fact she and John were the stars
of the show. The experience took a little getting used to, but
the Arkons moved with more natural grace and alacrity than
she'd expected. Dolly had always been good on her feet, but
keeping up on this occasion required a serious effort.

Although there was some initial shock, they showed no
reluctance about accepting her. Years later, when she looked
back on her time at the cabin, she recognized that the party
had played a major role in her overall success. She had, on
that night, become one of them.

Several returned over the next few days. Dolly let them see
she was happy in their company, and they enjoyed providing
assistance with her main objective. She was gradually acquiring skill in the language, and some of them began greeting

her in English. And then laughing at the difficulties, even though they usually got it right.

She returned a couple of times to Fort Totten to load up on watermelon and cantaloupe, which her hosts and their neighbors thoroughly enjoyed. She was disappointed, though, when nobody showed any interest in the pizza. They viewed the entire cooking process as odd. But any kind of fruit went well.

She also brought back two battery-powered table lamps and a box of batteries for her hosts. Solya and Morkim screamed with delight. They hugged her and told her how lucky they were to have her for a friend.

Along the way, she learned that her conclusion that the book was a collection of plays was correct. She'd brought along multiple copies of six of the Arkon plays. "I think I have a better way to learn to read these," she explained. "If you'd be willing to help."

"We will be happy to assist." Solya looked at her mate. Even Dolly could see that he was not excited at the prospect of reading plays, but he said yes, of course he would do what he could.

Dolly gave them each a set of the copies and kept one for herself. "I'd like you to pick one that you're familiar with. That you think I would enjoy. And read some of the parts for me."

They looked through them, conversed briefly, and decided on one. "The title," Solya said, "is *Lyka*."

Dolly settled back with her copy. "Okay. I'd like to get a feel for what it's about. How it reads. I can manage that best if I hear you guys delivering the lines instead of my trying to read them. We don't have to do the entire thing. We'll do some scenes, and, if you will, you can explain what happens between. Can we try it that way?"

They took a few minutes to assign parts and discuss other details. When her hosts talked to each other, feeling no need to include Dolly in the conversation, they spoke more quickly, so following them was much more difficult. But she welcomed it as a test of her progress. "We're ready," Morkim announced after a few minutes.

"Good," said Dolly. "Let's do it."

• • •

LYKA IS A young female, in love with Bakaro, who, as nearly as Dolly could judge, is a member of an exploration team. In the opening scene, Bakaro is brought home by rescuers after having been lost for years and given up for dead. His ship had gone down, and he'd been the only survivor, stranded on a remote island.

When he returns, Bakaro discovers that Lyka, with whom he had expected to mate, has committed to Aman Glam, his closest friend. She still loves Bakaro, however, and, after a struggle with her feelings, she agrees to rejoin him. Glam, heartbroken, and suffering from an overwhelming guilt for having pursued his friend's lover, frees her from all obligations, and tells Bakaro he has released her from all commitments, and that he regrets any complications he might have caused. Committing to mate, however, imposes a sacred obligation in the culture, and if Bakaro accepts the deal, Lyka's reputation will be ruined. But apparently not his. Furthermore, Bakaro perceives that Glam is hopelessly in love with Lyka and that life without her will be a disaster for him.

It's obvious from the start that there will not be a happy end.

The play was difficult for Dolly, though, simply because, even with Solya and Morkim reading and explaining as they went, she still didn't have the grasp of language and culture that would have allowed her to ride along and experience the emotions of the characters. Maybe if she could have stopped taking notes, at least. She remembered Mrs. Schriver in high school explaining that fiction writers don't try to tell a story. Rather, she'd said, they want to create an experience. When the girlfriend in the book tells the guy that she's sorry, but it's over, and she walks away from him, the intention is that the reader be left in tears. When you're struggling with the language, that's not going to happen.

Ultimately, Lyka refuses both males because she doesn't

want to destroy a longtime friendship, and also because she believes less pain will be inflicted if neither has to watch her give herself to the other. She accepts the destruction of her own reputation and leaves the community.

Dolly thought the play could work for an American audience, given a decent English translation. Add the fact that *Lyka* would be the first theater presentation of a work written by aliens, and it was a fair bet to become a megahit.

What she was beginning to suspect during her time with Solya and Morkim was that maybe there would be no aliens. Not on Eden and not anywhere else. They might look a bit different. And cultures would vary. But where it mattered, maybe they would all share the same core.

That feeling was reinforced when she accompanied her hosts as they went looking for food. The excitement and energy they exhibited picking fruit and vegetables off the vine was not unlike what she felt walking into an Italian restaurant.

• • •

LIFE IN SOLYA's home moved along. Dolly had virtually become a member of the household. She had her own room. The security escorts, who were in a tent nearby, came by occasionally and checked with her regularly by radio. James Walker had been unhappy with the situation and had resisted it from the start. But she'd stood her ground.

She was picking up the language without undue effort. She couldn't reproduce all the sounds, but she could get close. They sat and talked all through the day, laughing at occasional breakdowns. They did other plays, as well. And Morkim seemed to be acquiring enthusiasm for the project.

Her hosts were shocked when Dolly told them their world was a globe. "You say," Morkim asked, "it rotates, and that is how the sun descends into the ocean and comes back up next morning in the east. But how is it that we do not fall off during this process?" Dolly had gotten used to the smug smile that would have scared the daylights out of her a couple of weeks earlier but now implied only an Arkon sense of superiority.

Her hosts could not put down the books she'd brought.

At first they'd asked where the waterfalls and canyons and architectural marvels depicted in them were located. "They're very far from here," she said.

Morkim smiled. "They must be. We've never heard of them. And never seen anyone who looks even remotely like you and your friends. How can that be?"

She'd thought about trying to explain, but was prohibited from drawing attention to the Cupola. Not that it mattered. Trying to describe teleportation wouldn't have worked well.

"If you come from a place that is so far, how is it that you are able to bring fruit and food from there so easily?"

"It comes by boat," she said.

"Is the boat here now?" asked Solya. "Could we go down and see it?"

"It's not here at the moment. It comes now and then."

"Perhaps," said Morkim, "next time it comes, you could take us for a ride."

"It's big," she said. "The captain doesn't like just going for rides."

"I'm sorry to hear it." Solya appeared genuinely disappointed. "Where you come from, does everyone look like you?" She was trying not to give offense. But the photos of humans in the books had also surprised them. Dolly had the impression they'd expected to see Arkons running things.

"More or less like me, yes."

"And there's no one like us?"

That brought a smile. But she resisted the temptation. "No," she said. "If you visited us, my people would be as surprised to see you as you were when we got here."

"Truly remarkable," said Morkim.

• • •

SHE PHOTOGRAPHED EVERYTHING. Neighbors, animals, picnics, Morkim playing his guitar. She recorded a wedding and a religious event that appeared to be a christening.

"Do you believe that someone made the world?" Dolly asked afterward. They had no term, as far as she knew, for "universe."

"You mean Umbala?"

"Probably. He who controls nature."

"Yes. Of course. He provides meaning for our lives. Why do you ask?"

"The ceremony that we just witnessed." She wanted to refer to a spiritual dimension, but she didn't have sufficient command of the language. "And there's a suggestion of a presence that is more than physical in several of the plays."

Solya and Morkim exchanged glances, and Dolly wondered if she'd strayed into forbidden territory.

"I have no doubt," Solya said, "Umbala exists. That He watches over us, and holds us to account for how we live."

Morkim and Solya had a lot of free time. That happens, Dolly decided, when you're good at building a log cabin, and all the food you will ever need is hanging from nearby trees. Morkim spent much of his leisure pursuing his painting hobby. Dolly couldn't decide whether he was seriously talented, or she just didn't expect much from someone who looked like him.

"Why are you smiling?" Solya asked.

"Just thinking how much I enjoy being with you and Morkim."

The remark apparently touched her mate. "I would like," he said, "to do a portrait of you."

• • •

THEY STARTED THAT afternoon. Next morning, as they were getting ready to resume, Solya had a surprise announcement. "One of our friends told me that she saw you coming out of the cylinder several days ago. Carrying books."

She was referring to the Cupola. "Yes," said Dolly. "That's correct."

"Do you live there? When you're not here?"

"No. Why do you ask?"

"I was just wondering. Is that where you store your books?"

"Ummm, no." Here we go again. Dolly probably, despite the prohibition, should have told her the truth at the start. She'd known this might happen but had not been able to prepare a reasonable explanation. The best she'd come up with was to claim it was a washroom.

"You know how to get in and out of that place?"

"Yes."

"It has been there forever, but nobody was ever able to get inside." She obviously hadn't heard about Jack's experience. "How do you do it?"

Morkim was straightening his canvas, but she could see that he was listening. Dolly had become good at reading the nonverbals from her hosts, which told her that more lies would be a dangerous option. "We have an electronic key." It was close enough to the truth. The Arkons had no word for "electronic," so she simply used the English term.

"What is an electronic key, Dolly?"

She reached for her flashlight and turned it on. Both Morkim and Solya had seen it before, of course, but they were still struck by the large yellow circle of light that appeared on one wall. "This is electronic."

"So the key uses the same sort of power?"

"Yes."

"And we could use that to open the door?"

"Not the flashlight. You'd need a different instrument. Why do you care?"

"It is a relic of the past. Very mysterious. We've talked occasionally about breaking into it, but we have people who say it would be wrong. It's protected by law."

"That's good," Dolly said.

"You obviously know its secrets."

Morkim was still paying attention while he selected a brush and set up his pallet. He was doing it with deliberation. But he said nothing.

Solya's eyes focused on her. "Will you tell us who put it there? What it is?"

Dolly was trying to arrange herself in the position she'd assumed for the artist the previous day, hoping that he would get back to work. "We have no idea who put it there," she said.

"But it was your people, wasn't it? I understand it was a long time ago, so you might not know specifically."

"It wasn't us," she said. "At least we don't think it was."

"So who was it?"

Dolly shook her head. "We don't know. All I can tell you is that we use it sometimes to sit in the shade."

Morkim reached out to Dolly and lifted her shoulder slightly. Then indicated she should lean forward a bit.

"Dolly," said Solya, "you're not telling us everything."

Morkim finally intervened. "If she's not telling us, love, she has a reason. Let it go."

"We aren't supposed to talk about it," Dolly said. "I signed an agreement not to."

Solya's eyes closed momentarily. "With whom?"

"I'm sorry. That's as much as I can say. Do you want me to leave?"

"No. Please, I'm sorry if I offended you. It's just that the cylinder is one of the world's great mysteries. I'd love to know what it's about."

"Me, too," said Dolly. "We have a key, but not an answer."

• • •

RELATING THE ALPHABET to the spoken language was a whole new task. It would have been easier had Dolly not been required to sit for hours while Morkim produced her likeness on canvas. She wasn't even supposed to talk. During one of the breaks, Dolly asked about the drama collection she'd been given. "You've mentioned that you enjoy going to the theater. Where is it located? The theater?"

"It's in Korkis. It's only about forty minutes' travel time."

"Do you walk?"

She laughed. "It would be a long walk. No, sometimes several of us get together. We have a coach."

"There are animals that pull the coach?"

"Of course, Dolly. How else would we do it?"

Morkim walked in at that moment with some grapes, which he held out for them. "Do what?" he asked.

"Go to the theater."

He laughed. "Have you told Dolly about your own experience onstage?"

Solya rolled her head from side to side. "I wasn't very good."

"You were extraordinary." He smiled at Dolly, revealing a lot of teeth. "When we moved out here, though, it was the end of her career."

"I wouldn't have come here if I'd thought I had a future onstage."

"What kind of shows did you do?" asked Dolly.

"We were just a group that performed because we enjoyed it. We didn't make any profit from it. So I did it whenever they had a part for me. Strictly support roles."

Amateur group. "What's your favorite kind of show, Solya?"

"I love musicals," she said.

"How about you, Morkim?"

He had to think about it. "I guess," he said, "comedies."

She had finished the translation of *Lyka* and was anxious to get it back to Walker. "I have to leave in the morning," she said, "but if it's okay, I'll be back in a day or two."

"What about the painting?" asked Solya.

"Can we finish it when I get back?"

Morkim looked disappointed. "Yes," he said, "we can do that."

THIRTY-EIGHT

'Mid pleasures and palaces though we may roam,
Be it ever so humble, there's no place like home.

—J. H. Payne, "Home, Sweet Home," 1823

DOLLY STEPPED OUT of the light, smiled at James, raised a hand to the reporters, and gave him a laptop. "The English version?" he asked.

"Yes. It's a literal translation. So you wouldn't want to stage it as is, but a good playwright could probably fix it."

"How good is it?"

"I don't know. It feels decent, but I don't have enough command of the language to be able to appreciate the original. Let me work on it a bit."

"What's the title?" asked CNN.

"Lyka."

CNN frowned: "Is that *your* title?"

"No. It's theirs."

A young woman she hadn't seen before waved a hand and laughed. "A romantic comedy?"

"It's a drama." She waited, but nobody made any gorilla jokes.

• • •

WALKER WAS NOT a theater enthusiast. He'd been to only a couple of plays in his life, both when he was in school.

Nevertheless, he was interested in knowing what alien literature would look like, so he wasted no time when he got home. He collected some coffee, settled down on the sofa, and started reading. He was surprised to see that the play was divided into three acts. But, of course, that made sense. Presumably nature calls on alien worlds, too, so they'd have to allow intermissions to give the audience a break. And the actors. What surprised him, now that he held the script in his hands, was that the Arkons had developed stagecraft at all.

He stayed with it until he'd finished. He wasn't sure what he'd expected, but as he headed for the kitchen and a late snack, he felt disappointed by the ordinariness of the plot. It was a story line that wouldn't have been out of place as a rerun on any of the movie channels. Except maybe for the unhappy ending.

• • •

JOHN COLMAR CALLED him from the Roundhouse. "Got a question, Mr. Chairman. Dolly's getting ready to go back to Eden. She's taking eight lamps with her, and about sixty batteries. Is that okay with you?"

"Put her on, John."

"Hello, James," she said. "I didn't think this would be a problem. I've done it before."

"What are the lamps for?"

"They're for the Arkons. They're battery-powered, so they're okay. We've already given a couple of them to Solya. They love them."

"That's all?"

"Yes. There's nothing more."

"No chance they might electrocute themselves, is there?"

"No, there's nothing to worry about, James."

"All right. Put John back on."

• • •

SOLYA'S NEIGHBORS WERE entranced by the lamps. They insisted on bringing her to each of their cabins, showing her how their homes looked in the soft light. Dolly had become a beloved figure in the neighborhood. The one problem that was developing from living on Eden was the shortness of the days. It resulted in a more compressed sleep cycle. Dolly knew she was going to have difficulty adjusting to life back in North America.

Morkim finished the painting and unveiled the result. She'd seen enough of his work to suspect he'd do pretty well, but she was surprised at how effectively he seemed to have caught her in a pensive mood. How the fatigues, which were at best a modest work garment, contributed to the personality on display. She couldn't imagine a human artist doing as well with an Arkon subject. "I look pretty good," she said.

Morkim was delighted with her response. "Thank you."

"May I take photos of it to show my friends?"

"Yes. Of course."

She took the pictures, and Morkim closed his eyes and smiled at the heavens. "You are pure magic, Dolly," he said.

She hugged him and took several more photos, including one of the artist standing beside his work. Then Solya took one of her hugging Morkim. "So what will you do with it?" She was hoping he would offer it to her. Allow her to take it home. She could see Walker's jaw dropping when she came off the grid with it.

"Well," he said, "I cannot imagine that, at this moment, there is a more valuable painting in the world." His eyes were gleaming.

"Why do you say that?"

Solya responded: "Because it is probably the first painting ever of a visitor from a completely unknown place. He will be famous. Dolly, you have been very generous. You have brought us these books. Now you give us this. What can we do for you in return?"

That was easy. "I would love to have the portrait of Solya." It was on the wall in the dining room. Solya with a sweater wrapped around her shoulders, smiling, happy, completely carefree. Just like the person she knew so well.

Morkim hesitated. So Dolly withdrew the request.

"No," said Solya. "He can do another one of me. He's a

better artist now anyway than he was when he did that. All right, Morkim?"

"Of course, love," he said.

Dolly had grown tired of the fruit and vegetables. She needed some beer and pizza. And she was anxious to show April and the chairman Solya's portrait. So she had her security guy inform the Roundhouse that she was going back again. "The people at home would love to see this," she said, indicating the portrait. "I'll be back in a couple of days."

Everyone had by then seen the photos of the Arkons, but nevertheless when she arrived in the Roundhouse and held up Solya's portrait for them, the media people couldn't resist laughing. One of the TV guys stood in front of her and smirked. "She looks great in that sweater."

Dolly glared at him. "Idiot," she said.

"What?" He looked puzzled. "Come on. She's a *gorilla*."

She came close to slapping him.

• • •

WALKER HAD A different reaction. He wasn't at the Roundhouse when she arrived. She caught up with him in the parking lot at Mario's, where he usually had dinner on days when he worked late. "Beautiful," he said. "You're giving us exactly the kind of relationship we need, Dolly. Perfect. I'm grateful we're getting some good news out of that place. Dolly, I can't thank you enough. Is there anything I can do for you to repay your efforts?"

"Actually," she said, "I would love to see that planet with the rings."

Walker clapped his hands. "Yes! Absolutely! When would you like to go?"

"Well, I'll be going back to Eden tomorrow."

"Do you have time in the morning?"

• • •

WALKER WENT WITH her. And Adam. It was broad daylight this time when they came out of the tunnel, but it did not diminish the spectacle. They rode along the face of the cliff, above the alien sea, and all three cheered and raised their hands in celebration. The chairman had never before seen an unchained display of emotion from Adam.

When it was over, they were laughing and going on about what it would be like to have that kind of spectacle in the sky every day. When they returned to the grid and were waiting to be transported back home, they were still so excited that no one noticed the approaching shadow.

THIRTY-NINE

The first mistake in public business is going into it.

—Benjamin Franklin, *Poor Richard's Almanack*, 1758

THE DEVILS LAKE City Commission met twice monthly. Usually, the only persons present, other than the members, were those who had a business or political interest in the proceedings. But now, since the advent of the Roundhouse, meetings routinely filled the conference room.

Tonight's agenda included a move to reduce classroom size in the next school year, confront the ongoing flooding issues from Devils Lake, and an attempt to overturn the nuisance legislation that had made it illegal to neglect taking proper care of one's lawn and buildings. But the real issue had surfaced a few days earlier after the arrival of a petition from a consortium of visitors to the area who had not been able to gain entrance to the Roundhouse. More parking space was needed, and it would be helpful if the Roundhouse itself was open to the public. And, of course, that would mean an increase in security requirements.

The commission was headed by the mayor, Wilma Herschel. She had been talked into running for the position a year earlier and had been surprised at her success. Everything had gone well, and she'd been thinking about moving up the political ladder when Lasker had found that damned boat and the nightmare on the ridge began. Devils Lake had been getting rich in the wake of the thing, but the cost had been high. Traffic had overwhelmed the city. They were not able to accommodate the crowds. Drunks and hoodlums from other areas were constantly fighting in the streets, and people were parking their cars everywhere. One problem, at least, had been resolved: They were being assured that the floater was gone.

As a result of the Roundhouse, business had boomed. Motels filled up every night. Gas stations couldn't keep enough fuel in their pumps. Restaurants had to turn customers away. But now the Sioux had locked the doors. Herschel had talked with Walker on several occasions, asking him to back off and reopen the place to tourists. She understood the security issues, but the city was paying a substantial price.

He was not inclined to back off. "It's not just the risk from lunatics who want to blow the place up," he'd told her. "We had some disorderly behavior as well. The way things are now, if we were to reopen, we couldn't guarantee everyone's safety."

Herschel had her hands full simply calling the meeting to order. The crowd was unruly, a common characteristic in these uncertain times. She put the Roundhouse issue at the top of the agenda because once they got through that, most of these people would leave.

She read the proposal aloud, "that Chairman Walker be solicited to reopen Starlight Station to tourists and that funding be made available to the tribe to offset whatever additional expenses it might incur." She'd been careful, of course, to use the designator that Walker preferred. *Starlight Station.* If they were looking for something that would reflect reality, she'd have gone for *The Money Palace.*

"The meeting is now open for discussion."

Besides the mayor, there were four commissioners. Three of them, she knew, would argue in favor of the bill although two had informed her that the proposal wasn't applying sufficient pressure on the chairman. But before going to them, she solicited comments from the floor.

The comments were direct:

Doris Corley, who described herself as a mother of four, wasn't happy. "I know this isn't going to be a popular point of view in here, but some of us are tired of the drunks and the crowds. They've backed off a little during the past few weeks. But that's not enough. If we're going to send a message to Chairman Walker, it should be that Johnson's Ridge be closed off altogether. We should let nobody near the place."

That got a round of boos.

Alex Patchworth, owner of a major retail outlet, was more in line with the conventional view: "Look, this is a once-in-a-lifetime opportunity. We'd be damned fools not to take advantage of it. Make it clear to Walker that the Sioux stand to benefit as well as the rest of us."

And Calvin Kerr, a clergyman: "That's easy for you to say, Alex. You don't have kids running into some of these people in the streets. My son Joseph got assaulted a few weeks ago."

Herschel understood the request would have no effect on Walker. But the position she took would have political implications for her. No matter which way she went, it was going to cost her.

• • •

THE DAY ON which they were departing on the new mission dawned bright and clear. April and Brad were waiting at Grand Forks International Airport when Lynda Russell and Patrick McGruder arrived on their flights. They welcomed them to what they were calling the Galactic Mission and led them to a waiting helicopter. Both were excited. Lynda was so pumped, she couldn't find her seat belt.

She was a biologist, had written several books dealing with off-world biological issues for humans, such as the effect of zero gravity on long-range space exploration, radiation considerations, and a host of other topics. She looked about thirty, with brown eyes locked on a distant place.

Patrick appeared even younger. But he also had a faraway look. His specialty was cosmology, and he'd brought home last year's Fundamental Physics Prize from Geneva for his work in dark matter. He had done groundbreaking research in determining whether dark matter was responsible for differences in observed and theoretical speed of stars orbiting the centers of galaxies. Apparently, he'd come up with an alternative possibility, but April could not get hold of it. It had a quantum component, and she always tended to get lost when quantum theory became part of the conversation.

She was tempted to pretend she was up to speed by asking about the work but decided it was too early in the morning to try faking it. Instead, as they lifted off and headed west toward Johnson's Ridge, she asked how their flights had gone and whether their families were worried about what they were doing.

Lynda's husband was, she suggested without actually saying it, scared out of his mind. He'd tried to talk her out of coming, but ultimately he understood the significance of what they were doing.

Patrick wasn't married. But his girlfriend and his parents hadn't been happy either. They'd warned him against participating though they'd realized there was no way to change his mind. "They got seriously annoyed," he said, "when my fifteen-year-old sister Thelma asked if I could arrange for her to go, too."

It reminded April that there was nobody in her life who would be very severely affected if something happened to her. Nobody who really cared. Mike was long gone, and she had no kids. *Nobody to cry over me.* Well, she thought, at least she'd make some headlines.

"Is there anything that could go wrong?" asked Lynda. She meant it as a joke.

But April played it straight. "Nothing that we know of. The system seems to work fine."

Patrick was easygoing, armed with a natural grin and a laid-back manner, and no sign of the ego issues that one might expect from a young winner of a major award. "You've already done this several times, April, right?"

"Yes."

He was sitting across from her. She watched him prop his elbow on the arm of the seat and lower his face onto his fist. The excitement drained away, replaced by apparent bewilderment.

"Something wrong?" asked April.

"It's just hard to believe," he said. "We're going outside the galaxy today, but if we had to get to the Moon, we couldn't manage it."

• • •

THEY CAME IN over a crowd of tourists waiting outside the fence, descended into the parking lot, answered a few questions from reporters as they climbed out, and entered the Roundhouse. The two astronauts, Melissa and Boots, were waiting for them, and two members of the security team, George Freewater and John Colmar. Both carried rifles and telescopes.

While they were getting into their pressure suits, Walker appeared. He took April aside. "Got some news for you," he said. "We have the book title."

"The *Arkon* book? What is it?"

He smiled. "It's *The Great Plays*."

"Written by the Arkons?"

"Of course. Who else is there?"

"I'm having a hard time picturing them onstage doing *Hamlet*."

Walker was obviously enjoying himself. "I think we're learning a lot about ourselves."

They'd caught Brad's attention. "You say that's a book by the aliens?" he asked.

"It is," said Walker. "We also have the titles of the other books."

April knew there'd been ten altogether. "Are you going to tell us?" she asked.

"One's a dictionary." He fished a piece of paper out of his pocket. "She—Solya, that is—has two poetry collections.

And a book of short stories called *Chocolate Nuggets*. By the way, Paula said that Dolly wanted us to know she was making up the titles herself, but that she was trying to reproduce the Arkon titles as best she could. She says they don't really have chocolate, but there is a similar preparation that they use to coat various foods. And it's a similar color. Anyhow, the stories are by a writer who's been dead a long time. But we don't know how long that is because we haven't been able to figure out yet how they measure time. Solya thinks the stories are hysterical. Dolly's read a couple of them. She says they remind her of James Thurber."

April couldn't resist laughing. "Thurber would have loved hearing that."

"There are also books that she describes as being analyses of the social fabric, and a couple of histories, including one titled *The Gromingo War*."

"Okay," said Brad. "So much for a peaceful society."

"Not necessarily," said Walker. "Dolly says she's not sure about it. It might be an account of religious or political debates."

FORTY

Never greet a stranger in the night. He may be a demon.

—*The Talmud*, c. 200 B.C.E.

W HEN THEY ARRIVED on the space station, the galaxy was directly in the center of the long window. Lynda and Patrick couldn't stop staring at it. April understood and was in no hurry to move on. Brad took more pictures, and finally stopped to ask Patrick if there was any way to know for certain whether it was the Milky Way. The answer was the same one he'd heard before.

"I wish there was. If it's not the Milky Way, and it's something even farther, that just makes it still more of a mindbender." Patrick looked down at the deck. "The artificial gravity's another shock."

"There's more to it," said April. She explained about the inconsistency. "Whatever generates it is apparently broken."

After another several minutes of stargazing, they returned to the grid, wondering where they'd go from here. "Lynda," April said, "pick an icon." She indicated the three that were active.

Lynda studied them for a moment before replying. "The turned E."

April looked over at Patrick. "That okay with you?"

"Let's go with it," he said.

George was to lead the way. He pressed his fingertips against his helmet as if making an adjustment, approached the wall, the bulkhead, whatever it was, and got on the grid. "Good luck," said April. She pushed the turned E. The phosphorescent glow formed and gradually enveloped him. Then he was gone, and the light diminished and went out.

They waited. The glow came back and a pen appeared. "Okay," said April. "We're good." She picked up the pen and stepped onto the grid. John climbed up beside her, and they transported out. Patrick and Lynda went next, leaving Brad alone in the station. A sobering moment. It occurred to him that he was light-years from the nearest human being.

He pressed the icon, watched the luminous cloud form, and stepped into it.

• • •

HE ARRIVED IN a place that looked like the interior of the Cupola except that the walls weren't transparent. It had two windows, at ground level on opposite sides of the dome. They were filled with sunlight. Boots was looking at the images in the wall, satisfying himself that the rings icon was there to take them back to the space station.

"Do we need the suits?" asked April. Brad knew she wanted to be free of the encumbrance so she could taste the air and enjoy the sun.

"Keep it on," said Melissa. "It's hot. And there's not enough oxygen."

"So we're not on Eden," said John.

April opened the door. The sunlight was blinding. "I don't think so." She looked across a landscape composed of sand and rock. Gravity felt about Earth normal.

"Everybody lower your outer visor," said Boots. It was tinted, and Brad was happy to see that it blocked off the worst of the glare.

They walked outside into a desert filled with the remains of ancient structures. Plazas, domes, and low, curved buildings with collapsed rooftops were scattered across the landscape. Off to their right, the ground gave way to a crevice. A structure that might once have been a temple had collapsed into it. There were gasps and profanity as they looked around them. "My God," said Lynda. "What kind of place is this?"

Brad stared at the wreckage. So much for the theory this is a series of tourist spots.

There was no sign of life. No birds flew through the skies. No serpents crawled among the rocks. No tree, or bush, or blade of grass was visible. Brad couldn't believe anyone would ever have tried to live in such a place.

They started walking. "Be careful, everybody," said Melissa. "The ground's rough. If you fall and tear the suit, it will be bye-bye baby."

The sun was a swollen yellow giant. It was approaching the horizon, or maybe rising. No way to know yet. "Temperature's over a hundred degrees," said Boots. "Centigrade."

Brad did the math: That came to more than two hundred degrees Fahrenheit. "Where are we?" he asked. "Mercury?"

"I doubt," said Melissa, "they ever had any cities on Mercury."

There was no sign of water anywhere. The chamber in which they'd arrived was different from the surroundings in that it was in relatively decent condition. There was nothing else that hadn't at least partially broken down and been to some degree swallowed in the ground.

April knelt to look at a piece of rock or concrete, something, that had once probably been part of a building. "It's been a long time," she said.

George stood beside her. "How long do you think?"

"Can't tell. Millions of years, probably. Right, Patrick?"

"Looks like it," he said.

"Incredible." Lynda put a hand on Brad's arm as if she needed support. "I don't think there's likely to be anything . alive here."

Maybe. But neither George nor John showed any inclination to dispense with the rifle.

The ruins stretched across the parched land in all directions. Off to the right, a few miles away, a rocky ridge rose to several hundred feet. Some buildings had been crushed by it, pushed aside as if the thing had marched across the desert. Everywhere else, the land, except for the wreckage, was flat.

They looked at the broken walls and columns, hoping to find any sort of clue that would reveal something about the builders. Occasionally, they found a remnant of a chair or table, large pipes jutting out of the ground, melted vehicles lying dead in the sand. It was all so degraded, it was impossible to be sure about anything. Patrick stood staring at something that might once have been machinery. Beside it was a box-shaped piece of corrosion that might once have been a computer. Or an air conditioner.

"A TV," said Brad, trying to lighten the moment. But nothing about this place was funny. They came across a stone pillar that had fallen into the sand, carved to display something with wings. It was surrounded by a rock ring that suggested it might at one time have been a fountain.

"How could this be?" asked John. "How could anyone have lived here? This place is like a boiler."

"Conditions have changed," said Lynda. "I'd guess we're on a world that's gotten its orbit screwed up. It's probably dropping into the sun."

"And they all cleared out?" said Brad.

"If they were lucky." April raised her hands, indicating the ruins. "They probably had plenty of time to go somewhere else."

"Of course they did," said John. "They had the technology. Hell, they had a Roundhouse."

"I doubt it," said Lynda. "The Roundhouse—the one on the ground here—is in good shape. It hasn't been around nearly as long as this other stuff."

They fell silent for a moment. Brad was thinking how North Dakota had never looked so good.

• • •

THE RIDGE WAS puzzling. Broken pieces of buildings were scattered at its base. Why would anyone build at the bottom of a cliff? It would be an oppressive place to live, and dangerous as well. It looked as if it might have risen directly out of the ground, pushed up possibly by an earthquake. Was that possible? "I've no idea," said Patrick. "Not my field. But I'd love to get the age of this place."

George and John were peering through their telescopes. "Nothing out there," George said. "The ruins just look as if they go on forever."

They wandered through the desolation for two hours, taking pictures, shaking their heads, wondering whether the inhabitants had gotten clear. The sun gradually sank below the horizon. Stars were appearing in a moonless sky. Patrick was also carrying a telescope, a larger one than the Sioux had. He began using it.

"Recognize anything?" asked April.

"No," he said. "Not a thing." As the darkness advanced, the stars directly above them brightened and formed a river. On the other side of the sky, another vast arc of glowing stars was becoming visible. "Well," said Patrick, "that should be the Milky Way."

Brad looked for the Big Dipper. But he saw nothing he could recognize.

"So what's *this* thing?" asked April, indicating a cluster overhead.

"Never saw anything like that," said Brad.

"My God," Patrick said. "It has spiral arms. And look." He gave her the telescope.

She peered through it. "It's spectacular," she said.

"You notice the two clouds on either side of it?"

"Yes."

"Do you know what they are?"

"I've no idea."

They passed the telescope to Brad. The sky was being taken over by three circular groups of stars. "They look like galaxies," he said.

"Exactly," Patrick said. "I can't be sure, but I'd bet the big one is Andromeda. The other two are satellite galaxies."

Brad's astronomical knowledge was limited, but he knew Andromeda was the galaxy next door to the Milky Way. "We're pretty close to it," he said. "Where the hell are we *this* time?"

Lynda broke in: "That *can't* be Andromeda," she said. "You can't see it with the naked eye, can you?"

Patrick spent the next half hour watching it, until finally April said she couldn't see much point in hanging around any longer. "I don't think there's much left to look at here."

"Can we stay on for a while? A few hours?" asked Patrick.

"Why?"

"Maybe we could figure out where we are."

"Will the suits be able to stand this kind of heat for that long?" John asked. It had gotten dark, but it was still hot.

"No problem," said Boots. "They'll take the heat. But we've got less than three hours of air left. That's the real issue."

"Can you tell me what you're looking for, Patrick?" April said.

"I'm not sure. But I keep thinking about that star cluster."

"All right," April said. "Let's give it another hour. But I can't imagine what could happen here that would have any effect on those stars."

The hour passed. Andromeda, and the rest of the sky, moved westward. Patrick eventually sighed and put the telescope away, and it was time to go. They started back toward the transport station, but had gone only a short distance before John tripped over something, a rock jutting out of the ground. He went down hard. Melissa hurried to his side. She inspected the suit, and asked if he was okay.

"Yeah," he said. "I'm fine."

"You've got a tear. You're lucky. It's only a small one." She produced some tape and put two strips of it across his right knee. "That should take care of it. Everybody, please be careful."

Brad spent more time now watching the ground instead

of the collapsed buildings. He was disappointed. Was everything dead out here? He was suddenly aware that George was pointing off to the west.

Something was moving. An aircraft. It was low and it was coming in their direction.

They were passing a partially collapsed wall. "Get behind it," said John. "Everybody out of sight."

Patrick's voice broke in: "You don't think we should try to make contact? This might be the only chance we get."

April responded by pushing him forward. "Move," she said. "Everybody get down."

Brad agreed. They huddled behind the wall. The aircraft continued in their direction, losing altitude as it came. "Maybe they saw us," said Lynda and Melissa simultaneously.

"Couldn't have," said Brad. "We were too far away."

"I don't think we need to worry," said April. "There's no place they could land." There was no smooth ground anywhere.

Boots grunted. "That thing is *slow*. The way it's moving, I doubt it would need a landing strip. It might be a helicopter."

The wall was broken in several places, so they could watch without having to show themselves. "It looks kind of strange," said Melissa.

"How do you mean, *strange*?" asked George.

"I can't tell what kind of propulsion it has. But Boots is right: It's a chopper."

But it *wasn't*. They could see that much.

"They might be tourists," said Boots.

"Are you serious?" John laughed. "I bet the tickets are cheap."

"People love ruins," Lynda said.

"Listen, guys." George sounded worried. "We don't know that they aren't picking up our radio transmissions. It might be a good idea if we all shut up for a few minutes."

Brad was not happy. If they actually had to run for their lives, he knew he wouldn't have much chance in the space suit. The plane kept coming, and, while they held their breath, it passed almost directly overhead. Patrick started to stand, but April grabbed his arm and pulled him back down.

"It doesn't look very big," said Brad.

It continued forward and finally disappeared over the top of the ridge. April pointed toward the station. Let's go. Brad was happy someone had kept track of its location. For him, it was lost amid the piles of rock.

They moved out. Melissa held up her hands, trying to indicate caution. Uneven ground. Take it easy. But despite all attempts to keep calm and watch his step, Brad came very close to breaking into a run. So did the others. No reason to panic, he told himself. Even if they'd been seen, the occupants of the aircraft were not likely to be hostile. And they were probably safe in any case since they should be able to get back to the transport station before anyone could reach them. Nevertheless, they were all keeping their eyes on the ridge as they hurried across the battered landscape.

George and April led the way while John stayed in the rear. April used her radio: "Everybody please slow down."

They did. Slightly. And eventually the station came into view, its round dome rising out of the rubble, gleaming in the starlight. At that point all hope of restraint disappeared. Brad kept telling himself to take it easy, but he rumbled along at his best pace. George reached the place first, opened the door, and stepped aside. April waited outside waving the others forward.

Brad's heart was pounding as he followed Lynda into the building. He couldn't speak for anyone else, of course, but he was embarrassed as he leaned back against a wall and watched Boots, April, and John come in behind him. "Okay," said April. "Let's clear out."

Patrick lingered outside, still looking at the sky. Finally, he came in.

• • •

WALKER WAS WAITING in the Roundhouse when they arrived. He made no effort to hide his shock as they told him about the plane. "Okay," he said. "We don't go back there again. It's too dangerous."

"We can't do that," said Patrick. "I'm pretty sure we saw Andromeda in the sky."

"So what?" asked Walker.

"Let me see what else is there, Mr. Chairman. We might get the key to what this is all about." The only people in the Roundhouse, other than the six travelers, were the chairman and the security force.

"What else could there be?"

"Please, Mr. Chairman. Trust me. This is too important. We might also want to think about putting together a contact team. Eventually, we're going to have to do that. We can't just walk away from this."

Walker looked at April. "What do you think?"

"I have no problem going back in a few hours. I'm pretty sure they don't know we were there. And the area we were in isn't inhabited. So okay. But I'm a bit reluctant about going over to say hello when we don't know anything about who we're dealing with."

The chairman shifted his attention back to Patrick. "Why does it matter?"

"It *does*, Mr. Chairman." Patrick's eyes came alive. *"Please."*

Walker stood quietly for a moment, then glanced at April. She was nodding.

"Okay," he said. "Go when the time seems right to you. But take no chances. Understood?"

Patrick nodded. "All right, Mr. Chairman."

"When do you want to go back?" asked April.

"How about four hours? That might not work because we don't know how long their days are. But it gives us a decent chance."

She looked at George and John. "Is that okay for you guys?"

They both indicated yes.

Walker managed a pained smile. "All right. Just try not to get yourselves killed."

"Good," said April. "Meet back here."

Brad wasn't sure he wanted to go there again, but if Patrick could figure out where that place was, it would be an even bigger story than the plane. "April," he said. "I'd like to go, too."

Walker indicated he saw no problem. He glanced at the two astronauts. "I assume," he added, "we should also keep Melissa and Boots on board?"

"We're still not exactly experts with the suits," April said. "We'd like to have one of you guys. Or both, if it's okay."

They exchanged smiles. "Easiest space travel ever," said Boots. "I'll be here."

Melissa gave them a thumbs-up. "Me, too."

"All right." Walker seemed satisfied. "We'll meet back here at eight. Now we have one other issue." He looked toward the exit. Only Patrick and Lynda appeared uncertain what he was referring to. "The press," he added. "Let me handle it." He signaled Sandra Whitewing. She went over and opened the door.

The reporters flooded in.

The first question, as usual, addressed the issue of aliens. "Did you find anybody?" asked ABC. "Was anybody there?"

"They saw a plane," said Walker.

And that dominated the conversation for the next fifteen minutes. But everyone was embarrassed when they discovered they'd forgotten to get pictures of it.

Then they talked about the ruins. There were plenty of photos of those. "Most depressing thing I've ever seen," said the *Chicago Tribune*. "You guys have a name for this place?"

"How about *Comatose*?" said Melissa.

FORTY-ONE

I wandered through the wrecks of days departed
Far by the desolated shore, when even
O'er the still sea and jagged islets darted
The light of moonrise; in the northern Heaven,
Among the clouds near the horizon driven,
The mountains lay beneath one planet pale;
Around me, broken tombs and columns riven
Looked vast in twilight, and the sorrowing gale
Waked in those ruins gray its everlasting wail!

—Percy Shelley, *The Revolt of Islam*, 1818

WALKER PROVIDED ACCOMMODATIONS for everybody at the Spirit Lake Resort in Fort Totten. "What we need to do," said Boots, as they sat in the restaurant, "is go to the top of the ridge and see what's there."

"Do we have any mountain climbers here?" asked April. "We'd need a special team."

"You really think that's a good idea?" asked Brad. "Not sure how we'd get there in the suits. And if we made it, we'd be too visible and have no place to run if we got spotted."

"I agree," said Melissa. "I think Patrick was right. We should have let them see us. I wonder how they'd have responded?"

Lynda was chewing on a tuna sandwich. "Why don't we try that tonight?" she said. "Settle it. If we see them again."

Patrick was sitting at the far end of the table, nibbling on scrambled eggs. "I'm having second thoughts about waving at them. Maybe we should just try to see what's going on."

"You really think you can figure out where that place is?" asked Boots.

"Maybe."

Brad saw Lynda exchange glances with Patrick. She knew what this was about. And she tried to change the subject: "We need a name for it."

Melissa grinned. "You don't like *Comatose*?"

"Maybe *Desolation Point*," said Boots. "The place is a wreck. Why is it so important, Patrick?"

"I'll tell you after I've had another chance to look at the sky." He shook his head. "That place has been a wreck for thousands of years, probably millions. But it has a cupola. I can understand an advanced species putting star ports on Eden, or at the Maze and the spaceport. Even near Lake Agassiz if they enjoy boating. But I can only think of one reason why anybody would want to visit *that* place."

"And what's that?" asked Brad.

Patrick grinned. "Let's see if we can get a better look at the sky."

• • •

ADMIRAL BONNER FIRMLY believed that the solution to every problem was to bomb it. Despite that, Taylor kept him on because the guy was inevitably right in his threat assessments. He just didn't believe in talking his way through disagreements. He had earned his sobriquet *Bomber*.

He had a talent for making other people's opinions seem ridiculous. Taylor was sitting contemplating what Chairman Walker had told him about aircraft at this latest place, wishing it would just all go away, when his secretary announced the admiral's arrival.

"Send him in," he said.

He was tall, straightforward, and, given a Revolutionary uniform, could easily have posed for a George Washington portrait. "Good afternoon, Mr. President," he said.

Taylor looked up from the desk. He, of course, understood

what the Bomber's position would be. "Good afternoon, Admiral. Have a seat. Can I get you anything?"

"No, thank you, sir." He lowered himself onto the sofa. "I won't take much of your time, Mr. President. I wanted to inquire whether you've changed your mind?"

"About the Roundhouse?"

"Of course. We have to shut it down, sir. Seize the damned thing and get rid of it. Even if you were able to secure the technology, your successor, or *his* successor, will try to make the applications available to the military, and possibly even to American industry. That would be a disaster, as I'm sure you realize. We will not be able to keep it out of the hands of those who wish us only harm. The opportunity to get past this thing is here and now. It won't come again. And I assure you, sir, if we let it get away, we will all live to regret it. Or maybe not."

• • •

A PAIR OF vans took everyone from the Spirit Lake Resort to Johnson's Ridge. Walker arrived a few minutes later. John and one of the U.S. marshals came out to help him get through the media, who kept asking him about the desolation world.

He laughed and waved and said, several times, "We don't know anything yet. It's hot, it's a disaster area, and yes, there was an airplane." He wished he'd kept quiet about the plane.

The pool reporters were inside, taking pictures and conducting interviews. He talked to a few of them, explaining that he was hoping to see another aircraft. It was a lie, of course. He'd happily have sent six more missions to the place if he could get some assurance they'd see nothing but ruins.

"If the plane comes back this time, Mr. Chairman, will they get some pictures?"

"Probably," he said, "as long as we can do that without exposing our presence. We'd like to get a sense who we're dealing with."

Naturally, that brought questions about how they'd ever learn who they were dealing with until they made contact.

But he waved them off. "I can't keep repeating the same thing," he told them. "We're exercising due caution."

He watched April and her people get into their pressure suits, shook their hands, and wished them luck. "Be careful," he told them. "Don't let them see you."

It was almost nine o'clock before they were ready to go. April and George went first as the TV cameras locked in.

• • •

THEY PAUSED AT the space station to look again at the galaxy. It was at the bottom of the long window, almost out of view. Then they moved on.

John, with his rifle ready and a sidearm on his belt, went first. Moments later, the grid lit up, and John's pen appeared. Lynda picked it up. Then she and Patrick followed.

Brad stood off to one side and watched them go. The mood seemed different this time. It was probably the ancient ruins, the emptiness of the new world, the sense of decay. Whatever it was, the heady optimism was gone.

• • •

THE GOOD NEWS when they arrived on Desolation Point was that it was still dark. The lights had come on automatically when John stepped off the grid at the transport station. "Better turn them off," said Brad, assuming they knew how.

"Trying," said John. "There doesn't seem to be a switch here anywhere."

April was looking around, too. "Probably like the power in the Roundhouse," she said. "It activates with movement."

"So we have to go away to shut them off?" asked George.

"Probably."

Patrick was already out of the station, studying the sky, holding his telescope. "See anything?" Boots asked.

One of the galaxies was gone. The other two were sinking below the horizon.

"Not yet."

April was the last one out. A couple of minutes later, the lights dimmed and went off. "Okay," she said, "we better stay away from it until we're ready to leave."

Brad was also looking at the stars. He saw no Dipper. No Belt of Orion. Actually, those were the only two constellations he could have identified. He had no idea what Patrick was looking for. The mass of stars that Patrick had said was the Milky Way now dominated the entire eastern sky.

The landscape looked better in starlight than it had under the baking sun.

"We might need a little time," Patrick said.

"You haven't even used your telescope yet," said Brad.

He received no reply. Eventually, they picked out pieces of broken stone, all within fifty yards of the transport station, and sat on them. They started talking again about the galaxies. Were they really what Patrick thought? Why did Patrick not want to explain his motives?

"Because if I'm wrong," he said, "you'll think I'm an idiot."

The security guys kept looking around to make sure nothing was approaching in the dark. "I wonder," Melissa said, "why there's a transporter here?" It was the question they'd all been asking themselves. Who had been in the aircraft? Why would anyone want to come to this place?

The conversation went round and round. "I think," said Melissa, "as a next step, we'll need an archeological team to come in and have a look."

Lynda couldn't take her eyes off the broken buildings. "You think archeological expertise would have any significance once it gets away from Earth?"

Nobody knew.

"This is the gloomiest place I've ever seen," said Boots.

George was looking for somewhere more comfortable to sit. "I wonder," he said, "if the people flying the plane yesterday are visitors? Or just survivors? Maybe they're here because they have no choice."

"I don't think anybody could live here," said Lynda. "Why would anyone stay here when they have a transport station out?"

"I don't know," said George. "Maybe they don't know what

it is. Like the Arkons. Or maybe they like warm weather." He laughed.

Brad had seen a few end-of-the-world movies, but they always had to do with alien invasions or asteroid collisions. The end came quickly. But what, he wondered, would it be like on a world that, for some reason, was spiraling in toward its sun? Getting hotter every day? The streets would be filled with desperate mobs. Presumably nobody would be working, so there'd be no food, no water. "You know," he said, "I'm beginning to see why we should take NASA a little more seriously."

"Some of us," said Boots, "have been saying that for years."

George got to his feet and pointed at the sky. "Look. Another plane." Lights were approaching, on the wings and tail.

Headed toward the ridge again. Descending as it came. But unless it changed its route, it would pass well away from them.

"Get down," said George. They scrambled for cover behind a load of rubble.

April's voice: "Okay. Everybody stay put." She got up and started walking toward the approaching aircraft.

"What are you doing, April?" said George. "Get back here."

"You guys just stay where you are. Let's get this settled."

George hurried over and grabbed her. But before he could do anything else, she turned on her wrist lamp and pointed it at the plane. "Stop!" he said.

"Relax, George."

He lifted her off her feet and began to carry her back.

"Will you knock it off?" she said.

Brad wanted to tell him to put her down, but he didn't like the idea of drawing the plane's attention. He kept quiet and watched.

"I thought," said Patrick, "this is precisely the thing we didn't want to do."

The suits were getting in the way. April and George both

tumbled to the ground. Then she was up, and her helmet light was on. "I changed my mind. Anybody want to make for the station and clear out? You've got time."

Nobody moved. Had he been alone, Brad would have bolted. He suspected most of the others would have, too. But maybe April was right: Maybe it was time to settle things.

He couldn't be sure, but he thought the plane's angle of approach was changing.

"Toward us," said Lynda.

"Damn it." Patrick sounded annoyed.

"Everybody please keep quiet!" said George. "Stay off the radio."

"It's seen us," said Melissa. Brad would have said the same thing, but he didn't trust his voice.

April was back on her feet but still in George's grip. "It's seen *me*," she said. "And Hulk Hogan here. The rest of you stay out of sight." He finally released her, and she resumed walking.

George threw up his hands and chased after her. "Will you please back off?"

The aircraft was coming down with some forward motion, but mostly it was a vertical descent. "It's headed over there," said Boots, pointing at an open stretch of ground about a hundred yards away.

"April." Melissa sounded frustrated. "Slow down! You fall out there and tear the suit, and you're dead."

"Would everybody *please* stay off the radio," said George.

Lynda was next to Brad. She grabbed hold of his arm. She said nothing, but there was no mistaking the gesture. *It doesn't matter anymore.*

April stumbled. But she recovered her balance and stayed on her feet. George caught up with her and put an arm on her shoulder. She took the hint and stopped. The aircraft was descending into the open area. Brad and the others were still behind the rubble. There probably wasn't much point hiding, but he wasn't going to stand up. Nor was anyone else.

Brad still couldn't figure out what kept the plane in the

air. It had jets and wings. And it looked like an ordinary passenger plane, relatively small, like the one they'd seen earlier. He wasn't certain, but he thought the cabin had a line of windows. April and George stopped about halfway to the edge of the open area into which the vehicle was descending. Brad wanted to tell April to give it up, to come back so they could all get out while there was still time. But he knew that would accomplish nothing except getting yelled at for using the radio.

Briefly, a light in the cockpit came on and then went off. The fuselage had markings but nothing he could read.

The descent slowed and stopped at about a hundred feet, where it simply hovered for a minute. Finally, it settled to the ground. Its lights stayed on. A door opened in the center of the fuselage. April and George went a few steps closer.

They were all holding their breath. Brad saw movement in the cockpit. And then at the door. A figure in purple clothing— it looked like a jumpsuit—appeared. It stood several seconds, looking out at them. He couldn't make out a face, but it had human dimensions. It stepped forward away from the cabin and, incredibly, *floated* to the ground. It was in shadow, too far away to make out what it looked like.

Patrick put his telescope to his eye, adjusted it, stiffened, and gasped. "Oh, God," he said.

He handed it to John, who looked. And staggered. For a long moment, he kept the telescope pressed against the helmet, as close to his eye as he could. Finally, he gave it to Melissa, but even then he seemed reluctant to let go of it. She got it away from him eventually and, while she struggled to adjust it, John took the rifle down from his shoulder and put his finger next to the trigger guard.

The pilot was walking toward them now. April and George had begun backing away. Somebody said, "Make for the station." They all began to retreat. Melissa passed the scope to Brad. He looked, needed a moment to get it in focus. The pilot straightened its shoulders and tugged at a belt. The uniform started to glow, casting a dim light in all directions.

And Brad saw it had *fangs*. And horns as well. Its eyes burned with fire.

"My God," he gasped. "It's a *devil*!"

"It can't be real," Melissa said.

"Talk about it later." April sounded scared. "Everybody back to the station. Quick!"

Brad was on his way. They all were, except John, who'd gone out to one side so he could get a clear shot at the creature. April's voice rang in his ears: "Don't do it!" she said.

Brad stumbled through the sand. He fell once and barely touched the ground before he was on his feet again. April and George hadn't turned and fled like everyone else. They were backing off, but they were taking it slow and easy. If they ran, they would likely be pursued. The pilot watched their reaction and stopped. The thing raised a claw, in a gesture that Brad thought threatening. But it made no effort to chase them.

And Brad remembered that Matt would want photos. He pictured his boss's reaction when he came back with a story about a devil but with no photos. He caught his breath and stopped. Got his cell. Turned, lined up the demon, and captured it. Got a second one. It was probably the most courageous moment of his life. Then he jammed the cell back into his belt and began moving again, but more deliberately now, toward the station.

Meanwhile, the devil turned away. Maybe it had noticed John's rifle. In any event, it went back to the plane, and somehow rose through the air and reentered the cockpit doorway. The thing looked back at them over its shoulder and then closed the hatch.

When Brad reached the station, Lynda had already gotten it open. They piled inside. Boots called for Lynda and Melissa to get on the grid.

"*You* go first," said Melissa.

Lynda reacted by jumping onto it and pressing the rings icon. "This might not be the best time for a debate," she said, grabbing Melissa's arm and hauling her up beside her.

Seconds later, they disappeared into a cloud of light. Boots pointed for Brad to go. And Patrick. Okay by Brad. He got into position, but Patrick didn't move.

Boots was standing at the door, looking out. "What's happening?" Brad asked.

"The plane's lifting off. Going straight up." Then he backed out of the way to make room for April and George.

Brad looked back at Patrick. "Let's go," he said.

"No," said Patrick. "I'm not going anywhere."

George came inside. "What's wrong?" he demanded.

"We didn't get what we came for."

"I'd certainly agree with that."

"What are you talking about?" asked April. "What did we come for?"

Patrick threw his hands in the air. "This might be where the answers are. This place is probably at the center of everything."

"You've said that before," said April. "What do you mean?"

"You guys can leave. I need a little more time."

"For *what*?" April was exasperated. When Patrick hesitated, she looked over at Brad. "You might as well go," she said. "John, go with him."

John hesitated, but George broke in. "Do it, John. We'll be with you in a minute."

He joined Brad on the grid and pressed the icon.

FORTY-TWO

The end crowns all;
And that old common arbitrator, Time,
Will one day end it.

—Shakespeare, *Troilus and Cressida*, c. 1602

B RAD WAS RELIEVED to reach the space station. He and John backed away from the grid to make room, but minutes passed, and nothing happened. "I guess they're still arguing," said Melissa.

"What the hell's he expect to find?" asked John. Nobody had any idea. After another few minutes had ticked by, he got back on the grid. "I'll be back in five," he said. "If I don't show up, do not come after me." He pressed the icon and was gone while Brad, Melissa, and Lynda stood looking at one another.

They were all relieved when he reappeared almost immediately. "They're going to stay for a while. I don't know why. McGruder doesn't want to say what he's looking for. But he's not going to move unless George decks him. I'm going back. You guys might as well leave. It might not be a bad idea to let the chairman know what's going on." He raised a hand in farewell and faded out.

They hesitated. Follow him? Wait at the space station? Or go back to the Roundhouse? After a brief debate, they decided on the Roundhouse.

• • •

THE POOL REPORTERS were waiting. "You guys came back pretty quick," one of them said. "What happened?"

"Well," said Melissa, after she'd taken off her helmet, "we saw another plane."

The reporters broke into wide grins and hands started waving. "And—?"

"I guess some of us waved at it, and it came down. Landed right in front of us." They were on their phones already. Brad looked for the chairman but didn't see him.

"So what happened then?" asked the *Devils Lake Journal*.

"April and George went out to say hello."

"You're not serious?" The Associated Press looked shocked.

Melissa glanced at Brad. Did he want to take over? Brad liked audiences, but there were going to be repercussions over this. Anyhow, he was trying to get out of his space suit. They should have decided what they'd say to the media before leaving the space station, but they'd been so caught up in McGruder's action that they hadn't thought about it. "Go ahead," he said.

"The incredible thing," Melissa continued, "is that they pretty much came straight down. We thought at first we were safe because there was nothing resembling a landing field. But they might as well have been in a helicopter."

"But it *wasn't* a helicopter?"

"No. It was a plane. With jets."

Several people shouted the obvious question: "How could they do that?"

She shrugged. "I'd guess some kind of antigravity system." More questions came, but she waved them quiet. "This will go better," she said, "if you let me talk first, then we can do questions.

"It landed, and the pilot got out." She hesitated. "He looked a little unusual." More hand-waving. "We have pictures, so you can see what I'm talking about." She turned to Brad.

Brad nodded, finished disposing of the space suit, and walked over to the security desk. He tinkered with his cell phone and handed it to Andrea. "Can you put it on the TV?"

Andrea looked at the image on the phone, made a face that suggested she was about to swallow a worm, and connected it to the monitor. The plane blinked on. It was just a set of lights in a dark sky, and in another picture it filled the screen, and a third portrayed the aircraft on the ground.

The room was silent.

Then she had the pilot.

The reporters gasped and swore.

"It's a *devil*," said MSNBC.

"Well—" Melissa hesitated. "It had fangs. And horns."

The *Grand Forks Herald* said, "Yuk!"

"So we're clear: It made no hostile move. It got out of the aircraft and started walking toward us. To be honest, I got the impression it was inviting us to board the plane." She tried to laugh, but it sounded shaky. "It was a bit much, so we retreated to the transport station."

The *Fort Moxie News* found the story hard to believe. Even with the pictures. "This is for real, right? There are actually devils out there? But they never came after you?"

"No. It just stood there and watched us walk away." Brad was thinking how *walk* wasn't exactly the right verb. "When one of our escorts raised a rifle, it hustled back into the plane."

CNN: "It was scared of the rifle?"

"That's what it looked like."

The *Washington Post*: "Were there any passengers in the aircraft?"

"We didn't see anyone else. Just whatever that was that got out of the plane."

And a comment from CBS: "A plane headed for hell."

• • •

WALKER WAS GOING over some financial records when Andrea called. "We're on live TV," she said.

Her voice suggested something had happened that wasn't good. When he turned it on, the devil was front and center.

"What happened?"

"Three of them are back. Melissa and Brad. And Lynda. They ran into a devil out there."

"I'm looking at the pictures now. Look, if any of them show up at the Roundhouse, devils, I mean, don't hesitate to shoot. Okay?"

"Suppose they're not hostile?"

"You know what I'm saying. Look, I'll be over in a few minutes." Walker had to pause to catch his breath. "The others are still out there?"

"Yes, sir. They're looking for something, but nobody seems to know exactly what."

The story exploded across every network. News anchors took over, announcing that a team of scientists might have found Hell, that a team from the Roundhouse had been threatened by a demon, that devils were piloting aircraft across the latest Sioux destination. Images of the satanic creature were everywhere. One network even reported that some of the scientists had failed to return, but their situation was unclear.

Miranda was waving at him from the doorway. "The president."

"James." He didn't sound happy. "What the hell's going on?"

"I'm on my way now to find out, sir."

"I think it's time to take the damned thing down."

"I think you're right, Mr. President."

"Call me when you have something."

• • •

WALKER ARRIVED AT the Roundhouse and fought his way through an army of media. "Don't know yet," he told them. "You have as much information as I do."

Then he was inside. Melissa, Lynda, and Brad were still there, talking with the pool reporters. He took Brad aside. "What's going on? Are they in trouble?"

Brad explained while Walker listened with gathering impatience. "Okay," he said, taking a deep breath. "You willing to go back?"

"To do what, Mr. Chairman?"

"To take me there. Or if you want to back off, I'll ask Melissa."

"I've got it," Brad said.

• • •

LYNDA AND MELISSA both announced they wouldn't stay at the Roundhouse while Brad and the chairman proceeded to Desolation Point. "Please," Walker said, "can't we come up with a better name than that?"

"How about *Hellfire*?" said Brad.

They picked up a suit for the chairman, climbed back into their gear and, less than forty minutes after they'd returned to North Dakota, they were back at the space station. It was, as expected, empty. And this time nobody was interested in looking out at the galaxy.

Walker wanted to hurry up. As soon as he could, he got back onto the grid and looked at the icons. Melissa joined him. "Which one are we using?"

Melissa touched the turned E, and, a minute later, they were gone. This time there was no plan to send back a pen or something. They hadn't stopped to think about it. Brad and Lynda waited a couple of minutes and followed.

When they arrived, Walker was in the middle of an explosion. "—Any idea how this is playing out at home? You guys are *not* supposed to violate the protocols. I don't care *who* you are." He was facing April, glaring at her. Then he turned to Patrick. "So what the hell is it all about?"

April moved in to protect the young astrophysicist. "I'm sorry, James. We were just about to leave. But there's something you'll want to see before we go." She looked in the direction of the door, and Brad was surprised to see it was open.

Walker stared at her. "Is that devil out there?"

"No. It's gone."

George went outside to make sure. Walker followed. He looked around at the wreckage. "This place has been dead a long time," he said. April followed him out. Brad, Melissa, and Lynda joined them, while Walker continued to survey the broken landscape. "So what am I looking for?"

Patrick's voice: "Hold on a second, Mr. Chairman. Follow me." A large, crumbling structure blocked off the view to their right. Patrick led him around it until they had a clear view of the horizon. "Look at the sky."

"My God," said Walker.

Brad followed them, looked up, and saw a moon. At first the reason for the chairman's shocked reaction wasn't clear. It wasn't, after all, anything special. It was the same old moon that lit up the sky every night.

Earth's moon!

"What the hell is it doing out here?" said Walker. "We're not in the Middle East, are we?"

"No," said Patrick.

"Then what in God's name—?"

"Mr. Chairman, the Roundhouse doesn't just transport objects through space. It's also a *time* port."

Walker was stunned. "What are you talking about?"

"There was obviously a connection with us. Earth and this world both served as tour locations. Still do, apparently. Why? What did the two have in common? And why would anyone want to visit this place?"

"Why would they?"

"Because it's the home world. It's Earth."

"I don't get it."

"This is the future Earth. At least a billion years downstream."

FORTY-THREE

Happy the man, whose wish and care
A few paternal acres bound,
Content to breathe his native air,
In his own ground.

—Alexander Pope, "Ode on Solitude," c. 1700

"FOR GOD'S SAKE, *wait a minute*." Walker looked on the verge of a stroke. "You're telling me that inferno is the future Earth? That's where we're headed?"

"A long time from now." April was holding both hands in the air, trying to calm him.

"So the Roundhouse isn't just a teleporter? It's a time machine, too?"

"Yes, James. Either that, or somebody stole the moon and took it to that place."

"All right." They were in Walker's car in the parking lot. "Then whoever came here ten thousand years ago to go sailing—"

"Might have been *us*. Human beings from the future. Or the past."

"This is crazy." He stared out at the night sky. "So who are the devils?"

"We think they operate a tourist service."

"For whom? Who's going to go sightseeing on that hellhole?"

"That's a good question. You want an answer?"

"Yes. If you have one."

"Patrick thinks probably *us*."

"What?"

"Tourists visiting the home world. Maybe they like to go back and see where it all started. More or less the same reason they came to the Dakotas twelve thousand years ago."

"So there are still people a billion years from now?"

• • •

BRAD NEEDED AN hour to get past the media circus and reach his car. He started for home and turned on the radio. It was tuned to KLYM, which normally ran country music until midnight. But he was startled to hear his own voice: ". . . floated to the ground as if there was no gravity."

Then one of the reporters: "You're sure, Brad?"

"Yes, I'm sure."

And Matt: "Brad, of course, will be here tomorrow morning to describe in more detail what he saw on Brimstone. That's what they're calling it now, by the way, which should give everybody an idea what that place is really like. Tune in at seven for *Grand Forks Live*, which will be extended by an hour, until eleven, to accommodate the scope of the story. We'll also have the Rev. Jimmy Carstairs, host of The Evangelical Club, and neurologist Michael Fossel, who will chime in on all this. That's tomorrow at seven."

They went to country music. He tried other stations and discovered quickly that Matt was right. *Desolation Point* had been dropped elsewhere, probably everywhere, in favor of *Brimstone*. They've got a large surprise coming, he thought.

The streets were quiet. He took his time, trying to decide what he would tell Donna. She'd certainly want him to quit now. Stay away from the missions. Maybe he should. But he suspected he'd be on *Face the Nation* again Sunday.

He had been trying to play the role of a modest but heroic character. But it was going to be hard to forget that, at the critical moment, when the devil had come walking toward them, he'd panicked. They all had. Even George and John. But that didn't make it any easier.

Donna had left the lights on, of course. He pulled into the driveway, climbed out of the car, and collected his gear. A full moon floated over the rooftops, a moon that caused his heart to skip a beat. He was also happy to see that the Big Dipper was back in the sky. Inside, the TV was on. And Donna appeared from nowhere and threw herself into his arms. "Brad," she said. "I'm so glad you're—" It was as far as she got before stopping to choke back sobs.

He held on to her while a car swung into the driveway. Someone said, "There he is." A van showed up, and lights started coming on. He tried to persuade himself it was annoying. But, in fact, he loved it.

• • •

EVERYTHING ELSE THAT was happening on the planet, religious wars, racial strife, political scandals, all went away. Guests on cable news shows were denying that time travel was possible, a few preachers claimed that we had wandered into Hell, and politicians, depending on which side they were on, either damned the policies of an idiot president that put the entire nation at risk, or lauded the cautious approach of a smart leader that had kept all the dangers at a distance.

The phone rang all night at Walker's house. He and Carla retreated upstairs, turned off the second floor phone, and switched on the TV. Seinfeld was running. Just what he needed. They both loved the show. Jerry and Julia were sinking into a confrontation with the Soup Nazi.

They lay on the bed, watching the scene play out. Then Carla muted it. "You sure you're okay?" she asked.

"Yes. I just wonder what else could happen?"

"Maybe you should have kept it quiet. About its being Earth in the future."

"No way we could do that, love. It would have gotten out, and nobody would ever have trusted me again. Anyhow, it's such a huge story that everybody has a right to know about it."

"I suppose. But I hate to think that's the way the world is going to look someday."

"It's a long way off. And it's not as if scientists didn't

know it was coming." He fell silent. She put the sound back on. And they watched for almost an hour. The bedroom door was shut, and they had to concentrate to hear the phone ringing downstairs.

"What are you thinking about, Jim? It's not like you to be so quiet."

He hesitated. And turned on his side, facing her. "I keep thinking about the thunderbird."

"How do you mean?"

"The space station. It has to be the future, too. I'd like to think we did something here that people still talk about thousands of years from now."

"Jim—" She was shaking her head, smiling, groomed in her trademark tolerant expression.

"I know, babe. It's ridiculous. But I'm allowed to use my imagination, right?"

• • •

MATT WAS WAITING for Brad next morning when he arrived at the station. Brad couldn't remember the last time that had happened. But the boss was gloriously happy. Another rare occurrence. "Magnificent," he said. "Though I can't help thinking about the story we'd have if you'd tried to interview that thing." The smile grew even wider. "Just kidding. You're okay, right? How's it feel to have the biggest story anybody's ever heard of?"

"Pretty good, actually."

"Were you scared?"

"Not a chance. If he'd gotten near me, I'd just have taken him out." They both laughed.

Brad sat down and attended to his regular tasks. His three early-morning colleagues, a staff assistant, the news reader, and a secretary were all breathless with excitement. Todd Baxter, the reader, wanted to interview him on the next newscast, which ran at six o'clock. Brad would have gone along with it, but Matt intervened. "Not a good idea," he said. "We publicized *Grand Forks Live* as being an exclusive

opportunity for Brad's listeners to ask questions. We don't
want to spoil things."

"This would just give us a little more PR," said Brad.

Matt was wrestling with it. "All right," he said finally.
"Let's do it. But try to save something."

• • •

ALL THE OTHER news, the turmoil in the Middle East, the latest
political scandal, a mine cave-in, a massive rainstorm headed
east across the plains directly for Grand Forks, got barely a
mention. "KLYM's own Brad Hollister is with us this morning," said Todd, as the newscast opened at the top of the hour.
"Brad, in case anybody out there is just back from the North
Pole, you were a member last night of the Roundhouse team
that encountered something unusual on the world they've
begun calling Brimstone. Can you tell us what that was?"

Brad described the experience, trying to make it sound
relatively uneventful, the sort of thing you can expect when
you're visiting another planet. Toward the end, he was
explaining that the pilot was wearing a uniform. "Or a jump
suit. Something like that." Keeping in mind Walker's wish to
avoid talk about devils, he referred to it throughout the interview as "the pilot."

"We've all seen the pictures," Todd said. "It does look
very much like a devil, wouldn't you say?"

"I guess you could describe it that way."

"Did he have a tail? We can't tell from the photos."

Matt was watching him from the control room. He looked
gloriously happy. "I don't know," he said. "I didn't notice."

"Why not?"

"I was too busy getting out of there."

At seven, the conversation carried directly into *Grand
Forks Live*. The phone lines were overwhelmed before they
even got on the air.

• • •

"WHAT HAPPENED?" DEMANDED Walker.

"I was going to ask you the same thing," said Taylor.

"You were supposed to keep control of those missions. How the hell could you let all that goddam stuff get out? Devils? A dead Earth? You have any idea what you've done? The voters are not happy, James, and they are blaming me. I can name the Roundhouse a threat to national security, which it is, and demolish the damned thing. Or you can do it. If you elect to manage it on your own, I'll see that you and the tribe are rewarded. Not on the scale you would have been a few days ago, but, nonetheless, your people will never find themselves short of resources. I'm sorry it has to go this way, James, but I really have no choice."

Walker could not get the thunderbird out of his mind. He knew it was nothing more than a piece of artwork on a station that might have been abandoned for thousands of years. There was no connection to the Spirit Lake Sioux. But, nonetheless, there it was. Of all the pieces of art, of blooming flowers and beautiful women and planetary rings they might have found, they found instead a bird with lightning bolts gripped in its claws. It almost seemed like a message.

He stood at a critical moment. It was possible that his decision would alter the course of history. Keep the door open? Or shut it down? What chance was there to be remembered for backing away?

The only route that could lead the tribe into a bright future was to stand up. To resist the political pressure.

• • •

THE CHAIRMAN WAS listening to *Grand Forks Live* when one of Brad's callers asked whether the Brimstone action figures were realistic. "Is that what they really looked like?"

"What action figures?"

"The ones at Wal-Mart. The devils."

Brad responded that he hadn't seen them yet.

"I thought they looked pretty good," said the caller. "Like the pictures, I guess. Gives me a chill."

Walker googled them. They were packaged in plastic, armed with pitchforks, wearing a complacent smile.

Damn it, he was not going to cave in.

FORTY-FOUR

My friends, quit ye like men, and be firm in the battle.

—Homer, *The Iliad*, VI, c. 800 B.C.E.

WALKER MET DAVID Woqini the following day in the Main Street Café. "It's been a nightmare, David," he said.

"I can understand it, Jim. How's Carla getting through it?"

"She's okay. She's been by my side throughout this whole thing. Thank God. I wouldn't have made it this far without her."

"Tell her I said hello." Walker was eating a salad with some grilled chicken fingers. He had to watch his weight.

"I will. She'd want me to do the same with you."

"So what are you going to do?"

"I'm going to keep the Roundhouse functioning as long as I can. Look what we've learned. And we've walked on other worlds. I never would have believed something like that could happen in my lifetime. I mean, we went to the Moon, and then we forgot how to do it."

"There's certainly some truth to that." David was working on a trout sandwich.

"You still don't think it's a good idea, do you?"

"No, I don't, Jim."

"Well, we'll just have to disagree on this one."

"I know. And that's not a problem."

"This is a chance for the Oyate to have a major influence on the world. To make life better for everyone." Woqini took another bite out of his trout. "Go ahead," said Walker. "Say it."

"When you say 'everyone,' are you including the Arkons?" All these years since that high-school physics class, and somehow nothing basic had changed.

"Sure. Why not? I know a lot of people want to move over there, to Eden. But I'm not going to play the role of the Europeans. We aren't going to allow it. If they were able to get a court order or something, then I *would* destroy the Roundhouse."

"Jim, you've already had an impact on them. On the Arkons."

"How do you mean?"

"You've sent your people to talk to them. To let them know we're here. You've given them electric lamps. And a collection of books."

"That doesn't seem like a big deal."

"It wouldn't to us. But there's no way to know what the long-range impact will be on *them*. It might lead to a widespread belief in magic. Professor Proffitt says the Arkons were surprised to hear their world is round. That could start a religious conflict. We just don't know, Jim. It's why we should keep our hands off."

"Okay, David."

"You'll notice that the people in the river city haven't paid us a visit. Maybe they don't know we're here. Or maybe they're simply keeping their distance. Encountering a civilization that probably has a connection with the transport system would not be good for us. And I'd be surprised if they're not aware of that. We should have the same concern for the Arkons.

"Jim, I know you want to do whatever you can for the tribe. And God knows, after all we've had to endure, we deserve a break. But the risk to the world at large isn't worth whatever advantage *we* might get from all this. I saw the images of the thunderbird. And I know you well enough that I'll bet they've inspired you. But maybe the gutsy thing to do here, and the correct thing, is to walk away from it. Close the door. You'll take a lot of criticism, but I think you'll sleep well at night."

• • •

HE'D BEEN BACK in his office about an hour when Miranda told him there was a caller who wouldn't give her name. "She says she *has* to talk with you."

"Put her through." He sighed, waited for the buzz, and picked up. "This is Chairman Walker. Who's calling, please?"

"Mr. Chairman, I work for Dorothy."

He recognized the voice. It was Wasula Graybear, one of Dorothy Kalen's staffers. The Woodlake representative. "Yes, what can I do for you?"

"This is in confidence, Mr. Chairman. I don't want anyone else to know about this call."

"Okay."

"Dorothy and one of the other representatives, I think Les Krider, are going to file a lawsuit against you demanding that they get access to the Roundhouse. A lot of people want to be able to visit Eden. And some are even talking about moving there. Anyway, I wanted to give you a heads-up."

• • •

WALKER HAD HAD enough. He checked the schedule, saw that Jack Swiftfoot was off duty, and called him. "I need a pilot and a plane," he said.

"Back to old-fashioned travel, Mr. Chairman? Sure, I can manage that. When?"

"Wednesday afternoon if you can arrange it." That would give him two days.

"Hold on a second," said Jack. After a moment he was back: "Local flight?"

"Yes."

"Okay. Where are we going, and what time do we want to leave?"

"About noon be okay?"

"Two o'clock would be better. I'm committed until then."

"All right. Two o'clock works."

"I'll meet you at the airport. Where are we going, sir?"

"The middle of Lake Superior."

Jack hesitated. "I don't understand."

"I want to go out over the lake, then just come home. Okay?"

Jack didn't sound comfortable. "Sightseeing?"

"I've never been out there before. Oh, and I'd be grateful if you'd keep this to yourself."

When it was done, he called Ivy Banner. "Can you meet me at the Roundhouse?"

• • •

ANDREA HAWK WAS on duty when she heard from the chairman. "Who's out there now?" he asked, meaning off-world.

"Just the Eden mission."

"Dolly?"

"Yes."

"We still have two people with her?"

"Right. George is near the cabin. John's at the Cupola."

"Okay. We're going to close down the operation as soon as we can. Tell them all to get back here within twenty-four hours."

"We closing down permanently?"

"Yes. Nobody else goes out anywhere."

"Yes, sir."

"Have the marshals remove the package. If they have a problem with it, tell them to check with the White House. And one other thing, Andrea, I'd appreciate it if you'd keep a lid on this as much as you can."

FORTY-FIVE

Once more, farewell!
If e'er we meet hereafter, we shall meet
In happier climes, and on a safer shore.

—Joseph Addison, *Cato*, IV, 1713

ORKIM WAS OUT somewhere. They'd had visitors earlier, people from a town Dolly hadn't heard of before. Its name was Akar, which, in the native language, translated to *Oceanside*. There was a constant stream of visitors now, all coming to see Dolly and to look at the lamps and books. They were friendly but occasionally condescending. They asked all kinds of questions about North Dakota, and inevitably explained that they wouldn't want to live in a place much colder than Arkonik. Solya didn't complain, but it was clear she was getting tired of the traffic. She apologized to Dolly. "They mean well," she said.

They were beginning to show up at the Cupola, as well. That made the security people unhappy, but the Arkons were keeping their distance and giving the Sioux guards no trouble. Dolly regretted having admitted to any knowledge about the Cupola, but she'd been trying to win the confidence of her hosts, and lying to them wasn't a good way to do that.

"The City Council," said Solya, "has asked us to take you to Akar. They would welcome you appropriately."

Dolly had been debating how to ask Solya whether it

would be possible for her to visit the place. So she accepted without hesitation. She'd run the possibility by the security people. They'd recommended she decline any such invitation, but it was simply not an offer she could refuse.

"It would be very nice," Solya said. "You would have an opportunity to meet some of our most notable citizens. And I think I can promise you an evening you'll never forget."

"Marvelous. They won't be put off by someone who looks so different?"

Solya laughed. "That is where your charm lies, Dolly." Something outside caught her eye. "Your companion is coming." She frowned. "I do wish you would make it clear to him that he is welcome to stay with us."

It was George. "He's part of a security detail. The people back home won't let him do that."

"Because they do not trust us."

"They don't know you as I do, Solya."

"All the more reason their attitude is so odd. What reason have we given them to think we could be capable of rudeness?"

"It's a cultural thing." She was rising from her chair when George knocked. "We tend to be very cautious." She went over to the door and opened it. He looked upset.

"Dolly," he said. "We're being cut short. We have to leave."

"What do you mean, George? Cut short how?"

"The chairman's going to shut down the transport system. Tonight."

"Why? He can't do that. Why don't you come in for a minute?" Solya couldn't understand, but she realized something was wrong. Dolly switched languages: "Solya," she said, "you know George."

Solya extended a hand. "*Shalay*, George." And said how it was good to see him again. George got the gist of it without translation.

"We can't leave now," said Dolly. "I'm invited to be a guest at Oceanside tomorrow." She turned back to Solya and asked whether the invitation extended to George.

She said they would be delighted to have him come.

George shook his head. "I don't think you were listening to me. The chairman wants you back *now*." He checked his watch. "Listen, Dolly, I'm not clear on exactly what happened, but he's indicating events are not completely under his control, that if we don't get back quickly, we may be stranded here. Permanently."

"And you don't know why?"

"No."

Dolly lowered herself slowly back into her chair. "Solya," she said, "I'm being called home."

Solya's eyes widened. "I'm sorry to hear it. Is there a problem?" She could certainly see that both Dolly and George were upset.

"Apparently. It has nothing to do with you and Morkim. But I may not be able to get back for a long time. Maybe not at all."

Solya made a noise deep in her throat. "I am sorry. We have grown very fond of you, Dolly."

Dolly got back on her feet, crossed the room, and embraced her host. "I don't want to lose you, Solya."

"You understand, if you wish to stay, we will welcome you as a permanent member of our family."

"Thank you. That's very kind. But I have obligations at home. Whatever the problem is, maybe we'll be able to fix it somehow."

"I would like that very much."

She started toward her room. "I'd better pack. If we can set this operation back up, I'd like to have you come visit the Dakotas."

"Marvelous," she said. "I'd love to do that."

FORTY-SIX

The happiness of the domestic fireside is the first
boon of Heaven; and it is well it is so. Since it is
that which is the lot of the mass of mankind.

—Thomas Jefferson, letter to John Armstrong,
February 1813

THE SECURITY PEOPLE were not happy about the impending
shutdown, but they kept quiet about it. Instructions had
also been passed on to Dolly to say nothing. Walker was
present at the Roundhouse when she arrived. She performed
at her usual high level, taking questions from the media and
entertaining them with stories about the Arkons and their
new lamps. And she had pictures. When she left, all but a
handful followed her out.

Walker sat casually and talked with the remaining journalists until Jack notified him that Ivy's car had pulled into
the parking lot. He then explained they were going to be
doing some work on the electrical system, and suggested that
anyone who was staying should retire to the pressroom.

But he'd made it clear he had nothing to add to Dolly's
comments, so the place cleared out. Ivy Banner arrived
moments later, carried her toolbox in, said hello to the security people, smiled, and made for the grid. Andrea Hawk
had probably been the most upset among the Sioux. She
watched with obvious concern as Ivy opened a panel in the
wall.

She walked over and sat down beside the chairman. "When," she said, "are we planning to make the announcement?"

"Why don't you leave that to me, Andrea?" If it got out, Walker knew he'd be overwhelmed with demands to back off.

Her eyes narrowed. "Sure." Ivy was pointing a flashlight into the panel. "What is she doing?"

"She's going to remove some parts."

"It won't work without them?"

"That's correct."

"What are you going to do with them? With the parts?"

"Andrea, don't you have some preparations to make for your show this evening?"

"This is a mistake, Mr. Chairman."

Walker had to smother his anger. What the hell did *she* know about what he'd gone through these last few months. "I appreciate your opinion," he said.

Ivy needed about twenty minutes to remove the gray device that she'd called a collector. She also detached the control unit and the black apparatus whose purpose he'd forgotten. She wrapped each in a plastic bag, put the bags into a cardboard box, and handed the box to the chairman. "That's it," she said.

"Thank you, Ivy." He gave her the check he'd been carrying in his pocket. "Don't know what we'd have done without you."

"I'm glad to help, Mr. Chairman. Will you need me later?"

"Probably not." He instructed the security people to remain on duty, took the box outside, put it in the trunk of his car, and returned to Fort Totten, where he went back to working on the statement he would make after he got back from Lake Superior, announcing the Roundhouse shutdown. "We do this," he would say, "for the benefit of the human race."

• • •

HE WAS JUST walking into the Devils Lake Regional Airport when Jack called. "Been working," he said. "I'm about twenty minutes out. I assume this has something to do with the devils?"

"Not really," he said.

"You're shutting down the Roundhouse?"

"I'll explain when you get here, Jack."

"Fair enough. I've arranged an escort to bring you out to the plane when I get in. Where are you now?"

"Just coming in the front door."

"Okay. Good. Clear security and then just take a seat and stay in the area. They'll pick you up. They know what you look like."

"I hadn't thought of this earlier, Jack. I have some equipment with me that I probably won't be able to get through TSA."

"Okay, sir. Stay out in the lobby. I'll let them know you're bringing in some electronic stuff. Can you tell me what it is?"

"Roundhouse gear," he said reluctantly.

"Oh. How many pieces?"

"Three."

"Okay. Wait for your escort. He'll take you through."

The airport televisions were showing Roundhouse pictures and journalists talking to the Sioux guards. Banners were running stating that no one would confirm that a shutdown was imminent. Actually, the story had been contained longer than he'd expected.

A short, official-looking man in a brown suit arrived. "Chief Walker?" he asked.

"I'm a chairman. But yes. That's me."

He smiled. "Good. May I take a look at what's in the box?"

Walker showed him. He studied the equipment, frowned, and shrugged. "What is it?"

"It's electronic gear. Part of a transportation system."

"Looks okay, I guess. Come with me, please."

• • •

HE WAS TURNED over to a different escort, a young woman, who accompanied him out onto the airfield and took him to a blue-and-white Cessna waiting just outside the terminal. Jack was getting out of it.

"Good to see you, Mr. Chairman," he said. "I'm sorry this hasn't turned out better."

"Me, too, Jack. Are we ready to leave?"

"Whenever you are, sir."

"Good. Let's go." He thanked the young lady who'd come outside with him and climbed into the cabin.

Jack followed him and shut the door. There were four seats. "You can sit up front with me if you like."

"Sounds good." Walker put the box down and joined the pilot.

"You have any particular destination in mind, Mr. Chairman?"

"Just the middle of the lake."

"Yes, sir."

They waited several minutes for clearance while Walker thought about what he was doing. He'd considered just trying to hide the equipment, but he had no place available that wouldn't eventually be found. Best was to settle the issue.

He should probably alert the president, but if he did that, he would in effect be turning the decision over to him. And there was no way to know how that might go. Taylor had an election coming up next year, and whatever he did would cost him politically. By giving him deniability, Walker could also provide a shield.

Jack asked how the Tribal Council had reacted to his decision.

"I haven't told them yet," he said. "They know I've been thinking about it. And I guess they deserved a say in the matter, but to tell the truth, I'm tired of the argument. I'm going to get it done and end it."

"Good luck, James. I suspect you'll take some criticism."

• • •

THREE HOURS LATER, they landed in Duluth to refuel. Then they were back in the air, over Lake Superior. Gradually, the shoreline behind them disappeared, and they could have been out over an ocean.

"When did you decide to do this?" Jack asked.

"I'm not sure. I think probably when I looked up and saw the Moon."

Jack looked puzzled. "How do you mean, sir?"

"The one at Brimstone. The future Earth."

"Oh. I was surprised. How could you be sure that was *our* moon? There are probably a lot of moons that look like ours." It was a clear, bright afternoon. A few white clouds drifted below them. "I don't think you could really be certain about it."

"You wouldn't feel that way, Jack, if you'd been there."

His phone sounded.

It was probably the tenth or eleventh call he'd gotten since leaving Devils Lake. The calls were mostly from people with political connections to the tribe. He'd let them ring. But he couldn't ignore this one. "Hello, April."

"James," she said, "where are you?"

"Not sure."

"You shut down the Roundhouse." He couldn't miss the accusing tone.

"That's correct. And I'm about to destroy the transporter."

"Please don't," she said.

"I've no choice, April. We have to get rid of this thing. Everybody's worried about the economy. The president's scared of military implications after the technology gets out. And now we've got a dead Earth on our hands. And some people trying to move onto Eden. It's enough." He could sense Jack watching him.

"James, I've never known you to be so negative. You've been watching too much cable news. We have potential access to all kinds of technology here. Look, we're living in a seriously overcrowded world. We're up to our ears in fanatics. The climate's going to hell. Maybe we need to find out that the human race comes through okay. Patrick thinks that's what we'll discover if we go into Riverworld.

"Don't shut it all down, James. Please. Have a little faith. We've had problems before and gotten through them. Who knows what we might get from the transporter? Just give it a chance."

He glanced over at Jack, who was looking straight ahead. "Talk to you later, April," he said. "I have to go."

Below them, there was only water. "We're pretty far out," Jack said. "I doubt going farther would make much difference."

"Okay."

"You ready to do it?"

"Yes." Walker started to release his seat belt.

"Not yet. Let me lose a little altitude."

"Okay."

The plane slowed gradually. Dropped lower. Finally, Jack said, "All right. We're good now."

Walker got out of his seat and went back into the cabin.

"Let me do it," said Jack. He put the plane on autopilot and followed the chairman.

Walker removed the lid from the box.

Jack looked down at the three pieces. "Stay clear of the door, Mr. Chairman." He opened it. A blast of wind came in and almost knocked Walker into one of the seats.

He pulled himself up and offered to help, but Jack indicated he should stand clear. He reached into the box and brought out the collector. Just a gray cube with its wires removed. He looked at it and then back at the chairman. "You sure you want to do this, sir?" He had to raise his voice to be heard over the wind. "That might be the future in that box."

"The future is ours to take, Jack. We don't need anybody to give it to us." Walker looked out through one of the windows at the lake. It was immense.

Jack let go of the collector. The chairman could not see it once it left his hands. Next went the black metal device. And finally the control unit.

"Okay, Jack," he said. "Let's go home."

EPILOGUE

T WO DAYS AFTER the president announced that Walker had done no wrong, that the property he had destroyed belonged to the Sioux, and that consequently no action could be taken against him or the tribe, Jeri surprised her mother when she appeared in the kitchen, wearing a smile. "Hi, Mommy," she said. Her eyes moved to the toast.

June's heartbeat picked up. She took a deep breath, embraced her daughter, and walked with her to one of the living room windows. *Yes!* The tip of a tree branch was rising and falling, and leaves were fluttering to the ground.

Louie was back.

When she took a closer look, she saw movement also at the top of the tree. There were *two* of them.

Now available from

Jack McDevitt

COMING HOME

AN ALEX BENEDICT NOVEL

Thousands of years ago, artifacts of the early space age were lost to rising oceans and widespread turmoil. Antiquities dealer Alex Benedict and his pilot, Chase Kolpath, have gone to Earth to track them down. When the trail goes cold, they head back home to rescue the *Capella*, the interstellar transport that vanished eleven years earlier in a space/time warp.

Alex now finds his attention divided between locating the artifacts and anticipating the rescue of the *Capella*. As the deadline for the *Capella*'s reappearance draws near, Alex fears that the secret of the artifacts will be lost yet again. But Alex Benedict never forgets and never gives up— and another day will soon come around...

PRAISE FOR JACK MCDEVITT
AND THE ALEX BENEDICT NOVELS

"The logical heir to Isaac Asimov and Arthur C. Clarke."
—Stephen King, #1 *New York Times* bestselling author

"Jack McDevitt is a master of describing
otherworldly grandeur."
—*The Denver Post*

jackmcdevitt.com
facebook.com/AceRocBooks
penguin.com

From Nebula
Award-winning author
JACK McDEVITT

The Alex Benedict Novels

A TALENT FOR WAR
POLARIS
SEEKER
THE DEVIL'S EYE
ECHO
FIREBIRD
COMING HOME

"The Alex Benedict series is reminiscent
of some of the work of Isaac Asimov."

—*SFRevu*

jackmcdevitt.com
penguin.com